Afghan Ghosts

By:
Jeffrey H. Fischer
Colonel (Ret.)
Website: www.jeffreyhfischer.com
Facebook: www.facebook.com/ColonelFisch
LinkedIn: www.LinkedIn.com/in/jeffreyfisch/
Twitter: @jefffisch

Coalition forces have withdrawn from Afghanistan and the Taliban have again seized control of the nation. Back in the U.S., a welcome change enters Dr. Curt Nover's life but also surfaces powerful memories of combat he buried years ago. Curt and his friends soon realize that their only recourse is to confront these mental hellhounds via a trip back into the demon's lair, Afghanistan. Searching to find answers, former interpreters, and friends, the team unknowingly become pawns in a sinister profiteering plot, leveraging the Afghan opium market. Furious, the Taliban capture Curt and schedule his televised beheading; a lesson not to meddle in Afghan affairs. The race is on to save Curt, but is it too late? Do the demons that haunted him for years finally enact their revenge? Does Afghanistan consume the life of yet another U.S. serviceman?

DEPARTMENT OF DEFENSE
DEFENSE OFFICE OF PREPUBLICATION AND SECURITY REVIEW
1155 DEFENSE PENTAGON
WASHINGTON, DC 20301-1155

Ref: **22-SB-0095**
August 10, 2022

Colonel (Retired) Jeffrey Fischer

████████████████████████████████

Dear Colonel (Ret.) Fischer:

This is in response to your March 16, 2022, correspondence requesting public release clearance for the manuscript titled, "Afghan Ghosts." The manuscript submitted for prepublication security review is **CLEARED** for public release. This clearance does not include any photograph, picture, exhibit, caption, or other supplemental material not specifically approved by this office, nor does this clearance imply Department of Defense (DoD) endorsement or factual accuracy of the material.

This office notes that your manuscript may include personally identifiable information (PII) of former or active duty Service members, DoD employees, and third party individuals, the release of which could be a violation of the privacy rights of these individuals. As the author, you are solely responsible for the release of any PII and its legal implications. If necessary, you may wish to consult these individuals and obtain permission to include their PII in the manuscript.

This office requires that you add the following disclaimers prior to publishing the manuscript: "The views expressed in this publication are those of the author and do not necessarily reflect the official policy or position of the Department of Defense or the U.S. government." and; "The public release clearance of this publication by the Department of Defense does not imply Department of Defense endorsement or factual accuracy of the material." A copy of the first page of the manuscript with our clearance stamp is enclosed. Please direct any questions regarding this case to Please direct any questions regarding this case to ███

Sincerely,

MCCOMB.DOUGLAS. Digitally signed by
for   GREGORY.10426113   MCCOMB.DOUGLAS.GREGORY.10
      24   Date: 2022.08.10 10:51:52 -04'00'

George R. Sturgis, Jr.
Chief

Enclosure(s):
As stated

DEDICATION

To my fellow Veterans and service members who struggle with the wounds of war. Also, I dedicate this book to friends and family that know fully well that today I am a far different person than I was before partaking in the horrors of war.

To a man I admired greatly, Paul Flaherty, Sr. You are gone too early, leaving a void no one can fill. #FuckCancer.

ACKNOWLEDGMENTS

I am blessed to have a brigade of part-time editor. They find my errors (most, anyway), offer excellent suggestions, and charge nothing for their service. Thanks to all of them, far too many to name. *Read as* I make a BUNCH of mistakes.

NOTIFICATIONS TO THE READER

This book is the third in a series by the author. Some of the plot and character development would make more sense if the reader were to consider reading <u>LIVE RANGE</u> as well as <u>BALKAN REPRISAL</u> prior to this book. Just scan the QR code with your mobile device to find them in Amazon.

Chapters

* An Appendix of Acronyms is enclosed to assist the reader. *

Foreword by General (Ret.) Jeff Harrigian

I first met Fisch years ago on Ramstein AB, Germany. Our conversation was sparked by a personal common interest; not the standard shop talk that typically occurs at a conference. Back then as a General Officer, not a day went by that someone didn't try to pitch me something. Fisch didn't, and I always appreciated that about him. Since then, we've stayed in touch and while we haven't shared a beer recently, we've been able to stay connected.

When Fisch asked if I'd be interested in an early reading of *Afghan Ghosts*, I was all in. After my time as the Commander for Air Forces Central Command, and more recently commanding U.S. Air Forces in Europe and Africa, I, like many, had a lot invested in Afghanistan... so I dug in. As I turned the pages, I began to learn 'who' Fisch was, on a personal level. How he painted a picture, used lexicon I had heard for years and described details that service members immediately recognize. He not only penned an action-packed thriller, but one that exposes the wounds our veterans often keep hidden and the challenges military families face. Throughout the book, I found multiple chapters precisely describing the visual scene, the smell, the warfighter's emotions, and, equally important, the challenging military family life. At times, having seen the emotional attachment that naturally occurs in the throes of combat, the book reminded me how important it was to tell the story and listen to those that carry the burden of war. It's often a difficult story, with many incredible patriots and families doing amazing things... stories that are worth your time.

I've read many fiction and non-fiction books about Afghanistan. *Afghan Ghosts* is absolutely one of the best. It draws the reader in quickly, instantly bonding you to his characters. Then Fisch, in his own unique but sobering way, smacks the reader in the face with graphic warfare. Perhaps at a

1

higher level, he's crafted a mental conflict... attaching you to his characters with all their faults, battling in the hells of war. To a degree, Curt, Smitty, and Buck aren't just characters. To me, they were my brothers in arms... they are the folks I fought with, like Stuff, Corky and Pistol. I know them and the bond we share. A bond I've never been truly able to express, yet this book does it perfectly. A fiction thriller that explains our veterans' struggles is perhaps just what's needed to heal our nation from this 20-year war.

The storyline is without question, Afghanistan, exposing the kindness and loyalty of Afghans to the Taliban's unspeakable ruthlessness. Fisch concisely captures the spectrum... from those of an ancient society to those seeking to advance Afghanistan; from a challenged international policy on Afghanistan to the greedy who seek economic opportunity. It is an amazing read that pulls you into every chapter, every moment. It's all inside *Afghan Ghosts*.

My only criticism (debriefing myself) is that I must go back and read his first two books. While *Afghan Ghosts* stands on its own, his characters have drawn me in. I want to know the rest of the story! Bottom line, if you want an action-packed fiction novel that's as real as it gets, turn the page and start reading. You will love this book and won't put it down.

Gen (Ret) Jeff "Cobra" Harrigian

Chapter One
The Infidel's Punishment

The live internet video stream began with a solid black image. An audio clip played Islamic music, akin to what one would hear at a Mosque during any of the five daily prayers. This video, however, would not be a prayer. Eventually, the video transitioned away from black. The initial image was grainy, but eventually, the camera's autofocus corrected itself. In the middle lower section of the screen sat a human on his knees, hands tied behind his back, wearing an orange prison jumper. The man was large as the orange jumpsuit stretched over him. He was fit, but bruises, burns and other wounds covered his chiseled arms. A black burlap sack covered the entire head. The body remained motionless. If the torso was not erect, one could question if it were even alive.

For the world, such a scene was not uncommon. The Taliban were now posting two to three videos a day, mostly local Afghans who had broken the Taliban's strict interpretation of Islam. This video, however, would prove different. The person in this orange jumper was not an Afghan, but rather a foreigner, an infidel tried and convicted under the laws of Afghanistan. He would need to be punished. Word circulated around the globe and the curious had tuned in, trying to ascertain the nationality of the poor victim.

From the right side of the screen, another individual entered the picture. Based on the size, it was likely a male but determining this was difficult. He wore a large, black cloth over his mouth and nose. On his head sat a traditional Taliban turban headdress which matched his black 'man-dress,' or in Afghan terms, an abaya. He spoke in Pashto, reading from a piece of paper he held in his hand.

"All Praise Allah. When the Lord inspired the angels, saying I am with you. So, make those who believe stand firm. I will throw fear into the hearts of those who disbelieve. Then smite the necks and smite of them each finger. (Koran 8:12)"

3

He paused. Long enough to pull out a large dagger style knife, then continued. "Now when ye meet in battle those who disbelieve, then it is smiting of the necks until, when ye have routed them, making fast of bonds; and afterward either grace or ransom 'til the war lay down its burdens. (Koran 47:4)"

No longer quoting the Koran, the man continued, "The accused stands charged and guilty of numerous acts from being an infidel to treason against our ways. He must no longer walk among us in this life. We send him to the great Allah who shall judge his sins against Islam."

The man put the paper down and lifted the burlap sack off the head of the accused. As the bag came off, the victim's eyes squinted, blinded by the powerful lighting in front of him. His left eye was bruised, and the right side of his face had electrical burns. A few open lesions were covered with infected scabs, displaying the initial signs of infectious pus. Through all the wounds, it was still clear. The individual was Dr. Curt Nover, a former Navy SEAL turned medical doctor who somehow had an unfortunate knack for getting into such situations.

Now acclimated to the light, Curt held his head high. Staring directly into the camera.

The millions who had 'tuned in' to the live webcast were on the edge of their seats in disbelief. An angered and frustrated Admiral Hershey sat in the Pentagon, watching. Allison, now hospitalized, was in no condition to view the streaming video. She had been informed today's execution in Afghanistan would be Curt. She cried and begged God for help.

The Taliban executioner raised his blade...

Chapter Two

'+' One

(*Four Months Earlier*)

This D.C. morning was far from one of the year's best. The weather was overcast and cold for March. Spring could not arrive soon enough for most of the Capital's residents. Curt remained asleep in bed, snoring moderately. It was not too loud, and Allison still found it cute. Their bedroom was nice, but small, much like most other Washington, D.C. row homes.

Now settled in D.C., the two rented a three-story Lindy style row home near Eastern Market and the Marine Corps Barracks of '8th Avenue and I Street.' The ground floor had an entry door and a narrow staircase on one side, with a small garage on the other. Behind the garage were the utilities and a small room the two used for storage. The second floor was split between a living room and a kitchen with a small half bathroom. It was recently renovated with a stone fireplace. The place exuded warm charm. Finally, on the third floor, were two bedrooms and two full baths. Although their home was small, it was cute and had a unique character, a trademark of houses on 'The Hill.'

Curt slept alone, as Allison was not in bed. She'd gone to the bathroom minutes earlier. She sat still on the toilet, quietly, staring down at her right hand. In it was a white plastic stick which had a small window with a plus in the display area, designating a 'positive' indication. Allison was pregnant. It was her third test in a week, the first two also positive, but she had questioned their accuracy. After the third test, she accepted the notion she was, in fact, pregnant. Mentally, she was horribly torn. Part happy, part nervous, part scared, part confused. It didn't make sense.

'I'm on protection. How could this happen? Or, how on earth will I explain this to Curt?' She thought. Allison was right. When it came to family, Curt was a planner. Months before, they discussed raising children. Curt laid it all out as if it were some sort of major military operation. They would settle onto 'The Hill' of D.C. for a few years. Allison would be able to further her

5

career as a freelance journalist in the D.C. networks. Then, after saving up enough money and enjoying 'their' time together, the two would start a family, moving out to the Virginia suburbs, where the schools were better. A pregnancy now was not the plan.

She had to tell him, but how? It would definitely have to wait. Today, there was too much going on to include this news to the day's events.

Allison got up off the toilet, hid the pregnancy test under the bathroom sink, and went back to bed. She curled up behind her snoring love, gently placing her arm over his large shoulders. They'd be starting a family soon. She felt sick to her stomach and could not tell if it was nerves or morning sickness. 'Maybe both,' she guessed. She took a deep breath. The alarm clock would soon blare, and they'd need to begin preparations for the day's events.

Chapter Three
Crackin' Crabs

"Come on, Baby! Hurry up. We're gonna be late," Curt bellowed out up the narrow staircase of their row home. He stood at the front door, one foot in and one foot out, excited about their pending lunch date. It had been weeks since Curt and Allison had seen their friend. Smitty, Curt's long-time friend and also former Navy SEAL, recently finished his close security detail training and was assigned to the team that protected the Chairman of the Joint Chiefs, Admiral Hershey. It was the job the Admiral had promised him just months earlier.

"Curt, slow your roll. We're fine," Allison replied from the second floor living room. She gathered her keys, wallet, phone and shoved them into her purse, which was sitting on the kitchen table. She finally came down the steps. To Curt, she looked glowing.

"God, you clean up well, baby."

"Yeah, yeah. Get in the car, you crazy man," Allison dismissed Curt's compliment, but secretly loved to hear them - especially now.

The two jumped in the car and drove towards Annapolis out of D.C. It would take roughly forty minutes to arrive at The Boatyard Bar and Grill, a local favorite of Chesapeake Bay seafood.

As they drove, Allison asked, "What time did you tell Smitty we'd be there?"

"Interesting framing of that question, my amazing journalist wife. Did you mean to ask it that way or perhaps 'What time are we supposed to be there?'" Curt laughed, "I believe we all agreed to meet there at one, which is in thirty minutes." Curt smiled at Allison and, without speaking, relayed there was no way on earth to make it from Capitol Hill to Annapolis in thirty minutes.

"Curt, look at this." As if she were a game-show host, she waved her hand from her face to her feet. "This isn't natural. It takes some serious work to get this dolled up for you. I

7

sometimes think it's not fair. You take a shower, dry off, get dressed, do twenty pushups and you need to beat off the ladies."

"Beat off the ladies? Come on! I appreciate that, but we both know it's been weeks since I received more than a handful of numbers from ditzy D.C. interns." From the grin on Curt's face, he was clearly proud of his joke.

"Ha…. Ha…. Ha….. Funny, Nover." Allison wasn't amused and readily changed the subject. "Hey, have you heard from Buck lately?"

"Yes, actually. He's doing great. The NATO gig flying around senior officials seems to be picking up. He's getting more flight requests than he can service. He said something about getting another aircraft and creating a fleet. I'm happy for him. We should go visit. I miss that old ogre."

"I miss him too. Hey, why don't we try to get out there this fall?"

"Deal," he responded. Curt kept driving, now on Highway 50, headed east to the shoreline. Curt and Allison were perfect together. The two hands and continued the small talk. After everything they had been through, it was moments like this that made it all worth it.

Walking into the Boatyard Bar and Grill, the two immediately found Smitty. He was sitting at the bar with his back to the door, watching the Chicago Cubs play the Baltimore Orioles at Camden Yards, just a few dozen miles away. If his friends hadn't interrupted, Smitty would have been fine for the next three hours, oblivious to Curt and Allison's tardiness.

Curt tapped him on the back, deepened his voice to disguise it, and spoke, "Excuse me, young man, I believe this is my barstool. You're gonna need to move."

Smitty didn't flinch. He casually picked up his beer, took a long pull, and set it back down. Without taking his eyes off the ball game, he said, "Nover, you're an idiot."

Allison laughed out loud, threw her arms around Smitty, and squeezed him tightly. "Smitty! Congrats on finishing training and starting the new gig! And for always being able to put my husband in his place!"

Smitty leaned into her hug. "Hey sexy. When you're done with that model, I'll always be here, ready for ya."

"Easy Trigger," Curt jested. "Smitty, you realize if you tried to use such lines on single women, you may have better luck than, let's say, on your friends' wives?"

Smitty threw a $20 on the bar, stood up, and hugged his good friend. "Curt, you're probably right, but those chicks are unknown entities. If I could clone Allison, I'd do it in a heartbeat, buddy."

As the two separated their hug, Allison said, "Uh… Smitty, I love you like a brother, but dude, in today's society, I'd suggest that using 'chicks' as your female descriptor is not gonna get you too far." She knew trying to transform Smitty at this point was useless and changed the subject. "Hey, where's our table? I'm starving!" Curt and Allison laughed. Smitty just looked puzzled about his 'chick' comment, providing great insights into his single status.

The three moved to a large indoor wooden picnic table, ordered a pitcher of beer and a bushel of steamed Maryland Blue Crabs. After a few minutes, the table was 6 inches deep in cooked crabs, and the three diners held wooden mallets at the ready. Given the winter and spring cold water temps, the crabs were perfect. They smashed crab and ate it with their fingers. It was a local custom and great fun. The two men drank beer while Allison had a Coke. She was the designated driver and would let Curt drink with his buddy. Most importantly, as they ate and drank, the group caught up.

"Hey Smitty, how was training?" Allison asked.

"It was OK. Far easier than BUDS (Basic Underwater Demolition/SEAL) training. I'm happy it's over, though. Word circulated among the instructors that Squirts brought me on. They considered me the 'golden child' who could do no wrong. Not really fair to me or the other students, but it is what it is."

Curt took a drink of beer, then spoke. "Have you already started your protection detail on Admiral Hershey? You realize you probably shouldn't call him Squirts now that he's your boss. Right?"

Smitty chuckled. "Ha. Yeah. I gotta work on that. I started

already. Just a few days. Nothing big yet. Most of my efforts have been shuttling him from his residence on Ft. Myer to the Pentagon and back. That man puts in some serious hours. Hey Allison, what have you been up to?"

"Didn't Curt tell you? I got a job in D.C. with the Wilson Center," Allison said proudly.

"Wow. That's great." He paused, then started again. "What's the Wilson Center?" Smitty was truly impressed, but unsure why. The Woodrow Wilson Center for International Scholars was one of the best non-partisan institutions in D.C. For many journalists, it's a dream job.

Allison's answer was measured. "God, I love you. I'm doing research and analysis at this point but am hoping I can eventually get some of my work published through them. As with most jobs in D.C., the pay isn't great, but the opportunities are nearly unlimited."

"That's really awesome. I'm happy for ya! What are you working on right now?"

"Right now, a large effort of the international community is focused on Afghanistan. After the West's withdraw, the Taliban have an opportunity to become a better neighbor on the world stage. That's easy to say, but the 'how' is truly a challenge, and that's what I'm researching."

"How? That's easy. Turn Afghanistan into glass," Smitty said, referring to dropping nuclear weapons and heating the Afghan countryside to a temperature that would chemically transition it from sand to glass.

Allison was polite in her response, but also firm. "Smitty. I know you and Curt aren't fans of that place based on your history. But the world can neither nuke it nor ignore it. I'm not saying we're gonna get it right, but there's value in trying to make it better. Don't ya agree?"

"Well, I can say this. I'm glad *you're* working on this and it's not just a bunch of diplo-pacifists who fail to acknowledge the military as an instrument of hard power. D.C. has too many of 'em. That's for sure."

Curt just sat there, listening to the exchange, beating a crab with his mallet, eating the meat and drinking beer. Eventually, the first pitcher was drained. Curt raised it, looking at the waiter, signaling for another. As he set it down, he spoke, "Smitty, I don't disagree with you on the societal make up of D.C., but after America's two decades in Afghanistan, many of those were lost years for you and I in that shithole. I'm all good with other agencies trying their luck."

"Fair. Good riddance, shithole!" Smitty raised his glass and smacked it against Curt's.

"Good Riddance!" Curt responded.

Allison also raised her Coke, bumping it against theirs. She took a sip, a good designated driver. As she drank, the frustration surrounding Afghanistan for her husband and Smitty was deep and real. She changed the subject. "Smitty, did Curt tell ya about his new job?"

"Not much yet. Yeah, what's up with that, Doc?" Smitty smashed another crab and looked up with interest at Curt.

"Yeah. The new job is actually really excellent. From the first blush, it appears I have a huge amount of maneuver space. The Veteran's Administration officials and I talk regularly about my Florida incident. They've presented some interesting takeaways, and it's exposing some exciting research. Additionally, I have regular access to medical staff to help me personally. Because of that, Allison and I are in a great place. I owe a great deal to Admiral Hershey. Next time you see him, please tell him I am grateful beyond words for the opportunity he secured."

"Will do, Doc. That's impressive. I'm really happy for you both. Look at us! If only Buck was here, we'd all actually be normal humans doing normal shit!" They all laughed, but their past exploits validated Smitty's words.

As their crab feast ended, the two men fought over the bill, as they always did. Eventually, Smitty paid, but agreed the next meal was on Curt. Within a day, they would both forget the arrangement and fight again over the next meal. Allison enjoyed the entertainment.

On the drive home, Curt nodded off in the passenger seat. Beers and a belly full of crab meat served as a great sedative. Allison enjoyed watching the sunset in front of her. She exited the highway and approached D.C. on East Capitol Drive, which

11

circled around the now abandoned Robert F. Kennedy stadium. She continued on the beautiful tree-lined East Capitol Drive as the setting sun gently settled behind the Capitol building. It was a beautiful scene, near picturesque. A tear welled up in her eye and fell down her cheek. She could keep her secret from Curt no longer.

Allison turned off the radio. The silence awoke Curt, who was barely sleeping. "Hey, what did you turn the radio off for?"

"Because I'm pregnant," she replied.

"You can't listen to music when you're pregnant?" Curt asked, puzzled by her answer and completely missing the point.

"Curt! I am pregnant!"

The news hit him like a ton of bricks. "What!? But you're on protection? How? Are you serious?"

Allison stopped the car on East Capitol Street, just a few blocks from home. She lowered her head and began crying. It was exactly the reaction she feared.

Curt quickly realized what he'd done. He opened his door, jumped out, and ran to her side of the car. Opening her door and kneeling down to her level, he pulled her out of the car and held her. "Baby. Stop. Please. I am VERY excited, and I AM HAPPY! You just caught me off guard."

"But this isn't your plan. We've discussed this. We haven't saved up the money to move to the Virginia suburbs yet. We haven't had 'our' time together yet." She was growing hysterical, crying.

"What? Baby... That stuff is peanuts! Really! No plan survives first contact with the enemy!"

"Curt! It's a baby, not an enemy!"

"Stop, please! HA!!! I'M GONNA BE A DADDY!" Allison began to see Curt's sincerity, and it calmed her. "Allison. Seriously, I will now have someone I can legit say, 'Who's Yo Daddy?' too. It's what I always dreamed of!"

Allison let out a chuckle as she wiped away her tears. "You idiot."

Curt reached into the car and turned back on the radio and quickly streamed a song from his iPhone's Amazon Music app. 'Beautiful Crazy' by Luke Combs began playing . Cranking it up loud, he reached out his hand and said, "May I have this dance, Ms. Allision Nover?"

She accepted, and there, in the intersection of East Capitol Street and 10ᵗʰ Street, they danced. "Nover, you are one of the craziest guys I have ever met."

"My mom says that too, albeit I think for different reasons. Hey, I gotta get as many dances in now as possible before you get fat."

Her eyes widened and eyebrows pierced as Curt laughed. Somehow, Curt could get away with such statements that would have most husbands buckled over in pain. He pulled her close and held her tight.

From out of nowhere, a voice yelled, "Hey! Turn that down!" It bellowed out of a second-story window on East Capitol Street, somewhat ruining the moment.

"Sorry buddy!" Curt yelled back. "I'm gonna be a father!"

"I could give two shits! Turn the music off!" The angered individual screamed. Such was the love among neighbors on The Hill.

Curt yelled back, "Hey! That's not the line! Haven't you seen *It's a Wonderful Life*? You're supposed to say, 'Aww, youth is wasted on the young!'" Allison laughed, knowing exactly what Curt was referring to. It was a scene when Jimmy Stewart and Donna Reed were scolded by an angered old neighbor.

"Curt, ignore him. Kiss me," Allison said. He did just as she requested.

Curt turned down the music and helped Allison back into the car. He did so with far more conviction and concern than in the past. His wife was now pregnant. Allison was relieved, as if a wave of calm blanketed her body. *'Everything was going to be ok,'* she believed.

Curt circled around the car to the other side. As he was getting in, Allison heard him say, "Dude! I don't care what time it is there! I'm gonna be a dad!"

Puzzled, Allison looked over and saw his phone raised next to his ear. She grabbed his arm! "Jesus! You're a freaking doctor! You know the rules! We DON'T tell anyone yet!"

13

"Baby, it's just Buck! Who will he tell? He's in Belgium! Hey! Hold on. He wants to talk to you." Curt handed the phone to Allison.

Allison apologetically said, "Hey Buck. Sorry we woke you."

"What? No! It's all good! Congrats! This is so cool! What do you need from Europe? They have tons of cool baby shit here. Have you considered the name Buck?"

"Buck, I'm not sure it's really referred to as 'Baby shit' but thanks. If you don't mind, I'd like to try and calm my husband a bit and maybe we can get back to you on that?"

"Sure thing, kiddo! HA! Kiddo! Get it? You're gonna have a kid!"

"Yes. Quite clever, Buck." It was far from clever, but Allison had grown to embrace the juvenile humor of her husband and his friends.

"OK, Buck. Go back to bed. And please, I have one favor to ask. PLEASE do not tell anyone. Frankly, Curt shouldn't have told you yet, but I'm glad he did." She actually wasn't, but at this point, raising such concern was a moot point.

"You got it, 'Kiddo.' Just between us." Buck was still riding the kiddo joke, no matter how lame it may be.

"Thanks, Buck. Have a good night."

The two hung up, and Allison looked at Curt. He had a wide grin on his face. "Curt. I'm glad you're happy, but can we make a deal? Please let's not tell anyone else until I see a doctor and we get through the first trimester. OK?"

"Sure. Sorry. You're right. I wasn't really thinking. I am just so excited." He meant it. All of it. Allison drove the rest of the way home; a two-minute ride. They parked and entered the house. The evening was still young, but neither wanted to go out. They'd go to bed early and watch a movie. Soon to be parents, they wanted to practice playing the part. Plus, tomorrow would be Monday, and the work week would start. The day's events held more than enough excitement.

Chapter Four
Noorullah's Revenge

Allison had fallen asleep no less than halfway through the movie. She'd let Curt pick the flick and, as usual, he'd selected an old classic comedy, this time *Caddyshack*. They'd both seen it many times; Curt voluntarily, and Allison somewhat under duress. As she laid there, Curt looked down at Allison and quoted a line to her, speaking as if he were Bill Murray, "I don't think the heavy stuff is gonna come down for a while, Judge." Curt laughed. It was time to go to bed. He turned off the TV and curled up with Allison. Everything was going to be OK as Curt drifted off to sleep... and to his dreams. His eyes began to twitch. Curt was back on deployment in his mind...

The late morning sun was scorching, shining down on his Forward Operating Base near Qalat. It was a small town in Zabul Province, in southern Afghanistan, east of Kandahar. Curt had just finished showering as he heard HH-60 Blackhawks approaching. The ever-increasing rotor blade thumping was unique and a dead giveaway. Dozens of rotary wing assets transitioned through the base every day. There was no need for alarm. Curt went to his hooch and changed into his uniform.

As he dressed, he recalled the previous night's mission. It went well and soon he'd be writing up a situation report about it for submission to headquarters. Two EKIA (Enemy Killed in Action), and one HVT (High Value Target) captured. The mission's target, the HVT, had surrendered and would soon be moved to Bagram Air Base for questioning and interrogation. No friendly wounded, no friendly losses. The mission was a success.

Curt, now dressed, grabbed his M-4 rifle, slung it over his shoulder and began walking to the chow hall, hoping to catch a late breakfast or early lunch. As he did, a young sergeant medical technician from the base clinic ran up, "Captain, Captain! Can you come with me? We need an officer!"

The medical technician did not realize Curt was a Naval

15

officer. "Uh, OK. But I'm a Navy Lieutenant, not a Captain. What's the issue?"

"There is a small boy who needs lifesaving surgery! Now! And the Afghan father won't approve it! Please! You gotta help!"

The medical technician tugged on Curt's sleeve, and he began walking towards the clinic. He could see the commotion there. "OK, I'll go. But where is the base commander? Shouldn't he deal with this?"

"Yes, but he is out on a mission with the Zabul Governor and our other officers. You are the highest-ranking officer I could find. Please! There is not much time!"

As Curt approached the clinic, he could hear a childish voice, yelling in ear-piercing pain and crying. The screaming was repetitive, "ALLAH AKBAR! NO! ALLAH AKBAR!" That phrase, 'Allah Akbar,' was feared by every coalition military member. In most cases, it meant an imminent attack from a suicide bomber or another bad actor; chaos and death would soon rain down upon anyone within earshot. Most had mentally prepared for how they'd manage hearing such a phrase. Few had planned on hearing it from a four-year-old child clinging to life.

"Hello, I'm Lieutenant Curt," Curt said to the head doctor at the clinic. Last names for Special Operators like Curt were rarely shared. "What's going on?"

"Curt, I'm Dr. Matt Masquelle. Come with me." From his uniform, Curt could tell Matt was a Major and of senior rank, but in the military medical community, that mattered little. Curt recalled seeing Matt just weeks before. Unfortunately, Matt worked feverously to save one of Curt's fellow SEALs after an ambush attack. The effort was unsuccessful. It was war.

The screams grew louder. "OUCH! NO! ALLAH AKBAR! PLEASE STOP! ALLAH AKBAR!"

Matt took Curt inside the clinic. There, three medical staff were holding down the boy and pouring water on his left leg just above the knee, or what remained of it, which wasn't much. The fibula bone was still there, but the tibia was nowhere to be found, likely with the kneecap, which also was void from the boy's leg. His calf muscle was reduced to the width of a few bloody red shoestrings. At the lower end, the child's foot was partially intact, minus the entire section that had once been his toes. Matt spoke. "This is Noorullah. He's four years old and desperately needs an amputation. He, his six-year-old brother, Naimatullah, and seven-year-old cousin, Rahamatullah, were out in the desert kicking a scrap piece of metal that turned out to be a landmine. Rahamatullah is dead from massive internal organ damage. Naimatullah was lucky and only has superficial wounds."

"ALLAH AKBAR! ALLAH AKBAR! STOP! DADDY PLEASE!" The crying and screaming didn't stop.

Dr. Masquelle paused and then pointed outside the clinic. "Noorullah's father, Bakht Mohammad, is the man I was talking to when you walked up. He refuses to allow his son to have surgery. Since we are on a U.S. military installation, I must follow U.S. law. I cannot perform any medical procedure without parental consent. If we do not start soon, Noorullah will die."

"So, all you need is parental consent?" Curt asked, over the shrieks and screams of pain.

"Yes. That's all I need," Matt responded, somewhat sarcastically, that such a request should be easy. "We've tried for over forty-five minutes to get Bakht to agree. He refuses and demands fifty dollars and a cab to the Kandahar hospital."

"Is that an option?" Curt asked.

"I WANT MY DADDY! ALLAH AKBAR! PLEASE STOP! ALLAH AKBAR!" Over, and over, and over.

"For Noorullah, no. Kandahar is over an hour ride away and he'd be dead well before arriving. Bakht says he doesn't trust U.S. doctors, which, from his perspective, I understand. That said, I'm a Maryland National Guard soldier on rotation. My normal job is at Johns Hopkins Hospital where I am a pediatric surgeon. I'd be surprised if there was anyone more qualified to perform this surgery in all of Afghanistan," the doctor stated matter of fact. He was likely correct. Noorullah was lucky... or could be lucky, depending on his father's decision.

"OK. Got it. I'll go talk to Bakht," Curt said.

"Hurry, L.T. (Lieutenant). Time is not on our side."

Curt went back outside, where Noorullah's screams could still be heard, but no longer as loud. The poor child had lost his voice from screaming so harshly. Curt sent one of the many U.S. military members who'd gathered around now to fetch his interpreter. Most of the military surrounding the area were members of a Provincial Reconstruction Team (PRT), a unit tasked with bringing stability, governance, and security to the Afghan people. Seeing a little boy on his deathbed was completely counter to the mission goals and objectives. Concern for Noorullah was tearing them up inside.

Curt's 'terp' (interpreter) arrived and was quickly briefed up. He began speaking to Bakht in Pashto. The two started raising their voices back and forth. Curt's terp, Majeed, turned to Curt and said, "Sir, he refuses surgery. He demands $50 and a cab."

"Yes, I know," he responded to Majeed, then grabbed Bakht's arm and took him into the room. There, he pointed at Noorullah, laying on a gurney, medical staff pouring fresh water on the remaining pieces of his leg and Noorullah screaming in pain. Curt raged. "Is this what you want? Look at him! He's dying." Majeed did his best to translate it with the same intensity.

When Noorullah saw his father, the screams intensified over his increasingly hoarse larynx.

"DADDY! HELP ME! PLEASE! ALLAH AKBAR! PLEASE! ALLAH AKBAR!"

Majeed translated Noorullah's pleas to Curt, who stared into Bakht's eyes. It was strange. Curt could see true emotional pain in Bakht's face, the pain one would expect a father to feel, but Noorullah's cries did nothing to convince him.

Bakht spoke to Majeed, then to Curt. "Sir, he still refuses."

Realizing the direct and threatening approach had just failed, Curt brought Bakht back outside the clinic and changed tactics as the crowd grew even larger. "Bakht, I know you are saddened. You lost your nephew, and you may lose your son. I promise you to everything on Allah, our doctor is the best in Afghanistan. I beg you to sign the approval." Majeed again relayed the message. Curt didn't need to wait for his terp's response. Majeed answered in Pashto, but shook his head no.

Over and over, Curt tried different approaches. For nearly another hour they spoke, and nothing worked. Noorullah was still screaming, now fully hoarse. Noorullah had been without most of his lower leg for over three hours by now. Louder and louder, the little boy's screams grew in Curt's head.

"Sir," Majeed said. "Can I speak to you alone?"

"Yes, Majeed. Please." Majeed led Curt away from everyone where the two could speak.

"Sir, I don't think you understand. No matter what you do or say, Bakht will not allow his son to have surgery. You see, he is a Kochi (*Koo-chi*) tribesman. They are nomads or kind of like gypsies who wonder the Afghan deserts in clans." Majeed stopped there, hoping he'd said enough for Curt to understand.

"OK, Majeed. But what does that have to do with this?"

"Sir, Bakht doesn't want $50 to go to Kandahar. It's his excuse to get away from here. He wants a cab to drive his son to the desert and let him die."

"Die!?" Curt responded. "What do you mean he wants Noorullah to die? To kill him?"

"Sir, you don't understand our ways. In a nomad clan, a boy with one leg is not of no value. Actually, it is worse than that. He's a hinderance, a burden. He will hold back the clan and will be a drain. The clan elders won't allow Noorullah to remain. He will be kicked out of the tribe. Our nation doesn't have social structures like modern nations." Majeed paused, and then continued. "If Noorullah lives, it is likely he will become a homeless beggar on the streets of Kandahar. He will probably be beaten, abused and raped. That is not a life that Bakht wishes for his son. Letting him die now spares Noorullah such a life of suffering." Majeed said all this extremely matter of fact.

Curt was stunned. As a SOF (Special Operations Forces) officer fighting in Afghanistan, he'd taken his share of lives from the Taliban. To learn the paltry value placed on human life in Afghanistan, or at least in tribal communities, floored him. Curt walked away from Majeed, back into the clinic, and stared at Noorullah. Their eyes locked. Curt could not only see the immense fear in Noorullah's eyes but also a desire to live.

Curt stormed back out and addressed Majeed. "Tell him

19

that's why the U.S. promises to never leave! We are going to help them get there. Things are going to change. His son will have new prosthetic devices as he outgrows them. The social nets will come from Kabul once the nation improves!"

Majeed did not turn to Bakht. He didn't need to. None of what Curt just shared would be of value. Majeed spoke back to Curt. "Sir, forgive me. But these are the same promises the British gave our people in the 1800s and the promises the Russians gave our people in the 1900s. We've heard these too many times to believe they are real."

"Fuck this!" Curt said out loud. Sternly, he walked back to where Bakht Mohammed was standing. He pulled his phone out of his cargo pocket and placed a call to the Zabul Governor's chief of staff, Nazir.

"Nazir, L.T. Curt here. Look, I need you to tell this man to approve a surgery, or I'm closing down our base."

"Curt, I am with the Governor right now and your base commander. I don't know what you're talking about."

"Great, put the base commander on the phone." Nazir handed the phone over.

"Lieutenant Colonel Mark Flaherty," the commander said.

"Sir, Curt here. I don't have much time." Curt explained the situation. Lieutenant Colonel Flaherty wasn't only the base commander, but also the PRT Commander. A boy dying on the base was the last thing he'd want.

Within a half hour, Nazir would be on the Forward Operating Base. He would pull Bakht aside and speak with him. While Curt would never verify it, he was fairly confident a significant wad of money was handed over to Bakht as he shook Nazir's hand. After that discussion, Bakht signed the paperwork, and Dr. Masquelle began the surgery.

Curt returned to his hooch, alone. He could still hear Noorullah's screams. Curt was exhausted. He'd missed lunch, but he didn't care. Curt laid down and fell asleep. As he did, Noorullah's screams grew louder and louder and louder, until...

Now, experiencing a nightmare inside of a nightmare, Curt awoke... back at home, in bed with Allison. Neary hyperventilating, he sat up and screamed, "**STOP!!!!!!**"

Allision jumped out of the bed and stood up, as if ready to fight an intruder. As she calmed, she saw Curt in bed, covered in sweat, appearing as if he'd just run ten miles at a sprint. "Curt! What the hell? Sweetheart, are you ok? Who are you talking to!?" She turned on the nightstand light. There in the bed, she could now see his arms and legs were shaking.

She climbed back into the bed to hold him. He squeezed her tight. He couldn't talk just yet. She rocked him, quickly at first, and then slowed the pace.

"Curt. What happened? Did you have a nightmare?"

"Let's just go to bed," he responded.

Confused, Allison offered a bending ear. "Do you want to tell me about it?"

"No. Not at all."

"OK." Allison turned off the light and held Curt. She would try to sleep. Curt would not. The last place he wanted to be was back in Afghanistan, his last deployment. He'd stare at the ceiling, praying for the morning alarm to ring and get him out of bed.

Chapter Five
Ambassador's Granddaughter Skating

It had been well over a year since John Gerzema asked to meet Andrew Denney for lunch. John departed the Senate years ago, followed by a failed run for the White House. Without a need to raise campaign funds, there was little reason to meet with Andrew.

Andrew walked around his bedroom, curious as to why John would invite him to lunch. He lamented over it to his wife as he got dressed. "Do you really think he's gonna run again? For President? He's crazy if he thinks he can win." Andrew asked out loud.

"I don't know. Stranger things have happened in politics," Becky responded. She was correct, but if pressed, she couldn't name one. Becky was a loyal southern wife, but she wasn't much of a political insider. She loved being an old school southern homemaker, and she loved Andrew. Her husband was just happy that Becky, for the most part, had come to terms with their oldest son's suicide. Don had been dead for a bit less than a year, and she was finally moving on.

"Yes, my love," Andrew responded. "You're correct. Stranger things have happened. But he's older, and a run now, even for a Senate seat, would impact his future chances at the Presidency. Maybe he's starting a PAC (Political Action Committee)?" Andrew lamented.

"Well, whatever it is, I'm sure he will tell you soon enough," Becky said as she walked over to grab his fine Italian leather shoes. The maid had cleaned them days before and the shoes were a perfect match for his outfit. "Here," she said, as she handed them over.

"Yes, I suppose you're right. I wonder how much he knows about my falling out with the White House?" Andrew's question had relevance. Both Andrew and John had bones to pick with the current administration, especially after how things played out in the Balkans.

"Oh, I don't know," Becky responded. "It always seems to

me no matter how angry D.C. politicians get; their frustration magically disappears when money is to be made."

Andrew looked at his wife and kissed her on the cheek. "You are ever so right, my dear."

"Andrew, you need to leave soon, if you're going to make lunch."

"Right again," he replied. Andrew finished adjusting his belt, kissed Becky one more time, then departed.

The ride into D.C. was lovely as Andrew drove south on the George Washington Memorial Parkway, approaching the city from the north. The road paralleled the Potomac River, and a dense green tree canopy provided gorgeous views overlooking the river. Soon, the tall buildings of Georgetown University would come into view, stunning in their own right. Andrew would turn onto Francis Scott Key Bridge, cross the river, and enter Georgetown. Soon, he'd be at Filomena Ristorante, a small but popular upscale establishment.

Seated alone at a small table inside was John Gerzema. The table was tucked away in a back corner and relatively private by D.C. standards. No politician wanted to grovel for campaign funds within earshot of others. A crystal vase with a lone flower sat on a spotless and pressed tablecloth. Next to it was an elegant salt and pepper shaker set, along with utensils and napkins. As Andrew approached, John stood, "Andrew! It's been far too long. I'm grateful you took my call. Please join me."

Andrew shook John's hand, grabbed a chair, and sat. "I'm happy you called, John. You're right, it has been too long." Much of this was political politeness. Both knew if John didn't need something, such a meeting would never have taken place.

"How is Becky doing, Andrew?"

"Oh, she's doing fine. Thanks for asking."

"Before we go too far, I want you to know. I feel awful about your son's passing. It was truly a shock to many of us."

"Thanks, John. That means a great deal to me," is what Andrew said. What he thought in his head was, *'Really? Perhaps you can explain why neither you, nor anyone from the administration that I gave thousands upon thousands of dollars*

23

showed up at his funeral at Arlington?' It's D.C., after all. Andrew's reply would remain polite. He would inquire as to John's family, mostly out of courtesy. The initial conversational chess moves in D.C. were ever so obvious.

A waiter took both the drink and food order over the open volley of moves. After the drinks were served, Andrew opened up the chessboard. "So, John, how is time with the family? As I understand, that is the public reason you stepped down from being the Defense Secretary." Andrew knew this was a poor excuse for the truth and was curious how long John would tow the party line.

Turned out, John had no intent to do so. "Andrew, you and I both know that was crap. I got pinched between the President and the Chairman. To this day, I still don't know exactly how, but I think I may have a clue. Which is why I asked to meet you for lunch."

"Interesting. I didn't know about the issue with the Chairman. I've met Admiral Hershey. He seems like a good man. Surprised he'd be wrapped up in something nefariously political." Andrew, in fact, had met Admiral Hershey months ago when he shared the information about the Stojanovic family. Could John know about this meeting?

"Yes, well, I don't know exactly what Squirt's role was in this, but I know it's extremely uncommon for the Defense Secretary to not know about a Special Ops mission in a foreign land."

"Oh, you mean the Balkan thing. Yeah. I saw it on the news. Some super secretive mission," Andrew responded, knowing far more of the story than he'd let on about. Quickly, he changed the subject. "So, what is it you are looking to do? Are you putting together an exploratory campaign for the Presidency again? I'm actually somewhat confused as to why you brought me here."

"No Andrew. I want my old job back. I want the Secretary of Defense position."

Andrew chuckled. "John. I don't think I've ever seen that, nor do I think it's possible. In less than a year, you want back a job you supposedly stepped down from?" He took a drink of his water. By now the food was being served and they both paused

24

the discussion. As they awaited the waiter's departure, John pulled out his iPhone and began playing with it. Eventually, the waiter left, and the two were alone again.

"Andrew, I understand you think it's impossible. Hell, until I learned a bit of interesting news, I too believed it to be impossible."

"OK. So, what is this interesting news?" Andrew asked.

John handed over his phone. A video was paused on the screen with a file name 'Ambassador's Granddaughter Skating.' "Push play," John said.

Andrew did as instructed and watched, nearly in disbelief. Just as John did when watching the first time. The content was utterly unbelievable. The video was a graphic video of the U.S. President having sex with a woman other than his wife in the White House's private quarters. Unbeknownst to either, this video was a key reason the entire Balkan situation just months ago nearly spiraled out of control. "Where did you get this?" It was all Andrew could mutter.

"Andrew, that doesn't matter."

"With technology, John, this could be a deep fake."

"It's not. I've had it verified." John was convincing.

"And what do you plan to do with it?" Andrew responded.

John took a deep breath, sat back in his chair, and slowly took a sip of water.

"Andrew, do you mind if I be blunt for a bit?"

"Not at all. Frankly, I'd welcome it."

"I am pissed about my termination as the Defense Secretary. And I know you are pissed that not one member of the White House staff, or even the President, attended your son's funeral." John paused.

"Well, yes. Becky and I were..."

John cut him off. "Andrew, don't bullshit me. Since your son's death last year, you've stopped contributing campaign funds to the President. I've pulled each of their monthly disclosures. You stopped contributing the month after his death. I don't believe that's a coincidence."

John was correct. "OK, John. Go on." Andrew was intrigued. This meal had completely spiraled into an atypical D.C.

discussion. It no longer resembled the common chess match.

"I want my job back, Andrew."

"John, I don't doubt that video will get your job back. You don't need me for that."

"Yes, you're correct, Andrew, but what then? I get the job back through extortion. I won't be trusted, and I definitely won't be lined up to run for the White House at the end of the second term. I need someone to help me do that. I realize we haven't been the greatest of political allies in the past, but you are the only person I know with enough political power and a disdain for the current administration. Sharing the video is only step one. I need you for something far greater."

Andrew sat there. Power in D.C. is an addictive drug, and nearly all of Andrew's previous power was gone. While he couldn't be certain, it appeared what John was offering was a chance to regain that power. Andrew was interested.

"John, this is all fascinating, but bottom line, how much is this going to cost me?" Andrew knew his place in D.C. politics. He wasn't a politician. He was a money guy.

"Andrew, that's the beautiful part. This not only costs you nothing, on the contrary, it makes you millions. All I ask is that when my campaign begins in a few years, a fair portion of the money you make is funneled to my campaign."

Whatever John Gerzema was offering, Andrew was fairly certain it was at a minimum unethical, if not outright illegal. Neither would stop him from continuing the discussion. "I'm listening."

During the rest of the lunch, John laid out his plan. Other than the waiter's occasional trip to the table to refresh glasses, there was no one within earshot. After finishing, John said, "So, what do you think?"

"John, I think it could work. But I need to think about it. What you're asking is a big step. I'm not sure I'm ready to make it."

"Oh, I understand, Andrew. Take a little time."

"Thanks, John, I will. And I thank you for considering me in your plan." Andrew knew there were a few others John could have gone to, but he also knew John selected him because of his grudge. Revenge was not the norm in D.C., but it existed. John also knew that because of Andrew's feelings towards the White House, there was little chance he would expose any of this to the President or others.

The meal was over, and the two stood up. "Don't worry about lunch, Andrew, it's on me." Andrew knew when a politician and not a lobbyist bought lunch, the intent was significant.

"Thanks, John. I appreciate it."

"You're very welcome. One last thing. If you help me with this and I'm elected, you're my first Ambassadorial placement. Just tell me where you and Becky want to go. You deserve it, Andrew. The both of you."

"That's quite kind, John. Thanks. Again. I need to think about it. Have a good day."

"You too, Andrew. You, too."

Chapter Six
Healing a Soul

As expected, Admiral Hershey delivered on his promise. He'd pulled some strings and now, Curt was working at the Veteran's Administration in the head position, overseeing PTSD and related issues among homeless veterans. It was a good job, and on this day, Curt arrived at work early. It was an effort to shake off the prior night's bad dream. Technically, it wasn't actually a dream, but rather reliving his past. During his 2016 deployment, Curt met Noorullah. After returning to the U.S., this event would be one of the key reasons Curt separated from the military and went into the medical profession. It also was the foundation for much of his PTSD.

After a while in his office, Curt could hear his secretary, Jill, fumbling outside his office. "Good morning, Jill. When you get a chance, can you come in here?"

"Yes, Dr. Nover. Right away." Jill was a wonderfully amiable lady. She'd worked in the Veteran's Administration as a receptionist / secretary for years. She came highly recommended and qualified, and Curt was pleased with her efforts. After a minute or two, she entered with a pad of paper and pen in her hand, as always.

"Jill, can you call down to Dr. Delligatti and see if she has some time today? I'd like to come by her office and discuss something."

Jill wrote down everything and then said, "Yes, sir. Right away." She left the office, and Curt could hear her already on the phone.

A minute later, Jill returned and said, "Dr. Nover, sir. Dr. Delligatti is currently in her office and says you can come by before nine if that works for you. She has scheduled patients after that."

"Yes, Jill. That would be great. Thanks. I think I'll walk down there now."

"As you wish." Jill went back to her desk and provided Dr. Delligatti a courtesy call notifying her Dr. Nover was on his way.

As Curt was now a high-level governmental official, unscheduled visits were part of the perks.

Curt knocked on Dr. Georgia Delligatti's door. It was partially open, as if expecting Curt. "Dr. Delligatti, it's me, Curt."

"Dr. Nover, please come in. What can I do for you?"

"Well, Georgia, this is somewhat of a personal call. I was wondering if I could talk to you a bit."

Dr. Delligatti shifted around the office chairs quickly, transitioning it from a professional setting to clinical. She was a psychologist at the VA and one of the best.

"Sure, Dr. Nover. Absolutely."

"And, please, as a patient, call me Curt."

"Sure, uh, Curt." It was a bit odd to refer to a person with such stature by his first name, but Georgia would manage.

Over the next thirty minutes, Curt shared the events of his night. Much like all the other health care professionals he shared it with in the past, she was stunned how Afghan society valued life versus the western world. He also shared that Allision was pregnant, and that perhaps was the catalyst for the dream.

"Well, Curt, you are likely correct," Dr. Delligatti responded.

"Yes, my question is, should I share all this with Allison? I don't want my PTSD spiking again, but the last time I kept a secret from Allison, I almost lost her. Now, with a child in our future, I couldn't imagine losing her."

"Curt, I think we both know that since you're even asking this question, you likely know the answer."

Curt knew she was right. "I know. It's just so hard. Trying to explain this to someone who can't comprehend Afghanistan is..." Curt paused.

"Yes. It's challenging," Georgia finished his sentence.

"Dr. Delligatti, it's worse than that."

"OK, I'm listening."

"As scarring as that event was, when others learned of it, they'd all tell me that I did the right thing."

Dr. Delligatti was surprised. "Don't you believe them? Surely you do?"

"Frankly, I don't know. I was not prepared to make such a

decision, and ever since I did, I realize I decided based on my framework of culture and society, a Western one. A society in which Noorullah doesn't live. I agonized when I got back to the U.S. Is he still with the Kochi Tribesmen? Is he receiving new prosthetics as he grows like the PRT Commander, and the Governor promised? Or is he a beggar in Kandahar? Is his life a nightmare? Does he wish he'd died back then? Does he curse me? Now that the U.S. departed Afghanistan, what will happen? Is he even alive? I don't know the answer to any of this."

Dr. Delligatti sat there for a moment trying to digest what Curt had rattled off. She'd heard many horror stories from veterans. This wasn't the worst, but it was one of the more unique and mentally anguishing stories she'd heard in her years of practice. "Curt. I can't answer any of that, and even if I could, I don't know what difference it would make. You were forced to make a quick decision. You did so based on your cultural values and norms. May I ask you? Do you believe in God?"

"I did. But since this event, I've had little ability or desire to worship."

"I can understand that. But faith is an extremely powerful asset to help deal with such things. I'm not saying rush out and join a congregation, but perhaps consider talking to a priest or friend who is religious."

"Yes. I hear ya, Doc. It's the same advice I received when I was first diagnosed with PTSD."

Georgia looked down at Curt's hands. They were drenched in sweat, as was his medical smock. "Curt. What do you say we stop for today? I'm proud of you for sharing this. I recommend that when you're ready, you share it with your wife. Eventually, she needs to know."

"Yeah. You're probably right. I need to get a new medical smock, anyway. I appreciate you listening. You came highly recommended, and I can see why."

"Well, thank you Curt, er uh, Dr. Nover. I appreciate it. Please, if you need to talk again, here is my card. On the back, I have written my personal number."

"Thanks Dr. Delligatti. I will call if needed. Have a good day." Curt shook her hand and walked out. He wouldn't need to hit the gym today. That hour session with Dr. Delligatti burned the equivalent calories of a ten-mile run.

****

Allison had returned home from work before Curt. Through the day, she thought about Curt's bad dream and decided to make his favorite dinner, her soon to be famous homemade baked mac and cheese along with pesto chicken breasts. The pasta was so good Curt had nicknamed it 'Mac-crack.' The kitchen table was set as Curt entered the house at street level. As he climbed the stairs, he could smell his favorite dish. Allison was more than he deserved.

He kissed and hugged her, then the two sat down. It was exactly what he needed to open up.

"Allison," he said. "There's some stuff from my past that I want to tell you."

There'd be no need to delay sharing his horror. Over dinner, Curt told her everything. Allison tried as hard as she could to understand. As Curt talked about Noorullah, his descriptions reminded her of the young boys in Akjoujt. She tried to make it as personal as she could to help comprehend. For most of it, she understood. However, when Curt began to explain his second-guessing if he made the right decision, Allison struggled. She could not fathom how Curt could contemplate if he made the right decision. 'Of course you did,' she thought. Allison remained silent, nodding up and down as if to say she understood, but the episode was hard enough for someone who experienced it firsthand... It was exceedingly tough for a pregnant woman bearing her future child.

After sharing his challenging story, Curt was spent and could take no more. He'd just shared his deepest scar twice in one day. It was exhausting. Curt climbed upstairs to bed. Allison appreciated the brief break from Curt, providing time to both process what she'd just learned and a bit of time to clean up the kitchen. After placing the last dish in the washer, Allison sat down on the living room sofa, alone. The next day, she'd have her first medical appointment regarding the pregnancy. Originally, she'd thought of asking Curt to join her. Now she wasn't sure. Perhaps it was best to let this one pass. There'd be others.

After a while reflecting on Curt's story, Allison went to bed, finding Curt already deep asleep. There'd be no nightmares tonight. Dr. Delligatti appeared to be correct.

****

After his lunch meeting earlier in the day, Andrew Denney placed a call to John Gerzema. He'd decided. "John, Andrew here. My apologies for the hour."

"Andrew. Thanks for the call. No concern, we were up just watching TV."

"Thanks. Hey, regarding your question at lunch. I'm in."

"Wonderful news, Andrew." John executed a small fist pump.

"As you directed, I will begin buying the stock tomorrow at market opening. Once I have enough, I'll demand a meeting with the leadership."

"Perfect. Please keep me informed. I have a meeting with a lobby group tomorrow and will let you know how that goes. I'm glad you're on board."

"Yes. Well, there are many steps. Let's take them one at a time. Good night."

Chapter Seven
Financial Alignment

Andrew sat alone in his home office. His computer was on, a cup of coffee by its side, and a large blank pad of paper with a pen resting on the top. The sun had just risen, and he was ready. Today, massive amounts of his personal funds, as well as funds under his control, would move. A handful of secure financial websites were open in browsers on his screen. Across the room, a TV hung on the wall. On it, CNBC blared across the room, with the tickers scrolling across the bottom.

In pre-market sales, Andrew made a few minor sales, testing the market and ensuring not to spook it. After each sale, he watched for any unexpected reactions. There were none. As the New York Stock Exchange bell rang, Andrew leaned in for the kill. He began selling off a massive amount of his existing holdings. Orders to sell: Nike, Amazon, Apple, Tesla, Ford, General Electric and many, many others.

On his desk, the phone rang.

"Hello, Andrew Denney."

"Mr. Denney, this is Todd Smith, a private financial manager from Charles Schwab. There's some significant activity on your accounts today and we just wanted to ensure it was you."

"Yes, Todd. I am doing some restructuring of my account today. I appreciate the call."

"Well, sir. You are one of our most valued customers. We'd be happy to take care of these transactions for you."

"No, Todd. That's unnecessary." In most cases, he welcomed such monitoring of his accounts. Today, the courtesy call irritated him. He wanted little knowledge of his actions, and no meddling. It was an undue risk; he'd have none of it.

"OK, Mr. Denney. Well, we are here if you need us."

"Great, thanks. Good day." Andrew hung up. The phone call was not his focus.

Once Andrew amassed his war chest, he began buying. He placed an order for 1,000 shares of BAYN on the Frankfurt Stock Exchange. He'd set up his account to continue purchases, 1,000 transactions over the next three days, for a total of 1,000,000 shares. The German markets would soon close for the day as they were six-hours ahead of U.S. Eastern Standard Time. Buying stock in relatively small chunks limited the stock price elevation due to demand. On a regular trading day, BAYN only had a volume of 250,000 transactions. A single trade of 1,000,000 shares would set off bells, whistles and sirens... something Andrew wished to avoid, hence, the myriad of small purchases.

MYER, or Myer, Inc. from Germany, was one of the largest pharmaceutical companies in the world and had a long-standing existence. Andrew watched his computer closely. Approximately every 2.5 minutes, a trade order request was placed and filled. Slowly, his position in BAYN grew. As expected, Andrew's demand for the stock slightly drove the price up. In the end, it wouldn't matter. By the time he sold the stock, he'd more than double his money. It was a sure bet.

****

In D.C., John Gerzema was scrolling through his notes, preparing for the day. Dressed in a dark suit with a red tie, he planned to exude power. He'd asked for a meeting with the leaders of a large lobbying firm, KHG, or Kennedy, Horowitz and Graham. One of the senior members was an old colleague who welcomed the meeting with the former Defense Secretary. John stepped out of his Georgetown residence, carrying his umbrella. The rains in the capital are often unpredictable, especially in the spring.

He'd soon hail a cab for a ride to Clyde's restaurant on M Street. It was a brief ride. His contact would also have a quick cab ride. KHG was nested down on K Street, packed in with many other D.C. lobbying firms. John was confident he could pitch the deal today, but if he couldn't, it was not a major loss. At last count, there were over twelve thousand lobbying firms registered in Washington, D.C. If KHG didn't want his business, certainly another would.

John's cab stopped, and he strolled into Clyde's. The restaurant had a warm atmosphere. The décor shimmered with wood accents and a feel reminiscent of the 1920s and 1930s. John found his colleague, Steve Bryant, waiting in a high back booth.

"Steve! Great to see you," John said.

"John, you as well! You look great for a guy who just retired," Steve said in a small jest. They both knew John had neither wanted to retire, nor, in fact, had he retired.

Steve attempted to stand up in the booth as John reached out to shake hands. Over many years in D.C., they'd partnered a decent number of times on important legislation, many of which they recalled fondly. They'd also butted heads on other legislation, yet somehow seemed to forget such things at times like this.

Over the first five minutes of the conversation, it was the standard D.C. discussion. Family, kids, job, placing drink orders, placing food orders. Neither would confess, but just prior to the meeting, each had reviewed their 'dossier cards.' On each of these detailed cards, the names of family members, along with unique granular info unique to that individual. Little Katie Bryant, Steve's daughter, for example, had just started piano lessons the last time John and Steve spoke. John's inquiry about her lessons was a great way to demonstrate he truly cared about the Bryant family. They both did it. Heck, nearly everyone in D.C. did it. After the small talk, as well as receiving their food, the actual conversation began.

"Steve, I am quite grateful you accepted my lunch invitation. I think I have some information you will find quite beneficial."

"John, it's always a pleasure to catch up with you. With or without you imparting beneficial information."

"I mean it, Steve. I think this is a tremendous opportunity. You're the first one I came to."

"Well, I'm all ears. What do you have?"

"There's going to be a large, fast tracked Defense Department procurement effort in less than a month." John used all the key words. 'Fast tracked' meant that the contract would be 'sole sourced,' meaning only one vendor considered.

35

'Less than a month' meant money would flow quickly; far faster than the usual years it takes for defense contracts to mature.

"Quite interesting. And how do you know this contract is going to be offered?"

John just leaned back. "Because I'm going to be the one to offer it."

"John, no offense, but you're no longer the SECDEF. I'd also gently point out you have a one-year cooling-off period by law where you cannot lobby the Defense Department."

"Steve, I understand those concerns, but I can assure you, they won't matter. That said, any further discussion with details will take a bit of effort on your part."

"I'm listening," Steve replied, realizing nothing in D.C. was for free.

"I want a board seat with full salary for one year, paid up front, with a $1.5 million sign-on bonus." John had that line memorized. He had rehearsed it in his mirror a dozen times.

"John, I think retirement has affected you. That's a huge ask. The board seat is an easy do, and you know we'd love to have you." Steve was being sincere, if not soft balling a job offer. Every D.C. lobby group would welcome the chance to have the former Secretary of Defense in their strategy meetings.

"I can assure you, the opportunities I can lay out in under one year will make your clients one hundred times what I am asking."

"OK, let me take your offer back to my colleagues. Can you give me any more to entice them?"

"I wish I could, Steve. But we both know that's not how the game is played. Everyone assumes their portions of risk in this city. Again, I came to you first with this. If KGH doesn't wish to pursue the offer, I'll find a firm that does. You have many competitors in this town."

No lobbyist in D.C. welcomed discussions about the competition, but it was a fact. Steve looked at his watch. "OK. Got it. Hey, I gotta run. I appreciate the time."

John stood up to say farewell. "Sure thing. Let me know soonest. Opportunities like this have a rather short leash."

"Will do." They shook hands and Steve departed. John

pulled out his wallet and thought to himself, '*Poor form, Steve. Sorry.*' John could tell merely from Steve's body language that there was little chance KHG would pursue the venture. John threw a credit card down on the table to cover the bill, then scrolled through his phone. He called Andrew. "Hey Andrew."

"John, how did your lunch go?" Andrew queried with interest.

"Not great. Doesn't seem KHG is interested."

Andrew paused, digesting the disappointing news. He then responded, "So, what's the play?" He wasn't overly concerned. Rejection in D.C. was commonplace.

"I'm going to reach out to a buddy in the Abraham Project, Zach Peters. Let's see if they are interested." At his desk, Andrew scribbled down the name and the firm.

"OK. Sounds good," Andrew said. "All is progressing smoothly from my end," as he continued to watch shares of Myer, Inc. be purchased every 2.5 minutes.

"Great. I'll reach out to Zach in a few minutes. Need to settle the bill, hit the head, and check in with the wife."

"No worries. Let me know how it goes. Bye."

"Bye." They both hung up. Andrew quickly flicked his fingers in his personal phone and found the contact he was looking for. It simply said 'ZP.' He called the number.

"Zach Peters," the male voice answered.

"Zach, Andrew Denney here. Hey, I don't have much time. You're going to get a call from John Gerzema. I strongly encourage you to take his offer."

"The former Defense Secretary, John Gerzema? Hell, we'd love to talk to him. He doesn't need your push."

"I realize that, but he's coming with some big strings attached, a much larger asker than normal." 'Asker' over the years had grown to be a D.C. unique word. Originating from 'Tasker,' it was the merging with the word 'ask.' Almost everything in D.C. was either a tasker or an asker, and the lines between the two weren't always black and white.

Zach processed Andrew's comments. "I understand. Andrew, are you backing him on this?"

Andrew didn't need to think twice. "Yes, I am."

"OK," there was a pause. "Wow, Andrew, you work quick. John's calling on the other line."

"Good. Please don't mention my call."

"I won't. Take care. Gotta go." With that, Zach switched over to the call with John Gerzema.

"Zach Peters."

"Zach, hello there. John Gerzema here."

"Secretary Gerzema! Great to hear from you," Zach said. "How are you doing?"

"Ha. Zach, it's just Mr. Gerzema now. I'm good, thanks for asking. Any chance you'd be free for a few drinks at happy hour? I'd love to run something by you?"

"Sir, yes. I am free. Sounds good."

Zach would meet with John and listen intently. If Andrew's money was backing the effort, there'd be little concern about meeting John's asker. After drinks, John departed the meeting far more confident than he had been after the one with Steve Bryant; all of which he relayed to Andrew, who attempted to act surprised.

****

"He wants what?" the well-dressed elderly man said as he sat at the end of a long, dark walnut conference table with a handful of others seated along the sides.

"$1.5 million, a year's salary up front and a board seat," Steve Bryant relayed to the senior members of the lobby firm.

"Nonsense!" the elderly man bellowed. Louis Kennedy was loosely tied to that of the famed Massachusetts Kennedy family. "He may have been the former SECDEF, but that's just ridiculous. Tell him, no thank you."

At another conference room on K Street, a similar discussion was taking place at the Abraham Project. That meeting would progress in a much different fashion. Zach Peters would pitch the same request, this time with the backing of Andrew Denney. The association of that name to the offer made all the difference. Throughout the night, the Abraham Project began working up contracts and securing funding. If this venture would move as fast as John had indicated, they needed to be prepared to act.

Chapter Eight
Hello Again

Curt was finishing work for the day. He was quite productive, a byproduct of a good night's sleep. He was also happy he had taken the steps to share his story about Noorullah with Allison. There were only a handful of people who truly knew the full extent. To Curt, every time he told the story, he was exposing himself, a feeling he dreaded.

Changing into his cold weather biking attire, Curt left his office and headed out on his road bike. The trek back to Eastern Market would be roughly ten miles, a great mini workout for the day. The ride felt great and as he worked his way south on North Capitol Street, things could not have been more perfect. He began riding harder to get home.

Curt accelerated downhill into an underpass. As he hit the bottom and began climbing, he popped up and out of the saddle, grabbed the handlebars firmly, and began pumping the pedals hard, trying to maintain the impressive speed all the way up the hill. He nodded his head down and pushing harder. As he looked up, a silver Tahoe was pulling out in front of him. The driver hadn't noticed Curt.

"Hey!" Curt screamed, and the driver slammed on the brakes. The screech of locked brakes roared, and another car slammed into the back of the Chevy Tahoe. Curt parked his bike and ran up to the accident; the two cars now affixed bumper to hood. As he approached, he could hear a child screaming.

"Is everyone alright?" Curt asked.

The adults were fine, but unfortunately, in the back seat, a beautiful little African American girl had suffered an injury. She was in a child seat, but she had wrapped her left arm around part of the seat awkwardly. As her mother slammed into the back of the Tahoe, the young girl's body weight propelled her forward, trapping her arm and breaking both her ulna and radius. The pain was intense, and she screamed in pain.

Curt told the mother he was a doctor as he quickly began to examine the child. The swelling around the girl's forearm was

40

mushrooming. He tried to calm her down, but there was no use. She was scared, injured, and being treated by a stranger. Her cries started to weigh on Curt, reminiscent of Noorullah. He could take no more.

"Ma'am, I am going to have to leave. Your daughter is going to be fine. An ambulance will be here soon and when she gets to the hospital, I recommend X-rays. From there, the ER staff will assist you."

Before the woman had a chance to thank Curt, he was on his bike, riding quickly away. This time, however, he was not racing to get home, but rather to get away from the accident.

Once home, he found Allison in the living room. "Hey baby. Welcome home," she said as she saw him in riding shorts. "How was your ride?"

"Good. Hey, baby. It's great to see you." He grabbed her and hugged her tight. Curt chose not to share his recent events.

Allison kissed him. "I have a surprise for you," she said.

"I could use a surprise," Curt said. "Just promise it's good news."

"I think you're gonna love it. Here, look." With that, she handed over an ultrasound photo. Their baby, while indistinguishable from a kidney bean, was clearly in the womb. "Meet the newest member of our family!"

Curt took the image and stared at it. "You had a medical appointment today?"

"Yes. My first of many, or should I say, our first of many."

"Why didn't you tell me? I would have wanted to go."

"Curt, after the past few days, I thought it better to give you some space. I was trying to think of you."

Curt was upset. "Allison, come on. I'm a doctor. This is our child. Please. I don't need you protecting me. I'm a big boy."

"Curt, I know that. Come on. This should be a joyful event. The doctor says we have a healthy baby and everything about the pregnancy is perfect."

Curt tried to set aside the fact she hadn't invited him behind, but that wasn't the real issue. Curt's mind raced as he questioned how he could ever raise a child when he couldn't even help a young, beautiful little girl who needed him? "I'm

41

sorry. Look. I'm gonna go for a walk to clear my head."

"OK. Do you want me to get us some dinner?"

"Get something for yourself," Curt snapped. "I'm not hungry. I just need to get some fresh air. I'll be back later." Curt walked out of the house without kissing Allison. He walked along E Street Southeast towards Marion Park, a small city park, which housed a dog park and playground, nestled in the heart of 'row home' central. Curt grabbed a seat on one of the park benches. He watched kids play and laugh. He watched dogs frolic as their owners gabbed over trivial topics. To Curt, those adults were about as alien as Martians. *'Am I ever going to fit in?'* He thought. The sun had set, and Curt was still on the bench. He hadn't moved. Finally, he got up and went home. Allison had already gone to bed. She left a note on the kitchen table.

> *'Hey babe,*
> *I'm sorry I didn't tell you about the doctor's*
> *appointment. I promise to tell you about all the future*
> *ones. I bought you Chipotle for dinner. It's in the fridge.*
> *Your favorite. A carne asada burrito. Don't stay up too*
> *long.*
>
> > *I love you,*
> > *Allison'*

Curt went to the fridge, grabbed the burrito and ate it. He was lucky to have such a caring wife. Once finished eating, he climbed the stairs to bed, trying to remain quiet and let Allison sleep. He was able to prepare for, and get into, bed without disturbing her. Curt slowly threw his arms around her, kissed her gently and then tried to fall asleep...

He would sleep, but soon, he'd be in another dream...

The haze of smoke and smog was thick. Curt, dressed in nearly forty pounds of battle gear, was pulling point for his four-man team as they prepared to enter a building with potential hostiles. Silently, Curt motioned with his fingers. A countdown from five to one as the others watched through their night-vision devices. At one, they breached the front door, threw in a few flash bangs (noise grenades). Explosions rang out. Yelling to each, they continued in. Had anyone been in the entryway, it would have been overwhelming mayhem. They'd lost the element of surprise and raced professionally from room to room, clearing the structure. On the second floor, Curt kicked open a door. The room was empty except for a small child's body, lifeless. An electrical cord wrapped tightly around his neck as he hung from a light fixture in the middle of the room. A sheet hung from his shoulders to the floor, exposing only one arm. Curt slowly approached the body, which had it's back facing him. With the muzzle of his rifle, he shoved one shoulder and spun the corpse slowly. As the body turned to face him, Curt immediately recognized the boy. It was Noorullah. He'd been beaten repeatedly. Scars lined his face and neck. Some from abuse, others from heroin needle tracks. Open scabs and wounds lined the rest of his arm. Curt stepped back and gagged. He wanted to speak; to apologize to Noorullah. Curt grabbed the body, lifting it and desperately struggling to get it down, holding Noorullah face to face.

As he looked into the boy's face, Noorullah's eyes opened, staring directly at Curt.

"Hello, Curt," Noorullah said.

Curt froze. He couldn't respond. He held the boy's body but ceased his efforts to get the boy down.

"Don't worry about me anymore. I'm dead. I'm in Allah's hands."

Curt nodded. He still couldn't speak.

"I just wish I had gone when I first lost my leg. Why did you make me live?" Noorullah's face transitioned from one of kindness to that of anger. His eyes pierced into Curt and his brow narrowed.

Curt woke…

"I'M SORRY! I'M SO SORRY!" Curt screamed.

Allison jumped. "Curt! It's OK! It's OK! It's just another bad dream!"

Allison turned and held Curt tight. This was twice in under a week. Something was wrong. "Curt, what did you dream?"

Curt tried to catch his breath. He wiped away the sleepers from his eyes. It was either sleepers or tears; he wasn't sure. Finally, he was coherent and back in reality. "Oh, God. Sorry Allison. I woke you again. It was just a dream about Noorullah again. It's nothing. Please go back to sleep."

"Curt, are you OK? Seriously, please tell me. I'm here for you."

"Yeah. I'm fine. Just a nightmare. It's nothing, baby. Just go back to bed. You need your sleep."

Allison laid down while Curt got up to go to the bathroom. He splashed water on his face and stared at himself in the mirror. He repeated the process, bowing down to splash water again. This time when he looked up into the mirror, Noorullah was standing behind him with rope burns around his neck from his hanging. Curt quickly spun around, only to find he was alone. Noorullah was just a figment of his imagination. Curt closed the bathroom door, leaned back on it and slid down until he was sitting on the floor. He lowered his hands into his head. *'Is my PTSD ever going to go away? Am I ever going to be normal? What do I have to do, God! Or Allah, or Whoever! Please tell me!'* It was all he could think.

Chapter Nine
See Ya in D.C.

The time in New York was 0900Hrs and the large Boeing 757 painted with a U.S. Air Force VIPSAM (Very Important Person Surface Air Movement) Blue and White scheme landed at Andrews Air Force Base in Maryland. It had departed Brussels before sunrise, carrying U.S. Government officials assigned across Europe, who would participate in an interagency discussion on global air traffic management. Buck was on the aircraft, invited by the NATO delegation as a subject matter expertise on existing European Air Traffic Management issues. He hadn't told Curt, Allison or Smitty he was arriving.

A group of vehicles met the aircraft and transported the delegation from the ramp across the Maryland State line into D.C. Once in the District, Buck pulled out his phone and placed a call.

"Curt! Hey! It's Buck!"

"Buck? Dude, it's like three in the morning in Belgium. What are you doing awake?"

"Nope. It's about nine twenty where I'm at."

"What? Are you in Eastern Time?" Curt asked.

"Closer than that. I'm actually in a vehicle driving through D.C. on I-295 passing between Nationals Park and Eastern Market." Buck smiled. He knew he was less than a half mile from Curt's home.

"Buck, you idiot. What are you doing in D.C.?"

"I'm with some embassy folks attending some symposium at the Pentagon. We are staying through the night. Any chance you can round up Allison and Smitty for dinner? It's on me."

"Buddy, I'll rally them up, but we are buying. You're our guest. See ya tonight. Hey, by the way. You're the only one who knows Allison is pregnant. Let's try to keep it that way."

"What?!" Buck shouted into the phone. "Allison doesn't know she's pregnant?"

"Dude. Don't be an idiot," Curt responded.

"Ha. OK, sounds good. Our secret. As for paying, I'll arm wrestle you for the bill, and just know, I'll win. I haven't had sex with another partner for months. My right arm is in rare form these days. Ha!" Buck was loveable, but he'd never be a diplomat, and he was perhaps the only true connoisseur of his own jokes. Curt wondered who in the delegation made the awful choice to include him for the meeting.

"The quality of your jokes at least remains consistent, buddy," Curt shot back.

"Take care! See ya later! Buck, out!" Buck hung up. He was far more excited about seeing his friends for dinner than he was about visiting the Pentagon.

Buck and the rest of the delegation processed through the Pentagon visitor's center. They were all given a bit of time to grab some food and a coffee at the Pentagon food court. Buck snuck away, traveling up to the third floor 'E ring' or outer most ring. He again pulled out his phone to place a call.

"Smitty! Buck here! Are you OK?"

"Buck, why are you calling this early?"

"I just saw the news! Part of the Pentagon is under attack!"

Smitty jumped out of his chair and scrambled out of his office into the hallway outside the Chairman's office. There, standing in the hall, was Buck, smiling ear to ear.

"You're an asshole, Buck. A true asshole."

"You're right! I am! Hey buddy!"

"Buck, what on earth are you doing here?"

Buck explained the story. Smitty would be available for dinner. They'd all meet at a restaurant on 8th Street Southeast near Curt and Allison's row home.

The air traffic event Buck traveled to attend was far more boring than he predicted. He struggled the entire day to stay awake, drinking coffee from both Dunkin' Donuts and Starbucks in the Pentagon. At the lunch break, he walked into the middle courtyard of the Pentagon and took a nap in one of the large deck chairs. He finally made it through the day, looking forward to his evening with the gang.

After a quick shower at his hotel, Buck grabbed a cab to the Southeast section of D.C. at the corner of 8th and E Street. As he exited the cab, the street was alive with a mixed aroma of foods from places as far afield as Cuba, Belgium, Bosnia, the Chesapeake Bay, Mexico and Italy. Somehow, they blended to perfection. If one wasn't hungry when they arrived at Restaurant Row, they soon would be. It was one street away from Curt and Allison's condo, less than a thirty-second walk. Most of the residents in the area often had clean kitchens and empty dishwashers. The choices of food were just too many and the quality was outstanding. Tonight, dinner would be at Cava, an exceptional Greek restaurant that served dishes in tapas fashion, allowing for a wonderful group meal.

As Buck walked in, Curt, Allison, and Smitty stood at the bar. He could see their mouths moving, but the noise across the restaurant made it impossible to hear them. In true Buck fashion, he yelled, "SMITTY!"

His voice boomed so loud, the entire restaurant silenced, and everyone turned, staring at Buck.

From the bar, Smitty said at a normal level, "Buck, never one to pass up an opportunity at an awkward entrance! Welcome buddy!" The two walked towards each other and 'man-hugged' upon joining up. Following Smitty, Allison and Curt also greeted him in the same fashion. The restaurant background noise resumed as the other patrons were only slightly annoyed. The hostess, after Buck's display, changed their table from up front to the rear of the restaurant, stuffed away in a corner. To the gang, it didn't matter. They were together again.

"Buck! Seriously, what the heck are you doing in D.C. now?" Allison asked.

"According to the delegation from U.S. NATO, I'm an 'aviation expert.' It's some boring-assed conference. I dunno. They asked. I knew you all were here. It was a simple decision. We depart tomorrow afternoon. How are you doing, sweetheart? You look great, by the way!"

"Buck, you say that to all the women," Allison gushed.

"Yeah, especially Serbian spies," Smitty said, referring to Katarina, the honey trap Buck had fallen for in Austria, which nearly had cost him his life.

"Damn, Smitty! Too soon!" Curt jumped in.

47

"Not even close, Nover! Did you hear what this idiot did to me at the Pentagon today?"

Buck laughed, then told Allison and Curt in verbose detail about his prank earlier in the day.

Over the next few hours, the group ate, drank, chatted, and laughed. The discussions ranged from what everyone was doing now to memories of Akjoujt. Although Buck lived thousands of miles away, every time they were together, it was as if they hadn't missed a beat. After many drinks over the night, the bill came. Buck refused to allow others to pay and covered the tab. A minor fight ensued. Somehow Buck prevailed.

"Buck, thanks for the meal and the night. I gotta get back home. Early day tomorrow with the Admiral," Smitty said.

"All good, buddy. I'm really happy we got to catch up. When you coming to Europe?" Buck responded.

"Actually, I think Hershey is speaking at NATO soon. I'll find out, and when we come, I want to return the favor."

"Sounds great!" Buck was elated to hear about the potential visit. The two man-hugged. Smitty also provided his farewells to Allison and Curt, then walked away, leaving the three standing on 8th Street.

"Hey Buck, do you want to come back to our house for a nightcap?" Curt asked. "It's only a thirty-second walk."

"Do you have any cigars?" Buck responded.

"You drunk idiots are NOT smoking in the house," Allison said. Because of the pregnancy, she had not drank alcohol all night and had reached her fill of dealing with three drunk veteran Special Operator knuckleheads.

"Allison, come on... I wouldn't smoke in the house. You have a porch, right? We got jackets! All good! Plus, when we get to your house, I wanna feel that little baby bump!" Buck smiled with a shit-eating grin.

"Come on, Buck, ya damn drunk. Let's go. We'll figure it out when we get there," Curt said. The three walked down the street, back to the house.

Once inside, Allison kissed Curt goodnight and then hugged Buck. She'd had enough and wanted to sleep. Curt poured two glasses of Glenmorangie Scotch and grabbed a few Romeo et

Julieta cigars from his humidor. He and Buck walked out onto the back porch. "Buck, have a seat. I really can't begin to tell you how happy I am you're here."

"Me too, buddy. I really love living in Europe, but it gets lonely sometimes. I don't have many friends; you guys are really kinda it."

"Well, Buck, we'd love for you to move back. Cheers." Curt raised his glass, and the two clinked.

"Cheers, Curt." The two drank and prepared their cigars. Curt pulled out a lighter and within seconds, the two were drawing exceptional tobacco married with a wonderful single malt. Life was good.

"So, how is the business, Buck?" Curt asked.

"Actually, buddy, it's going really well. The replacement aircraft Admiral Hershey helped me acquire has really been a workhorse. The only problem I have is NATO has been asking for more capacity on flights than I can provide. For example, the flight here was a significant amount of folks. Because of this, NATO provided me with a stipend to perform a cost analysis regarding the procurement of a C-160 or even a C-130 for large movements. Frankly, I think that's cost prohibitive for their budget, but hey, I'll do the work and provide my report."

"That's really cool. I'm glad things are going so well. And what about all the drama from Natalie aka Katarina? Did NATO take any action against you?"

"Nothing really. I don't hold any clearances for NATO, Curt. I'm just a bus driver. I still get a few dirty looks, but that's understandable, and perhaps to a degree, deserved."

"Fair," Curt responded as he took a small sip of his scotch.

"What about you, Curt? How are you guys doing?" Buck asked.

"Actually, we are great, too. Allison has a great job she really likes. She's smitten with the baby. I couldn't be happier with the job that Admiral Hershey offered. I'm working daily with veterans that struggle. It's rewarding, Buck, and it's what I needed."

"Yes, the good Admiral has served us all well. To the Admiral," Buck raised his glass and the two again drank. "It seems Smitty is happy too," Buck continued.

"Yes. That dude is going to be an operator until he dies. He can't sit behind a desk. He loves action too much."

"I agree," Buck said. "I still don't understand how he got mixed up in Nissassa. I think back to Akjoujt and what they were doing. Bizarre."

"Buck, I think we all stumble in life sometimes. Even you," Curt said. He didn't have to expand further, given they'd just discussed Katarina.

"OK, fair point," Buck conceded. "Hey, different subject, what do you think about the Afghanistan pull out?"

"Well, I'm not a fan. As you probably recall, many of us who served there were continually told by the U.S. Government to continually promise the Afghans that the U.S. would never leave until their nation could stand on its own. Clearly, that didn't happen. I knew we couldn't stay forever. It was a difficult, high-level decision. Some days, I'm grateful I left the military when I did and didn't rise to a position where I was forced to make such decisions. A good number of the ones I made still weigh on me."

"I agree. It was a shit-show, and I dislike the way the departure made it appear many service members who made promises broke them. Washington broke the promise, but sadly, the everyday Afghans we worked with likely won't understand that nuance. What decisions did you make that weigh on you?" Buck asked.

"It's nothing, buddy. Not worth using the little precious time we have on it," Curt replied. Frankly, he didn't want to talk about it.

"Well, I tell ya. It weighs on me every night. One of my tours in Afghanistan was teaching members of the Afghan Army Air Corps how to fly C-130s. The Afghans received three aircraft through the Defense Security Cooperation Agency, and I worked hard to train them. I became close friends with an Afghan Major. Major Raz Mohammed. Up until the U.S. withdrawal, I would email or WhatsApp chat with him. He was a good aviator, and a great father to his children. He loved the West and what we were doing to advance Afghanistan. Now, he no longer responds to my emails or chats. I fear thinking about what happened to him." Buck's openness about his struggle was unbelievable to Curt.

"Buck, how do you do that? How do you just admit your struggles so openly?" Curt asked quizzically.

"I don't know, I guess... to be fair, I'm not in front of media cameras and bright lights. I'm with my good friend, perhaps my best friend. If I can't tell you, who can I tell?"

"Good point," Curt realized. "Well, you're not alone. I too have had nightmares and they seem to be increasing."

"About what?" Buck asked.

Curt shared his story about Noorullah. Buck listened intently and patiently. There were times he could be serious. This was one of them.

After Curt finished, Buck said, "When did the nightmares start? After our withdraw?"

"No," Curt replied, "After I learned Allision was pregnant."

Buck sat there for a bit, finished his scotch, and poured another for both of them. "Buddy. If your dreams are anything like mine, they feast on me. It's like they are killing me from the inside."

"Yup," said Curt. "I know the feeling."

"Well, there's perhaps no better place for you to work, given your flashbacks and nightmares. I wish I had something like that."

"Do you want an appointment?" Curt asked. He was partially embarrassed he didn't think to offer earlier.

"Nah. I think there's only one way I make them go away, and it ain't talking to someone."

Curt didn't understand. "What do you mean?"

"Curt, if this doesn't subside, I'm either gonna pay someone to go find Raz, or I'm going myself. I made a promise to him. I'm not breaking it, no matter what my stupid fucking government did." Buck was dead serious. It was in his eyes.

Curt thought about it. Would this be something he, too, would need to do? Should he pay someone to find Noorullah? The boy would now be around ten years old. Would he remember Curt? Was he abandoned by the tribe? Is he even alive? The only way to find the answers to these questions was the same way Buck was going to solve his problem with Raz.

"Buck, no disrespect, but you were a SOF pilot. You are comfortable at twenty thousand feet, but you'd be a hot mess on the ground. You can't go. Or you can't go alone."

"I wouldn't go alone. Curt, I have plenty of money thanks to Nissassa. I'd pay for a security detail. I'm serious. I'm really thinking of going."

Curt was quiet for a bit. "Yeah. I hear ya. I guess if I ever want to answer the questions that nag me about Noorullah, I may have to do that as well."

The two were quiet for a bit as they both took another drink. A loud SLAM crashed down from above. Quickly, they looked up. The sound originated from the forceful closing of the master bedroom window. It didn't' take Curt long to figure out what happened.

"What was that?" Buck asked.

"I have a suspicion Allison overheard our conversation," he said, pointing up to the bedroom window. He was right and merely the discussion of Curt traveling to Afghanistan after everything they'd been through was far more than she could process. Throw a pregnancy into the mix and the issue was akin to a nuclear explosion.

"Well, if you want, I'll try to find your Noorullah when I'm there," Buck said.

"Thanks, Buck. I appreciate it. Right now, I think I have some mending to do. Do you want to crash here tonight in the spare room?"

"What? And wake up to an angry, pregnant woman in the morning? Look, I love Allison, but I'm not married to her." Buck smiled. "I'll head out. Let's go back inside." The two extinguished their cigars and went back into the house. Curt walked Buck to the front door. "Goodbye, ya big lug," Curt said. "I love you, buddy."

"I love you too. Sorry about the discussion. I really didn't mean to cause any problems between you and Allison."

"It's OK. It's nothing we can't fix."

"Good. I'll shoot you a message about my future plan. Try to remember as many details as you can about Noorullah. I meant what I said. I'll go find him."

"I will. Thanks Buck. You're a great friend. I'm lucky to have you as a buddy."

"Same here, Curt, er uh... Doc." Buck walked away and shot a quick wave farewell. Curt closed and locked the door. He walked up to the bedroom, not knowing what he'd confront in Allison.

He opened the master bedroom door. The bed was empty and a mess. He looked towards the bathroom. The door was open, and the light was off. Allison was not there. He searched around and found Allison laying on the guest bedroom bed, clearly signaling she'd be sleeping alone that night.

Curt walked up to her, bent over and kissed her. "Good night, my love," he said.

"Curt, if you go to Afghanistan, I'm leaving. I mean it. I can't take it. I need you. Our baby needs you." Tears were in her eyes. She was dead serious.

Softly, Curt responded, "I understand, baby."

Her eyes clenched shut. It wasn't the 'I promise I won't go' she'd hoped for. She knew he was considering it, and it was killing her just as much as Noorullah was tormenting him.

Chapter Ten
The Naked Emperor

The crowd was lively as the President stood offstage. A local politician from Richmond was charging up the audience, preparing them for the President's speech. While it wasn't a Presidential election year, there was a midterm election for Congressional seats and fundraising was a never-ending effort. This year, Virginia was up for grabs.

As the host introduced the President, wild cheers and yells boomed from in front of the stage. Hail to the Chief played from large booming speakers. The scene made it hard to determine where Hollywood ended and politics began in the U.S. Both were filled with showmanship, yet more and more, only one seemed to have substance.

"Hello Richmond!" The President belted. He'd thank the crowd. He would then thank his colleagues for the gracious introduction. Then he'd stump for the local candidates. After a few good plugs for other candidates lower on the ballot, he'd shift the discussion to the national level. The ingredients for each speech had become the same. Identify an issue of concern, pour gasoline on it to amplify the flames, then accuse the other party as the arsonist. Of course, little proof would emerge. Why would they? Facts were often politically inconvenient. The crowd, firmly in the President's camp, desired no facts. He was 'their guy.' The similarities between voting bases and sports fan bases had become indistinguishable. Party affiliation was more important than policy, and the individual candidate trumped the importance of performance... always.

The President wrapped up his speech, waving to the crowd. Occasionally, he'd focus in on someone as if he knew them personally, offering a confident thumbs up. He, of course, didn't know members of the crowd; but it played well on video and was part of the game. After a while, he walked off the stage and was met by Steve.

"Great job, Mr. President. Nothing came through on your comm devices while you spoke."

"Thanks, Steve. God, I love stump speeches. The energy. It's infectious!"

"Yes, sir. Marine One is waiting for you about a mile away. The Beast is out back. We should get going if you're going to make your dinner appointment tonight." 'The Beast' was the nickname for the Presidential Limo.

The Secret Service was prepared for the Presidential movement. As the President shook hands backstage and started moving towards the exit, he looked up and saw his former Defense Secretary, John Gerzema, and Andrew Denney standing in front of him.

"John, Andy! Hey, great to see you here. What a pleasant surprise," the President said.

"Yes, Mr. President," John replied, "Like you, we need to do all we can to support the party."

"I'm glad to hear you say that. Hey, I need to get moving for a dinner back in D.C. I'd love to catch up," the President said as he turned to Steve. "Perhaps we can get John and Andy on the schedule?"

"Sure thing, sir," Steve responded, knowing full well it was a throwaway comment. There was no intent to meet.

"We'd welcome that, Mr. President. Hey, before you go though, I wanted to show you something." John Gerzema raised his phone and pushed play on a video titled, 'The Ambassador's Granddaughter Skating.' The volume was muted.

The President saw two seconds of it and nudged John's hand down, as to not raise too much suspicion. He'd seen the video before, courtesy of the senior Russian diplomat to the United States, Ambassador Tarlov, who leveraged it against the President a while ago. Angered, he had been assured this video would never again haunt him. He was wrong.

"Yes John, I've seen that video. Interesting." The President limited his words. He was still in public, surrounded by many supporters and donors.

"I agree, Mr. President. You know what? We don't have a ride back to D.C. Perhaps there's room on Marine One and we can catch up?" John's comment wasn't a request.

"Yes, sure John." The President looked at his Chief of Staff,

"Steve, please arrange for the former SECDEF and Mr. Denney to join me on the flight."

Steve scurried away, raising his phone, beginning the coordination effort.

"Great! Shall we go?" John asked, gently swinging his arm and hand in a fashion to suggest, 'After you.' The President worked the crowd a little more as he walked towards the vehicle door. The three entered The Beast. On the other side of the limo seating, Steve sat there, looking quizzically at the two. There would be no discussion.

Marine One's auxiliary power unit was humming, and the crew patiently awaited engine start for their VIP. As The Beast's doors swung open, the President got out and said, "Steve. I need you to ride back in the limo. I'm sorry. I'll catch you in D.C."

It wasn't a request. Steve knew there'd be no way to change his mind. "Yes, sir. I'll see you there." The limo door closed.

John and Andrew walked towards Marine One and entered the back door, reserved for visitors. A small press pool was on hand and in true showmanship, the President gracefully walked towards the helicopter, waving at the press pool. A young Marine snapped a salute as the President approached, returning the salute in a casual, civilian fashion. He climbed two steps, turned around, waved and said, "Thanks again, Richmond!" Seconds later, he vanished into the helicopter. A young Marine closed the door expeditiously, and the rotor blades turned, accelerating with every rotation.

The President settled into his chair. "So, John. May I ask you where you discovered this video?"

"You can ask. I'm not inclined to answer. Not yet, anyway."

"OK. Fair. I presume you want something. Do you want to discuss that?"

The helicopter lifted off, and the President waved to the crowd out the window.

"You fucked me. You know it and I know it. God Damn it! I did nothing wrong and to this day, I don't believe any of the bullshit that you orchestrated some super-secret Special Forces mission in Kosovo." John did all the speaking. Andrew just sat there, watching the show. It was enjoyable.

"John, my helicopter will be at the White House in around 15 minutes. Do you want to spend this time discussing the past or the future?" The President was right, and even in the most stressful situations, he could maintain focus on what was important.

"I want my job back."

"John. That's not going to happen. Never in the history of the Defense Department has a departed Secretary returned just months later. It's a bad look. We both know that. I can't even imagine how the other party would spin that in the media. Remember what you said back in Richmond, *Anything for the party*."

"Fuck the party," John retorted.

"John. I will work hard to find you something. You'll be back on the National Security Council. Just give me time."

"OK. While you do that, I want you to move forward with my proposal on Afghanistan. And I want the credit for it once the mission is accomplished."

It was the one thing the President didn't want to hear. For months, John continually tried to convince the President on an operational effort in Afghanistan that he swore had strategic implications. Never in his political career had the President heard of a Defense Secretary getting down into operational planning, which is why he continually dismissed John's idea. "John, again. I'll find you a new position in the administration. What about an ambassadorship?"

"I'm not screwing around. The mission goes within the next month AND I get a spot in the administration on the NSC. Much in the way you had U.S. SOCOM (United States Special Operations Command) lead that Kosovo crap, I'll oversee a planning cell and assets. I know if I don't, you'll do it without me."

"For Christ's Sake, John. Your idea is ridiculous. I have no idea how you'll be able to hide this effort, not to mention the fallout from our allies once they learn of it. Fine, I'll try to figure out a narrative to get you the Secretary position back."

John paused, "Look. I don't think you understand. You're

not in the driver's seat here. The effort in Afghanistan happens, and an NSC seat. It's not up for discussion."

The helicopter approached the White House as it overflew the Washington Monument. The President remained quiet. There was no response that would advance his discussion with John. Once set down on the South Lawn, Marine One's doors opened, and the President exited. As if old friends, he and John walked towards the White House while in the public eye. The media would be abuzz with speculation and rumors as to why the former Defense Secretary was with the President; exposing a public spat would only exacerbate rumors. The Press Secretary would simply point out the Richmond event was a political campaign where both the President and John Gerzema participated.

As the President neared the house, he stopped. "John, do nothing with that video. You don't share it. In the next few days, I'll figure out a plan to begin the process for your Afghanistan operation. I don't promise it will execute. But I will, at a minimum, start the process. Is that a deal?"

"Deal. For now," John said.

The President turned to Andrew, "Andy, it truly is good to see you. Steve relayed that we hadn't received your usual donation to the campaign yet. There are lots of tough races out there."

"That's odd, Mr. President. I'll ask my secretary to see where it might be." Andrew replied. From his tone, they both knew the payment didn't exist.

"Goodbye, Andrew and John. I presume you can show yourselves out." None of the three would shake hands. The President headed into the White House while John, accompanied by Andrew, would walk off the White House grounds towards 14th Street.

After exiting the grounds, John turned to Andrew. "Well, how do you think that went?"

"I've never seen him sweat before. It was entertaining. Do you think he'll agree to your demands and approve the Afghanistan operation? It's a bit of a stretch."

"Andrew, I don't think he has a choice."

"Good," Andrew replied. He'd taken significant personal risk moving money around.

John asked, "How are things going on your front?"

Andrew boasted a bit. "My funds are in place and you're looking at Myer's next Executive Vice President for U.S. Government Relations."

"Excellent," John replied.

"And you? What about the Abraham Project?"

"By tomorrow, I'll sign the contract. They didn't even try to negotiate. All the terms were agreed to," John stated. He was almost surprised there was no attempt to mediate.

"Good to hear. I'm gonna get a cab," Andrew replied. "I'm meeting one of the kids for drinks at the Elephant & Castle."

"Got it. Don't let me hold you up. I need to get back down to Richmond to get my car." It was a backup arrangement had they not flown on Marine One. "Let's catch up later this week."

The two said goodbye. The plan was progressing.

Chapter Eleven
The Unimaginable

In the Nover house, the next morning was not an easy one. Curt had woken early and prepared breakfast for Allison, hoping to make amends. As he heard her rumbling around upstairs, he was proud of the meal, admiring the eggs, toast, orange juice, and coffee. Then he heard her violently vomiting. The morning sickness had begun. Curt's pride in the meal quickly deflated.

Eventually, Allison made her way downstairs. She approached Curt, who was sitting at the dining room table. She kissed him on the head.

"Good morning, baby," Curt said. "Did you sleep OK?"

"I didn't sleep," she responded. It was not quite as cold of a response as it could have been, but it certainly wasn't the same way she wished him good morning after their first night together.

"I made you some breakfast, but I don't think you want any right now. Can I make you something else?"

"No, Curt. I'm good. I'll just have some coffee."

The two sat at the table and didn't talk. The awkwardness grew until Curt spoke. "Hey, I gotta get going. I have a meeting with the DoD medical leadership this morning at the Pentagon. After that, Smitty and I are going to run the mall during his lunch break."

"OK. Have fun. Tell him I said hi," she responded, as if neither wished to address the elephant in the room.

Curt got up, kissed her, and left. After she heard the door close, she sat there as tears rolled out of the corner of her eyes. She couldn't resist the urge to cry.

****

Curt's meeting at the Pentagon was productive. For years, the Defense Department had been trying to improve the transition of service members from active duty to either retirement or separation; however, transferring their medical data had always been challenging. Leveraging modern technology, a new pilot plan was being introduced and seemed promising. Curt was value added, and it made him happy.

After the meeting, Curt walked to the third floor E Ring to find Smitty, sitting at his desk, with obnoxiously thick glasses on.

"Yo, buddy, you trying to give your nose a workout?" Curt joked.

"Shut it, A-hole. I lost one of my contacts and now have to wear these until I can get a new one later today. Even with this extra five pounds on my face, I'll still kick your ass on our run. You ready?"

"Born, buddy. Born ready." The two walked down to the Pentagon Athletic Center, changed clothes, and then walked out the back of the facility, facing north. As if in unison, the two started the timers on their Garmin watches, which would track heart rate, distance, oxygen saturation, and many other stats. The watch had become a standard piece of equipment across current and older Special Operators. They ran north along Arlington Cemetery until arriving at Memorial Bridge, which they crossed, heading towards the back of the Lincoln Memorial. The chatter between the two remained limited. Smitty was pushing it and Curt was doing everything he could to keep up; however, externally, he tried to show no signs of wear.

As they came around to the front of Lincoln, Smitty tapped Curt on the arm and said, "It's on! Go!" as he started running up the steps of the Lincoln Memorial. The 87 marble steps that stretch from the reflecting pond up to Lincoln were always a great workout. Smitty held the lead the whole time. Curt didn't stand a chance but tried to keep up. Once at the top, Smitty turned and raced back down. Curt followed and once at the bottom, Smitty yelled as if he were a medieval Viking, "Again! Again!" He ran up the steps one more time.

Curt again turned to follow, but it was clear he'd not be passing, let alone catching Smitty any time soon. Once they were both back at the bottom, Curt asked, "Hey, any chance I can borrow your magic glasses?"

"It ain't the glasses, Nover. It's the engine. And it appears yours could use an overhaul." Smitty started laughing and then slowly began jogging towards the WWII Memorial.

Curt caught up. "Hey. Have we ever run the Memorials together before?"

"I don't think so," Smitty responded.

The running route was gorgeous. The tree-lined paths provided a cooling shade from the D.C. heat. On this day, a group of Honor Flight WWII veterans were welcomed to the memorial, escorted by active-duty service members. For veterans like Curt and Smitty, it was almost cathartic to see the old veterans being pushed around in their wheelchairs and tourist school children asking to get their photos taken with the WWII vets. The two ran around the WWII Memorial and returned towards Lincoln on the east side of the reflecting pond. As they neared the Vietnam Memorial, Curt said, "Hey, Smitty. Follow me. There's someone I want you to meet."

Curt now ran directly towards the Vietnam Memorial, then slowed to a walk. Running through the memorials is against the National Park Services regulations. At the Vietnam Memorial, Park Rangers strongly enforced the rule given how narrow the path was, as well as the location's somber character.

Smitty followed behind Curt as they walked along the wall of 58,319 names etched in stone. Eventually, Curt stopped. Softly placing his hand on the black granite, he scrolled down and found it. On plaque W10, line 35 was the name LCDR EUGENE W. NOVER. He looked up. "Smitty, meet my grandfather."

Smitty could see how proud Curt was. He gently touched the marble as well. "Very cool, buddy. It's an honor to meet him."

Curt smiled. "Thanks. Let's head back." The two walked out of the memorial grounds and then began running. They'd continue almost all the way to the Pentagon, only slowing to get a small cool down in before entering the building.

Curt would never share how his grandfather died in Vietnam, and Smitty wouldn't ask. Merely seeing the name on the memorial was more than enough. It was the way of the military.

"For the record, I kicked your ass," Smitty said, boasting proudly.

"Yes. You win. And I am utterly grateful you're so modest in victory," Curt responded with all the commensurate sarcasm.

"Not gonna lie. Feels good to beat you."

Curt quickly responded, "Not gonna lie. I'm still alive. And we will compete again."

Smitty was being ever cockier. "Oh, I welcome that more than you know."

The two kept up the banter in the locker room. They stripped down, grabbed towels and hit the large open bay showers, much like most other military bases. Other men walked in and out of the space while Smitty and Curt showered. The two didn't talk. It was part of an unspoken code among the other service members; one of the many 'man rules.'

As Smitty raised his arms to shampoo his hair, Curt slyly reached over and carefully snatched Smitty's enormous glasses from the shower shelf where Smitty had carefully placed them. In a graceful move, Curt walked out of the shower room, grabbed his towel and, from a distance, stood there watching.

Smitty finished his shower and instinctively reached for his glasses. They weren't there. Figuring they fell, he began skating his feet around the shower floor, hoping to find them. He was not about to bend over in the shower. Such a maneuver was far worse than talking according to man rules. Curt did everything he could to contain his laugh.

Smitty realized the glasses were not within reach of his feet, and squinted his eyes as much as possible to see if Curt was still in the shower. He could barely make out human shapes, let alone distinguish who it was. As he passed a blob, he would gently whisper, "Nover," holding his hands up as if he were a blind man, standing there stark naked. The three individuals near him stepped away, fearing the man was a leper.

Finally, Curt couldn't hold it in any longer and began laughing. "Smitty! Over here! I found your glasses!"

Smitty walked towards the voice, naked, with his hands out. Once grabbing his glasses, he quickly placed them on his nose and shuffled off to get his towel.

Curt watched the entire process and smiled. "Hey, really, congrats on the run victory today."

Smitty was furious. "Nover, one day I am truly going to relish killing you."

"Oh, I welcome that more than you know," Curt responded, mirroring Smitty's earlier comment.

The two changed into clothes and headed up to Smitty's office to grab a quick bite.

"So, how was the rest of your night with Buck? I'm sorry I had to leave."

"It was good. We had a great talk. Hey, get this... Buck is considering going to Afghanistan to see if he can find one of his old Afghan Army student pilots."

"What!" Smitty responded. "Is he fucking stupid? Well... wait. It's Buck. Never mind."

"Actually, he's not stupid," Curt responded. "Frankly, there is a part of me that wants to go back and try to find closure, too."

Smitty just stared at Curt. "Noorullah?" He knew the story. Curt told him once and the two never spoke of it again.

"Yup." Curt responded with a pause. "Noorullah.

"Buddy. After everything you've been through, I can't even begin to comprehend you thinking like this."

Curt took a deep breath. "Yeah, I'm not sure I truly understand. Frankly, it's not so simple."

"It never is, but I'll tell you, I almost lost it on my last Nissassa snatch and grab in Pakistan. I know in my heart that mission was the right thing to do, and we rescued the doctor who helped us kill Bin Laden. Because of us, he is now a free man. But for most of that mission, I trembled and shook through the whole 48-hour mission. It was all I could do to hold it together. If you went to Afghanistan, I suspect you'd be the same way. And I don't see you getting in and out of that shit hole in just 48 hours. It's gonna take at least a week. Seven days in hostile territory on your own? Brother, those days are behind us. Why not hire someone to go?"

All of Smitty's points were valid, but the longing in Curt for knowing what happened to Noorullah was overwhelming. "Yeah. I get it. But even if I sent someone, I'm not sure I'd buy their answer about Noorullah if it was bad news. I'd still need to see for myself."

Smitty stood up. "Look Curt. I need to get back to work.

Seriously, enough of this talk. You're chasing ghosts and that serves no one's interest. Yours, theirs, or Allison's. Let it go." Smitty smacked Curt on the back as if they were brothers. In a way, they were. He grabbed the lunch trash from the table and tossed it.

Curt also arose, said a quick goodbye, and departed. Walking out of the Pentagon, all Curt could think was, Smitty didn't understand. As the day passed, Curt was giving serious contemplation towards a trip to Afghanistan.

Chapter Twelve
Appeasing a Madman

The National Security Council (NSC) had convened to discuss some advances in China's space program, a fairly benign meeting for a NSC event. Since the President was delayed, sidebar meetings broke out in the room. Eventually, he walked in, and the room grew quiet as attendees rose. Walking behind the President was former Secretary of Defense Gerzema. Nearly every set of eyes in the room widened in surprise.

"Hey folks, sorry I'm late. I have some great news. Please, take your seats." Everyone sat after the President was in his chair. "Given some of the global security complexities, I have pushed John here to come out of retirement and serve as a special assistant to me on some specific security affairs. Initially, John was against it, but I think after a few days in retirement, he reconsidered and I'm grateful for it. Stacy," he was addressing the acting Defense Secretary, "John isn't going to come back into the Defense Department, but I'd like him to spearhead some of our efforts in the middle east and Afghanistan if that's OK with you,"

It wasn't a question, and in that forum, there was no chance Stacy Crawford could have said no. "Of course, Mr. President. Should we find space for him in the Pentagon?"

"No... no. I don't want it to be too awkward for folks."

As the President said this, Admiral Hershey began scribbling a note on paper in front of him, writing, *'Too late.'* He gently nudged it in front of Stacy.

The President continued. "John will work here at the White House or in the West Wing. John, did you have anything to say?"

"No, Mr. President. I appreciate the opportunity and that you pushed me so hard to return. I look forward to working with the team again."

"Good then. OK. Please start with the brief."

A relatively senior intelligence officer began the briefing on the Chinese space program, but Admiral Hershey wasn't listening. He was trying to put the pieces together on John Gerzema's return after being fired in associated with the Balkans turmoil. There were some missing pieces, and he would need to figure them out.

After the NSC meeting, the President called over Stacy to talk with John. The Admiral was not asked to join, nor did he believe it was his place. He realized the discussion was likely setting up lanes of operation between the two. Admiral Hershey walked out and moved towards his vehicle to depart. Smitty held the door open, who he almost didn't recognize in his huge coke-bottle glasses. As he passed, he said, "Thanks Smitty. You on Urban Sniper duty now?" Referring to the thickness of the glasses.

"Sir, please enter the car. You do realize the insider threat is real." The Admiral chuckled as he entered. Smitty jumped in the other side and notified all on the radio that the Chairman's convoy was ready to depart.

"Seriously, Smitty. Are you OK?"

"Yes, Admiral. I lost a contact and evidently these glasses have been quite entertaining for both you and Dr. Nover today."

"Ah... Curt. How is he and Allison doing? You know, I'd ask about your family... if you had one." The other two secret service officers in front of the SUV chuckled.

Smitty ignored them. "He's good. Crazy though. He and Buck are considering traveling to Afghanistan on a personal mission to find some kind of closure."

The Admiral looked out the window, thinking both about what Smitty said and what words he could carefully choose in response. He was still the Chairman of the Joint Chiefs after all. "Yes. I can tell you. There are many veterans and service members who are looking for closure. Your friends are not alone."

With the way in which the Chairman ended his comment, and continued staring out the window, made it clear the conversation was over. The passengers remained silent as the SVU crossed the Potomac and pulled into the Pentagon's South Parking.

As it stopped, Smitty flung open his door and ran around to

open the Chairman's door. Admiral Hershey exited the vehicle. As he did, he pulled Smitty towards him, then stopped. "Smitty. Don't underestimate Curt and Buck's urge. I know of a good number of vets who've gone to find either their old terps or seek some other form of closure. If they go, don't let them go alone. They'll need you." The only person in ear shot was Smitty. The Chairman continued into the building and fell under escort of another security team. Smitty stood there.

Admiral Hershey was right. To several vets, the withdrawal from Afghanistan broke a long-standing promise they'd made (on behalf of the nation). There were sporadic intel reports about veterans in Afghanistan. Most were corroborated as they exited with former Afghan Army service members or their interpreters, who were in jeopardy of death from the Taliban.

Smitty pulled out his phone and texted Curt.

'Hey, if you go, I'm in. I don't understand, but CJCS says I should support. Let me know if you're serious.'

The text popped up in Curt's phone. He had gone home earlier to check on Allison. Her morning sickness was fairly severe, and she had stayed home from work. Unfortunately, Curt's phone was on the table in front of Allison while Curt was in the bathroom. She saw the message come in and knew exactly what it was referring to.

Curt walked out of the bathroom. He'd cleaned it up after her last episode. "Baby," he said, "What do you want to do today? Can I give you a back ru..." Curt stopped speaking as he saw the tears coming down Allison's eyes. "What's wrong, baby?"

She pointed at Curt's phone. He grabbed it and opened the message. "Wait? What? I haven't even decided yet. I...." It didn't matter. Allison couldn't take it. The pregnancy was hard enough. She went upstairs and sent a message to her mom.

'Mom, I'm coming home for a bit, if that's OK.'

A reply quickly followed.

'Great! Your father loves to talk to Curt.'

Allison responded.

'I'm coming alone. Curt has work to do. I'll explain when I get there.

Love you, Mom
Allison'

She packed as Curt begged her to stay. It was no use. Even to Curt, it didn't make much sense. If he were in her shoes, he'd do the same thing. Allison went to the door.

"Can I at least drive you to the airport?"

"No Curt. I'll take a cab. There's a flight every hour to Chicago. I'll get on that, then continue to Tucson."

"Allison, I love you. Please. Is there anything I can say that will get you to stay?"

"Curt, I want you to promise me you won't go. But you can't. You didn't say it last night, nor this morning. It was thrilling to be around you in Mauritania and help you when you were in the Balkans. But you're going to be a father now. You dread what has become of Noorullah. I dread the possibility of telling our child that it doesn't have a father. You tell me where the common ground is?"

Allison's question was fair, and they both knew the answer. There was none.

"Allison. I don't know where it is. But I also know that if I keep having these nightmares and visions, the man you want to be a father to our child isn't the man you'd want in me. I want out of this. This morning, I asked how you slept. You didn't ask me. Well, I didn't sleep. I'm afraid to. Once asleep, Noorullah will be there, and my mind will continue to find ways to not only torture him, but torture me, too. That's no way to live."

"Curt, you're right. But you now hold a leadership role in a prominent VA hospital that deals with this. As a doctor, is your answer to every veteran suffering from Afghanistan induced PTSD to travel there and find solace? That makes no sense. You

69

could find another way if you wished. I believe that. I'm sorry if you don't." Allison kissed him, took her bag and walked to 8th Street, hailing a cab. Curt watched her walk away. He desperately wished to counter her points but couldn't. Allison was right. Curt closed the door, leaned against the wall and wept. The family he dreamed of having was walking away.

Chapter Thirteen
No Bucks, No Buck Rogers

John Gerzema had settled into his new office. In the West Wing, a junior staffer who was the son of a prominent donor stood outside what had been his office with his boxes rapidly packed.

John placed his first call to Andrew, relaying his new office contact information and check in.

"Andrew, how are things on your end?"

"Good, John. Everything is in place. Have you formally stood down from the board now that you are working for the government again?"

"Absolutely. Need to follow the rules. I was granted my bonus and a year's salary, then passed along all the pertinent information. They were a bit upset about learning I'd only be working for a few days, but they were more than happy to learn of the plan and put steps into place to capitalize." John was proud of himself for pulling off the first stage of his grand plan.

"Good. Now what?" Andrew asked.

"Today, I sat in an NSC meeting. Afterword, the President, Acting Defense Secretary Crawford and I met to discuss lanes of effort, so we don't overstep. She is amenable, but it's clear she's frustrated. It is an awkward structure, but I could not care less. My next step with her is garnering some sort of procurement and operational budget for our effort. The funding should be fairly easy. Acquisition, however, may be a challenge. Per Congressional law, we can't shift more than ten million dollars from any approved procurement program to another without notifying Congress. Clearly, we don't want to do that, so I'm trying to find out if there is another option."

"Well, you know the rules better than I. Just let me know when we can let the contract. I know our partners are already chomping at the bit to start production."

"I will, Andrew. Shouldn't be more than a week. Look, I gotta go. The Press Secretary wants to chat as she's sure there will be some questions about my new role. We hope to tamp

71

that down and move the press corps onto another piece of meat."

"Yes. I understand. Let's try to meet back up soon." Andrew was OK with the conversation but had concerns. He and John had put numerous entities on notice. Soon it would be time to deliver. He hoped that would be possible.

****

That night, Curt and Smitty met up at Trusty's bar. It was a local neighborhood dive bar in Southeast D.C. with literally a school bus upstairs for indoor seating. The beer was cold, and the food was decent. More importantly, it was one of the safest places to talk openly about information that fringed on classified.

"Smitty, thanks for offering to go to Afghanistan, but really, you have a job here and as you know, the larger we make the effort, the greater the chance we have getting caught."

"Fair, but if the team is too small, you also risk never finding him, nor being able to defend yourself in a small skirmish. Plus, Hershey said I can go. Look, I don't want to go back to that hellhole for any other reason than to ensure yours and Buck's safety. I've been thinking about the mission." Frankly, that was an understatement. Nissassa hired Smitty to perform mission planning. He was brilliant at it and extremely detailed. He'd done far more than 'just think about it.'

"Buddy, I remember you telling me you nearly lost it on your mission in Pakistan with Nissassa. You said you'd never go on an op again."

Smitty took a swig of his drink. "True. But that mission was for money and for an organization that conflicted me to the core. It's easier for me to do things like this, or even what we did in Serbia, as I know they are for a greater good. Mind you, I still am not fully comfortable, but perhaps that's a good thing."

Curt listened and thought about it. "OK. You said you've been thinking about it. I'm listening."

Smitty smiled. "To begin, we will need two different ops.

Last known location for Noorullah is near Kandahar and the last known location of Raz was near MiS (Mazar-i-Sharif). One team to operate in serial is too risky. Far better to have two teams operate in parallel. You'll lead the team in the Kandahar AOR, and I'll lead the one in MiS. I'd recommend three-man teams plus a terp, which means we are gonna need some firepower. I plan to start leveraging a few contacts for local support. I figure one trusted terp per team should do." To hear Smitty talk, it was as if he'd already drawn everything out.

"Alright. What about gear and getting into Afghanistan? It's going to cost a fortune, and although Buck is loaded, he can't fund this."

"I have a plan for that, too. Frankly, I think that Mr. Denney still owes us. I'm going to hit him up for funding without stating why. Also, I think Admiral Hershey or some of our other SOF contacts have open avenues in and out. Let's see what we can find."

"OK," Curt said as he took a deep breath and a long pull of beer. "What about Buck? Did you talk to him?"

"Yup. Buck's in. He's on my team, as he's the only one who knows what Raz looks like." Again, Smitty had it all planned out.

Over the next hour, they'd discuss what gear and firepower they'd require. Much of it was publicly available, however, they would need some hard to source items. Smitty had a plan for that as well. Every question Curt asked, Smitty had an answer.

"Smitty. No more questions. If all this comes together, when do we leave?"

"I need two weeks to pull all this together." Smitty was being conservative. If needed, he could likely pull it all together in three days.

"OK. Let's do it."

Later than night, Smitty shot a text message to Andrew Denney.

'Andrew, Smitty here. Need a favor. Can we meet for

coffee tomorrow AM?'

Andrew was awake and saw the note. He quickly responded.

'Sure, how is 0800Hrs at the Rosslyn Starbucks?'

'Deal,' Smitty wrote. *'See you tomorrow.'*

Chapter Fourteen
Building out the Plan

Allison's parents awaited her arrival in Tucson. She'd been crying on the entire flight and her mom could clearly see something was wrong.

"Ally, are you OK?

"Yes, mom. Can we just go home? I'll explain it all there," Allison responded. She hugged her mom quickly and then turned to her dad. That hug would last nearly half a minute. To Allison, her dad was a strong, caring, and intelligent father. To him, she'd always be daddy's little girl. "It's OK. You're home now. Let's go," he said. His arms and his voice alone were enough to make Allison feel comforted. She needed it.

They exited the airport and drove into Tucson. As they passed Davis Monthan Air Force Base's aircraft graveyard, Allison's stomach churned, thinking about the military-minded husband she had just left in Washington, D.C.

****

Smitty was early to the Rosslyn Starbucks. He hadn't slept well, mainly because he was so excited about building yet another military operation. As he laid in bed, his mind swirled. *'We need weapons, we need contacts, we need safe-house info...'*, he thought and much more. But first, he needed funds.

At the designated time, Andrew Denney walked into the Starbucks, wearing a well-pressed suit and highly polished shoes. For meeting Smitty, he was clearly overdressed.

"Mr. Denney, sir. It's good to see you," Smitty said. "Can I buy you a coffee?"

"Sure, Mark. Large, black. No sugar or milk," Andrew replied. Andrew was never in the military nor understood the value of nicknames. Smitty would just be 'Mark' to him.

"Easy day, sir." Smitty got up, placed the order. Andrew sat at the table, focused on his iPhone. Once the drinks were

75

prepared, Smitty returned to the table.

"Here you are, Mr. Denney," said Smitty.

"Great. Many thanks. How have you been, Mark? I understand Admiral Hershey brought you onto his security team?"

"Yes. That's accurate. He has been gracious to all of us who worked the Balkans operation. How are you doing, sir?" Smitty's question didn't include a query about Don's suicide, but clearly implied how Mr. and Mrs. Denney were coping with the loss of their son.

"Oh, we are good. The grandkids are growing, Mrs. Denney is happy and I'm still playing the D.C. game." Andrew was not ready to talk about Don, and Smitty understood. "So, why the meeting? Your dime, your time."

"Sir, I am looking for some help," Smitty said hesitantly. "I am building a military style operation and to make it happen, I need funding."

"OK. How much do you need?" Andrew asked.

"A half of a million dollars." Smitty watched Andrew's reactions closely.

"That's quite a big number. Can I ask what the operation is?" Andrew's answer wasn't a no, but it also wasn't a yes.

"I'd rather not get into that, given security issues," Smitty responded.

"I understand that, and I'm willing to accept the cliff notes, but for a half a million, I'd like to believe I can have the right to know what I am investing in."

"Sir, that's fair," Smitty said. "I am putting together two teams to go into Afghanistan. There's some unfinished business that needs to be taken care of."

"Is this endorsed by Admiral Hershey?" Andrew asked.

"Financially, no. But administratively, yes," Smitty said.

Andrew was curious, "When will it execute?"

"Sir, we are looking at two weeks to a month and then we are in country."

Andrew sat there for a while, mulling over the request. It was all an act. Given his efforts with John Gerzema, there was no way Andrew would fund Smitty's excursion. He liked Smitty and owed him. Placing Americans in Afghanistan now, even if covert, was putting them in grave danger. Further compounding the problem was Andrew needed to find a way to stop this mission from going altogether. Smitty's efforts in Afghanistan could disrupt his plan with John Gerzema, and that effort was worth millions.

"I understand," said Andrew, "But unfortunately, I can't fund that effort."

"Sir, I can share more if that's what you need."

"Mark, listen to me carefully. I am not funding this because I believe it's in your best interest. Do not go into Afghanistan anytime soon. Do you understand me?"

"Mr. Denney, do you know something?"

"Mark, let's be clear, you're asking for my money and therefore I ask the questions. You don't have that luxury."

Mark adjusted himself in the chair. Andrew could be an asshole if he wanted to and was bordering on that personality trait. "Sir, I appreciate your concern, but the teams I put together are well trained to operate in such locations."

Andrew grew stern and frustrated. "Look, I don't doubt your teams could survive months in Afghanistan. There are other things in play, and if you go soon, you are assuming far more risk than you realize. That's all I can say. Mark, thanks for my coffee. I hope you heed my words. Goodbye." Andrew got up and left, and so did his five hundred thousand dollars.

Smitty sat there, alone, still with an unfunded effort. He finished his coffee, got up, and headed to the Pentagon for work. It was curious to Smitty, though. Why did Andrew ask if Admiral Hershey was aware? Does the Chairman know about the pending 'increased risk' in Afghanistan? If he did, why would he push Smitty into that fire? None of it made sense.

As Smitty arrived at work, he saw the Chairman walking the opposite direction down the hall towards him, likely returning to his office. As they passed, Admiral Hershey said, "Good morning, Smitty."

In reply, Smitty said, "Good morning, Admiral. It's on. I'm going with Curt."

Admiral Hershey had passed Smitty by the time the

comments registered. He stopped, turned around, and said, "Smitty. My office. Now."

It was the exact response Smitty expected to get. Smitty followed the Admiral in and closed the door.

"Have a seat," Admiral Hershey said.

The two sat down. "OK. You have got five minutes. Explain it."

Smitty provided a rough overview of the two-team plan. He also shared the details about his failed meeting with Andrew Denney. Smitty watched the Chairman's reaction closely when he explained Andrew's 'increased risk' comment. There was nothing but surprise.

"Interesting. I don't know what this increased risk is. We have no other ongoing operation." The Admiral was being honest, but his suspicion that whatever Andrew Denney was referring to, it involved John Gerzema. Thinking through that would need to wait. "Smitty. How much did you ask Andrew for?"

"Half a mil," Smitty said bluntly.

"OK. I think I can get that. Don't focus on the funds, focus on the mission. Let me worry about the money."

A huge weight lifted off Smitty's shoulders. "Sir, thanks."

"Don't thank me yet. I don't have it, but I know where to look. Also, if Andrew Denney shares anything else, I'd like to know what's going on."

"Aye, boss," Smitty said as he departed the office. In the hallway, Smitty pulled out his phone and shot a text to Curt.

'Funding looks good. Not Denney but Squirts.'

Next, Smitty shot a text to an old friend, Jeremy 'Mule' Kasparov.

'Mule, Smitty here. Any interest in another game?'

The response came back in under 30 seconds.

'Hell, yes! Desk job is killing me. Happy hour at Elephant & Castle?'

Smitty was building the team.

Smitty responded with a thumbs up emoji.

Jeremy was a first generation American as his parents were Russian and moved to the U.S. in 1964, escaping political persecution for their religious views. He studied hard and was accepted to attend West Point. A gifted natural athlete, Mule had a brain to match. His only negative trait was a hint of stubbornness, likely tattooed into his Russian DNA. Nearing completion at West Point, he grew far fonder of the U.S. Marines, and cross commissioned to become a Devil Dog Lieutenant. The Army's loss was clearly the Marine's gain. Mule spent nearly a dozen years in the Marines, with tours in Iraq and Afghanistan. Towards the end, Mule was instrumental in setting up MARSOC (Marine Special Operations Command). Given his experience and intellect, Jeremy left the Marines and took a job as a military advisor to the U.S. State Department. While the money was good at main State, Mule longed for the days gone past of military operations.

Next, Smitty needed to leverage another old friend. Command Chief Master Sergeant Jason Cologne was a USAF Pararescue jumper or 'PJ' and part of the Air Force Special Operators. For years, Smitty had seen Jason at bases that, according to public record, 'didn't exist.' They grew to be friends, and Jason was always the guy who could get supplies. He was also serving as the Command Chief at the U.S. military base in Djibouti. From his Pentagon office phone, Smitty called Jason.

"Command Chief Cologne."

"Jason! Smitty here, your favorite Navy SEAL."

"Smitty. Great to hear from you. Are you calling from the Pentagon? The number is a 703 area code."

"I am. Actually, I'm now part of the Chairman's PSD

(Personal Security Detail), but that is nowhere near as cool as you now, being the Command Chief in the sandbox! I'm proud of ya, buddy."

"Thanks man. I'm loving the job. And good on you too," Jason said.

"Hey, looks like I am going to be near your AOR (Area of Operation) with a few teams. Any chance you might be able to help us get some gear?"

Jason knew Smitty was no longer on a SEAL team, but he also realized Smitty was working for the Chairman. If Smitty was going to be in the AOR and needed gear, he'd be a fool not to resource it. "Sure. Send me your email. I'm going to link you with Master Sergeant (MSgt) Jennifer Rose. She's one of my best logisticians. You let her know what you need. What she can't get, she'll come to me, and we can figure it out. Deal?"

"Perfect. Thanks Command Chief. I appreciate it. Look, I gotta go. I'll push you an email and look forward to hearing from MSgt Rose." The two said their goodbyes and within fifteen minutes, Smitty was linked up with MSgt Rose. Funding, manpower, logistics were all in the works. Next would be intelligence gathering. The pieces were falling into place.

****

"John, here is the information you requested," Steve Lewis said, as he entered John Gerzema's office in the West Wing. The document was a funding line, not through the Defense Department but rather the Department of Health and Human Services. The fund line allowed for discretionary procurement of medical and pharmaceutical supplies. It was exactly what John was waiting for.

"Thanks, Steve. I owe ya." There could not have been any more sarcasm in that statement had John tried.

The disdain on Steve's face wasn't hidden. He finally could no longer hold it in. "John, I don't understand. You're in the same political party as the President. You have a history with him. Why are you doing this? What do you have against the

President?"

John was fairly certain the President had not shared information about the video with Steve. Why would he? "Perhaps you should ask him," John said. "As for why... Steve, this is D.C. As one of my old mentors, Don Rumsfeld once said, 'A friend in D.C. is someone who will stab you in the chest.' Let that sink in."

Steve had no desire to continue the discussion and left. John got up from his desk and closed his door. He'd soon place a call and desired privacy. He scrolled through his phone and found his contact at Herbizid, one of the largest chemical and pharmaceutical companies in the world, which was the first to mix two phenoxy herbicides together, crafting 'Agent Orange.' It was the infamous chemical cocktail sprayed over Vietnam to eliminate foliage. It also caused significant illness and death in U.S. veterans who served there. John dialed the number.

"Yes, the funding is secured. I need thirty thousand gallons of your new herbicide mixture. The one we discussed with elements of diquat and paraquat." John waited while the other party spoke, then said, "Yes, delivery will be to Oman. Further details will follow. We will need it in two weeks. Hopefully that's not a problem, given we provided you some advanced information about the requirement."

Muffled, the other party replied, to which John Gerzema nodded and smiled. His operation was unfolding. It was already mid-March. For the mission to be a success, it must take place before the end of April. The clock was ticking.

Chapter Fifteen
Skol!

The Elephant & Castle was packed with Capitol Hill staffers and interns, just like every other day for happy hour. Alcohol flowed, stories were told, contacts were made, and networking took place. At the bar, Jeremy Kasparov was chatting with a few young female staffers. He bought their drinks, and the young ladies fawned over him. Jeremy was strikingly handsome and in exceptional shape. Every bar he walked into, the same scenario unfolded.

From behind Jeremy, a male voice spoke up, "Hey, Mule, did you tell them you finally got that herpes situation cleaned up?"

Jeremy turned around to find Smitty and Curt standing there, smiling.

The two ladies did not find the comment funny, nor were they even remotely interested in finding out if it was a joke. They grabbed their drinks and scurried away from the bar, freeing up spots for Smitty and Curt.

"Dudes. You really need to work on your approach. Easy to see why you're still solo, Smitty, with a right forearm like Popeye," Jeremy said, suggesting Smitty's only romance stemmed from an overzealous masturbation habit.

"Wrong. I'm Left-handed. Hey, I'm pleased with my personal life. Thanks for your advice. Buy us a beer and I'll call it even," Smitty responded.

Smitty laughed and hugged Mule. "Mule, this is my buddy, Curt. He's also a former SEAL and is now a doctor in charge of some VA department."

"Nice to meet ya, Doc," as the two shook hands.

"Same. Thanks for taking our meeting," Curt replied.

As they spoke, the three stood out like sore thumbs. Given their age, size, strength and physical shape, it was as if three Viking warriors had fallen into a college party. They would blend in far better at a bar near a military installation. Many of the young females across the bar were drawn to the three, while the young male staffers' jealousy was palpable. The three finally had beers in their hands and raised them in a toast.

"So, Smitty. I thought you were done with Nissassa." Mule said. "What gives? You back in the private military ops game again?"

"You're correct. Nissassa is done, but we have pulled together a potential job which may interest you."

"I'm all ears, buddy. Frankly, I don't know how much longer I can sit at my desk and merely advise over military and security issues on paper." Mule, like Smitty, was never meant to be a desk jockey.

"Good," Curt jumped in. "Op is two weeks total, one week in Afghanistan. No support. Two small teams. One is you, me, and a local terp. Payout is $100 thousand for you."

Jeremy nodded. "OK. I'm still listening. Keep going."

Smitty explained the entire mission from start to finish. While the topic was clearly sensitive, the surrounding crowd of staffers could not care less about military ops. Most, if not all, were young idealists or left leaning politicos which had little interest in kinetic warfare.

After he finished explaining the mission, Smitty and Curt awaited Jeremy's response. "Interesting mission. I have a counteroffer, though."

This was not the response the two expected, but at least it wasn't a no. "OK, Mule, what's the counter?" Curt asked.

"I'll cut my pay down to $80 thousand, but we change the mission a bit. I want to find my old terp and get him out of that hole as well."

Curt was more than willing to accept the terms, but Smitty, the planner, was concerned. "Mule, I don't know how many folks we can get out. Adding to that number now adds complexities."

"Yup. I get that. But just like you, I have unfinished business in that nation, and it needs to be settled. You have my offer. What do you say?" Jeremy queried.

Smitty didn't have much of a choice. "OK. You get one additional seat outbound. Do you know where your old terp is?"

"Nope. Last contact was Kandahar. I realize that's not what you want to hear. I lost contact with Saad once the U.S. pulled out." Much like Buck and many other U.S. veterans who maintained contact with former Afghan colleagues, Mule stopped hearing from Saad after the coalition's withdraw. It was a common theme. Many of these Afghans stayed off phones and the internet for their safety.

As they spoke, Smitty's phone buzzed with an incoming call from Admiral Hershey. This was rare, especially when Smitty was not on duty. "Excuse me, I gotta take this," he said as he stepped out of the bar. Once outside, he answered. "Smitty here."

The Chairman asked, "Smitty, where are you?"

"Sir, Elephant & Castle in D.C. Was I supposed to be somewhere right now?"

"No. But I need you at my residence ASAP."

"OK, sir. I'll be there soonest. I'm with Curt and another friend talking about plans. I'll ditch them and be there as quick as I can."

"No. Don't ditch them. Bring 'em. See you soon." Admiral Hershey hung up.

Smitty walked back into the bar and threw a credit card down. "Hey, we gotta go," he said.

"Who was that?" Curt asked.

"It was Squirts. He said he wants all of us to come to his house now."

"OK. Well, when the Chairman asks, we go," Curt joked.

Jeremy asked in a confused manner, "The Chairman? As in, the Chairman of the Joint Chiefs?"

"Yes. Who else?" Smitty smiled as he responded.

"Dudes, had I known you had that kind of firepower, I'd have asked for way more than $80k!"

Smitty smiled. "Even if you did, it wouldn't matter. We still don't have funding yet. Come on, Mule. We gotta go." The three slammed the rest of their beers, paid, and walked out of the bar, much to the disappointment of more than a few young ladies.

On Fort Myers, the three pulled into the Chairman's driveway after passing through a handful of security checkpoints. They rang the doorbell.

The Chairman answered the door, opening it with a beer in his hand and wearing civilian clothes. "Gentlemen, you're late."

"Yes, sir," Smitty said. He'd learned to be an extremely obedient subordinate to his new boss.

"Smitty, I'm screwing with you. Come in. I have a surprise for you."

The three followed Admiral Hershey into the living room. There, another gentleman was sitting, also in civilian clothes. His skin and hair were dark, but none of them recognized the man. That issue would soon be resolved. "Gentlemen," the Chairman said, "Let me introduce you to Lieutenant General Wahid Ghani of the Afghan National Army. He is my guest and I've told him of your mission. He maintains contacts and safe-house information across Afghanistan. He's offered to help you. I'd recommend you leverage his knowledge."

The three introduced themselves and thanked the Chairman. This was more than they could have hoped for. Curt and Jeremy both described the individuals they hoped to find. As expected, the General knew of neither, but had at least contact with whom they could begin. Curt also mentioned his old interpreter, Majeed. Again, the General was unfamiliar with him, but feverishly wrote all the information. As they spoke, Admiral Hershey pulled Smitty aside. "Smitty, I also have something for you." As the two walked out of the room into the kitchen, the Admiral handed him an envelope.

Smitty opened it. The first paper was a medical leave document allowing Smitty three weeks of vacation time away from work. The second, a smaller piece of paper, was a cashier's check for a half of a million dollars from the Afghanistan Embassy to the U.S.

"Sir, this is great, but I thought the Embassy of Afghanistan was shut down after the U.S. withdrew and the Taliban assumed control."

"That's correct. But I spoke to their last ambassador, Ambassador Adela Raz, who is still here in D.C. and unable to go home. I loosely told her of your plan to help Afghans. She assures me the check is good. I could think of no better funding entity than the Afghan government. Don't you agree?" Admiral

Hershey smiled as he said that last sentence, then took a sip of his beer.

"Sir. I agree. And I can't thank you enough." Smitty was truly appreciative.

"Smitty, just come back safe. And get your friend's closure. That's all I ask. Now, get in there and pick General Ghani's brain."

"I will, sir. Thanks," said Smitty.

Chapter Sixteen
Modifications

The Pennsylvania Air National Guard was much like every other air guard unit across the U.S. They maintained forces at a few different dual purpose (civilian / military) airports with many professional aircrew, maintainers and support personnel. At their base in Youngstown, PA, a squadron of C-130 cargo aircraft sat idle on the ramp. A good portion of their missions over the past few months were local efforts, flying cargo in and around the eastern portion of the U.S. as well as joint training with the Army performing para-drops in and around Fort Bragg, North Carolina.

Today, a message arrived at their Command Post, directing the Commander to call the West Wing. This was far from ordinary, and nearly every person in the chain of command questioned the directive.

Eventually, the message arrived on the Wing Commander's desk, and he dialed the number. The White House communications office asked the commander, Colonel Frank Hughlett, to verify some information and then placed him on hold. In a few seconds, he was connected.

"Colonel Hughlett here."

"Colonel Hughlett, good morning. This is former Defense Secretary John Gerzema, now the President's Special Security Advisor. How are you doing today?"

"Sir. I am good." Colonel Hughlett had never received such a call. Something was going on. "How can I help you?"

"Yes. I have a small team on their way to your installation. They are going to ask you to perform some modifications to your aircraft. They are nothing you haven't done before. Due to classification sensitivities, I can't discuss it over the phone, and I must also inform you, none of this can be discussed openly with anyone. Your unit will be in direct support of a no-fail Special Operations effort. I am confident you and your team can pull this off, and if you do, you'll be famous."

"Sir. I understand, but before we make modifications, I will need to discuss it with some of my leadership."

"Colonel, I am directing you not to do that. After we hang up, I will place a call to the Pennsylvania National Guard Adjutant General, Major General Glenn Carlson. I will tell him the same thing. Again, my team will arrive soon... if they are not there already. Follow their directions exactly, and should you have questions, you call me directly. Do you understand.?"

"Yes, sir. I'll await your team and further information."

"Great. Have a good day, Colonel. Your unit is going to be quite busy." John hung up.

Colonel Hughlett called his Maintenance Group Commander and directed him to pull in some personnel. While he was unaware at to what modifications were needed, he knew it would take manpower to make them happen. As he was on that call, there was a knock at his door. The knock was from his executive officer, Captain Nikki Pavnic. "Sir, there are some people here to see you from the White House?"

"Yes, please send them in."

Captain Pavnic did as instructed, and the two gentlemen entered. Once inside, they closed the door and opened their heavily secured briefcase. Inside, they pulled out classified documents and laid them on the table.

The required modifications, per the documents, were to fit four C-130s with a massive aerial dispersal system. It was a modification that the Youngstown Guard was familiar with. They'd flown with the system in the past. The dispersal system had two nozzles that expelled the agent, one on either side of the fuselage, under the wing line near the paratroop doors. Housed in the cargo bay, would sit a two-thousand-gallon tank of liquid.

In previous missions, the C-130s were used to spray overgrowth in and around aircraft training ranges. Killing off the overgrowth significantly reduced the risk of brush fires as military aircraft dropped ordinance and flares during training. That mission was amplified across the media as a good news mission for the area. This time, the modifications would allow for a vastly different mission.

Once briefed, Colonel Hughlett was asked how long the

modifications would take. His answer was two weeks. After he answered, one of them stepped out to place a call.

Chapter Seventeen
The Journey

As he sat on the Brussels Airport ramp, Buck's phone rang with an incoming video call from Curt. "Yo! Curt! What's shakin?"

"Hey Buck. All good here. Look, I'm with Smitty." Curt swung the phone around so that Smitty was in view. They were both sitting in Curt's condo at the kitchen table.

"Smitty!" Buck yelled, raising a mock salute.

"Buck!" Smitty returned the gesture.

"Hey! This is great! To what do I owe this wonderful call? If that freaking restaurant in D.C. says my credit card bounced, you don't know me." Buck asked.

"No, Buck. It's not your credit. We all know you're loaded. A bunch of things have been happening out here. Are you alone?" Curt questioned.

"Yup. All by myself."

"OK. Good. Turns out, Smitty and I have pulled together a plan to infil and exfil (infiltrate and exfiltrate) Afghanistan. I'm going in to find Noorullah. Given our discussion, we also built-in part of the plan for you to come with and find Raz if you'd be game."

"Get the fuck outta here. You gotta be shitting me." Buck was shocked and said out loud one of the more common military acronyms, YGBSM.

"Nope. It's legit. We depart the U.S. in a few days. If you're in, rally point is in Djibouti. What do you think?"

"Buddy. I just hired on a new pilot who's almost spun up. I think I can make it. How long are we in Afghanistan? I can't be gone from work forever."

"You'll be gone two weeks. One week in Afghanistan." Curt answered.

"Done. I'm in. I don't need to think about it. Send me the details about the meetup in D.J." (D.J. was the unofficial nickname among military personnel for Djibouti).

"OK. Great. Once there, we will spin you up on the plan."

Smitty said. Always the planner.

"Got it. Gotta go! Freaking sweet!" Buck was excited. They all hung up.

Curt turned to Smitty. "Hey. I gotta go. I got...

Smitty cut him off. "Yeah. I know. Tell her I say hello."

Smitty was right. And Curt appreciated him for it. Curt had already packed a bag. It wasn't big. He would be gone a few weeks, but most of what he needed wasn't at the house. "Make yourself at home. Lock up when you leave," Curt said. He left Smitty at the condo. Time was fleeting, and he needed to say goodbye to Allison, or at least try. Curt caught a flight out of Reagan National.

While in Chicago awaiting his connection, Curt wrote a quick note to Allison's father, Mr. Paul Flaherty, letting him know about the travel to Tucson and requesting, if not hoping, for a ride from the airport to their house. Curt wasn't optimistic and really didn't give Paul as much credit as he deserved. Paul served as a Marine in his early life and married Allison's mom years ago. Although he was her stepfather, he was one of the best. It wasn't hyperbole. Allison's friends all believed he was one of the coolest dads one could have. Paul had a quality that was far too rare in society. Even in Allison's rebellious years, he gave her the space she needed to grow, even more than her mom. After those rebellious years, she grew close to him. She would always be daddy's girl.

The flight into Tucson was uneventful, and it arrived on time in the late afternoon. As Curt exited the plane and headed out of the airport, he saw Paul standing there and was grateful. "Paul, hey. Thanks for coming."

"Why wouldn't I?" Paul queried quizzically, even gave Curt a hug. Curt was family and while Allison was hurting, Paul, being a Marine, knew the reasons she hurt weren't intentional on Curt's part. Curt was who he was, and what she fell in love with.

"Do you have a bag?" Paul asked.

"No, sir. Just this backpack. I won't be staying long. I depart tomorrow."

"I understand. Better for us. No waiting for luggage. But, if you call me sir one more time, I don't care if you are a former

SEAL, I'll drop you like a bad habit. Now, come on," Paul said, leading Curt to the car.

As they rode, there was little talk. Finally, Curt broke the silence. "How mad is she?"

"Well, I don't think she's gonna greet you with open arms and a sloppy kiss," Paul said. He tried to keep the discussion light, even though the issue was dead serious.

"Yeah. I wasn't planning on that. Maybe just a hello?"

"Eh. I give it 50/50. I didn't tell her you're coming. That way, her reaction can surprise us both." Paul chuckled.

The car was quiet again. And again, Curt broke the silence. "Sir, I hope you understand. I'm not trying to hurt Allison; I'm trying to heal myself."

Paul slowed the car and pulled over to the shoulder of the road until it stopped. "Buddy. I lost a bunch of friends in Vietnam. After we left, many of us said we'd never go back. And now, most of us realize we probably should have. I get it. But it's not me that you need to convince. Now, step out of the car."

"Excuse me? We aren't at your house yet," Curt said.

"You're right. But I told you if you call me sir one more time, I'm dropping ya." Paul smiled at Curt and Curt responded.

"Lesson learned, Paul. Jesus, you're a stubborn Marine."

"Oohra!" Paul belted out. Then he began driving again. They'd be at the house in five more minutes. Curt's heart raced.

As the car pulled in, Allison was nowhere in sight. The weather was warm and quite comfortable, as Tucson in the Spring is wonderful. Paul led the way into the house and Curt quietly followed. Allison and her mom sat at the kitchen table.

Allison looked up and saw Curt. "No. Not now," she said. "What in the hell is he doing here?"

Before Curt could talk, Paul took control of the discussion. "Allison, he's here to see you. I know you don't want to see him, but realize this-the last person he's coming to see before he departs is you. You can either push him away, or you can talk to him. The choice is yours, but you only get to make it once."

Had Curt told her that, she would have thrown a vase at him. But from her dad, it worked. She stayed in the kitchen, looked at Curt and spoke. "OK, Nover. What do you want to say?"

"Um. Perhaps we can go for a walk?" Curt was already uncomfortable. Trying to have a conversation with his wife in front of his in-laws was too much.

Allison got up, and the two walked out the front door, beginning a small stroll through the neighborhood.

"How are you feeling?" he asked.

"I'm OK. The morning sickness is slightly better. And I can eat."

"Are you seeing a local doctor?" Curt asked. It was a dumb question from most folks, but Curt was a doctor, and he knew she should be seeing someone.

Allison appreciated the question. "Yes, my mom's doctor is a friend of our family. I saw him a few days ago. Everything is going well."

The two kept walking. Curt reached over and attempted to hold her hand. As much as she didn't' want to, she took his hand, turned to him and cracked a small smile. For the rest of the walk, they did not speak. They just spent time together. It's was what they both needed. As they approached the house, Allison stopped and turned to him. "To be clear, I don't want you to go. But after speaking with my dad a few times, I realize it's something you need to do. I don't understand it, and probably never will. Just promise me one thing. You'll be careful."

Curt's heart burst. "I will... I will!"

"And you'll aways think about me and our child."

"Yes, yes. I will," Curt replied.

"And you'll try to contact us whenever you can.

Curt didn't answer.

"What? You can't try to call us?" Allison sternly asked.

"Of course I can, but you asked me to promise you one thing, and you're already at three!" Curt smirked.

As angered as she was by his answer, it was typical of the man she fell in love with. "Curt, damn it. What am I going to do with you!?" She threw her arms around him.

"I have some ideas, but I'm not sure you could keep quiet enough while executing them in your parents' house."

Allison laughed. Curt breathed a sigh of relief. Everything with Allison was gonna be OK. He could now focus on the mission.

Chapter Eighteen
Prepositioning

Jeremy, Smitty, and Curt sat at Dulles International Airport, awaiting the first leg of their flight. They'd depart to Frankfurt, Germany, awaiting their next leg into Djibouti. Overall, it would take them nearly two days to get around the globe. None of the three had packed much in the way of clothing. Mostly just personal effects. Each, however, was carrying in excess of $100,000. Once in Djibouti, they would be getting the majority of their gear in exchange for much of that cash.

****

In Bratislava, Slovakia, at the Herbizid Chemical plant, three tanker trucks sat, lined up, awaiting their load. Each was capable of hauling ten thousand gallons of liquid. One by one, they'd load their cargo and pull out of the factory onto the European highway system. Over the next few days, they'd make their way south from Slovakia, through Austria, and to the Italian port of Trieste. Once there, they'd wait at the port until approval to offload the liquid onto the awaiting cargo ship. The entire process would take several days. Upon completion, the ship would steam down the Adriatic into the Mediterranean Sea. From there, it would transition the Suez Canal, then into the Red Sea and then finally to a port in Oman, another eight days underway. In roughly two weeks, a key piece of John Gerzema's plan would be in place.

****

After flying for over 24 hours, Curt and the team arrived at the Djibouti International Airport. They were tired and looking forward to getting into a hotel for some rest and to clean up. After grabbing their bags, they walked out into the main airport area, hoping to find a cab. There, standing alone, was a female

U.S. Air Force Airman with a sign that said, "Dr. Nover."

Curt walked over to her, hesitantly, and said, "I am Dr. Nover, but I am not expecting anyone to meet me."

"Yes, sir. I'm aware. I don't know who you know, but evidently, you and your group are pretty important. I am Master Sergeant Rose. I have a van waiting for you. Please come with me."

Smitty walked over to her, "Jennifer? Hey! It's me, Smitty! I spoke to you about getting us some gear. Chief Master Sergeant Cologne linked us up. Great to see you today, but I thought we were to link up late tomorrow."

"Mark. Great to meet you. Yes, I did too, but my boss got a call from his boss who got a call from his boss. I'm supposed to drive you all onto the base. We have billeting already secured for you." Jennifer smiled at Smitty for a bit. She had previously not known what he looked like when they spoke on the phone, but now that she did, she was impressed. Smitty was oblivious.

MSgt Rose led the three out to a white van double parked in front of the airport. An airman sat in the driver's seat, and after all the bags were loaded and the team was inside, he drove off towards Camp Lemonnier, which sat on the other side of the international airport's runway. As they approached the gate, a small, Air Force blue pickup truck awaited them. The driver signaled to the guard, and the two vehicles proceeded in. After a short two-minute drive, they both stopped. Out of the truck emerged a bald, stocky, five-foot four man. Smitty saw him and immediately said, "Chief!" Smitty jumped out of the van, ran over, and hugged him. He'd not seen Chief Cologne for over a year.

"Smitty! You don't look like you've changed a bit. Great to see ya, buddy."

"You too! Hey, these are my battle buddies, Curt Nover and Jeremy 'Mule' Kasparov. Guys, this is the Chief I told you about, Jason Cologne!"

"Chief, great to meet you," Curt said. "And congrats. By the dressing on your sleeve, I see you're the Command Chief? Is that correct?" Curt recognized Air Force insignias, and was right. The dressing in the middle of his sleeve was, in fact, for a

Command Chief.

"Thanks, Doc, I believe it is," Jason said, brushing off the compliment. "Funny story, the Base Commander, my boss, got a direct call from high up in the Pentagon you were coming. I don't know what was said, but when he told me about your visit, I informed him that Smitty and I were friends and that I'd be happy to take care of ya. He appreciated my offer and said 'the sky is the limit' for you all. I presume you're tired and hungry. Let's get you into your quarters and cleaned up. After that, I can walk you to the Dee-FAC." (DFAC is the modern term for 'chow hall,' short for 'dining facility).

Mule reached out his hand after the Chief spoke. "Hey, Chief, Mule. Good to meet you as well."

"Absolutely, Mule," Chief replied. He turned to MSgt Rose, "Hey, Jennifer. Do you have those phones I asked for?"

"Yes, Chief, right here," MSgt Rose said. She handed him three old beat up Nokia phones. They were so old, sending texts required multiple presses of a number to scroll and get the right letter. Additionally, they only had one number programmed in, MSgt Rose.

"Mule, Doc, and Smitty, here are three phones for you. MSgt Rose's number is in there. Call her anytime. She has one job while you're here and that is to take care of you and outfit you tomorrow." MSgt Rose handed over the phones, somewhat flirtatiously when handing one to Smitty. Comically, Smitty didn't notice, but Mule, who normally garnered such attention, did. His jealousy was poorly concealed. Curt observed the entire event and just smiled.

The three took the phones and settled into their respective rooms. The team presumed Admiral Hershey had something to do with their treatment. While disappointed they'd not be staying at the Sheraton Djibouti, they all understood the base offered a far easier means to protect their cash and maintain a low profile—not to mention how much easier it would be to secure the supplies they'd require.

****

In the rolling hills of the Appalachian Mountains, a four-ship of C-130s flew in a spread formation that looked a bit like a lopsided triangle. They flew low, each aircraft no further apart from one and other than 300 feet and no higher than 250 feet. It was daylight, and the formation made quite the spectacle. Many locals raved about how impressive the flyover was. Others complained. While the responses were fairly standard, the flight profile was anything but. The crews were practicing for their upcoming mission. Today's practice would be during the day. The next few would be in the dark while wearing night-vision goggles.

Upon returning to the base, the crews all came into the debrief room. Standing there was the Wing Commander, Colonel Hughlett. At first, each of the four aircraft commanders looked at each other and their navigators, concerned they'd flown into a restricted zone or overflown known 'complainers' to the base. Neither was the issue.

"Sit down, folks," Colonel Hughlett said. They did as instructed. "I've received a prepare to deploy order for our aircraft. I'm telling you this because it originated in somewhat unique channels, clearly nonstandard communications. You are to deploy once the aircraft are modified, and you are not to tell anyone about your pending departure."

"Boss," one of the aircrew said. "Where are we going?"

"You'll find that out the day you depart. It's that secret."

"OK. But how will we know what to pack?" It was a fair question.

"Well, I can tell you it isn't the arctic, and it isn't the Sahara Desert. But if I was packing, I'd lean closer to the latter. Also, you won't be needing many civilian clothes. Flight suits and gear will be desert camo. Any other questions?"

No one raised their hands.

"One last thing. Before you fly out, the orders direct me to take your personal cell phones and provide each aircraft commander with one cellular phone for official business only. I realize that is far from how the Air National Guard works, so if any of you want out of the mission, now Is the tIme to tell me. No issues. I'll find you a replacement."

The four crews all looked at each other. If this mission was that secretive, the coolness factor had to far outweigh the ass pain of not having a cell phone. No one raised their hands.

"Good. Go home and get some rest. Tomorrow you're flying the same route on 'nogs.' I need you at your best." 'Nogs' was an old aircrew term for night-vision goggles. The current correct terminology was night-vision devices or NVDs, but no one dared correct the Wing Commander.

Chapter Nineteen
Three of Four

The next morning on Camp Lemonnier, a pounding on Curt's door startled him. It paused for a few seconds, then resumed. BAM! BAM! BAM!

Curt got up and partially opened the door. As he did, the door shoved into him, knocking him backwards.

"Hey jerkoff!" It was Buck. "I just spent the night at the Sheraton, waiting for you chuckle nuts to check in. I tried to call you. No answer. I tried to find you. I couldn't. I began to wonder if this was some elaborate practical joke. Finally, I got ahold of someone on the base who said some old Special Forces VIPs were here. I presumed it was you. So, when were ya gonna come get me?" Buck was far from the happy-go-lucky guy he normally was.

"Shit. Buck. I forgot. After the flight, we ate and fell asleep. Jesus. I'm sorry. Really."

Buck could tell Curt was sincere. Standing behind Buck was MSgt Rose, who felt horrible. "Dr. Nover. Sir, this was my fault. I should have asked if there were more in your party." It was classic MSgt Rose. She and Curt both knew the last person who deserved blame was her, but she was always the team player.

"No, Jennifer. This one's on me. Is there any chance we can get Buck a room? His real name is...

MSgt Rose cut him off. "Mark Thiessen. Yes, I know, and yes, we have a room for him. Again. I'm really sorry. Dr. Nover, since you're awake, I've prepared one of the logistics bays for you and the other three to check out your gear. I'll be the only one in there. Just call when you're ready."

"Thanks, MSgt Rose. I appreciate it," Curt said. He turned to Buck. "Well, I'm sure the breakfast at the Sheraton brunch buffet was far nicer, but would you like to grab some chow at the DFAC?"

"Sure. But you're buyin'."

"Mr. Thiessen, sir," MSgt Rose butted in. "The DFAC is free. You don't have to pay." She had not considered how many times the two had eaten in a DFAC over the years. The two just laughed. MSgt Rose blushed, realizing Buck's comment was sarcasm. "Sir. You knew that already, huh?"

"Yes. But MSgt Rose, I'm former Air Force, and I love ya! Thanks again for getting me here to harass Curt."

"Sure thing. I'm gonna go now before I say something else that's stupid." MSgt Rose smiled and left the two.

Curt put on some clothes and walked with Buck to the DFAC. "How was your flight in?"

"Actually, pretty good. I tried to get on your Lufthansa flight, but there was a cheaper routing through Istanbul that enabled me to upgrade to Business Class. Considering how things turned out, I should have joined you." It was another dig from Buck. Curt had apologized enough. He ignored it. "When do I get to learn the plan?"

"Probably after breakfast. Big picture, we are splitting into two teams. I'm going with Mule and you're with Smitty. You guys will track down Raz, and I'm going after Noorullah and Mule's old terp. We each have ten days, then we meet back up. We're not extending the mission. Smitty has much more for you, safe-house locations, and other stuff you'll need to memorize. Also, from a former Afghan General, there is supposed to be one terp/guide for each of our teams as we enter and check into our first safe-house. Frankly, I don't know much more. As those guys were memorizing the details, I flew out to Arizona to patch things up with Allison."

"Ouch. How did that go? Buck asked sincerely.

"Actually, pretty good. I'm lucky her stepfather is such a great dude," Curt said.

"Yeah, she told me about him once. Marine, right? Flaherty or something."

"Yeah. That's him. He was able to do some serious battlespace prep before I got there. I know she still wishes I wasn't going, but at least she's still there, and the baby is healthy. Honestly, even if things were perfect between us, I'd have recommended she go be with her parents."

"Fair point. I get that," Buck said. "Hey, where are you leading me to? Last time I was here, the DFAC was two streets back to the right."

"Shit. Sorry. I was just walking."

"Dude. Get your mind on the game!" Buck lectured.

"Yeah. I didn't sleep well again. Noorullah visited yet one more time. Gotta give it to him. He's a persistent little fucker. If he's anything in real life like he is in my dreams, he's not only alive, he's leading the Kochi tribe."

Buck laughed. "Don't worry. I get it. Come on. Let's head back to the DFAC. A cup of coffee and some powdered scrambled eggs will do you wonders."

Curt smiled. The two turned around and headed back.

****

Later that day, Curt called MSgt Rose, informing her they'd be ready to go to the supply warehouse around 1400Hrs. She'd have a van pick them up at that time. The four got into the van and the driver took them to the storage facility, parking in the back. He stayed in the vehicle and told them the open hangar door was where they should walk in.

The four men exited the van and walked into the hangar. Inside, four cleanly stacked mounds of gear stood in the middle of the floor, with two empty cargo bags on either side. "Sirs, I took the liberty of guessing your sizes and then providing you with a standard issue of combat gear. Check the boots, though. Not sure I got those right." Each stack also included two sets of pants and blouses of desert utility gear. She had nailed their sizing for clothes. Additionally, there were bullet proof 'Sappy Plate' chest and back body armor, knee and elbow pads, high-tech combat helmet with mounts for discrete radios and night-vision devices; both of which were also in the gear stack. Gloves, long johns, Under Armour wicking T-shirts. The list went on and on. MSgt Rose was extremely thorough.

"MSgt Rose, this is outstanding," Mule said. He was being honest, but also seeing if his charms were still there. She didn't take the bait. She kept staring at Smitty. Again, Curt chuckled, but said nothing.

"You're welcome, sir. Oh, and Smitty, Chief told me you were a fan of a specific dagger. I got that for you and gave the rest of the group standard issue U.S. KA-BARs. I hope that was right."

It was, in fact, correct. The blade was an Extrema Ratio "Special Edition" and standard issue for the Italian Army Special Forces. Smitty received one as a gift years ago and fell in love with it. Clearly, he had mentioned it at some point to Chief Cologne, who told MSgt Rose. Given her contacts on the multinational base, she 'sourced' the blade through one of her Italian friends in exchange for some U.S. gear. Such was the way 'down range.'

Mule looked at both Smitty and MSgt Rose with a befuddled look. While Smitty was handsome, he was anything but a ladies' man.

Smitty reached for the knife and unsheathed it. The blade was shiny, and the wooden handle fit his hand perfectly. The blade was thinner than a KA- BAR and slightly longer. Also worth noting, the top one third of the knife was double edged. Far better for quickly wounding and silencing an unsuspecting victim, but not as good for slicing. The KA-BAR was single edge but heavier. Both were great knives.

As Smitty was admiring his weapon, another Air Force enlisted member emerged from behind one of the racks of supplies.

"Gentlemen, this is Tech Sergeant (TSgt) Tonya Bruinink," MSgt Rose said. "She's a Security Forces Armorer and will help you select weapons."

"Sirs, when you're ready, please come with me."

The four didn't need to wait. Weapons selection was far more exciting than trying on clothing/gear. As the four passed around the large rack of supplies, they saw another section of the hangar that was decked out in weapons. Handguns, rifles, grenades, grenade launchers. It was like Christmas.

Smitty spoke up, "Hey, we probably should think this through. It may be wiser to have each team carry two different long guns, like an M-4 and AK-47. While there are disadvantages such as ammo mismatch, I think the benefits outweigh the costs.

Anyone else weighing in?"

It took about thirty minutes for each of them to get comfortable with the weapons they'd selected, along with their accouterments. Buck and Mule mounted Aimpoint Red Dot close combat optics on their M-4s while Curt and Smitty both went with a Trijicon Advance Combat Optical Gunsight. Each had their pluses and minuses. What was perhaps interesting is none of the four mounted a PAC-12 laser designator on the barrel. Common among many in the military, it was used when working with other units and an ability to 'paint' or illuminate a target for another asset. Given these four would be on their own, there was no point carrying the PAC-12, keeping significant weight off the weapon.

As they were building out their gear, TSgt Bruinink was recording the serial numbers for the weapons and gear. Much of it would be checked out until returned. In the worst case, if the teams didn't return, they would be dismissed as combat attrition. There was clear guidance from above to outfit the four men with whatever they requested.

As they ended up packing their gear into the duffle bags, Chief Cologne entered. "Gents, you all set?"

"Command Chief," Curt said. "This was awesome. Hell, if I'd known the Air Force was this generous with gear, I never would have joined the Navy."

"Hell, Navy? You should see the crap we got in the Marines," Mule belted out.

Jason laughed. "Well, we aren't normally this generous, but in your case, there's some top cover protecting you. Hey. One last thing. I have a special favor to ask you guys."

"Sure, Command Chief. You name it," Smitty said.

"I have some special coins. They are my Command Chief coins. I'd like you to take them with you. You're not the only ones who left people in Afghanistan. It would mean the world to me if I knew you took these in and then brought them back out. To be clear, I don't know where you're going, but I can guess, and if I'm right, you carrying my coin will at least give me some closure." Jason was almost tearing up. This was seriously important to him.

It was a simple request, and the Chief was right on his guess where they were going. He handed each of the four one of his coins. "Too easy, Command Chief," Smitty said. "It won't leave my side."

"An honor, Command Chief," Buck said.

"Same here," Mule followed.

"Easy day," Curt responded.

Jason began to well up a bit. "I'm serious. Please don't bullshit me. It really means the world to me if you keep this on you."

They all nodded, and understood. Warrior brotherhood was strong. They'd not let him down. Each put the coin in their pocket and would keep it on their person as if it were underwear. 'Challenge Coins,' or RMOs (Round Metal Objects) had grown in popularity across the military. Supposedly to have started under the WWI French flying unit, the Lafayette Escadrille, the U.S. mercenary pilots who flew with the unit carried Buffalo Nickels. After missions at the bar, they were often 'challenged' by colleagues. Today, challenges sometimes occur in military bars, and each aircrew member should always have their unit coin on them. That said, the tradition exploded over the past few decades, and now nearly every unit or senior person, to include the President, has a coin.

Ironically, the Chief's coin didn't really pass muster as an 'RMO' as it was not metal. It appeared to be plastic poker chip, with his rank and position listed on one side. On the other side was a silhouette of Elvis Presley and the phrase, '*If he's out there, we'll find him.*' It was a common phrase in U.S. Air Force CSAR units, and Jason had enjoyed his time as a PJ while assigned to CSAR. It was a decent coin, but clearly could have been better. Being plastic vice metal was likely yet another morale killing effort of the military's ever shrinking budget.

Chief Cologne helped the four men load their bags into his vehicle. He followed the van back to billeting and packed away all their gear into the rooms. Once locked, the six of them, to include MSgt Rose, went to the DFAC for dinner. It would be the last meal they'd eat on the base.

Chapter Twenty
Under Steam

The morning sun had not shown yet, as the time was 0400Hrs in Djibouti. The team wore civilian clothes, and their multiple bags of gear were on a pallet in the back of a large Air Force blue flatbed truck. MSgt Rose rallied the four into a van which led the truck off the base and over to the Djibouti sea port. There, the cargo ship, Maersk Freedom, was finalizing its load and the ship's captain was standing on the cement dock by one of the large bollards, chain smoking Camel cigarettes. In large letters, 'MAERSK' was inscribed on the side of the ship's hull. It was one of the many operated by the Danish shipping company. The vehicles pulled up, and Smitty got out, alone. He walked up to the captain and showed him a single piece of paper. Few words were exchanged. The captain nodded and Smitty pulled a sack out of his backpack, handing it over to the captain, who tucked it into his petticoat. Given the ship's planned route, having a few extra able hands onboard was well within the captain's interest, given the growing piracy in the region. He might have taken the four for half of what they offered.

After the captain made a few hand jesters and barked commands, a crane lifted the pallet onto the ship. The others exited the van, waiting with Smitty until they were cleared to board.

MSgt Rose tugged at Smitty's sleeve. "Smitty, Command Chief Cologne wanted me to give you this. It's my number. If you need anything on your transit back through Djibouti, or, you know, if you just wanna call?" MSgt Rose's head tilted sideways with a flirtatious smile. Smitty turned red, embarrassed by the scene. Curt and Buck laughed. Mule was baffled, being the one normally known as the lady slayer.

"Thanks, eh uh, MSgt Rose. Tell Command Chief I appreciate it."

"I will. And please, it's Jennifer."

"Yes... uh. Jennifer."

The ship's captain waved them over, and the four proceeded onto the gangplank. They would all be given adequate berthing, but the four would take turns between sleeping or guarding their cargo pallet. There was no chance of replacements, and given the captain's demonstrated ethical make up, the crew was likely not above theft.

****

The lights shone bright in the White House Press room, with the press pool awaiting the daily press brief. Much to their surprise, the President, not the White House Spokesperson, entered the room, followed closely by John Gerzema. John stopped a few yards short of the President, standing behind him and off to the side.

"Well, I bet you all didn't expect this today," the President belted out. He was right. They were stunned.

"Before the questions, I have a statement. Many of you have already started swirling rumors about my good friend and former Secretary of Defense, John Gerzema, after seeing him walking the halls of the White House. Well, I am here to put some of those rumors to bed. Over the past few months, I've asked John numerous times to consider coming back and serve in a less stressful role as a Special Security Advisor to me. Well, he finally relented, and I am happy to announce John is officially back on the team. I've brought him here to take your questions. John, come on up here."

John approached as they both smiled at each other. They were such excellent politicians that their mutual disdain for each other wouldn't have been noticeable to even the best face reader. "Thank you, Mr. President. Thank you." He turned from facing the President to the press pool. "As the President said, I came out of retirement to help him with a few unique problem sets. I am grateful to still feel needed and am hopeful I can help his administration advance their successful agenda. Now, does anyone have questions?"

The press pool exploded, firing questions faster than he could

107

respond. "Sir, why not just re-assume the role of Defense Secretary? You've already been confirmed, and the position is vacant."

"Yes, well as the President stated, that's more than I'm willing to take on right now." The answer from John was scripted, given the expectation of the question.

"Secretary Gerzema, what specifically will be your role?"

"Yes, I'm glad you asked. The President has asked me to examine Afghanistan and other Middle East nations, helping formulate our nation's long-term strategy now that we've pulled back and reset forces."

"Sir, given the questionable execution regarding the U.S. withdraw from Afghanistan, are you now coming back to repair that error before the coming elections?"

The question stung John deeply. The Defense Department given little ability to shape the Afghanistan withdraw. To the public though, none of this would be shared. The White House message on Afghanistan was consistent and stated all leadership, civilian and military, supported the effort. The notion that John was fixing HIS error, and not the President's, was frustrating. "No, No. Nothing like that. And as the President has long stated, we could not stay in Afghanistan forever. That was never the plan. I'm not here to 'fix' anything, as you suggest. I am here, however, to craft a long-term strategy that strengthens the U.S. and her vital interest in the region."

"Sir, will you be working out of the White House or the Pentagon?"

"The President suggested, and I agree it's best if I stay here in the West Wing, given my recent position in the Pentagon. Acting Secretary Stacy Crawford is at the controls of the Defense Department until a new Secretary is confirmed. She's an exceptional leader and both the Department and the U.S. are in very capable hands."

"Mr. Secretary, will you merely be making policy, or will you oversee any actions in the regions you are responsible for?"

Before John could answer, the President stepped in, "Folks, that's enough for now. John will be on the team for quite a while, and any further questions you have about his work can be vectored through my capable spokesperson. Thanks."

"Mr. President, did you..."

"Mr. President, how are the..."

"Mr. President, what are your thoughts...."

The questions flew fast and furious, all of them ignored by the President and John as they walked out of the room. Once out, John spoke. "Thanks Mr. President. I appreciate your support."

"John, you have two months in this position. No longer. Your presence is damaging to my administration. Do you understand? One month."

The President didn't wait for an answer and John didn't attempt one. It was clear to John the President's demeanor had shifted from one of embarrassment and defensive towards frustration and an offensive stance. The President was serious, but it didn't matter. In three weeks, the mission would be done.

****

The Trieste shipyard in Italy was bustling. Container ships were onloading and offloading containers via a massive system of cranes which orchestrated an impressive ballet of gigantic metallic boxes. Everything moved with purpose and balance. On the other side of the port, two tugs cleared the bollard lines as they slowly pulled and then pushed a large liquid tanker away from the jetty. The ship's draft clearly displayed she was steaming at capacity. She was not loaded with her primary cargo, aviation fuel. The main cargo for this trip was a hybrid concoction of Herbizid's 'Tillik' mixed with a chemical accelerant designed to rapidly suffocate plant life. Merely a hint of mist would deny plants an ability to absorb carbon dioxide, even robust plants such as weeds. America's EPA would never allow such a product into the nation. But where this ship was going, few would care about the environmental impact.

Slowly, the ship made her way to open water, where the tugboats released their lines. She steamed under a Panama flag, but it mattered little in the grand scheme of international logistical movements. In roughly a week, she'd be at her destination.

As two separate cargo ships steamed towards their destinations in the Indian Ocean, a few days would pass.

Chapter Twenty-one
Sir, You Have a Visitor

The last C-130 landed at Youngstown Airfield just as daybreak hit the Pennsylvania horizon. The crews were exhausted but had completed their training. They slowly stumbled off the aircraft into the crew bus, enroute to their operations center for debrief. Once seated, the lead pilot began the debrief, walking through the entire mission, providing compliments where deserved and criticism of mistakes. Such debriefs were commonplace in the Air Force. Aviation is a punishingly unforgiving profession, and it's no place for thin skin or hurt feelings. Overall, the four-ship of C-130s performed well. It was a spread formation, low-level night run, simulating spraying for mosquitos in the marshes around Lake Erie. The crews were on night-vision devices and as much as air traffic control would allow with exterior lights out.

After the debrief, the commander walked in. Everyone in the room stood immediately. "Seats, please." Colonel Hughlett directed, as everyone sat back down. "I just received word. Your deployment orders have arrived. You'll be wheels up in 48 hours. Maintenance crews are working to finalize the modifications and one other aircraft will need an FCF (functional check flight) tomorrow as we had to swap out two high time engines on the same wing. They're doing ground engine runs on her today. When complete and good, another crew will perform the FCF. If all goes well, you'll all be airborne as a formation in two days. And again, your orders stressed the sensitivity and secrecy surrounding this mission. I cannot state it enough. I'm offering you two choices. First, I can lock you all down here for the next two days and take your cell phones. The other option is to treat you like adults and let you go home."

His threat was not lost on the aircrew. They knew he was dead serious. They all opted for option two.

"Good. But know this. If I get one word, just one, from the press, the bro network, or the knives club (a common nickname for the 'wives club'), all your asses are back here in sleeping bags

111

until you depart. Is that understood?"

They all responded with, "Yes, sir." The commander departed the room, and they all stood again. For the Air National Guard, this was about as exciting as it got. The crews were pumped.

****

The weather in Tucson was exceptional for early May and the morning sunrise over the Catalina mountains was majestic. There was always a special shade of reddish, pinkish, purple that only an Arizona sunrise or sunset could produce. Allison, however, wouldn't know. Her face hovered over her parent's guest bathroom toilet bowl as she was yet again ill with morning sickness. Her arms were up on the sides of the toilet seat, holding on for dear life.

The door partially cracked open, and her father looked in. "Drive that school bus, girl," he said, as he peeked in.

"Jesus Dad! Here I am trying to give you a grandchild, and that's your comment?"

Paul thought about it for a second, shrugged his shoulders, and said, "Yeah. I'm stickin' with it. I'm going to the kitchen. Can I make you a cup of coffee and some plain toast?"

"Dad! I can't have coffee! I'm pregnant! Tea, Please!" Allison snapped at him.

"Alli, you're pregnant, not dead. But whatever you want. Tea it is. I presume you do what the plain toast. Right?" Allison loved her dad's coffee and, more importantly, she was grateful he knew just what she needed, even if she did change the order to tea. As a child, Allison suffered from a few intestinal tract issues. During that time, every day, Paul would get up and make her plain toast. It was all she could manage to eat. '*He remembered*,' she thought. "Yes, dad. That would be great. Tha...AARRGG!!!" Tilting her head down, she began vomiting again.

Paul walked to the kitchen and prepared her breakfast.

After roughly 10 minutes, Allison made her way into the room, looking as if she'd just been involved in a horrid wrestling match on the losing side. She was tired, with bags under her eyes, and moved slowly, as if every muscle ached, which they did.

"How did you sleep, Alli?" Paul asked.

"Not great, Dad. How about you?"

"Eh. I'm old. If I get five hours of sleep a night, I call it a win."

"Can I get you anything else? Do you want a Tums? Eggs? Cereal? A doctor?" Paul rarely showed it, but he was concerned for his little girl.

"Nah, dad. I'm good. What are you and mom doing today?"

"I think we are going to go walk the Sabino Canyon Trail. As you know, it's 'city hiking' as the majority of the path is paved. For your mom, that's about as outdoors as it gets." They both smiled. Paul continued. "Do you want to come with us?" He inquired.

"Dad, I'd love to, but I really need some more sleep. This kid is sucking the life out of me."

"I understand, Alli. I understand." Paul got up from his chair and walked over behind her. He put his hands on Allison's shoulders, bent partially down and gave her a reassuring hug. "We will have our cell phones if you need anything. Why don't you go back to bed? I'll rustle up mom and get us out of the house. You and Major can stay here. He'll stand guard for ya." Major was a large Weimaraner, the family pet.

"OK, Dad. Sounds good," Allison replied. She finished her breakfast and took her tea to the bedroom.

Allison could hear her parents preparing to leave. It was always the same routine from her mom. *'Paul, do you have your keys? Paul, do you have your wallet? Paul, do you have your phone? Paul, do you have a bottle of water?'* It drove her father crazy, but at least once a week, he'd forget something and then have to hear about it the rest of the day. Paul's departure questioning was routine, and to Allison, it was just another reminder she was home. She felt safe, and Major curled up at the foot of her bed as they both drifted off to sleep.

A few hours later, a large black SUV slowly pulled up in front of the Flaherty residence. A few men and a lone female exited the vehicle, approaching the house. Major jumped out of bed and began barking. Allison didn't see the vehicle or the people and knew it was far too early for her parents' return. She also knew they weren't the type of family to get many visitors.

She jumped out of bed and pulled back a window shade, seeing the men but not the female, as she'd already advanced too close to the front door to remain visible. The men were in dark suits and black sunglasses; about as far from 'normal Tucson attire' as it gets. Allison threw on some clothes and grabbed her phone. She was growing concerned, and Major could sense it. His barking became more intense, shifting from mere excited to aggressive.

The doorbell rang. Allison cautiously approached the door and then peered through the peephole. Her concern immediately washed away. It wasn't a stranger. It was Ms. Hershey. Kathy Hershey, the Chairman of the Joint Chief's wife from Washington D.C.

Allison opened the door. "Ms. Hershey! What on earth are you doing here?!"

"Good morning, Allison. It's great to see you. I'm really sorry to barge in on you, but my husband ordered me."

"Ordered you? I don't understand?"

"Please, may I come in? My security detail sticks out like a sore thumb here and I don't want to alarm your neighbors." Kathy was right. The security detail was out of place.

"My gosh! Yes, please. I'm sorry for not offering. Come in." Allison pulled Major back, who now sensed things were OK. He was excited to have company, but after a few sniffs, was satisfied and went to lie down.

"May I get you some coffee?" Allison asked.

"I'd love some. We just came over from Lowes Ventana Canyon Resort, and the coffee there was horrible."

"You're staying in Tucson? What brings you here?" Allison inquired.

"You do, my dear." Kathy replied.

"OK. I'm lost. What do you mean, me?"

Kathy reached into her purse and pulled out a handwritten letter. It was from Curt to Admiral Hershey. "Curt sent this to

my husband before he left, asking for a favor. You can read it."
Kathy handed it to Allison. "He asks if I would consider coming
to visit you while he's gone. He knew you'd not only be lonely,
but with a baby on the way, your acceptance of his travels would
be challenging." Allison read the letter, and a tear fell down her
cheek.

"Allison, don't cry. Here. Take this." Kathy reached into her
purse and pulled out a Kleenex.

"Thanks. This is all extremely nice, and I'm touched, but it's
all so unnecessary. Really, I'm fine."

Kathy served alongside her husband for decades in the U.S.
Navy. She'd heard those words many times, and also knew most
were untrue. "Sure you are. I understand. But, you see, when
Curt was in the Navy, he knew there were many entities to help
families through deployments. Family Support Centers, MWR
(Morale, Welfare, and Recreation), the Ombudsman program.
Now that he's no longer in the Navy, none of that is available to
you. He didn't want you to be alone. I agreed, and here I am.
Now, please. Don't make this a wasted trip. What do you say
we get you dressed and go have a great 'girl day?' It's on me."

Allison smiled. A good portion of the stress she felt washed
away with every word Kathy said. "Yes, Ms. Hershey. I'd like
that."

"Great," Kathy replied, "But Ms. Hershey is my husband's
mom, who isn't my favorite person in the world. Please call me
Kathy."

"Yes, Kathy. Thanks." Allison went to change while Kathy
finished her coffee. After a half hour, Allison was ready.

"Shall we go?" Kathy said as she led the way out the front
door. "Have you ridden with a security detail before?"

"No. Do they really take you everywhere?" Allison asked
quizzically, as one of the men opened her door to get in the SUV.

"Yes. Please don't perceive it as glamorous, though. They
annoy me more than I like." Kathy, now sitting in the back of the
SUV directed her attention up front, "Isn't that right Fredrick?"

One of the men turned and smiled, "Yes, Ms. Hershey." He
then turned back, grabbed a radio microphone, and said, "Daisy
on the move."

115

Allison was puzzled. "Daisy?" She asked.

"Yes, Allison. My security detail gave me the gracious codename of 'Ms. Daisy,' as in 'Driving Ms. Daisy.' Now just shortened to Daisy. I'm sure they find it cute."

Fredrick turned around and said, "Why yes, Ms. Daisy. We do." Kathy and Allison laughed. It would be the only personal interaction between the security detail and Kathy. At times, she wished there was less. Other times, she was grateful they were there.

"So, Allison, I've scheduled us a spa day at Ventana Canyon Resort. After that, we can grab some lunch. What do you say?"

"That sounds perfect. But really, can I please pay my way?"

"Are you crazy? If the Admiral found out, he'd kill me!" Allison found it humorous Kathy referred to her husband by rank. While some might consider this pompous, the way Kathy said the words, it was clear his rank was more of an annoyance than a pleasure. Allison knew she'd grow to like Kathy. She was good people.

****

The lunch hour had arrived in D.C. John and Andrew had scheduled a lunch to catch up on their plan. Now that John was back in the government, he'd made reservations at the White House Mess, an exclusive dining opportunity for anyone. The kitchen was run by U.S. military cooks, so expectations needed to be managed, but no one went there for the food.

The two entered and sat down. Both Andrew and John set their cell phones down on the table, a common practice in the beltway, almost a sign of importance. Immediately, a waiter stood at the table. "Good afternoon, Secretary Gerzema," the waiter said as he handed menus to both guests. "May I get you started with a drink?"

"Yes, please. I'd like a Coke. Andrew, what would you like?"

"I'd love an unsweet tea if you have it? Is that available here at the White House Mess?"

"Absolutely, sir. Right away." The waiter departed.

"So, John. How are the plans coming along from your side?" Andrew asked.

John could not contain his excitement. The individual pieces of the overall operation were coming together splendidly. "Andrew, I couldn't be happier. The crews out of Pennsylvania have received their orders, the aircraft will soon be airborne. The herbicide has been generated, transferred to the port, and is now on its way to Oman. I've sent a small team to Oman to bed down the aircraft once they arrive and to work the last leg of logistics, moving the herbicide from the port to the airfield." John smiled as he finished the discussion.

"Sounds great. I'm happy, but as you know, I'm not much on the military side. Where are we on the funding?" Andrew wanted to know about the money. It was his bread and butter.

"Yes," John said, as he leaned closer to Andrew. "I understand. The financing issues are also in place. We've transferred all the funds required to pay for the herbicide to Herbizid and their parent company Myer. We also secured a non-disclosure agreement that they cannot announce the contract details until the end of the second quarter, around early June. Once they announce, the stock is poised to jump significantly, as this is one of the largest contracts they've ever had. Did you purchase my stock into that offshore account?"

Andrew reached into his pocket and pulled out a single piece of paper. It was from an investment account in the Caymans, under the name Steve Perkins, the false identification created for John. "Yes. Here is the document. You can see the number and identification for Steve Perkins was created just as you requested-thousands of shares. As many as I could buy with the funds you provided. After the announcement of the contract award, there is a sale order in at market cost, for the close of that day."

Andrew looked over the document and passed it back. He didn't want to hold onto it. "Great, I appreciate it. Please, you keep this document. I'd rather not have it circulating around here."

"I understand," Andrew replied as he nonchalantly tucked it into his jacket pocket. "When do you think the operation will take place?"

"In roughly a week is my best guess. Timelines are fluid. We need to get the aircraft over there. The Pennsylvania National Guard intel officer is ranting about moon schedules or something, saying we should wait until there is lower illumination. I dunno. Night is night to me. We can't wait forever, as you know."

"How long does he want you to wait?"

"A few more days, less than five. Also said if there's a cloud deck, there's no need to worry about the illumination. We will see. Either way, it's gonna happen soon."

"Great," Andrew said. His phone buzzed, and he picked it up. "Damn. I gotta go. Issue at the house. Sorry. Gonna have to skip lunch." Andrew stood up, as did John.

"Is everything OK?" John asked.

"Yes. It's a minor emergency. Water leak in the house and Becky is far from prepared to deal with things like this alone. I really must be going."

"I understand," John replied. "Please give Becky my best, and thanks for catching up with me."

"Sure thing. Here's to wishing you good luck." Andrew said as he began walking out.

"You mean us," John replied quickly.

"Yes, sorry. Us." Andrew turned the corner outside the White House Mess and lifted his phone as if to call Becky and respond to the emergency. As he looked down at the phone, he gently tapped the red round circle, which directed the phone to stop recording. He then turned off the phone and walked out of the White House.

****

The lady's spa day was wonderful. Allison received a special 'pregnancy' massage, and Kathy was truly happy that she could be supportive. It was something she enjoyed from her early Navy days and now missed it dearly. As the wife of the Chairman, there were few opportunities to make a direct impact at a personal level on deployed sailors' families.

After the massage, the two ladies sat outside by the pool, looking up at the Catalina Mountains. It was Kathy's first visit to Tucson, as Navy personnel are rarely stationed in deserts. She found the view remarkable. To Allison, it was just a bunch more Saguaro, prickly pear and jumping cholla cactus, a bunch of scrub brush and the occasional quail darting by, chased by a road runner. It was her old home and still held a charm.

"Allison, in all honesty now, how are you holding up? I was told this is your second time where Curt has gone out on a mission."

"Yes, that's true," Allison responded, "But last time he went to a place that was far more civilized than Afghanistan. This time, it just hurts too much, especially now that we are starting a family."

"I understand. I remember when my husband was on a ship in the gulf during Operation DESERT STORM. We couldn't talk because the ship was ordered 'comms out' or whatever. I watched the news when the war started and prayed. Then, the news began reporting an Iraqi fighter jet had made it out to the gulf and was flying directly towards U.S. Navy ships in the Arabian Gulf. I panicked and turned off the TV. I couldn't take it. Frankly, I don't know which is worse. Watching everything unfold, or sitting idly by, fat, dumb and happy, hoping everything is OK. What do you think?"

Allison hadn't really thought about it. She knew she wanted to hear from Curt, but also knew that wasn't possible. As a journalist, she knew television media had skewed far towards 'over sensationalizing' the news, attracting far more viewers, but also causing worry and concern. "I don't know," she responded. "I just worry."

"Well, that's good. I'd be concerned if you didn't." Kathy picked up her margarita and took a sip. "Allison, we all worry. It's a matter of managing it, which is why I'm here."

"I get it. But why do they go? When they're young and dumb, I get it. But older?"

"Lord knows. Many women have asked that question thousands of times. Every time we talk about it at home, I'm told 'If not me then whom' or bible quotes or even John Stuart Mill. I think by this point, I can recite the entire thing verbatim." Kathy tried to imitate her husband's voice and said, "A man who has nothing for which he is willing to fight, nothing which is more important than his own personal safety, is a miserable creature... blah, blah, blah."

Allison laughed. "Yes! That's exactly how I feel!" She too took a sip of her margarita-a virgin one-because of the pregnancy. "Why don't THEY get it?"

"That's the thing, Allison, they are wired differently. One day, I sat there and wondered why I hadn't married the high school geek, who shamelessly followed me around the school hallways fawning over every move I made. Today, he's making a great living now, back in our hometown. But the truth is, I never would have been happy. My husband's is exciting to me because he has a thirst for adventure which is intrinsically tied to his thirst to defend freedom and his love for our nation. I can't remove one without destroying the other. Curt, I believe, is the same way. I remember when you told me how you met. He wooed you off your feet as a cocky and full of himself guy in the Mauritania Africa as the lead doctor on a humanitarian mission. Right?"

"Yes," Allison responded.

"OK, but do you think he'd have been as cocky and himself if he was working at a local medical clinic in his hometown?" Kathy asked. "Do you think he would have flown you back to Casablanca and propose? Do you think he'd up and move from Chicago to D.C. at the drop of a hat? These are all things you love in him."

Allison thought hard about it. Kathy was right. Allison loved Curt more than anything in the world, and she was beginning to realize 'what' Curt was, not just who. It didn't erase the pain of him being gone and in danger, but it did create a space in her brain to help manage the fear. Another tear fell down her cheek.

"Allison. Oh, I'm sorry, sweetheart. I didn't mean to make you cry. Are you OK?"

"I'm fine," Allison replied as she wiped the tear away along with a rub of her nose. "I just now realized I fell in love with freakin' MacGyver."

The two laughed and clinked their glasses.

"I can promise you two things, Allison. First, it gets easier, but never easy. And second, I am always just a phone call away. I like you, Allison. I hope we can become friends. Beyond the mandated orders of my husband." Again, they chuckled.

"Thanks Kathy. I do t…" Allison was interrupted by her phone. It was her father. "Excuse me. It's my dad."

Allison answered the phone. "Alli! Are you OK?" Paul was worried.

"Yes, Dad. Why?"

"The neighbors said a big SUV picked you up and now Major is out back barking. Where are you?"

"I'm at Ventana Canyon Resort."

"What!?" Paul exclaimed. "What are you doing there?"

"A friend came to visit and brought me here, Dad." Allison replied.

Kathy leaned over, "Tell them to join us if you want."

"My friend says you can join us if you want," Allison relayed as she mouthed 'thank you,' to Kathy.

"Lemme ask your mo… awe, never mind. She overheard the whole thing, and her eyes are as big as saucers. We'll be there soon. Just getting to the car at the end of the trail."

"Perfect, Dad. You're only about five minutes away. We are sitting out by the pool. If they ask, you are guests of the Hershey party."

"OK, Alli, but who do you know named Hershey other than through Curt… ALLISON! Are you sitting with the Chairman of the Joint Chiefs!?" Paul's pulse quickened.

"Better, Dad. Better. See you soon," Allison replied as she hung up the phone.

After fifteen minutes, Allison was with her stepfather and mom. Kathy was a meticulous and gracious host, sitting by the pool with the family for hours, talking and laughing. Every so often, Allison jabbed her father in the ribs as he kept asking questions about military operations or issues related to Admiral Hershey. Kathy didn't mind, however. It came with the territory.

That night when Allison prepared for bed, she reflected on the day, staring into the mirror as she brushed her hair. *'Nover, wherever you are, I love you. Today was everything it needed to be and more. Please come home safely,'* she said to herself.

Chapter Twenty-two
Infil(tration)

The Maersk Freedom slowly entered the port of Karachi, under tow from a few tugboats to navigate her safely. As the harbor bridge captain vectored the tugs, the Maersk captain pulled out his phone and placed a call. It was part of the coordination effort he'd promised Smitty in Djibouti. The call lasted less than thirty seconds, and one of the captain's best contacts would be at the dock, along with a jingle truck Smitty had requested.

Heavy lines were hoisted and anchored onto the dock's bollards. The Maersk Freedom was now still. The captain looked out onto the dock and saw his friend. Stepping out of the helm, now on the railings, he could better see his contact, who nodded up and down as he stood next to the customs official waiting to board.

The captain walked down the gangplank onto the dock, shaking hands with the customs official. Before the large cranes could start moving containers off the ship, the customs documents needed to be signed, and if desired, the customs official could request to inspect the ship. Today, that would not be required. The paperwork was quickly signed by the customs official, who walked away with a clear bulge in the front right pocket of his pants. He either found the captain an extremely attractive man or had been paid to ignore the ship. Smitty, Curt, Buck and Mule watched from above. To them, it didn't matter, they'd soon be on land in Pakistan.

After roughly an hour to get their pallet off the ship and onto the jingle truck, Smitty shook hands with the captain to ensure they were square, then joined the other three in the back of the truck. The jingle truck was truly a unique experience, as such vehicles were unique to the region. Truck drivers decorated the windshield and front of the truck with tassels and many little trinkets, making each vehicle unique. There was so much stuff hanging off some trucks that as they bounced down the uneven roads in the region, the truck literally 'jingled' on its way.

123

Three of the men sat in the back. It was sweltering hot and uncomfortable. Curt rode up front, trying to get the driver to understand he wanted to go to a Range Rover, Toyota, or any other large auto dealership. It took about 15 minutes, and a few $50 bills until the driver understood.

The jingle truck pulled up outside the Range Rover Showroom in downtown Karachi. The contrast between the car lot's new, beautiful Range Rovers and the jingle truck could not have been starker. As the truck stopped, the three men rolled out of the back, covered in sweat, while Curt was only lightly perspiring.

"Hot back there, huh?" Curt said to the three, who found his humor ill timed.

"Suck it, Nover." Mule said.

As the four walked towards the dealership, a well-dressed Pakistani man approached, clearly providing greetings in the local language.

Curt addressed him. "Sir, good day. Sorry, we speak English. Do you speak English?

"Yes! Oh Yes! Happily, gentlemen. I'm Ravi. How are you today?" The dealer asked. His English possessed a strong British accent. Understandable, given the history and relationship between the two nations.

"We're good. Thanks," Curt said. "We are looking for a fairly good-sized vehicle, perhaps used a bit. Not sure we need a new one."

"Yes, of course. I have a 2014 Range Rover Sport, right this way." He led the four into the dealership.

A 2014 was a little older than Curt desired. The miles and mission would be demanding, but at least it was a start to see how things might progress.

The vehicle was decent, but the color was black, which would draw heat. It only had seventy thousand kilometers (forty-two thousand miles). If it was all he had, it would do. "Ravi. This is nice. Do you have anything in a lighter color?"

"Oh, sir, yes, but those are the new cars. May I show you those?" Ravi was excited.

"Maybe, before we do that, what's the price on this vehicle?"

124

Curt was unsure how much such a vehicle actually cost in Pakistan.

"Yes, sir, it is 7,500,000 rupees which is a VERY good deal I must say."

As Ravi rattled off the cost, Smitty stood there with his iPhone. It was in airplane mode, just like all the others for security reasons, but for this activity, he wouldn't need the internet. Smitty typed in the last known exchange rate, then the amount of rupees. He handed his iPhone to Curt with the number $91,221. Curt gasped.

"Ravi, let's stay here for now and not go see the new vehicles. You said this was a 2014, right? Do you have anything perhaps older?" There was no chance Curt could even afford the 2014.

Ravi's excitement dissipated, but he still wanted to make a sale. "Sir, we do have an older vehicle. It is not a Range Rover, but rather a Toyota 4Runner. A 2005, but in relatively good condition." Ravi took them back outside the showroom out onto the lot. There was an older, white 4Runner with a roof rack and a bumper bar. It was exactly what they needed, albeit far older than Curt wanted.

"Great, Ravi. Now we are talking. What's the price on this?" Curt asked.

"Good Price! Sir, this one is only 4,500,000 rupees," Ravi responded.

Again, Smitty held out his iPhone. It displayed $54,875.

Curt looked at Smitty and said, "Jesus, are you serious? Are you off by a zero or something? It's a freaking 2005."

Smitty sat there in his sunglasses, covered in sweat. "Buddy. Welcome to Pakistan. It is what it is. Drop $60k for plates and a loose registration and let's get moving. I'm not fond of being in this city for too long. By the way, that's coming out of your portion of funds." Smitty smiled.

Smitty was right, and after a bit of haggling the price down to $50,000, Curt offered another $5,000 for an immediate purchase under one of the false passport identities he had in his gear. Within an hour, they were on the road, with the jingle truck behind them. They'd drive for the day, stopping in a small

125

Pakistani village halfway to Afghanistan. Once there, again, one would sleep in the jingle truck with the pallet of gear while the others would secure hotel rooms for the night. They'd pay cash and use false identification. Slowly, the team was disappearing from the real world and transforming into their combat roles.

* *

As the two teams drove north out of Karachi, four C-130s made their way out of the U.S. on their way to Ramstein Air Base, Germany. They'd bed down there for the night, and then continue on the next morning. Ramstein was a perfect location for their layover, as it was the primary hub for C-130 operations across Europe. Should any of the aircraft have maintenance issues, they'd easily be resolved.

* *

The next morning, the C-130s departed Ramstein, while the teams in Pakistan awoke for another long drive. Concurrently, a large chemical tanker was pulling into the port on Masirah Island, Oman. The port was in the airfield's vicinity and such tankers were common, as most provided aviation fuel for the base. The ship came to a full stop as lines were passed to secure the ship. On the dock stood John Gerzema's point of contact, Ashton Beasley, orchestrating the offload of what most onlookers believed to be aviation fuel. Trucks had lined up to begin the offload as new, empty fuel blivits were prepared on the airbase alongside the existing ones. These blivits, however, would welcome not fuel, but a far more sinister liquid.

* *

The team drove north along the Indus River and then between that river and the Chenab River. The valley between the two rivers was lush and quite stunning, a far cry from what one might first imagine when thinking of Pakistan. However, once they approached Islamabad, the terrain changed dramatically. Mountain ranges began sprouting up, and the lush green landscapes transitioned to barren brown. Again, the team would spend another night in Pakistan, this time on the outskirts of Islamabad. That evening, Smitty reached into his gear and pulled out a binder. He also cracked open one of his burner phones, loading a SIM Card into it. The text message he sent was provided by Afghan Lieutenant General Ghani back in D.C. Smitty followed the instructions as laid out. Within five minutes, the text response he expected arrived. They'd meet his first contact tomorrow, and the team would enter Afghanistan. Smitty relayed what had transpired to the team. There was a silent pause as they looked at each other. The gravity of the mission finally began to set in. It was now real.

Chapter Twenty-three
The Game is Afoot

The U.S. Embassies in Berlin, Germany, and Muscat, Oman, worked for days to secure overflight clearance, or 'Dip Clearances,' for the C-130s out of Pennsylvania. It was a common practice, and there were few questions about military cargo aircraft not declaring hazardous cargo. C-130s were far easier to approve than fighter aircraft with weapon's load outs.

The four Air National Guard C-130s lumbered into the air out of Ramstein, Germany, early in the morning. Spring dew covered much of the ground and the air was chilly, albeit not freezing. Tulips had popped and the ground cover at least was beginning to display some color. To the average onlooker, the gray military aircraft looked just like any other C-130, but to the expert, it was clear they'd been modified with some external systems, not common to 'slick' C-130s assigned to Ramstein. The trip from Ramstein down to Oman would require one stop along the way for fuel. To leverage U.S. overseas basing, the crews filed a flight plan to fly into Naval Air Station, Souda Bay, Crete. The crew was disappointed that their gas-and-go was such a quick stop. Greece in early May had perfect weather and a Mediterranean Sea bountiful with amazing sea food.

After refueling the four aircraft was complete, the crews cranked the 'four fans of freedom,' a common nickname for the C-130's engines, and departed Greece. They'd fly over Egypt, with a view of the Suez Canal, cross the Red Sea, and then over much of the barren Saudi desert before nearing Oman. Many of these sights were something the Pennsylvania Air National Guard aircrew had never seen, and their cameras in the cockpit capturing the unique opportunity.

At roughly one hundred miles from their destination, Saudi Air Traffic Control handed off the flight of four to Oman approach who directed their initial descent into Masirah. The approach was uneventful, and a few handpicked C-130 maintainers send a day prior from Ramstein Air Base were on the ramp awaiting the opportunity to catch the aircraft and bed them down. The maintainers didn't know much about the mission and their orders were more secretive than those provided by the Special Operations community. There weren't many, but enough with the right expertise to fix any minor issues and keep the mission on track. The maintenance crew chiefs marshaled the aircraft to parking. The engine's hum ceased, and the props slowed to a stop. As the crews exited the aircraft, a man in khaki pants, a white button down, blue blazer and tie waited to greet the crew. He was sweating profusely, destroying his Brooks Brothers attire. As the crew from the first aircraft approached, he reached out his hand and said, "Hello. Welcome to... wherever this is. I'm Ashton Beasley, or just Ash. I'm from the White House West Wing and will be overseeing your mission."

The lead aircraft commander, Lieutenant Colonel Pete Sanchez, was also the deployed commander. He had never seen such a thing in his ten years of active-duty service or fifteen years in the National Guard. *A civilian in charge?'* He thought. Clearly, LtCol Sanchez had fallen in under some sort of alternative command structure. While strange, he was not about to ruffle feathers. "Hey Ash. I'm Lieutenant Colonel Pete Sanchez, but my callsign is Dirty. Thanks for the welcome."

"A callsign? So cool! Kinda like Top Gun, right? Dirty?"

It took no less than twenty seconds with Ashton Beasley for Dirty to conclude this kid was in over his head. "Yeah. Kinda. Hey, what's the plan for our bed down and chow? The rest of the crew is downloading gear now."

"Yes. Well, we have secured CONEX billeting for you. I believe there is enough for each of you to be two to a CONEX," he replied. A CONEX was the military's response to a rapidly expanding billeting requirement in the Middle East with few resources to build an adequate facility. They took old shipping containers and retrofitted them with a bed on either end. The middle of the CONEX was a common space for the two inhabitants. It was not ideal, but far better than tents that had served the military occupants at Masirah Island for years.

"Great," Dirty replied. "How do we get there?" Lieutenant Colonel Sanchez and his crew, just like the rest of the Air Force, were accustomed to crew buses. Ash, not being familiar, had overlooked this.

"Yeah. Well. I just walked out here. So, I guess y'all can just walk back with me?"

"So, you have no transportation for any of the crew or any of the bags?"

Ash was clearly embarrassed, and also clearly not displaying any sense of leadership commensurate to the position he was filling. "No." he said sheepishly.

"Got it," Dirty replied. He turned towards the crew and shouted. "Folks! Bag Drag! Follow me!" He turned back to Ash. "Well, Ash. Lead the way."

There in the hot afternoon sun, a young, overdressed civilian who could easily pass for a college fraternity pledge led a team of four C-130 crews, grumbling, across an open military ramp towards the base compound. *'What on earth could possibly go wrong?'* Dirty sarcastically thought to himself. As everyone dragged, Dirty headed back up onto the flight deck of his C-130. Alone, he pulled out his personal cell phone and turned it on. Once it connected, he fired an iPhone iChat message to a long-time buddy he'd met back at U.S. Air Force Undergraduate Pilot Training, now Brigadier General Tony Moorehead. Dirty felt like something was amiss with this entire operation, and he wasn't wrong.

'Cravin — I'm sitting on the ramp at KMSH, under the command of a fraternity kid. YGBSM. WTF are we doing?'

He turned off his phone and would check it in the middle of the night in his CONEX.

****

Curt and his gang had checked out of their no-name hotel and would soon load up and drive. That night, they paid for the jingle truck driver to have a room as well. Unfortunately, he overslept a bit, enjoying the uncommon luxury. After roughly a

30-minute delay, the two vehicles made their way up from Islamabad toward Afghanistan.

Roughly fifty miles shy of the border, the mountains on either side of the road rose dramatically to the sky, and the road twisted along the valley floor between the two. "It's a slaughterhouse killbox," Smitty said as he looked up at the dramatic cliffs.

"You ain't kidding," Curt replied. The four knew where they were from the road signs. It was the famed Khyber Pass of Pakistan. The location sadly gained notoriety in 1842, when British forces in Afghanistan were ordered to return to England. Soldiers, along with their gear and families, traveled south through the Khyber Pass. Once in the pass, Afghans attacked from the elevated positions on either side. With nowhere to retreat, 4,500 British service members and roughly 12,000 support personnel as well as family were killed. One British Officer, Dr. William Brydon, was spared and sent by horseback to Jalalabad, Afghanistan to report the massacre.

The four men in the car remained eerily silent, as if there was some anticipation yet again that the Afghans would attack. Slowly, they continued through the pass, less than five miles from the mouth of the pass and the border with Afghanistan. Smitty pulled out his map as Curt drove. "OK. About three miles up, there's a small village on the right called Torkham. Drive into the village and beyond it. Seven hundred meters past the village on the left is an abandoned madrasa. That's where we meet our contact."

Curt understood the instructions but was reluctant. "So, we are supposed to just trust this link up is legit? To be fair, I'm not a fan. I'd rather be able to stop short of the linkup point and observe it for a while, but that's not possible because I'm not freaking stopping in the middle of an Afghan border town."

"Hey, chuckles. I didn't see you putting a shit ton of elbow grease into the plan. Now you wanna critique it?" Smitty replied.

Mule, from the back seat, popped up, "Yeah. This is helpful. Three minutes out and we wanna discuss the plan? Sorry. No time for that." Mule reached over the back of his seat into the

4Runner cargo area. He rustled through a bunch of bags and finally found two M-4 rifles, handing one to Buck and holding onto the other. "Curt," he said. "Drive past it like we are regular traffic and the other three of us will observe. Continue to a safe distance, then stop. I'll use my ACOG (Advanced Combat Optical Gunsight) and monitor it for a while." Buck pulled out a long range Leopold scope for long range observation, it was the same one SOF snipers often used.

The plan, under the circumstances, was about the best they could come up with. Curt drove slowly, trying to keep his head faced forward. Smitty, in the passenger seat, quietly said, "Building on your left, fifty meters."

Curt replied. "Visual. I got it." Without changing pace, Curt continued towards the building with the intent of passing it. Just 10 meters before the building, a man in a brown Afghan robe stepped out from the door of the building quickly. Mule switched the select switch off safety on his M-4 and began raising it, then lowered it, realizing the man was just tossing out a bucket of water, or urine... one couldn't be certain in the region.

Curt saw the entire thing, then his eyes locked on the man. From that moment until Curt slammed on the brakes of the 4Runner was milliseconds. He'd stopped so fast, the jingle truck driver almost slammed into the back of their 4Runner. Curt couldn't believe it. The man standing next to the 4 Runner was Majeed, the interpreter he had on his last mission to Afghanistan.

Curt slammed the gear shifter into park, jumped out and ran up to Majeed, bear hugging him. "Majeed! HA! YES! It's YOU!" He could not contain his excitement. The randomness of such an event was remarkable.

"Yes, commander. It is good to see you." Majeed was clearly taken aback. Such types of hugs and affection between adult men were uncommon in his culture.

"Damn, Curt," Buck said. "Let the guy breathe!"

Curt let Majeed go and introduced him to the team. After that, Majeed said, "Commander, can you please pull your vehicle around here to the side of the madrasa? Then come inside and join us."

"Sure, Majeed. I'll see you inside." Curt did as instructed. As he parked, he noticed eight donkeys tied up behind the madrasa. Once inside, he noticed there was one other Afghan in the room that he did not know. Majeed was speaking with Smitty and the other Afghan.

"Commander," Majeed interrupted Smitty. "This is my friend and other helper. His name is Usman I Bagrami. I was told by our colleague you were coming and need two interpreters. Your friend here, Mr. Smitty, says that's true."

"Yes, yes, Majeed. You are correct."

"Good, sir. I would like to go with you, and Usman can go with the other team. His family is from the Bagram area, where he grew up. I was also told the other team will go in that direction. You wish to go to Kandahar."

"Well, not exactly," Curt said. He looked around at the other three, who were also slightly concerned with how much information Majeed knew. "Majeed, who told you all this?"

"Commander. When Lieutenant General Ghani wants something, he gets it. Even if he is eleven thousand kilometers away. We pray he comes back someday and when he does, things will be better."

Curt was partially relieved. At least Majeed named the individual the teams had confided in.

"We will stay here until dark. Usman and I will drive your vehicle across the border with our legitimate papers. Your jingle truck and truck driver will follow us. We will unpack anything that can't legally cross the border from the jingle truck and place it on the donkeys. The four of you will ride the remaining donkeys across the border. Once across, we will link up and go to our safe-house in Jalalabad."

"Donkeys?" Mule said. "To be fair, I'm not opposed to donkeys, or horses, but without you two, how on earth are we supposed to know where to go?"

Buck chuckled. "Mule questioning a donkey. Priceless."

Majeed looked at Jeremy and dispassionately said. "We paid good money for these donkeys. They are trained to travel between the two border towns of Torkham, Pakistan and

Torkham, Afghanistan. Many times, they make the trip with just supplies and no humans. Their instinct leads them. You will be fine."

It was true, and none of the four wanted to dive deeper into 'what' kind of supplies the donkeys smuggled. They likely knew the answer was opium.

The four looked at each other. There was no other choice. They began unloading the weapons and ammunition from the vehicles and loading the donkeys. Many of the items could remain in the SUV and truck. Once the donkeys were packed, Majeed opened a duffle bag that he'd stashed in the building's corner. Inside were a handful of Afghan robes or 'perahan tunbans' in local slang. To the four Americans, they'd been referred to as 'man-dresses' for over a decade. The outfits were customary attire for Afghan males. The four didn't argue, realizing this attire would be the best camouflage available in Afghanistan. The four had also been growing out their beards ever since agreeing to the mission. Their facial hair was nowhere near as long as others in Afghanistan, but they were long enough to avoid questioning eyes.

It would be a long night. The four laid down on the floor of the madrasa and tried to get some rest.

Chapter Twenty-four

Exposed

Brigadier General Moorehead checked his phone as he drank morning coffee at home in Virginia. He scrolled through the news, some emails from work. It was well known that any Flag Officer stationed in the Pentagon could not be more than three feet from his phone, other than when in a classified vault. And in that case, one must give the General or Admiral twenty minutes upon exiting a secure vault to catch up on all the message traffic they missed.

As he opened his text messages, he saw a new one from Dirty. It was a welcome sight. They hadn't exchanged communications for a few weeks. It would be nice to hear how Dirty and the family were doing.

As he read the text, his eyes bulged. *'What in the hell are C-130s doing in the Oman?'* he thought to himself. Cravin shot a few emails and texts to friends. As with any General, the messages were far from alarmist, as if perhaps he'd possibly missed the memo or slept through that part of the operations brief.

Cravin's questions spread like wildfire through the Air Staff and the National Guard Bureau. As the information climbed from the one-star to the two, then three, then four, each level was even more cautious in the way they framed the question to their superiors. It started with, *'Why didn't you tell me we were forward deploying four C-130s?'* to *'Sir, were you aware there are four C-130s in KMSH?'*

At each higher level, there was also a sense of befuddlement that turned to anger. Each could not fathom how they were unaware. Eventually, the news made its way to the Central Command Commander, who is, in theory, responsible for every military asset in the region. He fumed at the notion something was in his battle space outside his purview. He placed an immediate secure call to the Chairman.

"Squirts. Hey. Got an issue here."

"Yeah. I heard. Hey, I'm in your corner. This is a huge process foul. Gonna meet with the Acting SECDEF and ask her

W.T.F.O." (What The Fuck, Over?)

"Thanks. Before we go too crazy, I tried to reach out to Glenn Etcher over at SOCOM, thinking it may be one of his ops. He hasn't gotten back to me, but even if he did, that's a boatload of tanker assets. Where's the associated operational aircraft? It's not clear to me yet."

"I hear ya," Admiral Hershey said. "And my SOLO (Special Operations Liaison Officer) assured me this isn't SOCOM. Give me a few hours and I'll get back to you.

"Copy. Standing by down here at MacDill. Out."

Admiral Hershey disconnected from the Video Conference. His staff had coordinated a 1000Hr meeting with the Acting SECDEF, Stacy Crawford, but this couldn't wait. Admiral Hershey walked out of his office, into the greeting area where his admin staff worked. He kept walking, headed towards the door and said, "Call the Secretary's admin. Tell them I'm coming." Without stopping, he kept going. He'd be there in under three minutes. The Admiral's staff scurried to make the phone call before he arrived.

As the Admiral walked into the SECDEF's greeting area, he saw the secretary hanging up the phone. *'Good,'* he thought. *'My staff still has some moxie.'* Also, in the SECDEF's front office were a few different Congressmen and other folks the acting Secretary intended to meet that day. Clearly, things were stacking up. Perhaps this issue was related.

Secretary Crawford heard her staff welcome the Admiral. As she heard it, she said relatively loudly, "Hey, Admiral, can you come in here a minute?"

It was all he needed to hear. He walked in and said, "Good morning, Madam Secretary."

"Yeah. Sure." She was beyond the point of pleasantries. "I believe I know why you're here, and I want you to know I had nothing to do with this. Evidently, Gerzema at the White House was given a funding line and ordered four C-130s from the Pennsylvania Guard to Masirah Island, Oman. I am just as caught off guard as you, and also just as angry. Rotary wing lift is on its way right now, and I'm going to the White House. Will you accompany me?"

"With pleasure," The Admiral responded. He knew Gerzema was up to no good and didn't trust the President farther than he could throw him. The Chairman leaned his head out of the Secretary's office and asked her administrative staff to notify his office of the new plans. The Chairman's front office scurried to get a security detail in place and began canceling and rescheduling meetings.

The green UH-60 'Blackhawk' helicopter with a distinguishable white top signifying a VIP flight, gently settled onto the White House South Lawn. Upon landing, SECDEF Crawford unstrapped and walked with authority into the White House. The Admiral needed to shuffle quickly to keep up. He didn't want to miss this.

Stacy threw open the door of Gerzema's office, bypassing his temporary secretary completely. "John! What in the freaking blue blazes are you doing!?"

John knew exactly what she was referring to. He knew the secret wouldn't last forever. They never did in D.C. "Well. Good morning to you too, Stacy... oh, and Admiral Hershey."

His greeting made her fume. A first name for the acting Defense Secretary, yet the rank of the Chairman? It was intentional. She knew it, and so did John. Stacy was smart, though. She'd get her revenge, just not yet. *'Keep your powder dry,'* she thought to herself. *'No fireworks now.'*

"Stop the games, John. I'm curious. Why is there a military order, signed out from you, with funding to place four C-130s in Oman?"

"Stacy. Slow down. The order was not signed by me. It's signed by the President. In case you forgot, he is the one who can authorize operational deployments, not me. I think your anger is misdirected. Perhaps we should go talk to him."

"Perhaps," Stacy said with enough sarcasm to light a Christmas tree.

The three walked to the Oval Office where the President was in the midst of a meeting with the Lithuanian Ambassador and Secretary of State. To the White House, it was mundane. To the Lithuanian Ambassador, it was the chance of a lifetime. So were the ways of the Executive Branch.

The three stood in front of the President's secretary's desk, demanding the chance to see him. Also in the reception room was the Secretary of Transportation, who's shoulders slumped at the sight. He'd been trying to meet with the President for weeks attempting to discuss transportation policy. Unfortunately, his issue was far less sexy and far less important than national security. From the moment he saw the three enter, he knew his meeting would be rescheduled.

Stacy turned to him with at least an apologetic appearance, mouthing the words, 'Sorry' to him. Reluctantly, the Transportation Secretary nodded.

The Lithuanian Ambassador departed, not missing the opportunity to greet the former SECDEF, acting SECDEF and the Chairman of the Joint Chiefs. From her perspective, it was an unbelievably fortuitous opportunity, oblivious to the pressing issue. She even took time to request a photo, as it would play well back in Vilnius on social media. Little did she know the three had zero interest participating in informal pleasantries. After the photo, the three walked toward the Oval Office. Steve saw them coming and immediately knew the gig was up. Given his contempt toward John, Steve exuded delightful anticipation as to how this would play out. If he'd have had time to make popcorn, he would have. As they all walked into the Oval Office, the President looked up. The look on his face lacked happiness. Everyone took their seats.

Stacy began laying out the issue, mirrored by Admiral Hersey, who also elaborated on how military assets in a COCOM region without the Combatant Commander's knowledge is a huge process foul, and the military lives on process.

The President turned to John. "Well, I think it's time you spoke."

John explained the plan, starting with the buildup and deployment of forces. He then continued. "Those four aircraft have been retrofitted with an insecticide / herbicide sprayer system that's a unique ability, one that the Pennsylvania Guard can perform. Currently, tons of a special herbicide are sitting in the Masirah port. In under 24 hours, the C-130s will start a two-night campaign that will spray, and thus wipe out 95% of the

Afghanistan Poppy crop. At present, the poppies are nearly in bloom, and intelligence says the harvest will begin in two weeks. This effort will eliminate opium profits and bring the Taliban to their knees. With their existing finances frozen and no future revenue to look forward to, they'll have no choice but to come back to the negotiating table, and this administration will salvage their Afghan security policy."

Both Stacy and Admiral Hershey could not believe what they just heard. Slowly, they directed their attention to the President, who signed the deployment order.

"Mr. President," the Chairman said. "Is this your wish? Did you direct this effort?"

John stared at the President with eyes that could rival Medusa. He had no choice. "Yes, Admiral. It's a risk, and I understand that."

"Risk?" Stacy responded. "Mr. President, we are still trying to evacuate Americans. Did you at least give the State Department or any other entity within the U.S. Government a heads up this is going to happen?"

The President hadn't, and Stacy made a good point. He needed a way around this and, as an exceptional politician, he hatched an answer quick. "Secretary Crawford, you are absolutely right. And that is why Steve and I had it as the first item on the agenda for today's NSC. I think we are all over-reacting here. The start of the spraying isn't today, and even if it were, it will take a day or two for the herbicide to take effect, isn't that what you said, John?" He looked at Gerzema who gave a convincing, but smug nod.

"Frankly, I'm glad this is out in the open, as I'd like to bring the full force of the Defense Department into this mission and ensure its success. Can I count on you to do that, Secretary Crawford? Admiral Hershey?"

The two looked at each other. They'd been had, but what do you say to such a question proposed in such a manner?

In unison, as if beaten, they replied, "Yes, Mr. President."

Steve sat in the corner, amazed. The outcome of this meeting was the polar opposite of what he'd envisioned. John knew this and as he stood up, he shot Steve a shit-eating grin.

The group left the President's office. The Transportation Secretary was still waiting, perhaps the only other person in the Oval Office reception area with a smile on his face.

Secretary Crawford and the Admiral walked through the White House corridors and were greeted by their aides. "Ma'am, sir. The helicopter is broken. We called two separate motorcades to take you back. Both are waiting out front." *'What else could go wrong, today?'* Squirts thought.

The Admiral and Stacy agreed to call a quick meeting when they returned to the Pentagon in order to salvage some level of support for the mission. The two departed the briefing, and Admiral Hershey walked to his SUV. Holding open the door was a Kosovar Albanian turned American named Veton. He was an intimidatingly large man who filled the role of Security Detail perfectly. "Good morning, Mr. Chairman," he said.

The Admiral had stifled his anger. There was no reason to transpose it onto others. "Hey, Veton. Good morning. Hope you're well."

Veton closed the back door, leaned down to the cuff of his sleeve to transmit the departure order, then got in the front passenger seat. Once inside the vehicle, he continued the conversation. "Yes, Admiral. My family and I are good. I haven't heard from Smitty for a bit though. Hope he's enjoying vacation."

The Admiral's heart stopped. *'Holy Shit! Smitty! Curt! Buck!'* The Admiral pulled out his phone and called his staff. "Hey. I need a meeting with Lieutenant General Ghani today." He didn't wait for an answer and hung up. Given this mission, the three were in immense danger and completely blind to it.

****

As the Acting Secretary and the Chairman departed the White House grounds, John headed to his office and closed the door. Once inside, he pulled out his personal cell phone and placed a call.

"Hey, Andrew. John here."

"Yeah, John. How are things going? Is there a problem?"

"No. Not really. Just wanted to let you know our plan has been exposed among senior levels and the National Security Council. It's nothing to be concerned about. We knew this was eventually going to happen. It remains highly classified, and I don't see any concern about it leaking out. Everything is still on track."

"OK, John. If you say there's nothing to worry about, I'll believe you. That's your lane."

"Yes, it is. And I put one of my closest confidants forward deployed to ensure the last few legs of the mission are executed."

"Is the guy a military officer you met when you were SECDEF?"

"No. I couldn't chance using a military member. I sent a civilian who's loyal to the core. The perfect guy."

Andrew replied, "OK. If you say so." Although, in his mind, he realized a civilian controlling operational efforts downrange was a recipe for disaster.

Chapter Twenty-five
Prayin' & Sprayin'

The sun had set in Pakistan, and the four men clad in local garb mounted their donkeys. Underneath their outfit, however, each was armed with enough ammunition for a gunfight against a dozen men. Additionally, the four had discrete communications gear and handheld thermal imaging devices. Owning the night was a common theme among Special Operators. The four had grown accustomed to night-vision devices 'shades of green' as well as the newer thermal and electro optic imaging. They'd stared through them enough that it was akin to daytime for them.

The eight donkeys slowly lumbered on the path into the night as the madrasa disappeared behind them. Buck looked down along the side of his donkey through the thermal imaging device. The cliff was nearly straight down, and the path was less than eighteen inches wide. The donkey showed no signs of fear. Buck, however, put the thermal device away, clutched the donkey's saddle and prayed. As a former Special Ops pilot, he would have rather had a dual engine failure in the C-130 at ten thousand feet than ride this donkey along a narrow cliff. "Dudes," he said. "Word of advice. Don't look down."

His headset cracked to life. "Buck. Word of advice. Don't speak English that loud out here, or it won't be the Taliban killing you," Mule said. Curt and Smitty smiled.

Buck had forgotten he had a comm device. Under the conditions, it wasn't hard to understand why.

As the donkey convoy meandered through the Hindu Kush, Majeed and Usman drove the 4Runner towards the border checkpoint. As they approached, two men in black attire rose from folding chairs with AK-47 rifles around their necks on slings.

In Pashto, the border guard ordered the vehicle to stop. Majeed, who was driving, did as instructed.

"Good evening and may Allah be with you," Majeed said.

"Yes. Your papers." The guard replied. He clearly was Taliban. The border guards under the former Afghan government were killed or had abandoned their posts to avoid certain death.

Majeed handed over his papers along with Usman's. He also passed over the vehicle registration. It clearly would not match his name.

The guard took a few seconds and noticed the issue. "Whose vehicle is this?" He asked.

"It belongs to a British Paki who sympathizes with our form of Islam," Majeed said, implying strict, if not radical Islam. "He bought it in Karachi and has sent it up here. We are on our way to Jalalabad with the car and some supplies. Look for yourself. He also paid to rent the truck behind me." Majeed pointed to the back of the SUV and also the jingle truck.

Given the commotion, the second border guard arose and walked to the truck's rear. He pulled back the worn plastic / canvas cover and saw large duffels of items. Climbing inside, much of the gear they found was water and supplies, piled on top of gear that, while legal, would draw unwanted questions.

The second guard jumped out of the truck and gave a nod.

The first guard looked at Majeed and said, "You take this stuff to Jalalabad? For the Taliban? Right?"

Majeed nodded.

The guard opened the back door, reached into the cargo area as the seats were folded down, and took a bag indiscriminately. He said, "I am Taliban, too," as if this were a justification for his theft.

After taking it, he handed Majeed back the documents, and they were cleared to continue. Majeed and the jingle truck driver slowly passed through the checkpoint. In under ten minutes, they'd be in the Afghan part of Torkham. Although the village was small, it straddled the Pakistan and Afghanistan border. The overall trip for them took less than an hour. For Curt and his amateur nomads, it would take three hours.

The night grew colder as the four continued. The stars were extremely bright, although there was nearly no moon. They all knew tomorrow would be a full eclipse. Curt, in front, continued to scope out their path with his thermal imaging device. Smitty was in the rear, covering their six. Mule watched both left and

143

right flanks. His original task was just left, but Buck, who was far from a ground pounder was doing everything he could to stay on the donkey and convince himself he would not die. Not tonight, anyway.

The eight donkeys started to accelerate, and the path widened. Smitty, who'd grown up on a farm, knew what that meant. "We're close," he said into his mic.

"How do you know?" Mule asked.

"They're speeding up. They know they're almost home and they wanna get your fat ass off their back." Smitty replied, pleased with his dig on Jeremy.

Smitty was right. Curt saw a discrete set of flashing lights ahead. It was Majeed who was also using an IR strobe to assist with night vision. The donkeys nearly trotted into a stable and began eating. Their owner patted them on the head, and rewarded them with some exceptional food, especially by donkey standards. The owner was well dressed and had two sparkling clean Mercedes Benz out front of his large house. He made no effort to hide what was most likely his ill-gained wealth. Why should he? His assets were a critical piece to a well-formed logistical system and had been for years.

The team unloaded the donkeys and the jingle truck. From this point on, Usman would drive his truck with supplies and the jingle truck would return to Pakistan. Before heading to Jalalabad however, the team would sleep for the night, finally in Afghanistan.

As they prepared for bed, Majeed and Curt were alone. Majeed asked, "Commander, why did you come back? Are more coming?"

It was clear from Majeed's questions, Lieutenant General Ghani had not shared everything, nor would the answer be easy. Curt knew there were no more Americans coming, at least not in numbers that Majeed was hoping for. "Majeed. I came back to see you and take care of some unfinished business. I'm sorry to say, at this time, there are no more coming. Let's talk more tomorrow. Why do you call me commander? Please call me Curt."

"Commander, when you were here before, you were my

commander. I called you, commander. To me, you will aways be my commander."

Part of Curt was humbled. Majeed remembered. Through years of being apart, never calling, never writing, never sending Christmas cards; Majeed never forgot. The other part of Curt crumbled inside as he remembered he, and many others, promised Majeed and many others that the U.S. would never leave. That promise was now broken. And promises in Afghanistan are more important than money or blood.

'How much can I trust Majeed?' Curt thought, as he went to bed. He prayed the answer was 'completely,' given there were few other options to help find Noorullah.

The next morning, the team woke up, packed up and traveled into Jalalabad where their safe-house awaited. Once inside and unpacked, Curt and Smitty started explaining the plan to meet up with Raz, Noorullah, and Saad. Majeed's face grew puzzled when the last name was mentioned.

"Majeed," Curt said. "What's the matter?"

"Do you mean Saad, the interpreter who worked for U.S. in Kandahar?" Majeed replied.

Mule's eyes lit up. "Yes! Do you know where he is?" The team was paying close attention.

Somewhat matter-of-factly, Majeed answered. "Yes. He is with Allah. The Taliban killed him days after the U.S. pulled out. They hung him in the streets for being a traitor." Majeed looked down at his phone. "I have a photo if you wish."

Curt put his hand over Majeed's and pushed down the phone gently. "No, Majeed. We believe you." Curt said softly. Mule walked out of the room. The person he'd just traveled thousands of miles to save was dead.

Without Mule, the team would go over the plan, and then go over it again. Both Majeed and Usman took good notes and also wrote out a list of things the teams would need, as well as contacts they would need to make. Once they were beyond Jalalabad, there would be little time to fix a mistake.

Curt explained the communications plan that would rely on burner cell phones and SIM cards, used at specific times. Usman asked, "Mr. Commander, what should Majeed and I do with our cell phones?"

"Keep them. When you are out performing scout missions, I want you to look as normal as possible. Afghans have cell phones. That's normal. Just please make sure your call lists and text messages are always void of anything linked to us."

Majeed and Usman shook their head in acknowledgement. Curt continued, also explaining when the teams were together, discreet wireless comms would be used, demonstrating the systems to the two terps.

After going over the plan, Curt walked out to Mule, "Hey buddy. Sorry about the news."

"Yeah," Mule replied. "It is what it is. Frankly, I think we all knew this could have been a possibility for any of the folks we came to get."

"You're right. And to be fair, we don't know the fate of Noorullah or Raz yet. It likely could be the same. I'd offer you my cut of the mission if I felt it would make any difference, but I'm not sure it's about the money." Curt paused then felt compelled to ask. "You're still in, right?"

Mule was slightly surprised. "Of course I'm in, and buddy, it isn't about the money." Mule took a deep breath. "But when we return to the states, if you buy me a steak dinner and stiff drink, we can call it even."

"Sure, Mule. I'll even get you some fries." Curt put his hand on Mule's shoulder.

"Hell then," Mule chuckled. "If you can afford French fries, can you cover the in-ground pool I want to eat them in?"

They both laughed. Mule nudged Curt's arm off his shoulder and gave him a man hug. Mule would be OK.

****

The morning sun shone into the CONEX windows on Masirah Island's base operations area. Most of the crew were already awake trying to fight off jet lag and circadian rhythm issues. Dirty turned on his personal cell phone. Text messages from his wife and other national guard friends popped in, then one from

Cravin. It merely said the mission was legit with high-level visibility, but that many in the chain of commander were not pleased. It also told him to be careful. Just as he'd presumed. In military terms, this was gonna be a 'goat rope.'

Cravin turned off his phone and rolled back over. He'd sleep until 1400Hrs, then get up and perform his normal military three 'S's, shit, shower and shave. The crew briefing for the mission would start at 1500Hrs and the planned take-off time would be 1800Hrs.

As Dirty was getting ready, maintainers were loading up the aircraft. Ash had arranged that each would be given a full load of chemicals and fuel. There'd be no tanking support.

Roughly, the plan would be a two-hour flight to Afghanistan, a one-hour spray mission, then two hours back. Ash had read his Wikipedia about the C-130 and calculated that five hours was a bit of a stretch but believed it could be done.

The crew briefing started, and Ash explained the mission. The four C-130 Navigators quickly did the math and realized the mission was impossible. The aircraft would likely run out of fuel and crash into the Indian Ocean upon return. One of them raised their hand.

"Mr. Beasley, sir. You realize this is a suicide mission. Aside from our requirements for divert fuel and minimum landing fuel, I don't even believe there is enough to fly the mission?"

Ash, who was fairly certain that Wikipedia and other Internet sources hadn't let him down, responded, "Well, I was told there may be some pushback from the crew, but I have done enough homework to believe this is possible. Right here on this website, it says a C-130 can fly this far and for this long. I am sure I can get some waivers regarding those other fuel thingies you talked about." Ash showed some documents to the C-130 crews.

Finally, Dirty spoke up. "Ash. Look. Once we get to Afghanistan, we need to descend to perform the mission. For correct employment, the spray must be disbursed at 500 feet or lower, which burns tons of gas. Then we need to climb back out. My crews are right. This is a suicide mission. We aren't going. You can fire me, court martial me, or put me in jail. Don't care. Ain't going."

Ash hadn't thought of the points Dirty raised. Given his experience, it wasn't surprising. "Uh. OK. Let me make a call." Ash stepped into the hall and called John back in D.C. It was early morning. "Sir, the crews refuse to fly. They say there isn't enough gas?"

John was angered. "Are they bullshitting or are they right?"

Ash was afraid to answer. "Sir, I think they may be right, but I'm not sure."

"Ash, for Christ's sakes. I told you to have this wired. Let me call you back."

John hung up and dialed Admiral Hershey, the only man he felt could solve the issue. Also, the man from whom he really didn't wish to ask for any favors.

Admiral Hershey was in a scheduling meeting with his front office staff. Alfi saw the phone ring and noticed it was from Gerzema. "Admiral, it's the call you were expecting from Former Sec..."

"Thanks Alfi, I know who it is. Alright staff, BOHICA" (Bend over, here it comes). The Admiral turned on his speaker phone for the office to hear. "Admiral Hershey."

John took a deep breath, "Admiral, sorry to bother you."

"How many?" The Admiral cut him off.

John was confused by the question. "Excuse me?"

"How many tankers are the crew asking for? I know they can't do the mission you've ordered them to do on organic fuel only. I may think little of you, but those are my airmen out there, and I'll be God damned if I'm going to let them down. Two tankers out of Al Udeid Air Base are on standby, launching soon. My staff will pass you the coordination radio frequencies so that the Herk bubbas can contact the tankers. They'll set up tanker tracks in the Indian Ocean south of Pakistan in international airspace."

John scribbled down as much as he could. "Uh, thanks Admiral. This is good stuff."

"Save it, John. You've made a fucking mess. It's infuriating that I'm the one to have to clean it up." The line went dead. The Admiral smiled at his staff. "That actually felt good."

John called Ash, who relayed the information to the crews.

The mission was back on. Dirty was astounded. In under a half hour, this snot-nosed kid just locked down two of the most limited assets in theater. Some heavy hitters were overseeing this mission. He quickly realized the priority of this mission.

The crews stepped to their aircraft and a full preflight was performed. The cargo areas held 'blivets,' large soft skinned containers designed to hold liquid. The fuel tanks were filled. Everything checked out. All four mighty Hercules fired up their engines and taxied to the runway. The weight of the aircraft stressed the main landing gear to the point it looked like they were riding on flats. One by one, they took off to the northeast, making their way directly towards the Pakistani coast. Each aircraft, once safely airborne and over the water, performed a quick 'test fire' of the dispersal system. Each worked perfectly, creating a massive mist off the tail of the aircraft.

As they flew northeast, the sun set behind them. The lead navigator worked a rendezvous plan with the two KC-135s on the radio and, like clockwork, the aircraft joined up and transferred the fuel. During the connection and not on the radio, Dirty spoke to the other aircraft commander via the boom intercom system.

"Hey boys. Thanks for the gas. We needed it."

"So, we heard. What in the heck are you guys doing all the way out here?" The tanker aircraft commander asked.

"Buddy, I wish I could tell ya," Dirty responded.

"Yeah. Gonna guess it's not hauling Cinco De Mayo Tequila to the Muslims," the tanker commander responded, "but given those odd sprayers on your fuselage, maybe you're gonna spray down Islamabad with tequila."

Dirty laughed. In his mind, that would be a far better mission than the one he was on. "Yeah. I'm with ya." He responded, then returned the conversation to be professional. "Texaco 51, we show a full bag. Thanks for the gas. Request Disconnect."

The tanker boom operator jumped in. "Clear Disconnect."

Dirty pulled the throttles back and dipped the nose. "Disconnect," he said.

The KC-135 Boom flew up into the air and away from Dirty's C-130. Another herk would snuggle in under the KC-135 and take on their fuel, while the entire same operation was being performed about three miles away with another tanker and two C-130s. It took roughly twenty minutes for the evolution and the sun had finally set.

As the crews approached Pakistan, they turned off their external lights, turned off their civilian transponder, leaving only their military transponder to function. They flew in a battle box formation, and either were not noticed by Pakistani airspace controllers or, more likely, were ignored because of some other efforts in their favor. Less than a hundred miles on their nose was Helmand and Nimruz Provinces-the two largest regions of poppy cultivation. Over a secure radio, Dirty again briefed the flight, repeating the overall spray plan he had briefed on the ground. Each crew member put on their night-vision devices and the load master armed the chaff and flares systems just in case they were spotted and fired upon by a surface-to-air missile system. Once inside Afghan airspace, Dirty led the four herks down from cruise altitude approaching 500 feet above ground level. Ahead, he could see the rows of poppies out in the open fields. Four abreast, the aircraft turned on their dispersal systems, running for nearly a mile. At the crossroad, Dirty on the radio commanded, "off," and they all secured the system and climbed out at max power. Roughly 15 seconds later, they all began a turn, arching to the west, flying a perfect 180, offset by roughly a mile. Descending back into the same field but a mile abreast from where they just sprayed, Dirty again came on the radio and commanded, "On," and the dispersal systems fired. For the next hour, they'd blanket most of Helmand and Nimruz Provinces, the two southwestern most in the country. The mission would only take fifty minutes, and Dirty continually checked with the navigator to make sure they had enough gas to get home. With merely 75 gallons left of herbicide in the tank, they climbed out and headed south, back over Pakistani airspace and towards the Indian Ocean. Once they were up at a safer altitude, the aircraft performed buddy checks and ensured all was well. The flight home would take a few hours and over the ocean was no time to discover a problem. Dirty knew this and also was aware that over Pakistan was no time to find a problem, but such was the mission.

On the ground in Afghanistan, locals heard the roar of aircraft, something quite uncommon since the U.S. and other coalition nations had departed. While they could not see the aircraft, they could hear them, many pulling out cell phones and telling their friends and neighbors. The next morning, rumors swirled as to what aircraft were doing in Afghanistan. The two which gained the most traction were some Special Operations Force extracted a high value personnel, or the aircraft were part of an infiltration mission dropping off U.S. military to restart the war. Neither was right, but to most Afghans, it was clear the West was back in Afghanistan was the theme.

As the sun came up, the four aircraft were tucked away by maintainers on the Masirah ramp, repairing minor items that either broke or required replacement.

The aircrew were already fast asleep. They'd awaken again at 1600Hrs this time, 12 hours after they'd gotten back from the second half of their mission. Dirty sent a quick text to Cravin, letting him know the mission was successful. Then he turned off his phone again, going to sleep.

Chapter Twenty-six
Lines of Departure

The morning air in Jalalabad stunk, just as the team of four remembered. It's impossible to forget that smell. Curt considered going for a jog in the early AM but decided against it partly because of security concerns. The other reason was that he'd been told before that Afghanistan had the second highest airborne fecal content in the world. Many U.S. military members deployed to Afghanistan had heard this, often wondering, *'Jesus, what nation is number one?'* It was far from ideal running conditions and likely why the Kabul didn't have a similar attraction as Boston or New York for their annual marathons.

The day prior, Majeed had secured a second 4Runner so the teams could split up. The second vehicle was far more worn that their first, but it at least had an Afghan license plate making it easier to pass through checkpoints.

After breakfast, the two teams stood outside the main building of their Jalalabad compound. In Afghanistan, most homes were surrounded by brick, stone, or stacked mud walls. As the Afghans say, *'Good walls make good neighbors.'*

Curt turned to Smitty and Buck. "Hey, you two, be careful. And Buck, listen to Smitty. You may be the ace aviator, but he'll keep you alive on the ground. Got it?"

Buck nodded. "Buddy, after that donkey ride, I have no problem admitting I'm out of my element."

Curt reached out and man-hugged Buck. The two smacked each other's backs, twice, in unison. He then turned to Smitty, "Buddy, keep moving and keep your head on a swivel. I wanna drink a beer with you again and my kid's gonna need an uncle. Don't forget that."

Smitty looked puzzled. "Kid?"

Buck's eyes widened. "I didn't say it!" He yelled.

Curt smiled. "Yeah. Allison's preggo. I'm gonna be a dad."

"Good for you, Doc," Smitty said. "Good for you. Hey, never forget, buddy... The only easy day was yesterday." The grin on

Smitty's face let Curt know there was no place else Smitty would rather be right now. The two embraced. Then Smitty said, "You guys be safe, too. Lord knows you're the only one Allison can put up with. We need you back."

Curt smiled. Mule, new to the team, also hugged the others farewell, but with far less fervor. Both teams saddled up and the main compound gate swung open as the two 4Runners departed. The vehicles traveled together until they were near Kabul. Once close, they split. Curt, Mule and Majeed would avoid Kabul and join up on the ring road headed towards Kandahar. Smitty, Buck and Usman would take back roads outside of Kabul north until they, too, were on the ring road headed towards Bagram. The ring road was a highway of sorts, 'National Highway 01.' There was no 02, or 03. It was the only 'main road' in the entire nation. It was at least paved and, in a few places, had more than one lane in each direction. The highway made a ring around the country, linking each major city. The vast majority of other roads, especially outside cities, were dirt or gravel.

The travel for Buck and Smitty would take only a few hours and Usman had already established a safe-house for their stay. The compound was nice; the walls were tall, and the host family provided a barn of sorts away from the main living quarters. The host family would not meet their guests. It was their desire. But under Afghan tradition, the man of the house would fight to the death defending his guests if need be. An odd custom of sorts, but honor and protection are puzzle corner pieces of the Afghan mind.

Once in the compound, Smitty and Buck unpacked the 4Runner in the old barn. Usman took the car out to the town. He'd drink coffee in some cafes, ask questions, and try to find out as much as he could about Raz Mohammed, Buck's long-lost friend. As Usman was working, Buck sat on one of his duffle bags, gazing into the compound courtyard. Two young children, a boy and a girl, played together without a care in the world. They had a soccer ball, kicking it, laughing, running and chasing each other. 'Strange World,' Buck thought to himself.

Curt and Mule's travel would take far longer. Their trip was nearly eight hours of driving under normal conditions on the ring road. But since Majeed would avoid checkpoints via old back dirt roads, they would be traveling for over ten hours. Now that the jingle truck was gone, the 4Runners were loaded down with military gear that could get all of them killed, should they be found out. After traveling through Ghazni, the next province was Zabul, where Curt had once served. The terrain had transitioned from mountainous to flat, brown desert, eerily similar to southern Arizona without cactus. As they came closer to the capital city of Qalat, things looked familiar to Curt. He was amazed at how much new infrastructure had been built in the area. There were power lines hanging overhead and a few of the roads in the villages had been paved. That said, there was no mistaking it for a third world country.

On the eastern edge of Qalat, Curt recognized the old turn off for Forward Operating Base Lagman, the place he was stationed. It sat roughly 200 meters back from the ring road. Now abandoned, a few goat shepherds shuffled their flock through the base to rummage for grass.

Mule looked at Curt, "Old memories, eh?"

"Yeah," Curt replied. "Were you there, too?

"Never assigned there. Bedded down overnight a couple times as we were on the tail of a few HVTs (High Value Targets) out of Kandahar."

The 4Runner passed the FOB (Forward Operating Base) entrance and Curt kept driving. Ahead was a large dirt mound, standing nearly three hundred feet tall. It was extremely out of place in the flat terrain.

"Mule, do you know what that is?" Curt asked.

"Nope. We drove by it many times. Frankly, I thought it's where we buried dead Taliban."

"Ha," Curt chuckled. "Nope. It's Alexander the Great's last fortress. Do you want to see it?"

"Sure!" Mule replied.

Curt turned around to Majeed in the back. "Majeed, how safe is it up on top now?"

"Sir, no one goes there. You'll be the only one. No Afghans find this impressive. Conquerors from every country came here

154

and left things. This is just one of many."

Curt vectored the car to the top and parked. He and Mule exited the vehicle, with Majeed following close behind. The view alone from the top of the fortress was worth the trip up. As they passed old wall ruins, some rooms were still visible. Historians could differentiate which was a bakery, a jail, a tailor, and a blacksmith. Curt had received a tour once but had forgotten most. The tour was given by a visiting scholar who had studied every book written about the fortress. He was finally visiting it. The man was mesmerized. The ruins were a wreck, but to him, it was the Taj Mahal. To Afghans, it was just another pile of rocks. At the top, Curt and Mule could see down onto the FOB.

"Mule, I remember evenings watching the sun set over this large mound of dirt and stone. Back then, I couldn't help reflecting that this was the spot where Alexander the Great, at 18 years old, sat and sent his recon elements out into the Hindu Kush over there," Curt pointed. Many considered the Hindu Kush to be the most rugged and desolate place on the earth.

Curt continued. "After his scouts returned from the mountains, they told him there was nothing worth conquering out there. And at this point, on this mound, before Christ was born, that 18-year-old leader made the announcement there was nothing of value beyond this point. He had conquered the world and turned around, leaving Afghanistan." Curt paused for emphasis. "Yet, since that time, empire after empire after empire with world leaders presumably older and wiser have come to conquer this place only to deplete their blood and treasure. It's utterly amazing to me. Afghanistan truly is the graveyard of empires."

Mule looked at Curt. "Good story. You jockeying for a teaching license if the medical thing doesn't work out?" Mule smiled at his own sarcasm. Majeed laughed. To both of them, the story was just that, but to Curt, it was more.

The three returned to the 4Runner and drove down the fortress back onto the ring road. It was a brief stop in a long day, but one well worth it to Curt. The remaining journey would be completed during sunset and night. As they drove, the famous Afghan poppy fields were sprouting along the ring road. There was no hiding them. They were out in the open for anyone to see. The first few were small, but the further they pushed into the desert, the larger the fields became. Eventually, they would arrive at their destination, a small village east of Kandahar, named Bamizay. Their safe-house was located there, actually closer to Qalat than Bamizay-out in the middle of the desert. It would serve as an excellent location for tracking down nomadic Kochi tribesmen.

As the 4Runner pulled into the compound, it was clear the location was too far to even see the lights of Bamizay and at least a mile off the ring road to the north. They'd passed a few small poppy fields along the way as well, all unguarded. A woman walking along the outside wall of the compound did not look up at the car as it passed. She was wearing a blue burka with a mesh netting covering her eyes, nose and mouth. The compound door swung open, and Curt drove the 4Runner inside. He looked in the rear-view mirror, and the woman he'd just passed also walked into the compound. She grabbed the gate and shut it. Once out of the public's eye, she lifted her burka off, tossed it on a railing next to the gate, and walked into the house. To her, Taliban rule ended at the boundary of her property.

A man inside the gate put his hand out as if ordering the vehicle to stop. Curt did as instructed, and the man walked up to the side door.

"Welcome," he said.

"Thank you," Curt replied. "You speak English?"

"Yes. I went to school in London years ago," the man replied. "I understand you will stay for roughly ten days. Majeed has secured your accommodations. I am happy to have you. If you need anything, please let Majeed know."

"We will, and thank you. I'm sorry, I didn't catch your name."

"Yes, you're correct. And I didn't offer it. Under our conditions, it is perhaps better if neither knows such things. Have a good night."

The man walked away towards the house, then inside. A guest house on the compound was where the three would be staying. They unpacked the car and explored the compound. It was impressive for Afghanistan-fresh running water, electricity, and Wi-Fi. None of them would use the last luxury, however. There was no telling who was monitoring it.

****

The midday heat of Oman was excruciating, and one could barely be outside longer than an hour. Dirty left his 'hooch,' the informal name for his CONEX accommodations and headed to lunch.

After grabbing some food, he saw Ash sitting alone and decided to join. As he got closer, he couldn't believe what he was seeing. The Omani heat had gotten to be too much for Ash. He'd cut his Khaki pants just above the knees. It was an extremely poor attempt to convert them into Bermuda shorts. His hand-sewn hem line was atrocious. "Mind if I join you?" Dirty asked.

Ash looked up and his eyes opened. He tried to hide his excitement but failed miserably. "No! Yes! Please! Join me."

"Great. How are things going?" Dirty asked.

"Decent, I guess. I understand two more tankers are already lined up for tonight's mission. Sorry about that."

"No worries, Ash. Trust me. I've had far better men come far closer to trying to kill me in the aviation world than you. Seriously. Let it go." Dirty picked up his glass and pushed it forward. "Cheers. OK?"

Ash responded in kind. "Cheers. And thanks."

The two kept eating and Ash finally spoke. "Hey, your name is Dirty, right?"

"No. That's my callsign."

"Yeah," Ash said. "That's what I meant to say, your callsign. How did you get it?"

"Ash, given my last name, it was my destiny. Let's just leave it at that while we're eating."

Ash didn't understand but agreed. "OK, but how do you all get callsigns? To civilians, this is really interesting."

"Well, a callsign can be based on several things. For example,

I knew a guy with the last name 'Barrett.' His callsign was Grinnin'…. Grinnin' Barret, as in 'Grin and Bear It.' See that guy over there?" Dirty pointed and Ash looked. "His callsign is Q. The dude's a walking Texas Instruments Calculator. He's brilliant. Sitting next to him is one of the most religious guys I've ever met. Devout Catholic with three kids.

Ash asked, "Is his callsign 'Preacher' or something?"

"Nope," Dirty responded. "That's what he wanted his callsign to be on name night, but he lost out. He's 'Tripod.' Dude has a Johnson the size of an NBA center's forearm."

Ash was puzzled. "Why did you tell me he's religious, then?"

"The fact he's religious makes his callsign even funnier given it's sexual nature. Look. A callsign can be about anything. With Tripod, it's hilarious because I think the porn industry really missed out. They could have made a fortune with that guy."

"So, there's a 'name night?'" Ash asked. "What happens there?"

"Well, as a new guy comes to the unit, he or she brings their callsign with them, kinda like Preacher did. Then, after a few months, a name night is held, and they try to defend that name. There's a significant amount of alcohol involved and many things your mother should never know. After the new person presents their defense to keep that name, the guys already in the squadron discuss it, offer other options and in the end, the judge rules. If you're lucky, you keep your callsign. If not, you get a new one."

Ash couldn't take it any longer. "I want a callsign." He blurted out.

Dirty looked up at him. "Really?"

"Yeah. But I'd need to get to a base and go through the whole thing."

Dirty's mind came up with a plan. "Hey, I tell you what. After we return from tonight's mission, tomorrow night we will hold a callsign night just for you. We don't start our flights back for another day or so. This will give the crew something to do."

Ash could not be any happier. For completely other reasons, neither could Dirty.

"Sounds GREAT! Really? You'd do that?" Ash asked.

"Buddy, if you want a callsign, we'll make it happen. But you need to go get some supplies. As you know, on the base here, we can't drink alcohol. Since you're the closest thing we have to a commander, I guess if you say we can drink, and you provide the alcohol, all should be good, right?"

Ash thought about it. 'Yes,' he thought. 'I AM in charge. And what could go wrong? It's just some drinking on the base.' "I'll do it," he said to Dirty.

"Sounds good. I'll let the guys know this afternoon at the mission brief. I'm heading back to my rack for a bit to get a little nap. Thanks for the company, Ash."

"Yes, sir, er uh, Dirty. Thank you, too." Amid all his excitement, Ash was having a hard time remembering who was leading and who was following. Ash was in way over his head, but nothing Dirty couldn't manage. Name night was going to be a lesson Ash would not soon forget.

Dirty was able to get another hour of sleep before his alarm clock rang. He stumbled out of the rack, splashed some water on his face from a plastic bottle, the CONEX's didn't have bathrooms or sinks. After putting on his flight boots, he made his way to the operations briefing room. The two-night mission was half over, and he wanted to get all his aircrew home safely. Tonight would be far riskier than the previous one. The element of surprise was gone and there could be the chance the Taliban had uncovered the plan, lying in wait.

The briefing went as planned. Tonight, they'd focus spraying the Kandahar and Zabul Provinces. Getting to the planes, preflight checks, engine start and taxi out were all routine, just like yesterday; however, this time, Dirty briefed up a nonstandard departure. The number two aircraft would take-off first, then three, then four. As they took off, two would go out to five miles, then start a large turn to the left. Aircraft three would start the turn at four miles with a tighter turn radius. Then, aircraft four would start their turn at three miles and pull an even tighter turn. If it all worked out, the three aircraft would circle around and come out of their 180-turn joining up on Aircraft One, Dirty's aircraft. And then, as a four ship, head out across the ocean. The effort was spectacular, however, the only witness other than the aircrew was a small Omani fishing trawler that was out at the time.

On the radio, Dirty directed all the aircraft to turn on their spraying systems. Each did, and he looked back to see a fog being generated... except from the third aircraft.

"Hey three. You, ok?"

"Sir, we have a malfunction. Working it."

"OK. What are your chances of getting it fixed? I don't want you over Afghanistan if all you're gonna do is be a cheerleader."

"Copy. Give us an hour."

"WILCO," Dirty answered. (Will comply).

The crew on aircraft #3 worked feverishly to troubleshoot the problem. The control panel showed everything working fine, but the discharge system appeared to have no power to open the valve and release the fluid. The copilot, Captain Thomas 'Niblet' Cobb, had accepted this mission back in Pennsylvania, getting approval from his civilian employer, IBM where he served as an electrical engineer. Niblet unstrapped and went back to the valve control motor. He stripped the wires and put them together, then told the load master to turn on the dispersal system. As the load master flipped the switch, nothing happened. It was clear no power was getting to the valve.

Niblet got out from behind the valve control and turned off the main circuit box. He then started following that wire all the way towards the control. On top of the blivet, he noticed one wire was connected via a screw clamp, which had failed, releasing one side of the wire from the clamp. Niblet crawled slowly across the blivet and carefully put the two wires together and then reseated the clamp over both. Once he was satisfied it would work, he slowly crawled down, turned on the power to the dispersal circuit panel and then climbed back up into the cockpit, taking his copilot's seat.

"Pilot, Co," he said on the intercom. "I think we're good. Was a loose connection."

The pilot looked over at Niblet. "You wanna tell Dirty, or do ya wanna show him?" Niblet's eyes widened.

"My aircraft," Niblet said.

"Co, your aircraft," the pilot in command responded.

Niblet pushed the throttles forward and sped up to the front of the four abreast formation.

Dirty saw their aircraft getting grossly out of formation and was about to say something, but before he did.

Niblet called out on the intercom, "Fire it off, Load!" (Short for load master). The load master hit the switch and the dispersal system showered a mist behind the aircraft. Dash three was back in action.

"Nice work, three," Dirty said on the inter-flight radio. "Now, get back into formation."

"Sure boss! Just showin' off," was transmitted over the radio.

Seconds later the intercom cracked to live inside the aircraft. "Good job, Niblet. My aircraft."

"Your aircraft," Niblet replied.

It was the most fun they'd have until arriving at the tanker over an hour later.

The two tankers again waited, and the fuel was transferred. Given the crews had just performed the same task the day prior, Dirty had concerns some of his crews could be lulled into a false sense of security. As they crossed into Pakistani airspace again and then into Afghanistan, he prayed that he'd emphasized the threat of complacency enough in the flight briefing.

Slowly, the four aircraft descended and, just like the night before, the low-level air ballet over the poppy fields commenced.

Mule and Curt were relaxing as the quiet night air was disrupted by the indistinguishable sound of C-130s engines. They jumped out of bed, grabbed their thermal imagers, and ran outside. They raised the devices and clearly saw four C-130s' engines with the heat signatures blaring.

The four were climbing out after a spray. Curt now realized it was likely they were not the only non-Afghans in the area. He grew suspicious other western forces were operating special forces missions in the area.

As the four aircraft turned and descended for their last run, Curt and Mule weren't the only ones aware of the aircraft. Over cell phones and repeater tower radios, Taliban officers had tried to coordinate and pinpoint the location. Two Taliban with AK-47s waited at the ring road, watching up into the sky. They could hear the aircraft coming and, once close, began firing wildly into the sky. The load master on Dirty's plane watching out the aft paratroop door window, saw the ground fire and called it out on the intercom, "Small arms fire, low, eight o'clock."

Dirty looked and saw the distinct strobe light flashing appearance of ground fire. Immediately, he and two other aircraft started popping off flares, lighting up the night sky.

The aircraft were too low for Curt to see them, but when the flares went off, he could see the night sky illuminate in that direction. It wasn't uncommon for flares to be shot off to protect the plane, and he did not see a following fireball or hear explosions. *'They're safe'* he thought. For the most part, he was right.

As the flares hit the ground, they set a small section of a poppy field ablaze. Taliban villagers might be angered by the C-130s overhead, but they were far more concerned about the fires in poppy fields. For the aircrews sake, the fire luckily diverted the Afghan's attention.

After the last spray run, the four C-130s climbed out southbound from Zabul Province and continued into Pakistan, reaching their cruise altitude in about ten minutes. They'd fly the rest of the way back to Oman without incident, albeit their hearts were racing just a bit more than they were from the previous night. Dirty was happily relieved there would not be a third night on this mission.

At 0300Hrs, the planes landed and taxied in. Ash was asleep, choosing to rest up for his callsign name night in lieu of greeting the crews when they landed-another poor leadership choice.

The crews, now exhausted, went to bed. Dirty broke out his phone, turned it on and shot a quick text to his buddy.

'Cravin – night two mission complete. 4 birds bedded down safe. Misison successful.'

Before Dirty could turn off his phone, a response came back.

'Dirty, good to hear. Thanks for the update. And DUDE! I'm a Flag Officer now. You can't call me Cravin anymore!'

Dirty chuckled, then wrote back:

'Sure, Cravin. Whatever you say.'

Dirty would never fit into the new Air Force at the top ranks. A key reason he chose to join the Air National Guard and keep flying.

Chapter Twenty-seven
Orientation Rides

As the morning sun shone down on Bamizay, Curt stepped out into the courtyard for a quick workout. He did sit-ups, pushups, and burpees. It was his stationary fitness routine, as running outside was just too dangerous. The 4Runner was gone and Curt presumed Majeed had already headed out to track down information on the Kochi tribes. Curt anticipated this mission would take days, but both he and Mule needed to stay alert and prepared to move. Once they had actionable information on Noorullah, they'd move fast.

Majeed had little luck at the first coffee shop. No one had seen any Kochi for weeks, and only one man suggested he'd seen them near Qalat. Majeed thanked his informant and headed to Qalat. Luckily, it was Thursday, which meant the open market would be set up. Perhaps some of Majeed's old friends would be there, he thought. Some were also old friends of Curt, who had visited the market every week during his previous missions in the area, using the market as a litmus test to understand the local societal concerns and feelings. Before heading to the market, Majeed chose to go back to the safehouse. He pulled in as Curt was finishing his workout.

"Commander," he said after parking the car. "Good morning. I have possible information. The last sightings of Kochi were in Qalat. I will drive there now, but it is market day, and I thought you may wish to go."

Curt's eyes lit up. Mule overheard as he was inside the house at the kitchen table with the window open.

"Bad idea, boss," Mule said. "The less engagement we have with locals until we have actionable intel, the better."

"Yeah. I know. You're right, but I'm willing to take the risk. If you don't want to come, I get that," Curt said to Mule.

"What? Really? And enjoy all the excitement here? No thanks. Let's grab our gear."

The three packed up their vehicle, then headed out about twenty minutes later. They'd be at the market by 1100Hrs, as it was only forty minutes away. As they pulled into the market, they noticed it was moderately full, bustling with business.

Majeed parked the SUV, and the three began walking around. Majeed separated to be on his own and queried the locals regarding information about Kochi's whereabouts. Curt and Mule strolled around cautiously. A good number of the vendors were new, but Curt recognized a few of the old timers. One particular vendor, Hakem, hadn't changed. Every week, Curt had tea with him. This time, Hakem's father was with him. The two ran a rug shop, selling some of the finest Persian carpets one could imagine for a fraction of what someone would pay in the Western world.

After roughly a half hour, Majeed returned to Mule and Curt, informing them no one had information on the Kochi tribe.

"Thanks, Majeed. It's OK. It's the first day. Hey, that is Hakem over there. Do you remember him?"

Majeed looked to his left and saw Hakem. "Yes. Of course. You bought carpets from him."

"Yes. Can you go ask him to go to the back of his area and pour five teas? Give him this."

Curt handed Majeed a $50 bill. Majeed did as he was asked. Curt and Mule watched the interaction, and within a minute, Hakem went to the back of his shop area and poured the tea. After five minutes, Curt and Mule walked into the rug store and towards the back. As the two approached the owner, Curt looked up, lifting his pakol.

Hakem's eyes lit up and as he was about to yell out a greeting, Curt's hand rose to his lips, asking Hakem to remain quiet.

"Hakem. It is good to see you," Curt said as he performed the traditional 'double hug' of Afghanistan. Once left, once right.

"Commander, sir. It's good to see you. Are you here for a rug? I thought all Americans left. It is not very safe for you here."

Hakem was right. It wasn't safe. "Hakem. It is good to see you too. Today, I do not seek carpets, but I am trying to find Kochi."

"Oh. The gypsies," Hakem said. It was clear they weren't his favorite. "They never pay," he continued.

"Yes. I know. I see your dad is here. Please, let's all drink your tea. It's part of the reason I came back."

Hakem poured the tea for five and all of them drank.

"I thought you said your father no longer works." Curt continued.

"Yes, but today he was sad, so he came to work." Hakem replied, matter-of-factly.

"Oh. Is he sick or is something wrong?" Curt's voice showed obvious concern.

"No, he's fine. One of my brothers died last night. We were celebrating a wedding, lighting fireworks and shooting our guns into the air. Unfortunately, one bullet fell back down and hit him in the head. He died right there."

Mule about choked on his tea as he heard the story.

"Oh my gosh," Curt said. "That's horrible. Don't you want to close your shop and grieve with your family?"

"We grieved already. It is over. There is little we can do. Better to have the business open. So, we are here." Hakem's muted emotion and matter-of-factness was almost frightening to Curt and Mule. To Majeed, it was normal. This was the way of Afghans.

"Hakem, earlier you asked why I was here. Do you remember the little Kochi Tribe boy I helped get a new leg?"

"Yes, commander. Many remember. We are grateful," Hakem replied.

"Well, I'm trying to find him, not the entire tribe. Do you know anything about what happened to him?"

Hakem did not. "No, sir. I'm sorry. But I can ask around. Kochi come to the market often. Maybe other vendors know."

"Great. I'm sorry I cannot stay any longer. It is best if I go. I am quite happy to see you again and sorry about your brother. Please give your father my condolences, too." Curt, Mule and Majeed stood up, hugged Hakem again and walked out.

As they departed the shop, Mule realized the two were being watched... and gawked at. They were not regulars, and this raised suspicion. He whispered, "Dude, we gotta get out of here."

"Yeah. You're right. Let's go."

Once back in the car, Mule shared his frustration. "Doc. This isn't 'old home' week. I didn't sign up for that. What just happened in the market? That was bullshit."

Curt wanted to argue but couldn't. Mule was right and their market visit wasn't smart. If anyone recognized them, there would be a decent bounty on any American soldiers in Afghanistan. "I'm sorry, Mule. It won't happen again."

"Fine. But the next time we expose ourselves in public, it's for actionable intelligence on the target. Deal?" Mule was calming down.

"Deal," Curt replied.

Nothing more was said on the way back to the compound. Majeed dropped them off. He was planning to head out to a small village north of Bamizay, which had a small mosque. He wouldn't be back until late.

Similarly, Usman from the other team was working the local area between Bagram and Kabul. He hung out in mosques, coffee shops and other gathering places. The good news was that he quickly learned that one C-130 was sitting on the ramp at Kabul International Airport. It was not flyable, heavily damaged and intentionally sabotaged by the U.S. military as they pulled out. The bad news was that trying to get any information from locals about former Afghan National Army or Air Force members was challenging. The Taliban were also inquiring about soldiers and airmen. Even if the locals knew something, they were wise to just say they knew nothing. While most Afghans feared the Taliban, they also did not want to be responsible for another's death if they could avoid it.

Usman came back to the Bagram around 1400Hrs. Buck was waiting for him in the courtyard, and Smitty was taking a nap in the barn. "Any luck Usman?" Buck asked.

"I found a C-130. It is sitting off the end of the runway, damaged in Kabul." Usman said.

"OK, interesting. Did you find out anything about Raz?"

Usman was hesitant to answer. "No, sir. Nothing. It is not easy at this time to ask about former Afghan Army members.

And even if you do, the answers are unreliable. They are all in hiding."

Buck assumed this was the case. Many of them had gone into hiding; likely the reason he hadn't' heard from Raz.

Smitty overheard the commotion and went outside. "Any luck?" he asked.

Buck relayed the info to Smitty, who also was not surprised. He then said, "Hey, it's only two o'clock. Can we throw on our man-dresses and head to the Kabul airport? I want to see the C-130."

Smitty was OK with it, as long as they didn't talk to anyone.

The three prepared, then departed the compound. Eventually they came upon the airport, driving a road that paralleled the perimeter fence around the flight line. The car slowed to a stop once they were at a place that had the best vantage point of the aircraft. Buck wanted a better view and jumped out of the vehicle. He walked along the road as cars passed. He wasn't alone. Other Afghans had gathered along the fence line to watch planes take-off and land, a popular pastime in Kabul for locals. Smitty had also exited the vehicle, far more discretely than Buck, who'd he be keeping an eye on. Buck was fixated on the broken-down C-130 abandoned on a barren ramp. He had a discrete set of binoculars and tried to see how much damage it had sustained. Each issue he found was like a bullet to his heart. Years ago, he'd flown that very aircraft while teaching others to fly it. The two port-side main landing gear tires were flat as the aircraft listed to the left. A few windows in the cockpit were cracked and appeared to have bullet holes through them. Puddles and stained concrete had formed under two of the engines, suggesting a fluid leak of some kind. Additionally, a significant amount of battle damage was visible along sections of sheet metal, likely from bullets, rockets, and shrapnel. Usman was right. The plane would not fly.

Buck had lost all sense of awareness around him. He was now openly staring through the binoculars non-discretely. Smitty kept his watch. An Afghan man noticed Buck and began staring.

"Buck, put the fucking binoculars down now. You're being

observed." Smitty said on his radio.

Buck did as instructed and looked down at his feet.

"Fuck. Dude. He's still watching you. Your three o'clock for fifty meters," Smitty said, then continued. "OK, slowly start moving towards me." Slowly, Smitty began reaching up under his Afghan robe, grabbing his weapon.

Buck had another twenty meters to the vehicle where Smitty was standing now. "Usman! Start the car now." Smitty said almost coldly into his radio.

"Buck. I need you to pick up your pace. He's jogging towards you. Roughly ten meters now."

Buck began walking faster. His heart raced. He'd acted stupidly, and now was likely to pay for it... possibly with his life. Suddenly, he froze.

Behind him, he heard a faint voice call out. "Buck!"

Buck turned around. It was Raz! He, too, had been standing along the fenceline, admiring the C-130, and dreaming about days past.

Buck raised his arm, which had the discrete microphone in it up to his mouth and said, "It's Raz! Stand down!"

Smitty smoothly released the weapon from his hands as the weight of the weapon fell back onto its concealed shoulder strap under his clothing.

Raz hugged Buck, in a distinctly American style, clearly not Afghan. As scared as Buck was just minutes ago for failing to blend in, he was doing it again. They were talking in English.

Violently, someone grabbed both their arms. It was Smitty. "Are you fucking nuts? Both of you! In the car!" Smitty threw them in, and Usman drove away quickly. Locals had noticed the commotion but made little of it. Luckily, there were no Taliban officials along that fence line.

Smitty turned around and chewed on Buck for a while. To Buck, it didn't matter. He'd found Raz. Tonight would be a great night. Usman drove back to the compound while Buck and Raz chatted in the backseat.

"Raz! What happened? You never wrote back when I asked if you were OK."

"Buck, I destroyed my phone and got a new one. I am sorry,

but I received no messages," Raz responded. "I also never logged back into my old email. People say the Taliban is monitoring everything. I am sorry. I couldn't risk it. But I am very pleased to see you! What are you doing here?"

Buck understood and ignored the question. "That makes sense. What happened to the C-130? It's in terrible shape."

"It is," Raz said. "The Americans destroyed much of the military assets as they departed. I don't know what the cockpit looks like, but the outside damage seems extensive, but mostly superficial. It makes me sad to see her like that, but I go back almost every day and just stare at her. I miss being in the sky. I miss flying. I miss what our nation was supposed to become."

"I hear ya," Buck said. "Do you know about any of the internal issues?"

"Not much. My Taliban friends..."

As soon as Smitty heard that phrase, his eyes widened. *'Taliban friends?'* he thought. *'Shit! This guy IS Taliban!'*. Smitty swung around from the front passenger seat with a Glock semi-auto 9mm handgun, pointing it directly into Raz's face. "Get the fuck out."

Raz raised his hands. "Don't shoot! Don't shoot! Look. I am not Taliban. But one can't survive in Afghanistan today without knowing Taliban. Afghan loyalties are a strange creature. People are more loyal to clans than they are to any form of government, be it Taliban, the U.S., the U.K., the Soviets. Yes, I know Taliban. But I grew up with them in my clan and that loyalty outweighs all. They would never turn on me, and I won't turn on them."

Slowly, Smitty withdrew his weapon, wishing he'd searched Raz before allowing him to enter the vehicle. For the rest of the ride home, Smitty was certain he was going to get a few rounds through his back.

After that episode, vehicle discussion fell mute. Buck and Raz chose to shelf the rest of their conversation for dinner.

****

Night set in the Bamizay compound. Majeed had not yet

returned, so Curt and Mule climbed up onto the guest house roof and watched out over the desert with thermal imaging and night-vision devices. Off in the distance, a few fires burned. As they scanned across the land, they both saw it at the same time. Some of the local livestock farmers and others were holding a Bachi bazi event. U.S. military personnel who'd served in Afghanistan called it 'Man boy love Thursday.' To Westerners, it was a sick and immoral ritual where elder men would have their way with the male youth of the village. It was a rite of passage and for Southern Afghans and Northern Pakistanis. It was as normal as Americans having a Friday BBQ boys' night out, minus the sex acts. Neither Curt nor Mule would keep their night optical device on that scene for long. Neither would say anything about it. Eventually, they saw headlights coming towards them from the ring road. Both presumed it was Majeed. The two climbed down off the roof to greet him and find out what he'd learned. Sadly, the answer was nothing, yet again.

Chapter Twenty-eight
What's in a Name?

On Masirah Island Air Base, the operations room was being prepared for Name Night festivities. At the front of the room were five chairs, the nicest one in the middle. That is where Dirty would sit. The other four chairs would be filled by the next highest-ranking officers, comprising the board. On either side of the room were many chairs for the younger officers and onlookers. And in front of the ranking court was one table with a bottle of tequila and a single shot glass. Off to the corner was an iPhone, affixed to a stand, recording the event. It belonged to Ash, who wanted to capture the festivities and share it with friends. At this point, he did not know how bad of an idea that was, but he'd soon learn.

Scattered around the room were coolers full of beer and other spirits. Ash had done well at securing alcohol for the event.

At 1900Hrs, aircrew and guests filled the chairs along the sides of the room, already well into the libations for the night. The room was called to attention and in a horrible display of pomp and circumstance, the five officers entered the room in a single line, with Dirty entering last. He was in his flight suit, with a makeshift crown, scepter, and sash. The crowd erupted in laughter and cheer.

Once Dirty sat, the entire room sat. Dirty pounded the end of his scepter against the floor three times, then spoke. "Hear Ye! Hear Ye! Who is it that comes before the Gods of Callsigns tonight?"

Standing alone in front of the table with tequila was Ash, wearing a navy-blue sports coat, white button down and tie, with his now homemade Bermuda shorts and dockers. He spoke up, "Lieutenant Colonel Sanchez, I do, Ashton Beasley."

"DRINK!" The officer next to Dirty screamed. "How dare you use unknown names in this forum!"

Dirty raised his hand. "Now, now. We must have leniency. Our guest is a virgin and unknowing to our ways." Dirty paused and directed his attention to Ash.

"Good, sir. Let me share with you the rules for this evening. First, you will refer to me as Lord Dirty. Should you wish to address any of the officers to my left or right, you will place Lord in front of their callsign as well. Next, you must never use the words…," Dirty stopped and looked at his fellow Lords. "Gentlemen, a training event requested, please." The Lords all nodded. "Thank you. You cannot say the words 'Head' or 'Box.' Do you understand the rules so far?"

"Yes, Lord Dirty," Ash replied.

"Good. You must also not point using your finger. You can, however, point with your elbow. When I or any other Lord order you to drink, you must drink one shot, an entire shot. Quibbling is not authorized. Breaking any of these rules results in a drink. Do you understand?"

Ash nodded. Wondering if he'd bitten off more than he could chew.

Dirty continued, "If you have a callsign already, you may defend it should you wish. If a majority of the Lords vote to endorse that callsign, you may keep it. However, in the course of the evening, if another callsign arises and the Lords vote for that name, you must take that name as your own. The decisions of this body are final. Do you understand?"

Timidly, Ash replied, "Yes, sir."

Dirty raised his voice and addressed the forum. "You see, now our guest understands the rules, therefore any error from this point on will result in a drink." The four other Lords nodded. Then Dirty said to Ash, "Now drink. I am not 'Sir' to you, but Lord Dirty." The crowd applauded.

Ash poured a glass of tequila and slammed it. The room howled.

Dirty continued. "Young man. Do you have a callsign you wish to defend?"

"I do, Lord Dirty."

"Good. You may state it and begin your defense of that callsign."

"Lord Dirty and other Lords…"

"Drink!" the officer to Dirty's left screamed. "You don't

simply address me as 'Lord' but rather, 'Lord Arnie.'"

The room howled and Ash chuckled a bit. "Yes, Lord Arnie. But how am I to address the other Lords if I don't know their callsigns?"

Arnie asked Ash, "Which Lords do you not know names for?"

Ash almost raised his hand to point, but at the last minute flipped to his elbow, pointing at the other three. "Lord Arnie, the remaining three." The crowd applauded him. He was learning. Ash was proud. He felt he was getting the hang of it.

"Those men are my good friends, Lord Squiggy, Lord Tupper, and Lord Mo. Now, please continue. We do not have all night."

Ash took a deep breath. "Lord Dirty, Lord Mo, Lord Tupper, Lord Arnie and Lord Squiggy, tonight, I defend the callsign 'Apollo.'"

The room roared when the requested callsign was announced.

Eventually, the room quieted down. Dirty said, "OK, present your case."

"Thank you, Lord Dirty. Apollo, the Greek God, and I are of one. Apollo's name is derived from the Greek word for destroyer or destruction, exactly what the mission I directed would do to Afghanistan's opium crop. He was born the bastard son of Zeus, the head of all..."

"DRINK!" Dirty yelled, as did half of the room.

Ash was confused. "Why am I drinking?"

"You are drinking your first shot for using the word that is spelled H. E. A. D. You're drinking the second time for not addressing me as Lord Dirty, and you may thank me for not making you drink a third time for quibbling."

Applause raged from the sides of the room. Ash poured his first drink and pounded it. He wiped his lips, poured a second and drank it." The cheers were impressive. Three shots in under fifteen minutes. He was doing well, but it was nowhere as much alcohol as others had drank at previous name nights.

"Thank you, Lord Dirty, for limiting my errors to just two drinks. May I continue?"

"You may."

"Zeus, who was the greatest of all Greek Gods. Again, like

Apollo, my mother was a single parent. While I know who my father is, his identity to the rest of the world is sealed by court mandate, presumably because of the power he wields in the U.S."

Dirty and the others looked at each other. Ash's story could be legit. Clearly, he was way out of his league to be the one to come run this mission, sent by the former SECDEF.

Ash continued. "Additionally, the U.S. named one of their premier space programs after the Greek God Apollo, which was a rousing success, much like our mission. Therefore, Lord Mo, Lord Tupper, Lord Squiggy, Lord Arnie and Lord Dirty, I respectfully request to be named, 'Apollo.'"

Many along the sides of the room booed, hoping for a far better story. It lacked lewd behavior, criminal involvement, or many of the other inappropriate activities often heard in a callsign night, but again, Ash was a virgin.

Dirty raised his hand. "Distinguished members of this auspicious forum, does anyone here have other suggestions for the individual wishing to be known as Apollo?"

Hands shot up around the room.

Dirty, using his elbow, pointed at one of the aircrew. "Lord Dirty. I propose he be called Ash 'Knees' Beasley, because... I mean. Jesus! Look at those knees in those crazy-assed pants!"

A howl of laughter shot up from the crowd. Ash even chuckled. *'It was witty,'* he thought.

Dirty called on another, "Lord Dirty, I propose the callsign Ash 'Sleazy' Beasley because he's not in the military but in politics and man, those folks are Saaaahleeeeeasy!"

Another roar. Ash voluntarily poured another shot. Things were clearly going in a direction he had not intended.

There were still more suggestions from the crowd. Dirty called on another aircrew member who responded, "Lord Dirty, enough with the efforts to pair a callsign to his last name. We're overlooking the far better name for the pairing, which is his first. I propose the callsign, 'Hole.' Ash 'Hole' Beasley!"

The volume of the next crowd roar nearly set a decibel record. Even the Lords began chuckling. As the laughter settled, even more hands fired up across the crowd.

The proposals got worse. Ash 'Kisser' Beasley. Ash 'Licker' Beasley. Each recommendation drew a ruckus and encouragement from the crowd. Ash began turning red. Once the evening was over, he would rush to the iPhone he had previously set up to record the event. The world did not need to see him humiliated.

Dirty raised his hand, "Dear forum members, I propose we now take a five-minute break while Lord Mo, Lord Tupper, Lord Squiggy, Lord Arnie, and I decide."

Aircrew in the cheap seats jumped up for a bathroom break and to refresh their beverages. A few approached Ash and congratulated him, offering to drink a shot together. While he was partially embarrassed, and now quite buzzed, there was a sense of camaraderie that he felt from them that was hard to explain. He had just been humiliated in front of them and yet; they were now welcoming him into their culture, a far warmer welcome than the one he'd received when the aircraft first landed.

In a quiet voice at the front of the room, Dirty spoke to the other four, "So, what do you guys wanna go with?"

Arnie responded, "Hey, do you think that story about his dad is true?"

Mo answered, "I don't know, but I don't want to find out. If he knows someone in D.C. that has that kind of power, we'd be wise to be gentle."

"I agree," Dirty said. "The dude shit two KC-135 tankers out of thin air. That's Houdini style magic. Let's toss out all the 'ass' connected names."

Already drunk, Squiggy giggled. "Ha! Toss... Ass. Damn, someone could have said Salad as an option too!"

"Dam it, Squiggy, focus. You lightweight." Dirty said. "OK. How about this? We tell him he will have a choice." Dirty explained the entire plan and all five agreed.

Dirty's voice boomed. "Distinguished forum! We have a decision." The crowd yelled back in agreement, scurrying back to their seats and hoisting their drinks in the air.

"Individual who wishes to be known as Apollo, please rise out of your chair."

Ash stood.

"I must inform you; the Lords were unanimous in their decision. And the decision is perhaps most unique. You, Ash Beasley, have a choice."

The room got quiet. *'A choice?'* They thought. *'No one ever got a choice.'* This was unique.

"You will herby be known as Kisser. OR. You will drink three shots of tequila and you'll be offered a second name we chose."

Aircrew around the room looked at each other. *'What a great idea,'* they thought.

"Lord Dirty. Before I decide, may I know the second callsign you all agreed to?" Ash asked.

"You may not." Dirty answered bluntly.

"DRINK! DRINK! DRINK!" the aircrew chanted.

Ash grabbed his glass. Kisser was not the worst callsign he had heard through the night, but it was also far from the better ones. He prayed the second callsign was not hole or licker. These, to him, were the worst. *'Fuck it,'* he thought. *'It's just three shots.'* Ash picked up the glass and pounded three shots back-to-back to-back.

When he finished. Dirty stood from his chair and slowly walked towards Ash with his hands raised. Unbeknownst to Ash, two aircrew were approaching from behind him with two large bottles of champagne.

"Individual FORMERLY known as Apollo. You will either be, 'Kisser,' or you will be 'Sleazy.' The choice is yours."

Ash, now completely obliterated on booze, smiled. He poured one more shot of tequila and raised it to the sky. In a proud, yet slurring voice, he commanded. "I am Sleazy Beasley!"

A final roar from the crowd erupted as champagne bottles popped. The aircrew rushed Sleazy and poured the bubbly over his head. The four other Lords walked down to congratulate him and shake his hand. Dirty bear-hugged him. Someone turned on some music and the place morphed into an aircrew bar in mere seconds. The smell of popcorn and jalapenos wafted through the room as everyone began munching down on the popular aircrew bar staple. Many asked if there was any way to get some Jeremiah Weed, which is not a brand of marijuana, but rather a somewhat foul yet unique tasting liquor found in many aircrew bars across the Air Force.

The rest of the night was fun and something the aircrew deserved. Back in his hooch, Ash was vomiting, but as he did, he reflected on his new callsign. *'Sleazy Beasley,'* he thought. It was not what he considered, but perhaps that's part of the point. Prior to that night, he was solely focused on 'what' his callsign would be. He'd completely overlooked how much of a memory he'd formed in 'how' his callsign was derived. Eventually, he'd tell his friends about the night. They wouldn't truly understand because they hadn't lived it. But it didn't matter, Sleazy lived it, and that's all that mattered. He never, however, shared the video. Unbeknownst to Sleazy, another aircrew member had turned off his iPhone camera and deleted what had already been recorded. There's good reason few videos from call sign nights exist.

****

In the Pentagon, a note sat on Admiral Hershey's desk. It was from Colonel Andrade, his executive officer. It simply said:

> *'Admiral,*
> *We are still working to get hold of Lieutenant General Ghani. He's departed the country to visit his family in Switzerland. Once we get contact, we will set up a TCON ASAP.*
>
> > *Apologies, sir.*
> > *Alfi'*

Chapter Twenty-nine
Diquat and Paraquat

The leaves on the Afghan poppy crop were turning brown and the budding bulbs were wilting. Most of the farmers dismissed these traits to the lack of rain over the past few days. Managing the irrigation better would surely eliminate the problem. This solution would quickly be dismissed and the true origins of the poppy crop challenges, however, would soon circulate southwest Afghanistan.

One farmer, who received his chemistry degree in London, went out into his massive poppy field. He'd been in Afghanistan for years as part of a failed U.N. agriculture effort to grow crops other than poppy. There, he retrieved some soil and plant samples. Within an hour, he'd identified the problem. Somehow, the poppies were exposed to diquat and paraquat, two herbicides known to aggressively attack plants like poppy, prior to bulb flowering and harvest. There were traces of other chemicals he could not identify but realized they were likely accelerants. He was furious. There was no chance to save his crop. All would be lost.

The farmer pulled out his phone and notified the Taliban contact, who planned to buy his crop. Before noon, the information was across the nation. Samples from other fields presented the same results. Taliban leaders were frantic, blaming the west, mainly the U.S. According to them, "There would soon be repercussions."

Majeed and Usman had been to coffee houses that morning in their respective regions. Both rushed back to their compounds and notified the teams of the situation. It didn't take long for the Taliban authorities to link the reported night aircraft sounds to the crop destruction. It also didn't take long for Curt to add it up as well. He was now in far greater danger than he'd originally expected. The Taliban wanted American blood, and there were only a handful of Americans in Afghanistan.

As Majeed stood in the courtyard relaying the news to Curt

and Mule, a black Mercedes Benz roared into the courtyard and stopped. It was the compound owner Curt had met a few nights ago. He exited the vehicle, slammed the door, and demanded, "What the hell is your country doing?"

Curt was surprised by the confrontation. "Sir, I assure you. I had no knowledge of this. Are you even sure this was the United States? I promise, what I am doing here has nothing to do with whatever is going on with the poppy crops."

The owner's eyes raged with fire. He turned and stormed into his house. Curt had no clue how much money the safe-house owner had lost in potential poppy revenue, but it must have been substantial.

"Majeed," Curt said. "Are we still safe here? Will he expose us?"

"Commander. I don't believe he will. But I must warn you. Our planned route out of the country is gone. I've known that man and his donkeys for years. If there are no poppies for his mules to carry, he'll lose a large amount of his annual income. If the poppy crop was destroyed by Americans, he will do nothing to us at this point."

"OK. Well, we will cross that bridge when we get to it," Curt responded.

Majeed looked confused at him. "But commander. There is no bridge there. That's why you need the donkeys."

Curt smiled. "It's OK, Majeed. Never mind. It's just a dumb American expression."

Curt looked at Mule, who was smiling.

The two teams had agreed to check-in occasionally, and tonight was one of the prescribed times. While it was only two nights into the operation, it provided an opportunity to ensure each team made it to their safe-houses and started their efforts.

At 2000Hrs, Curt called a coded number in his handbook. It was the sim card #1 that was in Smitty's gear. In five seconds, Smitty's phone rang. He answered. "Domino's Pizza."

Curt chuckled. "I guess you haven't been captured or compromised yet?"

"Not yet, but my idiot partner is trying. Any luck on your side finding Noorullah?" Smitty asked.

180

"No. Still working on it. We were upended today from our search, given the news of the poisoning of the poppy fields." Curt replied.

"Yeah, Usman and Raz told us about it in the local news up here. Seems like a big deal."

"You guys already found Raz!?" Curt asked.

"Yes," Smitty said. "It took a day. Frankly, I'm shocked you guys aren't ready to get out of this hellhole like we are."

"Well. That's another piece of bad news I have. Majeed says that because of the poppy issue, we likely lost our ride out of the country and will have to find another solution."

Smitty smiled. "You mean no donkeys? Buck is gonna be disappointed."

"Yeah. I bet." Curt said.

"OK. Look. I don't want to talk too long. Glad you guys are fine. Until the next check in, stay safe." Smitty said goodbye, as did Curt. The next check in would be a few days away.

Smitty walked back to the barn. "Bad news, Buck. Looks like we lost our donkey rides out of the country."

"What do you mean, Smitty?"

"Well, that poppy thing that Raz here was talking about earlier today, that's a bit of a bigger thing than we may have realized. The owner of those donkeys is now pissed at America."

"Well shit," Buck said. "How are we gonna get out of here?"

"I don't know," Smitty said.

"It is getting late. I must get back home," Raz said. It was the second night they were together now, and he'd ridden his moped to the compound. "I'll come back tomorrow if that is OK."

"Raz, you are why I came. You are always welcome," Buck said.

Raz started his moped and drove off.

The two teams were separated by hundreds of miles and now had no way out of Afghanistan. The danger had increased significantly, yet the night sky was clear, the air was cool, and the compounds were peaceful.

****

As Admiral Hershey entered his office after lunch, his executive officer, Colonel Laura 'Alfi' Andrade, jumped up out of her desk. "Admiral! I got ahold of Lieutenant General Ghani!"

"Great. When can I talk to him?"

"Sir, he's sitting on hold on your line right now."

"He's on hold?" the Admiral asked. "How long has he been on hold?"

Alfi looked at her watch. "Sir, about an hour and nine minutes?"

The Admiral looked at his exec. "*About* nine minutes? You have a second's count on that too?"

"Actually, sir," the executive officer replied, "I do." She looked down at her watch, "45, 46, 47... but didn't think you wanted it." Alfi smiled.

Admiral Hershey returned it. "Thanks Alfi, good job." He went into his office and grabbed the phone. "Admiral Hershey here."

"Admiral," Lieutenant General Ghani said. "Glad to hear from you."

"I'm happy to hear from you as well. Wahid, though, you didn't have to wait on hold. I could have called you back."

"No. Nonsense. You gave me a great reason to get away from my wife and family. They are driving me crazy here in Geneva."

"Wahid, you are in Switzerland right now and sat on hold for over an hour?"

"Yes, Admiral. It's nothing. This is my cousin's phone. He has more money than sense."

The Admiral laughed. He knew quite well the Afghan war caused significant poverty and despair. It also created millionaires, mostly via illicit means. Such was the way of conflict. "General Ghani, you are a special character, that is certain. Hey look, the reason I wanted to speak with you was to see if I can get ahold of the folks you met with at my house. Do you know what I'm referring to?"

"Yes, Admiral, of course. I will try to get a phone number, but it will take a few days."

"However fast you can get it. This is important or I wouldn't ask." The Admiral replied.

Lieutenant General Ghani paused. "This wouldn't have to do with a poisoned poppy crop, would it?" He paid close attention to the Admiral's manner of response.

"Wahid, the team we worked with were not part of any such thing, if such an effort were to exist." He chose his words carefully. True, Curt and Smitty had nothing to do with it, but the Admiral knew the United States did. The Admiral ran the comment again through his head. Yes. It was what he wanted to say. It didn't confirm or deny the event and it didn't implicate the team or him.

"Nice answer, Admiral," Wahid said. "Again, give me a few days. Goodbye Admiral." Wahid hung up.

While Admiral Hershey wasn't certain, he had a hunch Lieutenant General Ghani or perhaps his family profited in some way from the poppy harvest, or he likely wouldn't have asked in the fashion he did. If he too lost expected revenue for the year, counting on him for help could become a challenge.

As the Admiral sat in his office, an email popped up on his computer screen from the Acting SECDEF, Stacy Crawford.

'Admiral Hershey
Just heard through channels, Taliban leaders have declared they will kill any American they capture. All Americans are accused of the herbicide event, merely by nationality. There's already been a kangaroo court trial, and all Americans have been found guilty.

Stacy'

Chapter Thirty
Plan B

As Raz approached his village, he passed the entry to his residence and continued further up the road. He parked his moped in front of another compound. It was the residence of his childhood friend, Abdul-Baqi, who was now the village's lead Taliban official. Both Raz and Abdul-Baqi knew the Taliban had a bounty on Raz's head, but clan loyalty outweighed Taliban orders.

Raz knocked on the door. It was late, but Abdul-Baqi answered. In Pashto, he greeted Raz. "Praise be to Allah. Greetings Raz. It is good to see you."

"You as well. I must speak to you about a proposal."

"Of course. But it is late, and if this is your same plan to turn yourself into the Taliban to save your family, I will hear nothing of it. You are safe forever in our village as long as I am in charge."

"No, Abdul, that is not the plan. I have heard about the poppy crops, and I know the Taliban will desperately need money. I have a proposal for you."

"Interesting," Abdul-Baqi said. "Let me make us some tea and I will listen." Tea was made, and Raz explained the plan. Providing loose facts, Raz believed it was possible to rebuild the damaged C-130 at the Kabul airport, making it flyable and, more importantly, sellable. While the Taliban would not recover the roughly billion in lost opium revenue, an operable C-130 could fetch $20 million on the international market which was far better than nothing. As they spoke, Raz reminded his friend that Afghanistan at one time had four C-130s, and with a little luck, there could also be a chance to sell three of the four: the one in Kabul and another two up in Tajikistan. By selling all three, along with all the parts in depot, the Taliban might get around $75 million. The fourth plane was in the United Arabic Emirates, where it was under repair during the rise of the Taliban. Getting this aircraft back would not be possible. The UAE had no plans to let it go until receiving payment for the work performed. The

Taliban neither had the funds nor did they have the desire to get it back.

As Raz continued his discussion with Abdul, Raz had a request should he be able to repair the C-130. Raz asked that the Taliban remove the bounties on Afghan's who served in the military, providing them amnesty to live their lives peacefully.

After hearing the plan, Abdul-Baqi was interested. He was a small-town Taliban politician with far greater ambitions. Surfacing proposals to the Taliban leadership which generated revenue versus expenditures were always popular. Abdul-Baqi agreed to raise the idea in the morning to the Taliban. The two said goodnight, and Raz went to his home, only five minutes away. He prayed hard to Allah that night to accept his plan, help the Taliban see the value, and set hundreds of his friends free.

****

The next morning, poppy crops across southwest Afghanistan wilted even further. Flowering bulbs were visible only on roughly one in fifty plants and those also looked sick. The crop was a complete loss.

Curt and Mule woke and found Majeed outside in the courtyard on a small rug, performing his morning prayer. They did not disturb him. From inside the main house, they could also see the owner looking out the window, watching Majeed. The owner did not perform his required prayers per the Quran. He was not a devout Muslim, but he was Afghan by blood. After prayer, Majeed joined Curt and Mule in the guest house. "God be great," he said. "Hakem has sent me a text message and says the Kochi tribe was last seen about three kilometers north of Shahjoy."

"Shahjoy?" Mule answered. Isn't that on the other side of Qalat? I thought they stayed in between Kandahar and Qalat?"

"It is true that's where they normally stay, but they sometimes go as far north as Ghor Province in the summer to get out of the heat and find food. This Spring has had little water, and Shahjoy is farther northeast up along the ridgeline. I

185

will go immediately and see if I can find them if you agree, commander."

Curt looked and Majeed. "Yes. Of course. That's a great idea."

As they finalized their plans, a black Mercedes Benz roared out of the parking lot. The owner of the compound had departed and ensured everyone knew.

Roughly a half hour later, Majeed took the 4Runner and headed to the ring road, turning north towards the village of Shahjoy.

Curt and Mule were bored senseless. After another stationary workout, the two climbed onto the roof for a while and looked out over Bamizay. There was no movement for nearly thirty minutes. Then Mule got excited as he saw a nomad herder moving in the distance, slowly, with a handful of goats. It was so far away, he and Curt argued whether it was seven or eight goats and were considering a small recon mission just to see who was correct.

Three hours had passed. Curt and Mule challenged each other to pushups. Mule won by a long shot and for the next twenty minutes would mercilessly berate Curt for getting soft. Again, they climbed to the roof and looked out. This time, however, there was some traffic in the distance on the ring road. Zabul Province was waking up.

A small compact car turned towards the compound on the dirt road, with a jingle truck behind it. Both were speeding towards the compound. Boredom quickly turned to concern as they jumped down off the roof, grabbed their body armor and rifles, then quickly climbed back up to assume firing positions.

Both vehicles entered the compound and screeched to a halt as the driver's side door of the compact car flew open. The aggressive driving kicked up a substantial dust cloud, masking the car and its occupants from recognition. Curt stared through his gun scope, waiting to see if the man was armed, or showed any aggression. Eventually, he lowered his weapons and was relieved to not see an army of Taliban jump out of the jingle truck. Curt called out on his tactical radio. "Stand down. It's Hakem from the market." Mule lowered his weapon. Hakem ran towards the gate and opened it.

"Commander! Commander! Are you here!?" He called out quietly.

"Yes, Hakem, up here," Curt said from the roof. "Hold on, I'm coming down." Curt climbed down while Mule stayed up for overwatch. He still was unsure of the situation.

"What's wrong, Hakem. Are you OK?" Curt asked.

"Yes, commander, I am fine, but you are in great danger! Please grab your things! We must go now!"

"Hold on, please explain. Slow down." Curt was not ready to just un-ass the team from the safe-house over a hysterical carpet seller.

"Sir. Your host! He's a dangerous man! He's in Qalat right now, negotiating with the Taliban to expose you for money! He is not a real Afghan! He lived in England for years, then came back to buy a poppy farm. He won't protect you. I will. You pack now into my carpet truck. You have little time! Please!"

Curt couldn't take the chance Hakem was wrong and Mule was already packing. Quickly, Curt checked by the front gate. The burka was gone, meaning the man's wife was out. No one saw Hakem come.

Expeditiously, they packed the truck and departed. They turned onto the ring road and headed towards Qalat. After driving for about five minutes, a dozen pickup trucks filled with Taliban, machine guns and rocket-propelled grenades sped past them, heading the other direction. At that moment, Curt and Mule realized Hakem had saved their lives. Mule's trust in him increased considerably.

"Hakem, we have one problem. Majeed is in Shahjoy looking for the Kochi tribe. We can't let him return to the compromised safe-house. They'll kill him."

"Commander, Majeed is already on his way to my shop. I sent him a text immediately when I found out, but he said he was not with you, which is why I drove here. Everyone is safe, Inshallah."

"Well," Mule said. "Praise be to freaking Allah, then." Part of his tone was sarcastic. Part was honest. '*If there was one consistent thing about Afghans, it's that they'd always surprise you,'* Mule thought to himself.

The Taliban vehicles stormed the safe-house compound in Bamizay. They'd find the place empty. After roughly ten minutes of searching, the head Taliban official addressed owner, "I don't understand. You brought these Americans to your house to turn them into us?"

"Yes, sir! And God Willing, I was hoping you'd catch them." The owner's story was a lie, and he was quickly learning he'd let his rage and anger get the better of him. His story was quickly falling apart.

"If you are telling the truth, you should have told us about them earlier."

"Sir, I could not do that, or they may not have come." Again, the owner's comments made little sense to the Taliban leader.

"Why? How would they know if you told us?"

The owner had no answer and paused. Then, he said, "Maybe there is an insider in the Taliban!" It was a horrible answer.

Roughly fifteen minutes later, a cloud of dust kicked up as the Taliban pickup trucks drove away. As the dust settled, an image slowly emerged. It was the owner, hanging from a noose slung over the archway of the compound's entrance gate. An hour later, his wife would discover him dead as she walked home from the village. She, too, was in danger. There was little time to grieve. She hastily packed a suitcase and fled to her parents, the only place she might find safety. It was Afghanistan.

Hakem did the best he could to provide shelter for his friends. His compound was smaller than the original safe-house. There was no guest area but rather a storage room that had an overhang. Inside the storage room were dozens of Afghan carpets of all shapes, sizes, and colors. The team would sleep on top of the rugs which were comfortable, but musty. Ironically, the accommodations were modest for Afghanistan, but in the U.S. that stack of Persian rugs would easily be worth over $200,000.

"Hakem, I can't thank you enough for your efforts. If there is any way I can repay you, I will do it."

"Sir, you do not need to repay me. You bought many carpets

from me. You were one of my best customers. And you are my friend. And you are alive. That is all that matters."

Hakem invited them into his house, where they all drank tea. After another hour, Majeed returned from Shahjoy. He had good news.

"Commander!" he said excitedly. "The Kochi Tribe was north of Shahjoy and moving along the base of the ridgeline south, this way. I tried to spot them as I drove along the ring road, but the ridge line is too far off in the distance."

"This is excellent news, Majeed." Curt replied. "And I am glad you are safe."

"Oh," Majeed paused. "Safe. Yes." In Majeed's world, as with many Afghans, he saw himself just one day away from potentially being killed by the Taliban. 'Safe,' was a relative term. "Well, we are safer here than in our last location. The Taliban already boast that they hung the owner for being the infidel that invited Americans to Afghanistan. He deserves it," Majeed said matter-of-factly. "But, commander, they now know you are here, and eventually they will know I am helping you."

Majeed was right. He was in danger and could not stay in Qalat. "Majeed. Tonight, I want you to take the 4Runner and drive to the other safe-house with Smitty and Buck. I want you to tell them what happened and have them plan to call me tomorrow at 1900 hours. Can you do that?"

"Yes, commander."

The plan did not enamor Mule. "Hold on, boss. You want to give away our only mode of transportation and cut our team by 33%. Should we talk about this?"

"Sure. But you realize, Majeed will soon be a marked man by local Taliban. If they don't see him, they'll assume he left, as did we. Then they'll stop looking. And speaking of looking, the walls of Hakem's compound are just over a meter high. They don't provide enough coverage for the 4Runner, an unfamiliar vehicle in the area. Eventually, the Taliban will also know that's our vehicle. Both Majeed and the 4Runner need to disappear."

Mule hated it, but also knew there was little other choice.

"Sir," Hakem said. "I can build my walls up higher for you if that helps."

It was a kind gesture, but also one Curt could not accept. "Hakem, you are a generous and giving man. I thank you for your offer but must decline. I also beg you not to do it. As the Taliban look for us, they'll seek any activity out of the normal. Any increased fortifications of any residences in the area will be looked at with scrutiny. I cannot let you put your family at risk. Do you understand?"

"Yes," Hakem said reluctantly. He'd wished his walls were already ten feet high, and he wished he could offer more to Curt and Mule. True Afghans were amazing hosts, and per their custom, they would fight to the death to protect any guest that stayed the night, even a stranger. So were the ways of Afghanistan.

Night approached and Majeed prepared for his trip. Curt and Mule helped him get into body armor, wanting to take no chances. Hakem gave him one of the many weapons that were stored in his basement. It was an old German semiautomatic Ruger handgun. Not perfect, but it worked.

Once ready, Majeed drove off from the Qalat compound onto the ring road. He drove well into the night and did not stop until he passed Ghazni Province. No one would know him there. It would be safe. Majeed passed checkpoint after checkpoint. Each time he was concerned they'd detain him. At each location, they searched the car and asked about American Special Forces. He acted surprised and returned the question to the Taliban guard, curious about the infidels. Some of the guard's descriptions were close to those of Curt and Mule. Others were wildly fabricated stories about multiple Special Ops teams that parachuted in when the C-130s were flying, preparing to retake Afghanistan. While fabricated, they somewhat mirrored how the U.S. invasion back in 2001, starting with Special Forces insertions. This was likely the basis of their extravagant claims.

Eventually, Majeed was in Ghazni Province, and the checkpoint interrogations became far less concerning. He'd not yet grown tired, and chose to drive through the night, all the way to Jalalabad. He wanted to sleep in his own home and see his family. It had been a crazy few days.

Chapter Thirty-one
Sacrifices Must Be Made

The next day, Raz did not return to see Buck as he said. He waited at his home for Abdul-Baqi. Around 1400Hrs, there was a knock at this door. As he opened it, Abdul-Baqi stood with a smile and a warm greeting. The two performed the ritual left / right hug, and Raz welcomed him into the house.

"Raz," Abdul-Baqi said. "I have good news. The Taliban would like to hear more about your plan."

"That is great! Praise be to Allah!" Raz said. "Yes! And what did they say about eliminating the bounties on the Afghan soldiers and airmen?"

"Raz, I tried my best to negotiate, and they have made an offer." Abdul-Baqi knew it wasn't exactly what Raz wanted, but he was being honest, and had negotiated to the best of his ability.

"OK," Raz replied. "I am listening."

"Anyone with the rank of Lieutenant Colonel and below will be freed with no further charges. Those with the rank of colonel must accept forty lashes in public and profess their loyalty to the Taliban. Anyone with the rank of General will remain an enemy of the state. I know it is not what you wished to hear. But it was all they will give."

"And you believe they will keep their word?" Raz asked.

"Yes. They said they will make the decree as soon as you accept; then you will receive your forty lashes." Abdul-Baqi looked at Raz, knowing he neither wished to receive the lashes, be publicly humiliated or pledge loyalty to the Taliban.

Raz sat there. "I must take time to think about this."

"Raz, I am sorry, but they want an answer quickly. Please, this truly is the best offer you will get."

"OK," Raz said hesitantly. "Tomorrow, I will receive my lashes, but the decree must be public before that, and I must have assurances they will allow me access to the aircraft and to a handful of former Afghan maintainers."

"This they've already agreed to. I shared your plan," Abdul-

Baqi answered. "You will need to be in Kabul tomorrow morning in front of the courthouse at ten in the morning to turn yourself in, after the decree is announced."

"I will be there," said Raz. "Thank you, Abdul, and may Allah be merciful."

"Praise be to Allah," Abdul-Baqi said as he walked out of the home.

Raz drove his moped to see Buck. Upon arriving, he said, "Buck, tomorrow, I have a surprise for you. Your team must travel to Kabul. You'll witness something great."

"Raz, I hate surprises. Please tell me," Buck demanded.

"I cannot. I will stay here tonight with you. I will leave early on my moped and I will tell Usman where to go. I will meet you there at nine forty-five. OK?"

"Sure. But again. I hate surprises."

"Yes. It must be this way. Let's talk about something else," Raz offered. Understandably, he had no desire to even think about the events he'd experience the next day.

As they spoke, another vehicle pulled into the courtyard. It was Majeed, alone.

Buck and Smitty ran out to the car immediately, concerned.

"Majeed. Why are you here? Where are Curt and Mule?"

"Sir, everything is fine. Please, let me explain. Also, prepare your second SIM card. You must call the commander at 1900 hours local." Majeed got out of the car after his initial statement and explained everything to the team. He was introduced to Raz. Neither had met before.

Raz asked Buck, "How many are with the other team?" It was his only concern.

"Now, there's just two of them and they're looking for a boy. Why do you ask?" Buck inquired.

"No reason. I was just concerned and curious."

1900Hrs came around and the call was placed. "Curt, Smitty here. Dude. You guys, OK?"

"Actually Smitty, we're great. We are having Afghan Chicken Kabobs loaded with garlic and turmeric along with Afghan flat bread."

"Well, I guess I'm a dumbass for being concerned," Smitty

replied.

"Just screwin' with ya. Obviously not ideal, but I needed to get Majeed out of here. Smitty, I hope you understand."

Smitty understood the risks, but offered a counter-plan, "Look, we found our guy. Why don't we all pack up and move your way? We can put Usman to work down there, as he's not compromised, and he has Afghan tags on his 4Runner."

"Smitty," Curt replied. "You know this area. It's desolate, with ridiculously small villages dotting the desert. An even larger group of all of us will be a sore thumb. Stay there. Seriously. Hakem has already agreed to work as our interpreter and scout."

Curt paused, then continued, changing subjects, "While you're there, let Majeed and Usman work up a plan to get our asses out of here once I find Noorullah. Our original one is out."

It was a good idea. They needed a plan to get away. "Alright, boss. But I'm recommending we call every other day now. We need better comms than every few days."

"Agreed," Curt replied. "You got anything else?"

"Nope. We are going to Kabul tomorrow with Raz, who has some sort of surprise. Not sure what it is. We will lie low."

"Got it. According to Majeed, a group of nomads were moving our direction along the northern ridgeline to the southwest. I'm hoping we can interdict them in a few days," Curt was hopeful of this plan, even though he knew there was a chance this tribe was not the one he was looking for.

"OK. Solid plan," said Smitty. "I'm signing off. Take care, buddy, and stay out of Qalat. Sounds like they're already onto you."

"Will do, buddy. Out here." Curt signed off.

****

In the morning, Raz did as he said and jumped on his Moped and rode to the center of Kabul early. It would take far longer than the normal 40 minutes at regular traffic speed.

Usman and Majeed loaded the 4Runner. Each put on body armor and took weapons, minus Usman, who did not have one.

They drove into Kabul and parked. Walking around in a group of four gave the two Americans decent coverage. As they walked in, a crowd was gathering, far larger than normal. The four moved back away from the crowd, off to the side. They were alone and could speak comfortably in quiet English without being heard.

"What's going on?" Smitty inquired.

"I don't know, sir. There appears to be some sort of announcement coming that people are expecting," Usman said. Majeed nodded at Usman's comments but also didn't understand why the crowd had gathered.

At 1000Hrs sharp, a man in a clean black Afghan outfit walked out, and the crowd hushed.

Majeed whispered, "Taliban."

The man began speaking and, true to form, Majeed tried to translate as quickly as he could. "On this day, the Taliban renounce the criminal charges against all Afghan National Army and Afghan National Airmen from the ranks of lieutenant colonel and below. They are free to live in our prosperous country and abide by the laws of the Taliban. Former military members with the rank of colonel or below will be granted their freedom once they publicly pledge their allegiance to the Taliban and receive their just punishment of forty lashes in public. General Officers will remain enemies of the Taliban and should they be caught; will be punished by death under the eyes of Allah."

Quizzically, Buck and Smitty looked at each other. This was significant news, but how did Raz know what would happen? Then Buck saw Raz. He was brought out to the middle of the crowd and pushed down to his knees. His hands were tied in front of him. The individual controlling Raz spoke in Pashto. "Today, former Colonel Raz Mohammed turns himself in for the crimes he committed against the Taliban and the great nation of Afghanistan. He will speak."

Raz's voice was somber, but steady. He did not shake, he did not cower, he was not afraid. He held his head high. "I, Raz Mohammed, in the eyes of Allah and everyone holy, profess my love and devotion to the Taliban and request forgiveness for my sins under the former puppet government of the U.S. and the

West."

The crowd chanted a bit, happy to see justice being served. Buck and Smitty could hardly watch. Their stomachs churned. Another Taliban official approached with a large, old switch. He reared back his hand and struck a blow to Raz's back. Raz winced in pain, but maintained his composure. He looked around the crowd until he saw Buck. Once he did, he smiled and winked, wincing through another lashing. There would be many more. Raz's back was bloody, but his spirit was not broken. He was taken back into the government building until the crowd dissipated. In Afghanistan, there were times that some believed the punishment was not severe enough to match the crime. On such occasions, these individuals would take matters into their own hands, literally, with stones or other items. Luckily, Raz had suffered enough and wanted to ensure he could safely get to his moped and out of the city.

Before the full forty lashings were completed, Buck had seen enough. He turned and walked back to the car, dragging the full team with them. Once in the car, Buck said. "Next time Curt calls, tell him we're ready to go. Enough of this horseshit. I freakin' came all the way out here and the fucker joins the Taliban right in front of my God damned eyes!"

None of the other three knew what to say. The car ride back to the compound was silent. Once back, Buck sat alone in the courtyard, stewing over the day's events. Slowly, Majeed approached. "Mr. Buck, sir. May I sit with you.?"

"Majeed, thanks, but I'm not really in the mood for company."

"I understand, sir," replied Majeed. "But please let me tell you. Things in this country are never as easy to understand as they appear. Your anger is just, but in our country, Raz has a right to explain himself. I am sure he will seek you out in the next few days. I pray to Allah that you listen to him."

Buck heard what Majeed said but was a stubborn soul. "Thanks, Majeed. I'll make you a deal. After I punch him in the face, then I'll listen to him."

Majeed nodded and trudged away. He'd said what he had to. Buck would eventually digest it if he were smart, which he was.

****

That night, a car pulled up in front of the compound. Two younger Afghan men pulled Raz from the car. He struggled to walk and winced with every movement. The three knocked on the door, and Majeed opened it.

"Mr. Raz," Majeed said in Pashto, "Now is not a good time. Mr. Buck needs time to calm."

"I understand, Majeed," Raz said. "But there isn't time to waste."

Buck heard the commotion and rushed outside. He walked fast towards Raz saying, "How could you..." But before he could lay a hand on him, the two younger Afghans pulled knives against Buck, who quickly stopped.

One began screaming in Pashto as Majeed tried to translate as quickly as he could.

"Mr. Buck, he says he will kill you if you harm Raz. These men see him as a hero."

Buck looked at Majeed. "Tell them this: Hero, huh? He pledged loyalty to the Taliban."

Majeed began translating it and one quickly answered in English. "Fuck the Taliban!"

Buck was a taken back. "Excuse me?"

Raz finally spoke, faintly as full breaths hurt. "Buck. He said Fuck the Taliban. As I told you before, loyalty to the Taliban for most is not based in the heart but necessity. What you saw me do today secured the freedom of many. I also showed the Taliban that I am at least loyal enough to stand their punishment. What you didn't see was the rest of the story."

Buck interrupted. "Which is?"

"Tomorrow morning, you, I and nine Afghan Air Force former maintainers will begin work to make the C-130 at Kabul flyable." Raz said, as he smiled at the end.

"Come again?" Buck was speechlessly overwhelmed.

196

"You need a new plan to get out of here. Well, I have it. Once we fix it, you and I can fly it. Like old times."

Smitty was impressed, but he wasn't an aviator and had no idea how badly the aircraft was destroyed. "OK, but can the thing fly?"

Buck didn't know. He'd not been inside the C-130. Neither had Raz.

"Mr. Smitty," Raz said. "I do not know the answer to this, but I do know that my good friend from South Africa here (pointing at Buck and winking) is a former aircraft expert who I've asked if he can help. Tomorrow, we can at least look at the aircraft and see what's possible." Smitty was surprised. Raz, referring to him as South African, was strange. Now was not the time to question.

Buck was still angry. It was hard to overcome his hatred for the Taliban. All the fellow friends and warriors the Taliban killed, how horrid they were and how they treated women. And now Raz was one of them.

"Buck," Raz finally said. "If this isn't your wish, I will go, and I'll forever understand why you cannot accept my actions today. I pray to my God and yours, though, that someday, when your anger and rage for the Taliban calm, you can see I did this for you."

Raz turned around and walked towards the car. Blood seeped through the back of his tunic shirt. His two partners tried to help him walk.

"Take your shirt off," Buck said.

"Excuse me?" Raz replied, as he stopped.

"I said take your shirt off. Those wounds are gonna get infected and if by some miracle we get that elephant off the ground, I need your ass to be comfortable in that copilot seat."

Raz smiled and began walking back. "Thanks Buck."

****

The next morning on Masirah Island was a challenging one for Sleazy. His head pounded. By the time he arrived at the operations room, the four flight crews were already planning their flight back to NAS Sigonella.

"Good morning, Sleazy!" Dirty yelled. Knowing the decibels would act like a hammer on his skull.

"Good morning, Dirty. You really don't have to be so loud."

Dirty laughed. As Sleazy walked around the room, multiple airmen said,

"Hey, Sleazy!"

"Good morning, Sleazy!"

"Sleazy! How you feeling?"

"Great job last night, Sleazy."

There were more and more.

As crews prepared to leave, Ashton Beasley for the first time felt like part of the team.

The aircrew stepped to the aircraft and Sleazy watched as the engines began to windmill. He listened to the run ups and all the checks. One by one, the aircraft taxied out. Sleazy waved at each crew in the windows, wondering if he'd ever see them again. After taxiing for five minutes, he watched each aircraft climb into the air, lumbering skyward. As the last aircraft disappeared from sight, he drove back to the operations building.

Sleazy parked and slowly walked in. The mission was over, and given the news emerging from Afghanistan, it was a success. He took a deep breath and looked at his phone for potential flights back to Washington, D.C. As he sat in one of the planning rooms, the door flew open and one of the Omani air controllers yelled, "Mr. Beasley, sir! One of your aircraft is coming back with an in-flight emergency."

Sleazy put away his phone and ran to the operations desk. "What happened?" He asked.

"Sir, we don't know. The call came from Roach 01. They claim they had an engine over-temp, have discharged the fire bottle, and secured the engine."

"What!?" Sleazy asked. He was confused. "The engine wasn't 'secured' before they took off!?"

"No, sir. They shut down the engine. We say secured." the Omani said, almost wanting to laugh at the stupid American.

"Oh. Right." At that point, Sleazy realized just because he

198

had a callsign, he still was no aviation expert.

Sleazy moved towards the window and watched the C-130 slowly approach the base, the blades of the number two engine stationary in the wind as the other three spun normally. He looked at his information sheet. Roach 01 was Dirty's aircraft. Sleazy was worried. Dirty had become his friend.

Crossing the threshold, Dirty set the bird down on the runway. He, the copilot, and the flight engineer all confirmed only engine one and number four for reverse thrust. Two engines would be more than enough, and had he grabbed all four, only three would work given one engine was shut down. Three engine reverse thrust would induce significant asymmetrical yaw, driving the aircraft off the runway and making a relatively minor emergency far worse.

The aircraft lumbered slowly to a stop, using the entire runway. The aircrew performed a landing at max weight, placing significant stress on the landing gear and the brakes. One option to alleviate this would have been to dump fuel before landing, but because of the already high engine temp warnings and the potential for fire, Dirty wanted to be back on terra firma as quickly as possible. Under the conditions, there were many things an inexperienced pilot could have done to exacerbate the problem. Dirty was no novice. He would create no additional problems. Once the aircraft stopped, he waited until the fire crews confirmed there were no visible signs of fire. Once they gave him a thumbs up, he slowly taxied back to parking. It was clear Dirty and his crew would be staying on Masirah Island for a few more days. After shutting down, he shot another text:

'Cravin,
Minor issue with one aircraft. 3 of 4 got out. I drew the unlucky short straw. Stuck on KMSH.
Dirty'

Chapter Thirty-two
Something Smells Doggy

As news spread about the 'Great Poppy Crash,' the price of opiates, both legal and illegal, rocketed. Existing supplies of heroin remained decent, but the markets were already reacting to the pending shortfall expected in the next year.

The increasing price of legal opiates also rose for drug companies that could fill the need. Both John Gerzema and Andrew Denney would watch their investment portfolios grow. It was the most extreme example of insider trading, by the insiders crafting the demand upon to their prearranged supply themselves.

****

The next morning in Bagram, Usman, Majeed, Raz, and his two escorts prayed together, each on a prayer rug, facing Mecca. Buck and Smitty left them alone, making some morning coffee. Once the prayers were complete, the team loaded up into both vehicles and headed to the airport. Buck, Raz, and his assistants, both of which had been trained in C-130 maintenance, were excited to once again see their aircraft.

Raz showed a piece of paper to the airport guard, authorizing both vehicles to proceed to the C-130. As they pulled up and saw the wounded Hercules up close, Buck questioned whether this thing would ever fly again. Smitty, Usman, and Majeed remained with the vehicles as the others approached the aircraft. Lowering the crew entrance door, an awful stench bellowed out of the cabin as fluid rushed out from the base of the door. Buck nearly vomited. Raz barked something out in Pashto and one of his helpers scrambled into the aircraft, opening the pilot swing windows, the overhead escape hatches both fore and aft, and opening the paratroop doors. The smell from the aircraft made its way towards Smitty, who also could barely control his stomach. One of Raz's assistants exited the plane, carrying the carcass of a dead dog by the tail with pride, sharing the cause of the stench. Raz waved him along, and the man took the dead dog away from the aircraft.

As the cabin and cargo area aired out, Raz and Buck walked around the outside. The first blaring problem was a set of left main landing gear flat tires. Buck looked at it closely. There was a slit in the tire between the treads. Luckily, the sidewall was fine, and the tire could be repaired. From the main landing gear, Buck walked away from the fuselage, looking up at the wing and engines.

"Buck, there are bullet holes and some damage to the wing's leading edge and to the flaps," Raz said, pointing up at the damage.

"You're right, but I think those are manageable. Hey, how much do your two maintainers know?"

"They're like your crew chiefs, but other than what they said last night about the Taliban, they speak no English," answered Raz.

"OK. Can you see if they can find a power cart? Let's see if we can get power on the old girl. Also, maybe start the air conditioning. The hotter this aircraft gets, the worst that smell is gonna be."

Raz barked out some orders in Pashto and one of the two scurried towards the 4Runner, asking Usman for a ride. Soon the vehicle left, looking for a power cart.

"Raz, the prop blades are all in good shape, but I see some bullet holes around the engine cowlings. I'm hoping the engines aren't damaged. Until we get a ladder, I won't be able to know. Any chance we can get a cherry picker, ladder, or scaffolding?"

Again, Raz barked out another order. The second 4Runner with Smitty in the back seat went to find a lift. Smitty left and tried to get some fresher air.

Luckily, the empennage (tail section) was in good condition. Other than the wings, this section housed the other control surfaces for both elevation and yaw. Buck closely looked over the elevators and rudder. All the control surfaces looked to be in far better condition than he had imagined.

Raz followed Buck up the right side of the aircraft from the rear. Before he got much further, Usman approached, honking his horn and towing a power cart behind the SUV. He was excited and under a misnomer that it would only take a power cart to get the aircraft flying. Raz and Buck abandoned the rest of their walk around as Usman positioned the power cart at the 10 o'clock position in front of the aircraft. Raz's helper pulled the power cable off the cart like a pro and laid it on the ground. He opened some panels and fidgeted. After a few chugs and belches, black smoke emitted from the cart as it loudly hummed. The power gauges jumped to life and were all within tolerance. He walked back over, picked up the end of the power cord, popped open the aircraft's power panel and plugged it in.

There were no major sparks and things looked OK. He said a quick prayer to Allah and depressed the button which would allow the aircraft to accept the power. As he did, the Hercules came to life with the common sound to C-130 crews around the globe... 'vrrrrrrrrrrp.' Ticking sounds, altitude alarms, a hint of burnt ozone in the air, and many other warning bells and whistles began firing off from the flight deck. All this was normal. Aircraft were meant to fly, not sit still on a ramp. This was partly the reason for the multiple sounds. Raz and Buck clapped at the young Afghan, who was now quite proud. He had awoken this old girl from a long slumber. The smile on his face was as wide as the C-130's wing line.

After getting power onto the aircraft, the man ran up to the flight deck and began resetting and or securing the alarms and warnings, just as he'd been taught by U.S. instructors.

Buck and Smitty continued their external walk around the aircraft. Then, the entire area grew quiet. The power generator died, as did all the power on the aircraft. 'Not good.' Buck thought. The two walked back around to the front of the aircraft to find the young maintainer feverishly trying to reset the power cart, unplugging the power cord and reseating it. Nothing worked. He was frantic and angry. Buck suspected what was wrong.

He walked over to the power cart and screwed off the gas cap, looking inside. It was empty. Buck pointed inside the hole as both Raz and Usman laughed. The young maintainer sighed in tremendous relief, then talked Usman into another run, this time for gas. Buck and Raz again continued their walk around. The starboard wing line was in better shape than the port one. There was no visible damage, but the number three engine had a massive fluid leak with a puddle directly under the engine cowling drainpipe. Buck bent down and wiped his fingers in the fluid, then smelled it. Raz asked, "Hydraulics or Fuel?"

Buck responded. "Both."

They continued around the outside of the aircraft, unaware that another vehicle had approached. A man wearing black approached the vehicle from the other side. He was clearly Taliban.

In Pashto, he declared, "Hello, Raz. May Allah be with you."

Startled, Raz responded, "Praise be to Allah. Hello."

Buck just stood there. He was white as a ghost. The man was likely Taliban. His weapons and body armor were in the vehicle, and Smitty was gone. Raz and the man spoke in Pashto for a while. Then Raz pointed at Buck, continuing the discussion.

The man looked at Buck, "Hello," he said in English.

Raz cut in. "Daniel," he said while addressing Buck with the alias, "I have informed my friend about you yesterday, and he came out to see our progress. He's impressed with your knowledge of C-130s from your time in South Africa." Raz turned back towards the Taliban official. "Sir, this is Daniel Hejda."

Buck quickly recalled his cover story. All he could think to say was, 'G'day, mate!,' in response, albeit Australian and not South African. In the end, he wisely just nodded.

"Yes. Well, what do you think about this aircraft?"

Buck was far more comfortable talking about C-130s, even if it was in a horrid British accent. He struggled, but the Taliban official was quite impressed with his C-130 knowledge. As they spoke, Usman had returned with the fuel for the power cart. In front of the Taliban official, they filled the cart and again fired it up, applying power to the aircraft. As she again roared to life, the Taliban official was pleased.

"I am grateful, Daniel, for your work. What can we get you to help with your efforts?"

Buck was stuck and blurted out in a horrid British accent, "I suspect right now, good, sir, we could rightly use some contraption to jack up this aircraft and get those flat tires off and repaired. It would be banger if we could get scaffolding to pull some of the wing panels and engine cowlings to have a go at those as well."

"I will have both of them to you before the end of the day," the man said. "May Allah be with you in your efforts." He bowed and walked away.

Buck had survived. The two went up onto the flight deck. Their optimism from seeing the outside of the aircraft quickly dissipated when viewing the flight deck. The navigation station was stripped of the inertial navigation system as well as the GPS. Only one HF and one VHF radio remained, as the others had been pulled by the Americans. The U.S. did not want radios which had embedded encryption systems to fall into the wrong hands. Buck sat in the pilot seat and grabbed the yoke. He could move it far easier than he should be able to. He continued moving it, then noticed the control cables must have been severed, likely part of the sabotage committed by U.S. forces as they evacuated.

He got up from the seat and walked back into the cargo area. Hanging from the ceiling were the control cables, clearly cut before the U.S. departed.

Outside, Majeed and Smitty returned, towing an aircraft scaffolding, driving about five miles an hour across the ramp, honking as they approached. Majeed was pleased and smiling now, thinking it would merely take scaffolding to get the aircraft aloft.

Buck, now outside the aircraft, disconnected the scaffold from the vehicle and placed it in front of engine 3. Raz barked orders again and his maintainer ran up the scaffolding and began pulling engine cowlings.

"Smitty," Buck said. "While you were gone, I met a Taliban official and pulled off my cover." Proud of himself.

"You what!?" Smitty screamed.

"Yeah. It's fine. Even Raz says it's fine. Right Raz?"

"You did OK. I wouldn't say great," Raz replied.

"Shit. Majeed! Usman! Come with me." Smitty grabbed

Buck's arm and threw him in a 4Runner. The four drove away quickly. They were headed to the black markets of Kabul.

Raz and his team continued working on the aircraft, pulling off damaged panels, removing the port wing's leading edge and trailing flaps. All the items were laid on the ground relative to the area they came off.

Roughly an hour later, the same Taliban officer came back with two other Taliban henchmen. "Raz, hello again. Where is your South African man? Some of my friends would like to speak with him."

"Oh, sir. I am sorry. He's run to town to find some circuit breakers for the aircraft. Should I have him come to you when he gets back?"

"No, that's fine. I'll be back. By the way, look there." The Taliban official pointed across the ramp. An old aircraft tug was slowly moving their way, dragging a massive hydraulic jack system and blocks. "You will soon be able to fix your tire."

Raz winced as he looked up. The scars, scabs and wounds on his back had not healed. He tried to hide his pain. "Allah is great! Praise be to Allah!" Raz said.

"Yes. Allah always provides. Again, I will return." The man walked back to his car, and they drove off.

After a few minutes, the tug and jack arrived. Raz directed both of his men to get the aircraft jacked up from the jack point. Once up, the three went inside and pulled the maintenance manuals which were stored with the aircraft. They argued extensively over where to place the block under the aircraft, as none of them could read English. Luckily, they got it right, and soon had pulled the flat tires.

The day was drawing to an end. Much work was done, and the team could be happy. Raz released his two workers and told them to ask their old C-130 maintenance friends if any others would like to help. After they left, he pulled out his phone and began typing out a text message.

****

Smitty was furious with Buck as they drove off the base. He

ordered Usman to drive to the outskirts of Kabul, where they could be safe and away from people. Once stopped, Majeed and Usman feverishly worked their cell phones, trying to find a counterfeit South African passport. Many could forge a U.S. passport, but South African was proving challenging.

"What on earth were you thinking!?" Smitty demanded

"It's not that bad," Buck replied.

"Buddy, you might be a wizard in the air, but you're acting like a freaking court jester on the ground," Smitty scolded. "Do you have any clue how close you came to getting caught?"

"Really, I think you're exaggerating here. I was a bit scared at first, I'll admit. But once I explained the problems with the aircraft, he really took a liking to me." Buck said proudly.

"Buck," Smitty said. "You should have stuck with your first feeling of fear. I swear, if the Taliban don't kill you, I may."

Usman walked back towards the car. Smitty smiled, hoping there was a line on the passports. "Mr. Smitty. Raz sent me a message. It's somewhat convoluted, but says that his friend came back to the aircraft with others, asking to speak to Daniel? Who is Daniel, sir?"

Buck grew uneasy in the back seat.

"Usman, before I answer your question, can you tell Buck and I, how are things between the Taliban and Americans in the country?"

Usman was reluctant.

Smitty insisted. "Tell him!"

"Sir, the Taliban have killed about five Americans in the past few days. It's in the news. They say they will kill any that are caught."

Buck's bowels almost released into the backseat. In an instant, he knew how serious the situation was, how right Smitty was, and how naïve he had been.

Smitty just glared at him.

"Sir? And who is Daniel?" Usman said again.

"Usman, I'm staring at Daniel." Smitty replied as he glared into Buck's eyes.

It didn't take long for Usman to realize he needed to get back to finding a South African passport quickly. The two tried for over an hour without luck. Eventually, Smitty loaded them all into the 4Runner and drove back to the safe-house.

****

In Qalat, things were far less exciting. Curt and Mule stayed in the small compound, kicking a soccer ball with Hakem's son and daughter. Hakem was out for the day, delivering some carpets to customers. He would also drive towards Shahjoy scanning the ridgeline for Kochi. While it would be hard to see individual people, the Kochi normally traveled with a herd of camels, which would be far easier to spot. Unfortunately, there was no sign of people, sheep, goats, or camels.

Hakem turned around and headed back home. A smile crossed his face as he drove. He'd be going back to see his American friend. A good man.

Chapter Thirty-three
Hold the Flight!

The morning briefing for the Chairman and his staff heavily focused on the national security concerns associated with the Taliban losing one billion dollars over the next year. After the U.S. withdrew, most of the foreign bank accounts held by the Taliban leaders were frozen, angering them greatly. Poppy revenue was expected to allow the Taliban some relatively fast cash until they could unfreeze those assets. Intelligence analysts were trying to determine how much misery the funding loss would impact the average Afghan.

The next slide of the briefing showed many media quotes from Taliban leaders and sympathizers, many of whom blamed the United States for the crop destruction. In the room, a handful of folks knew the accusations were correct. Also on the slides were comments from allies, not accusing the U.S. but presenting open questions to the world, asking who could have done this. *'Eventually, POTUS will have to come clean,'* Admiral Hershey thought. He enjoyed thinking about how horribly that would go for the President.

Another portion of the PowerPoint slide caught the Admiral's attention. The Taliban had executed five Americans. Two were Mormons on their mission. The third was a former USAID employee who married a local Afghan years ago and stayed in the country. The other two were dual nationals who'd not been to the U.S. for years. To the Taliban, it didn't matter.

The Admiral also noticed on the bottom of the slide was a small photo clearly from a satellite that was a top-down image of a C-130. Next to the photo, an intelligence assessment was written so small the Chairman couldn't read it.

The briefer flipped to the next slide.

"Hey, back up." The Chairman said. "What's that image on the bottom? I told you guys, I'm old. I need big text. I'd rather have three hundred slides with huge text than one slide with small text. Come on!" The Admiral chewed a bit of butt; however, in reality, he had also told his staff that briefings could contain no more than ten slides. Often saying "If you can't get your point across in ten slides, it's not ready for me." His slide deck length and font size were conflicting guidance, but no one was brave enough to point that out. It was good to be an Admiral.

The briefer flipped back one slide and said, "Admiral. Intel is assessing that the Afghans are taking some initial steps to repair the sabotaged and abandoned C-130 on Kabul airport."

Under his breath, the Admiral said, "Son of a bitch...."

The briefer, presuming the comment was directed at him, responded. "Sir, I assure you. I'll make the text bigger."

Admiral Hershey ignored the comment. He turned to Alfi, his executive officer, "Get me the CSAF (Chief of Staff of the Air Force) on the phone after this meeting."

Alfi nodded and left the room. "Continue please," the Admiral said to the briefer. He let the briefer speak through the rest of the slides, status of the forces, existing global force postures, and many other issues. None of them would capture the Chairman's attention. He was thinking through his pending discussion with the Air Chief.

The briefing ended, and Admiral Hershey quickly got up and moved to his office. As he passed Alfi's desk, he said, "Is he on the line?"

"Yes, sir."

"Great," The Admiral replied. He shut his door and picked up the phone.

"Scammer. Squirts here. Hey, are those herks still at Masirah Island?"

"Admiral, let me check. I have a force laydown slide from yesterday. Here it is. Sir, my slide says they flew out yesterday. Why do you ask?"

"Damn. Do we have any folks still on the ground in Masirah?" Admiral Hershey ignored the Chief's question as to why.

"I don't believe so but give me some time to check." The Chief of Staff of the Air Force was responsible for the largest Air Force in the world, to include worldwide space and cyber assets. The location of four C-130s was not even close to being on his daily tracker, but he knew who'd have the info.

"Great. Get back to me soon." Admiral Hershey hung up.

The Air Chief called Brigadier General Moorehead, remembering he was the original source of the information regarding the C-130s on KMSH. It was the same Brigadier General that was Dirty's friend and confidant in the Pentagon. "Cravin, Scammer here."

"Chief, sir. Yes, what can I do for you?"

"Hey, Chairman called and asked if we had anyone left at Masirah airfield. I saw we flew out the four aircraft yesterday, but were there any maintainers left?"

"Well, General, that's not actually accurate. One aircraft had an in-flight emergency after take-off and circled back. It was the detachment commander, my buddy Lieutenant Colonel Sanchez."

"Callsign?"

"It's Dirty. Dirty Sanchez." Brigadier General Moorehead replied.

"Ha! Funny. He must be old school. That guy has zero chance of making General in today's PC world. Anyway, Cravin, listen to me. Don't let that guy take-off and send me his contact info," the Chief said.

"WILCO," Cravin said, doubting the idea of having shared a politically incorrect callsign with the Chief of Staff of the Air Force. No matter, the Chief was running with it. Cravin pulled out his cell phone and pushed Dirty's contact to the Chief's executive officer.

Within a few minutes, the phone rang in the Chairman's front office. "Chairman of the Joint Chiefs Office, Colonel Andrade. May I help you?" Alfi answered.

"Yes, Air Chief here. Returning the Chairman's call."

"Please hold, General," Alfi said.

Admiral Hershey overheard Alfi. He quickly picked up the phone and asked, "Scammer. What did you find out?"

"Sir, one of the C-130s is broke down at Masirah. It's the detachment commander's bird. Callsign is Dirty. I'm sending your exec his contact information."

"Scammer, many thanks," the Chairman replied and hung up.

"Alfi!" The Admiral yelled.

"Sir," Alfi responded as she walked into the office, already knowing what the Chairman demanded. "I have Lieutenant Colonel Sanchez's info right here."

"Excellent." Admiral Hersey took the info and dialed the phone number.

After a few rings, the other party answered. "Lieutenant Colonel Sanchez."

"Dirty?"

"Yes. Who is this?" Dirty inquired.

"Dirty, this is Admiral Hershey, the Chairman of the Joint Chiefs," he said.

"Jesus Christ! It was just an engine over temp! Seriously! Sir, I don't know who..."

Admiral Hershey cut him off. "Son, I have no clue what you're talking about, and frankly, I don't give a shit. I need you to listen. Two direct orders. First, you'll not take-off from that Island until you hear directly from me. Second, I need a full inventory of all C-130 parts on the island in storage. Got it?"

Dirty had no clue what was going on, but quickly realized the Chairman's call had nothing to do with his in-flight emergency. "Yes, Admiral," he replied.

"Good. I will call you back tomorrow." The Admiral hung up.

"Alfi!" He screamed again.

Colonel Andrade again hastily entered. "Yes, Admiral."

"Call Lieutenant General Ghani. I need the information I requested from him immediately."

"Will do, sir." Alfi left the room.

The Chairman leaned back in his chair and again muttered. "Ha. Buck. He truly is a crazy son of a bitch. He's gonna fly that herk out of Afghanistan."

Back on Masirah Island airfield, Dirty gathered the few airmen that were from his crew and asked them to work with the Omanis, searching the airport for C-130 parts. He also let Sleazy know the aircraft would not be leaving anytime soon.

Sleazy welcomed the information and, like any obedient servant, he passed that information along to John Gerzema.

'Quick update -
One aircraft had a fire after taking off or something and is now back. The pilot of that airplane said the Chairman called and told him not to leave for a while. Don't know what's going on. Should I stay?
Love,
Ashton'

A quick reply alerted in Sleazy's phone:

'Ashton,
Yes, remain there and try to find out why they are staying. You're doing great. I'm proud of you.
Love,
Dad'

Chapter Thirty-four
He's Gone

Curt was sitting around the compound, staring out to the north, watching feverishly for any signs of movement in the foothills. Eventually, the Kochi tribe would pass, and he was determined not to miss them. Mule was working out-burpees, pushups, and sit-ups. With the lack of booze, TV, and internet over the past days, he was getting into spectacular shape.

"Mule!" Curt screamed. "Camels!"

Mule scrambled up onto the roof and looked through the binoculars. Curt was right. A group of camels was visible.

Curt scrambled down the roof and pounded on Hakem's door. "Hakem! Hakem! Camels!"

Hakem opened the door. "Yes. I hear you. My neighbors hear you! Everyone in Afghanistan hears you! Be quiet! It is early still." Hakem put on some clothes and came out. He would drive up to the Kochi encampment and ask if they knew anything about Noorullah.

"I'm coming with you!" Curt insisted.

"No, commander. You are not," Hakem responded without hesitation. The response bordered on insubordination, but Hakem didn't care.

"What do you mean?" responded Curt.

"Curt," Mule jumped in, "He's right. Let's find out what's going on. Dude, they're on foot and we know where they're at. They're not going anywhere fast."

Curt still wanted to go, but it was two against one.

Hakem drove off the compound, and Curt scurried onto the roof. He watched Hakem continue towards the tribe. After a few minutes, all he could see was the dust kicked up from the compact car. Waiting for the next few hours would be some of the longest hours of his life.

****

Majeed and Usman still had not found a South African

213

passport, but it would not stop them from working on the plane. Smitty and Buck would sneak out to the aircraft every day as one of the now over ten maintainers would serve as a lookout for Taliban. If they saw a car approach, the two non-Afghans would pull away a section of fiberglass insulation and jump into a rib section of the fuselage. They would then drop the canvas covering over them to the floor, presenting the appearance of an empty cargo area. It would take a keen eye to see the discrepancy, and should someone suspect something, both were hidden with their Glock handguns. A shootout in a plane one is trying to repair isn't ideal, but should the situation arise, they were ready.

Throughout the day, Buck worked with Raz and the team. Everything seemed in place for an engine start attempt, a critical piece of the puzzle if this C-130 was going to fly. Buck and Raz sat in the pilot seats, with the swing window open. They performed the appropriate checklists. When ready, Buck displayed a thumbs up to the crew chief on the ground, who returned it.

Buck reached up and said, "Turning," at the same time he pushed in the start button for engine one.

"Timing," Raz said immediately and stared at his watch.

Buck looked out and saw the propellers slowly turn. *'Come on, old girl. Come on,'* he thought.

The propeller slowly began to spin. Faster and faster it rotated. A puff of smoke burst into the air as she lit off and the RPMs, engine temps, oil pressure... all the gauges for the first engine began climbing.

"Allah Akbar!" Raz screamed.

Buck ducked, fearing for his life. Once he realized nothing exploded and he wasn't dead, he screamed, "Don't say that!"

"But it means God is Great or Glory be to God."

"Raz, Sorry. I mean no disrespect, but to U.S. military, hearing that phrase means someone is immediately going to die. Could you please find something else?"

"Sure, Buck."

The two watched the engine parameters, which were clearly in tolerances. Buck prepared to start engine two. He had far fewer expectations about this engine given the visible engine cowling combat damage.

"Turning." Buck

"Timing."

The propeller didn't budge. "Stop start," the ground crew chief said in broken English. Buck reset the engine for a start and tried again. The engine wouldn't budge.

"OK. Let's move onto engine three," Buck directed. The crew chief ran around to the other side and held up his thumb when the engine was clear.

"Turning,"

"Timing."

The crew chief immediately yelled on the intercom in Pashto, which Raz translated. "Stop! Fluid is leaking all over the place."

Buck obliged and that effort was terminated. "Well. I guess we'll move onto number four," Buck announced.

"Turning."

"Timing."

The propeller windmilled, faster and faster. Another puff of smoke and she lit off. Two of the four engines were running. *'Fifty percent,'* Buck thought to himself. *'Not bad.'*

After checking the operating parameters, Buck shut down the engines and looked at Raz. "Well, we got two out of four. Let's see if we can find the leaks on number three. As for number two, I'm worried something under that cowling is destroyed and jamming the propeller from turning. I wonder if there's another engine in Afghanistan. Are there still spare parts back on our old base?"

"Buck, I don't know, but I will send someone to look. I'll also have the maintainers work on number three's plumbing."

After a few hours of watching the Afghan maintainers, Buck was impressed. For many of the broken parts, they'd done an excellent job transporting them off the airfield and having them re-fabricated from local shops. No doubt, this is what they'd do with the pipes and hoses from the number three engine as well. Unfortunately, many of the larger or technical parts, such as a new engine, could not be locally fabricated.

Buck climbed down off the flight deck and went to the cargo

area. A ladder stood in the middle of the compartment with a crew chief on top working to reconnect the flight control cables. Slowly, the old girl was coming back to life. Every day, Buck was increasing the odds she'd fly again. He was up to 60/40 on his internal estimate, up from 30/70 just days prior.

Outside, one maintainer began yelling. Buck jumped into the cargo rib, fearing it was the Taliban. Raz ran into the aircraft, "Buck! It's safe! Come look! Come look!"

Buck exited the aircraft and looked outside. The main landing gear tires were repaired and under pressure. With Buck observing, the workers meticulously placed the wheels back onto their hubs, cranked down the lugs, and slowly let the jack down. For the first time in months, this C-130 was standing level on her own legs or landing gear. *'OK, 70/30 now,'* Buck thought. There just might be a chance that this old girl would be their ticket out of Afghanistan.

****

After a few hours, Curt could see Hakem driving back to the compound. He jumped off the roof, eager to hear the news. Hakem pulled into the center, parked the car, and got out.

"Well?" Curt said. "What did you find out?"

"Hello commander. Where is your friend, Mr. Mule?"

"He is in the carpet shack," answered Curt.

"Can we please get him? I'd rather only say this once." Hakem was somber.

Curt shook Hakem. "Tell me. Now!"

Hakem stared into Curt's eyes. He was in no mood. "Get Mule."

Curt feared the worst. He ran to get Mule and drug him back. "OK, Hakem, go."

"Sir. It was the Kochi tribe that Noorullah's family is in. I found his father, Bakht." Hakem looked down.

"Damn it! Tell me!" Curt demanded as he grabbed Hakem by the shoulders.

"Bakht said Noorullah was becoming too much of a burden and that the Kochi elders forced him to get rid of Noorullah."

Curt's eyes watered. "What does 'get rid of' mean? Did he kill his own son?"

Mule stood there, ready to either catch Curt should he collapse, or pull him off of Hakem if he attacked. Either was a viable option at this point.

"Sir, he took his son to Mirwais Hospital in Kandahar, which specializes in care for amputees, a few months ago. He told Noorullah it was a regular medical visit. Once Noorullah was with the doctor, Bakht left him."

Curt let go of Hakem and went to the carpet shed. He began grabbing his body armor, weapons, and gear.

Mule approached him, "Curt, what are you doing?"

"What do you think I'm doing? I'm going to find Noorullah," Curt answered with authority.

"No. You're not. And I'll fight you until you relent. I'm not going into Kandahar with you without better details and a plan. I also am not letting you go."

"The fuck you aren't." Curt was determined.

"Buddy, before we throw haymakers, listen to me. I got here and learned Saad was killed, hung by the Taliban. It was hard for me, and I am sure this is hard for you. That said, you're letting your emotions control you and putting yourself at significant risk. I'm not going to let you go."

Curt stopped packing. He knew there was little chance he'd win a fight with Mule, and even if he did, he would be in no condition to travel afterwards. It was all too overwhelming. His chin fell to his chest and tears trickled down his face. "I fucking missed getting him by fucking months!"

Mule put his hand on Curt's back. "It's OK buddy. It's OK." Mule walked away and went back to Hakem. They talked a bit, both expressing concern for Curt. As they spoke, Curt laid down on the carpets. He would try to fall asleep.

****

Alfi walked into Admiral Hershey's office with a small note in her hand. "Admiral, here is a number that Lieutenant General Ghani passed for you."

217

The Admiral looked up from the staff package he was reviewing and took the number. "Awesome. Thanks, Alfi."

He picked up his phone and dialed the international number.

Majeed's cell phone rang. As he looked down, it was a U.S. number. He answered in English, "Hello?"

"Hello. Who am I speaking with?" The Chairman asked.

"My name is Majeed. Who are you?"

"I'm Admiral Hershey. I'm trying to find a few Americans named Curt, Mark, or a guy named Buck."

Majeed was unaware that Smitty's first name was Mark, and he also knew Curt was far away, but he knew Buck, who was about twenty yards away. "Hold on, sir."

"Mr. Buck. It is a man for you. Some Admiral Hershey?"

Given Buck's brush with the Taliban, he was leery of any calls and was fairly certain he'd not be receiving a call from the Chairman. "Hello?" he spoke quizzically.

"Hey... Buck, is that you?"

"Yeah. Who is this?"

"It's Admiral Hershey."

"Yeah, and I'm Jack Daniels. Sorry buddy, I don't believe it for a second." Buck hung up the phone and tossed it back to Majeed. Within seconds, it rang again.

"Hello," Majeed said. After listening for a bit, he said, "Yes, sir," into the phone, then looked at Buck. "Mr. Buck, the man says I should call you Pooh Bear."

Buck froze. Only one person in his life called him that, and it was Admiral Hershey, a name he'd earned from his Balkan honeypot escapades. "Fuck!" Buck yelled.

Smitty raced around the front of the aircraft from where he was serving watch. "What? What are you saying 'fuck' to?" he yelled to Buck, concerned the Taliban were approaching.

"Nothing, Smitty, really. Other than I just hung up on the Chairman of the Joint Chiefs of Staff."

"You hung up on my boss?" Smitty asked quizzically. "Why in the hell would you do that?"

Smitty grabbed the phone from Majeed, who was still holding it out. "Boss!" he said. "Smitty here! How are ya doing?"

"I'm good. How are you guys? And before you speak, be cautious on this net."

"Sir, we're good. Just working on some things."

"Yes, I have seen photos to suggest that. I want you to know, should you run into any snags and need a gift or two, please reach out, but don't do it piecemeal. I need one list in one message, preferably from a random email account. Also, don't ask for something I can't deliver. Small things. Do you understand?"

"Yes, sir. And thanks. It's good to hear your voice."

"Yours too. Stay safe. This poppy crop thing is a mess, and I don't want you to get sucked into it."

"Yes, sir. We're trying to avoid that fray."

"Good. Let's break contact. Don't want to talk too long."

"Yes, sir. Out here." Smitty said. The line went dead.

Smitty threw the phone back to Majeed. "Majeed, delete that number out of your call logs." Majeed did as instructed and put his phone away.

"Well, it looks like Santa is coming early for us," Smitty said to Buck.

"Why's that?" Buck said.

"Appears Squirts is watching from above and has seen our efforts." Smitty pointed into the air when he spoke. It didn't take long for Buck to understand. "Should we need anything, he's asked for us to make a list and send it."

"Parts!" Buck yelled.

"Yes, Buck. Parts," Smitty replied.

Chapter Thirty-five
Not Without a Fight

Curt's watch vibrated, startling him out of his sleep at 0100Hrs. He'd set it before going to bed. Slowly, he arose from the carpets, not disturbing Mule. He put on his gear, packed up Hakem's car, opened the compound gate, then pushed the car out until it was 50 yards away. Once there, he started it, and drove away, heading southwest on the ring road towards Kandahar. He put the Mirwais Hospital in his Garmin GPS and followed the route.

Ten miles ahead, Curt knew there was a checkpoint at the border between Zabul and Kandahar province. He turned off his headlights, dropped his night-vision devices over his eyes and approached to approximately one mile. At that point, he cautiously left the highway and traversed on the sand, slowly around the checkpoint, watching to make sure he wasn't seen. He preferred not to have to kill anyone tonight, but should they try to impede this mission, they'd be facing a heavily armed and irrational man.

After skirting the checkpoint, Curt drove the car back up onto the ring road, turned his headlights back on and continued towards the city of Kandahar. As he entered, the streets were mostly empty. No cars, as the shops were all closed. He found the hospital. It was closed, of course, except for the Emergency Room. Curt parked the car and went in. Under his Afghan robe, he had both an M-4 and sidearm.

The receptionist, a male, greeted him, likely in Pashto, but Curt wouldn't know.

"Hello, I'm sorry, I only speak English. Do you speak English?"

The man nodded but was not sure who Curt was or what he was doing. Curt tried to put him at ease. "I'm from England and am here studying the Kochi tribe. I understand a few months ago a teenage boy was brought here missing a leg. His name was Noorullah. Might you have any information on him?" As Curt finished speaking, he lifted his hand, which held out a $100 bill.

The man's eyes widened. Again, he nodded, taking the money. He searched through the records. It was time consuming, as they were paper files. A computerized medical filing system had not yet reached Afghanistan.

He found Noorullah's file. "Mister. He has been here many times. I remember him. Months ago, he came in and then his father abandoned him. He was furious and cried, but we couldn't keep him. He was released. Since then, he comes here now and then, hoping his father has returned to get him. He's often crying, and I think he may now be into drugs. His is Kochi and others like... you know... Djipts.. Dji."

"Gypsies, I think you mean. Like Nomads," Curt helped him.

"Yes, 'Djipsies.' They leave the hospital and then are on the street.

"Sir, do you know where such a person would go here in Kandahar?"

The man nodded, then scribbled out something on a piece of paper. After he was done, he passed Curt a small hand-drawn map with three locations where the homeless typically congregated in the city. "Sir, I haven't seen him lately, but one of these three places is your best bet at finding a homeless djipsy."

"Thank you. I truly appreciate it. Please, I will give you this if you promise not to tell anyone I was here." Curt pulled out another $100. The man took it and nodded, having made more money in a few minutes than he would normally make in three months. Frankly, he wished Curt had more questions.

Curt walked out of the hospital judiciously, then stopped. He took a deep breath. A fast-paced walk at this hour would be alerting to observers. He needed to fit in. Slowly, he strolled to the first location on the map. It had at least fifteen homeless beggars, drug addicts, and vagrants. All were adults and clearly none of them could have been Noorullah. As he passed each, Curt looked closely at them. Some yelled in Pashto at him, then settled back down. *Was that a question? Am I supposed to say something in response?* he thought. His Pashto abilities were long gone, and he just didn't know. Curt was fearful to a degree, but there was no turning back.

221

He cautiously walked another few blocks from the hospital, following the map. As he strolled, two men passed him on the street, offering a small greeting. Both appeared drunk and disobeying Taliban law. Frankly, anyone out at that hour was likely disobeying the laws of the Taliban. Curt nodded with a smile and hoped it would be enough as he passed. It was.

In front of him were five homeless bodies, all knotted together in a web on the ground tucked next to a building. Curt looked over at the group. There was a teen-age boy, missing his leg from the knee down. He was asleep. *'Could it be Noorullah?'* Curt thought? Curt said the boy's name, softly at first. "Noorullah." Trying not to wake everyone. It grew louder. "Noorullah. Noorullah."

The boy awoke and looked at Curt. Once again, Curt said, "Noorullah? Kochi?"

The boy didn't know Curt but realized the man had accurately guessed his name and his clan. Noorullah nodded and managed a soft response, "Noorullah." As he did, his head fell sideways, and the boy tumbled over. Noorullah was clearly drunk or on drugs. He passed out again. Curt lifted his arm. There were a handful of fresh heroin needle tracks. Noorullah was starting his downward spiral to death.

By now, one other body had awoken and saw Curt. Slowly, Curt pulled out his Glock and before the man could say or do anything, Curt smashed it down on his head, knocking the man unconscious. Curt then picked up Noorullah, slung him over his shoulder and carried him away, back towards the car.

One arm over Noorullah, and one hand on his Glock, Curt continued, trying to recall the map by heart. He couldn't. He set Noorullah down, pulled out the map, kept it in his fingers, then threw Noorullah back up over his shoulder, still with the other hand securely on his Glock. As he walked, things were getting more familiar. There were only a few more blocks.

As he turned one of the last corners, a man approached from the opposite direction. *'Shit!'* Curt thought. There was really no discrete way to carry a limp body down a city street. Curt kept walking, waiting for the man to make a move or yell. Before he did, Curt thought he might also knock this man unconscious as well. It would be his first option should the man say anything.

The man was now within ten feet. Curt could see his face. The man smiled at Curt and said something in Pashto then smiled. Curt smiled back but couldn't understand a word. If he had, there may have been trouble. The man had said, "You found one for the night. Congratulations."

Curt could not understand a word of it, but realized there'd be no threat as he returned the smile and nodded.

The two passed. Curt's car was two hundred yards ahead. He continued as fast as he could without making a scene. Once at the car, Curt loaded Noorullah in and began the drive back to the compound. Again, he would circle around the checkpoint. It was 0400Hrs as he arrived back. Luckily, no one heard him leave. He pushed the car in and quietly grabbed Noorullah, carrying him to the large carpet outside. Laying behind Noorullah, Curt held the young boy next to his body to keep him warm, as if Noorullah were his own son. A tear fell from his eyes. The reason for his mission was now secure. Noorullah was safe. Noorullah had woken slightly and felt a warm body behind him. As he did, he reached back and began pulling his robes up, exposing his bare butt. At that instant, the man's smiling comments in Kandahar grew suspect to Curt. He pushed Noorullah's hand back down. *'My God,'* he thought. *'What horrors has this child lived through?'*

As the dawn shone over Qalat, Hakem exited his house and saw Curt laying there with a young boy. Enraged, Hakem began screaming, "No! Not in my house! You pig! You're filth! May Allah curse you!" Hakem started smacking Curt on the head and body.

The commotion awoke Mule, who exited the carpet storage area. He quickly grabbed Hakem, attempting to stop him.

"Hakem! No! This is Noorullah!" Curt yelled.

Hakem and Mule looked at Curt as if he were crazy. Curt calmed them down and explained what had happened.

"Doc," Mule said. "You are a freaking idiot."

"Yes. I know. But my soul is now at peace." Curt answered.

Noorullah laid there, sleeping through the entire episode. Curt picked him up and laid him on the carpets in the storage area, out of the sun. He checked the boy's breathing and pulse nearly every minute. As Noorullah lay there, Curt also tried to clean his wounds and lesions, many of them on his stump of a leg.

After a while, Noorullah awoke, scared. Hakem talked to him in Pashto, explaining what had happened. He detailed who Curt was and asked Noorullah if he remembered Curt. In fact, Noorullah did. Noorullah began to cry and said in Pashto, "You. Will you take me?" as he gestured to Curt. For months, Noorullah was alone, abandoned, and helpless. Anyone expressing even a hint of interest in him was a sign of hope.

Hakem translated the boy's comments. Curt put his arms around Noorullah and said yes. It was a touching moment, but Curt knew Noorullah needed significant help. He'd soon experience drug withdrawals from whatever he was high on back in Kandahar. If Noorullah was to get to America, he would need to learn English. They also needed a way out of Afghanistan before the Taliban found them. All this, however, would wait. Curt continued to hold Noorullah. He needed that hug more than he'd ever realized.

Chapter Thirty-six
Highest Highs, Lowest Lows

A day passed and the small fleet of Afghan maintenance workers had performed a number of additional repairs. Damaged panels were patched or replaced, and engine number three had the fuel and hydraulic lines replaced. The old lines laid on the ground under the wing, each with bullet holes or shrapnel tears clean through them. The maintainers had prepared a display for their 'South African' friend.

Buck arrived with Smitty and the interpreters. He looked at the progress made as well as the removed parts. Compared to the first time he saw her; the aircraft was impressive. Buck walked through the cargo area. He looked up and observed the flight control cables were repaired. Each had a screw tight crimp holding the separated cables back together. *'Well done,'* he thought. *'I just hope he matched the cables correctly.'* It was a valid concern. Cross controlling an aircraft proved fatal for an F-15 pilot back in 1995 that killed one of Buck's flight school classmates. Buck would check and double-check to make sure the cables were matched correctly.

As Buck looked up into the cockpit, all the broken glass windshields were replaced. Buck climbed up and ran his fingers over the glass seams. They were installed well. He smiled. For a brief moment, Buck reflected. He was proud of what he and the others had taught Afghans. The efforts were not in vain. They had learned and learned well.

"OK, Raz. Let's fire her up." Buck said.

Raz barked out orders, and the power cart was started. Power was applied, and the aircraft came alive. Buck and Raz sat down in the pilot seats and began the process to start engine three. The ground crew reported a small leak dripping out of the saber drain under the engine cowling. Buck dismissed this fault as residual fluid in the engine compartment and continued the process. With a massive burst of white smoke, the engine lit off. The propeller rotated faster as the RPM indicator climbed. The engine would settle well within tolerances and all the associated gauges jumped to life; except one. The main hydraulic system had pressure. The booster hydraulic system pressure gauge, however, remained at zero. The needle hadn't budged. *'I'll worry about that later,'* Buck thought. *'It's just the booster. I have the main hydraulics. All good.'*

"Disconnect power," Buck commanded for the first time. He wanted to see if the aircraft's internal power was sufficient. Normally, after starting one engine, it would be common to disconnect power, but clearly this situation, and this aircraft, were anything but common. A maintainer disconnected power. The distinctive 'click' in the headsets indicated when the aircraft switched to internal power. The power panel indicators were in tolerance and the generators were providing steady juice. All was good.

"Alright!" Buck said. "Good power." Buck pointed down at the primary hydraulics. "We have some hydraulics. Let's see if the flight controls respond," he said to Raz. Buck pulled back on the yoke. He watched the crew chief on the ground who gave him a thumbs up. He pushed the rudder left and right, also watching in his mirrors to ensure that the distinct large C-130 barn door rudder was swinging the correct way. The cross-cable concern was eased. The flight controls were moving correctly. Buck slowly put the controls through their paces, providing further inputs on the yoke and rudder. Turing left and right, the elevators responded smoothly. And the rudder pedals easily swung the monster barn door on the vertical stabilizer. As he moved the yoke and rudder pedals, the pressure indicator jumped around a bit. It was normal. Again, he tapped the hydraulic booster indicator with his index finger, hoping the issue was a loose wire. Nothing happened, it was dead. He would not let that minor issue get him down.

"Hot Damn, Raz. We got flight controls. Let's push our luck and try to start number two again."

With just number three spinning, the ground crew chief walked from the starboard side to the port side and ensured the number two prop was clear of personnel and gear. Once confirmed, he passed along a thumbs up. "You ready, Raz?"

"Ready." Raz replied.

Buck pushed the starter button as he gazed out the window at the propeller. "Turning."

"Timing" Raz replied.

"Stop Start," Buck said. And pulled his hand back. The engine again didn't budge. "Hold on, God Damn it. Crew chief, can you get the stand and see if some of you can move the prop just a bit? I want to know if it's truly frozen."

The crew chief did as instructed. After a few minutes, the stand was in place. Four Afghans pushed and pulled on the prop, one hanging on a blade, trying to get the thing to turn. With enough force, they were able to move it. Their efforts possibly unfroze the gears, an uncommon problem for C130s that regularly fly. A potential problem for an aircraft that has sat for over a year.

The crew chief reported that he had in fact, moved the propeller, if only inches. The stand was pulled away and Buck tried the start sequence again. The prop didn't budge. Buck gave up, shutting down number three and putting external power back on the aircraft. "Raz, can you get them to put the stand back in front of engine two? I want to look at it."

Raz would do as directed, and the scaffolding was returned. While that was taking place, Buck walked back to the cargo area. The young maintainer who repaired the flight control cables stood there, next to his ladder. Buck took the ladder and climbed up, grabbing the flight control cables firmly with both hands. He kicked away the ladder and hung there. The repair didn't budge. Buck let go and fell to the cargo bay floor. "Great job." He said to the young man.

The Afghan maintainers eyes were wide as saucers as he watched Buck's unorthodox method of quality control. He didn't understand English but given a stocky Buck didn't rip the cables apart, he smiled with pride. His work hadn't given way.

Smitty ran into the cargo area. "Buddy, we gotta hide. Get your handgun."

The two jumped into the ribs of the aircraft. The same local Taliban official again approached with his two henchmen. They approached Raz.

"May Allah be with you today, Raz."

"Yes, sir. Allah has been with us greatly. We have done a great job."

"Yes. I see, and I heard. The engines were recently running."

"Yes, we were able to get three of the four engines running, but one just won't start. We don't know why yet but are troubleshooting."

Smitty and Buck could hear the conversation, albeit in Pashto.

"Interesting. And I presume again, your South African friend is not here."

"No, sir," Raz replied. "He has been sick today."

"I understand. Well, you wouldn't have a problem showing me the engines running, would you? It must have been you who was recently running them if your colleague is sick."

Raz gulped, hard. He couldn't imagine starting the engines without Buck. "Sir, I can, but I must tell you, at some point, we need more fuel. We are too low to even do engine ground runs." Raz hoped this would appease the Taliban official.

"Raz, if you need more fuel, you shall have it. Show me you can start the plane."

It was a direct order and Raz knew if there was any way to save himself and Buck, he'd need to start the aircraft alone-a task he'd rarely done other than a few times long ago in the simulator.

"Yes, sir. As you wish." Raz barked out some orders. The scaffolding would be removed and all the external equipment other than the power cart would be removed.

"What's going on?" Smitty said.

"I think Raz is trying to start the freakin aircraft," Buck said. "That's the same phrase he used when I started it."

"Can he do it without you?"

Buck shrugged his shoulders. "We'll soon find out!"

Raz sat in the aircraft commander's seat, the only one that can reach the start buttons. The Taliban official stood on the flight deck, along with his two goons.

Raz called out the checklist in his lap, alone. There was no copilot to provide responses.

He looked out the window at the crew chief. They both knew

exactly what was wrong but continued the best they could. They traded two thumbs up. *'Turning One,'* Raz said in his head as he pushed the button. Out the window, he saw the propeller turn. He diverted his head back into the cockpit, watching the number one engine gauges come to life. Faster and faster, the RPM climbed, then the engine lit off.

Buck pumped his fist while still hiding behind the mat.

Raz was elated. He ordered the crew chief to disconnect power, growing more confident by the minute. Next, he directed an engine start on number three. *'Turning three'* he thought, and again the gauges came to life.

Looking back at the engine from the copilot window, the Taliban Official yelled, "There is fluid dripping from that engine." Raz didn't hear him. It was too loud. Next, he tapped Raz on the shoulder and yelled it again. Raz reached over his left shoulder, grabbed an extra headset and gave it to the Taliban Official, showing him the push to talk button. For a third time, the official repeated it.

"Yes," Raz replied. "We know. It is far less than what we found. If you look under the engine, there is a huge puddle. There were bullet holes in the lines."

The official nodded.

Raz was unstoppable. Into the mike, he ordered the crew chief to clear engine four. The man scurried to clear the engine and together they'd start it. "Turning," he shouted into the headset, growing more confident, and ensuring the Taliban official could hear. RPMs climbed, and the engine came online just like before. After they ran for a bit, Raz directed ground power to be reconnected and then cut the fuel to all the engines, slowing the windmilling and winding them down.

Turning around, he said to the official, "Is there anything else you'd like to see?"

"Yes," said the Taliban official. "I'd like to see your South African friend and thank him for this work."

"Sir, you will. I'm sorry he's been sick. On another note, who should we talk to about fuel?"

"I will send someone out later today. He will coordinate your request." The three Taliban climbed off the flight deck and drove away.

Raz ran back into the cargo area and ripped back the canvas cover. "I started the engines! I started the engines!"

"You're a rock star!" Buck said as he hugged Raz.

They celebrated, but Smitty stood there. He knew that time was not on their side, and eventually, the Taliban would catch them. He couldn't let that happen.

"Raz, have them put back the scaffolding in front of number two," Buck directed.

It was done and Buck climbed up. He pulled the cowling and tried to find the problem. The bleed air ducts had some superficial scarring, likely from shrapnel. As he looked under the engine, he finally found the problem. Two holes were clearly visible on the starter box that were not supposed to be there. It appeared as though a projectile round had pierced right into the starter and out the other side. It was toast. Only a new starter box would suffice. So far, it was the only piece Buck knew they could not source locally. Hopefully Admiral Hershey could come through.

****

The day in Qalat was progressing well. Through Hakem, Curt was able to learn much about Noorullah, and also share his personal story. Numerous times, Curt promised Noorullah that he'd care for him. The child was understandably insecure and scared. Yet, as the hours passed, he grew more and more at ease.

Mule walked over. "Here, have him try this on." Mule handed Curt a makeshift prosthetic he'd crafted out of scrap wood, one of his T-shirts for padding, and worn scraps of leather for anchoring it onto the leg. Noorullah's eyes lit up when he saw it. He blurted out something to Hakem, who translated that Noorullah hadn't had a prosthetic for years. He just learned to hop on one foot with a crutch.

Curt put it on, making slight adjustments, until he was satisfied it was good. "Hakem, tell him to stand up." Hakem did as instructed.

Noorullah stood up on both legs with no crutch. He smiled, and he cried. Hakem's son gently kicked a soccer ball at Noorullah, who used his prosthetic to kick it back. The wood struck the ball and redirected it. The pass was horrible, but it was the most exciting feeling Noorullah had experienced in years. The entire group smiled, clapped, and cheered. Noorullah grabbed Mule in a massive hug. It was clearly a 'Thank you' for his new leg.

After all the chatter, Noorullah was tired and asked Hakem if he could lie down. Hakem translated, and Curt obliged. Noorullah went into the carpet shed, leaving the others out front.

Hakem, Curt and Mule played soccer with Hakem's son. They could not have been happier with the way things were going. Later that night, they would have a call with Smitty and could start working a way to get out of the country.

Out of the corner of his eye, Curt saw the carpet shed door open and also saw Noorullah scurrying out of the shed, trying to jump over the compound wall and leave.

"Noorullah!" He screamed, quickly catching him and pulling him back off the wall.

"Noorullah! What are you...?" Curt stopped speaking, remembering the boy couldn't understand English. Noorullah was shaking. His eyes were dilated. The boy was anxious and fidgety. After a few seconds, Curt realized the problem. It was the same thing Curt experienced back in the Key West Hospital after being drugged with heroin.

Mule had run over, "What the hell? I thought he wanted to stay here!?"

"He does. But he's addicted to heroin. He'll do anything for a fix," Curt said. "Hakem, do you have any methadone? Or can you get some?"

"Commander, I do not, but I can run to the pharmacy right away!" Hakem directed his son into the passenger seat. He could not allow his son to witness the situation. The car roared away, leaving the gate open. Curt kept holding Noorullah, who was struggling to get away.

Mule went into the house, looking for water or anything else that could calm the boy.

As Curt and Noorullah sat in the middle of the courtyard, two trucks flew into the compound. Two Taliban from each truck jumped out and onto Curt. Noorullah scurried away while Curt continued the momentum of the roll from one attacker until Curt was on top. Just as he was about to punch him, gunfire erupted into the air. Curt looked up and saw AK-47 barrels pointing at his head. Slowly, he raised his hands in defeat. The initial four Taliban searched the facility, finding all their gear and taking it. They also searched the house but would not find Mule. He had swung out a window and climbed onto the roof of the house, hiding just behind the crest. As Curt held his hands up, he saw Mule's head crest over the roofline.

'*Damn it, Nover!*' Mule thought. Curt discreetly swung his head from side to side as if to say no. Mule looked deep into Curt's eyes. His desires were clear. '*We are outnumbered. Do not intervene. Just take care of Noorullah and take care of Allison.*'

The Taliban loaded Curt into the truck, kicking Noorullah to the side. One Taliban soldier would remain behind to question the owner upon return. Once questioned, the Taliban thug would likely kill Hakem. There was no place in Afghanistan for traitors who harbor Americans.

The trucks drove away. Mule stayed on the roof, watching the one remaining Taliban. After a few minutes, he slowly crawled down to the back side of the roofline to the bottom edge. Once there, he took off one shoe and threw it into an open window, then scurried back up the roof.

In the courtyard, the Taliban soldier was bored and entertained himself by kicking Noorullah. Startled by the shoe's clanking around in the house, he walked cautiously towards the house with his AK-47 raised to investigate. Once under the roof's edge, Mule jumped, falling directly on him. With a single blow filled with rage and anger, Mule knocked the man unconscious. As the goon laid there, Mule quickly tied up both the thug and Noorullah. He couldn't take a chance the boy would run again. Five minutes later, Hakem arrived with the medicine.

Hakem had seen the Taliban trucks go the other way, and his worst fears were confirmed when he spoke to Mule. Hakem fell to his knees, praying to Allah and begging for forgiveness. The failure he felt would be hard for a Westerner to understand. In Afghan culture, one who hosts a guest is responsible for them with his life if need be. He had failed. He was embarrassed and filled with shame. No Afghan would ever see him the same. He disrespected his clan, his home, and the way of the Afghan. Hakem's son tried to comfort him.

"Hakem!" Mule yelled. "Please, not now! Get the methadone into Noorullah. Then get Usman or Majeed on the phone. NOW!"

Mule started inventorying the gear that was left. There wasn't much. The weapons, ammo, night-vision devices and other items were gone.

Hakem walked over with his phone and handed it to Mule. "Hello!" he said.

"Yea, Smitty here, what's up?"

"Taliban got Nover." Mule said tactically, as if matter of fact.

"When?" Smitty asked, just as calculating.

"Five minutes ago. In Qalat."

"Alright. I'm on my way. Bringing Majeed." Smitty hung up.

Hakem took the phone back. "Mr. Mule. I am so sorry. It is all my fault. I am shamed more than you know."

"Hakem. Listen to me. I understand Afghan culture but stop. Seriously. I need you now, more than ever, to be the Hakem I knew just an hour ago. Curt needs you to be that man. Please!"

Hakem nodded. "I shall try."

"Good. Did you give Noorullah the methadone?"

"Yes, Mr. Mule. And he is in my house with my son, who is watching him."

"Good. Now, where is your wife?"

"She is at the market, like normal this time."

"We need to get her. The Taliban will eventually be back. They'll hurt you, her, and anyone who lives here, including your son."

Hakem began realizing the threat to his family and snapped out of his sorrow. He directed his son to run to the market and

233

retrieve his mother. Hakem ran into the house and started packing, just the essentials for now. When his wife returned, he told her what was going on. She broke down in tears. Hakem shook her. She eventually understood and began to pack.

Hakem departed the compound, retrieving his jingle truck from work. He quickly returned, pulling it into the courtyard. Rapidly, they threw everything they could into it. Once full, Hakem made one last trip into the house, carrying numerous rifles and shotguns. Most were bolt action, single shot, old models, but they were the best he had. He then put Noorullah in his compact car, along with his wife. Throwing the jingle truck keys to Mule, Hakem said, "Mr. Mule, you must drive the truck. I will drive the car!"

"Got it." Mule jumped up in the jingle truck. In the passenger seat was Hakem's son, who spoke no English. Hakem led the way out of the courtyard onto the ring road. They'd drive twenty minutes to a small farmhouse in the middle of nowhere. As they drove, Mule looked out at the poppy crop. It was completely dead by now. *'Jesus,'* he thought. *'What the hell did the U.S. do?'*

Once in the farmhouse, Hakem closed the gate and locked it. A man emerged from the dwelling. Mule recognized him but couldn't recall from where. After a few seconds, Mule realized it was Hakem's father. He lived alone; his wife had passed years ago. The farmhouse was all he had.

Mule, Hakem, and his son helped unload the truck and set up rudimentary fortifications. On his makeshift prosthetic and full of methadone, Noorullah also tried to help. They all feared the Taliban and had every justification to do so.

Once things settled down, Mule asked for Hakem's phone. He slowly typed out a text message, using the old keypad style of three letters for each number. It took nearly five minutes to get it right.

> *'Smitty –*
>
> *SH & Supls compromised. Tban has Doc. Stop 10k short of Qlat. Ring.*
>
> *Mule'*

Nearly instantaneously, Majeed got the message, but didn't understand most of it. He told Smitty it came in and handed the phone over. Smitty looked at it and said aloud. "Smitty. Safe-house and supplies compromised. Taliban has Nover. Stop 10 clicks short of Qalat. Call then. Got it. Thanks, Majeed."

In under an hour, Majeed would begin his long drive towards Qalat. He'd drive a bit over the speed limit, worried about his good friend, the commander. In the back, under the cargo and supplies, Smitty laid there, concerned he was leaving Buck, but at least Buck had a way to avoid the Taliban. Curt was captured. They drove through the night, passing checkpoints with little problem. Smitty knew that with Majeed at the wheel, checkpoints were easy. The next steps would not be.

Chapter Thirty-seven
The Interrogation

The Taliban covered Curt's head with a black sack as they drove him down the road. He could sense the driver's aggressive nature. As the truck swerved, Curt slid across the truck bed, rolling towards the feet of Taliban who were sitting on the bed walls. As he hit their feet, they kicked him back to the middle. He was only wearing a pair of Under Armour running shorts and a T-shirt. Eventually, the scuffs on his arm and legs began seeping blood from the superficial scrapings.

The ride lasted roughly an hour, and once the vehicles stopped, the Taliban pulled Curt out forcefully and threw him to the ground. The sunlight shone through his hood, and he could see he was in a suburban area. Buildings were casting shadows. He began to hear more and more traffic and construction work in the distance. He tried to absorb as much information as he could. There was only one place this large and an hour away from Qalat. He was confident he was in Kandahar, but where?

Eventually, he was picked up and dragged into a building. It was dark at first and then well lit. The Taliban threw him into a chair, then pushed it forward until the edge of a desk smacked against his ribs. Around him, the Taliban kept chatting in Pashto. Curt was annoyed and confused. They hadn't stopped their jubilant screaming since they first captured him.

The sack was eventually ripped off his head. Curt's vision was blurry, but soon cleared. He was staring at two men armed with AK-47s on either side of a man sitting right in front of him. The man was burly, clothed in a black robes and headdress. He was clearly Taliban.

"Hello," the man in black said, speaking perfect English.

Curt just sat there.

The man smiled. Then he said, "Hello, for a second time. And I won't say it again."

As he finished, the butt of a gun smacked Curt across the back of the neck.

Curt softly said, "Hello."

"Good," he responded. "You are American. Yes?"

Curt didn't answer. He knew he had no passport or identification on him. He had no weapon. Faking another nationality was an option, but that was not likely wise. He had nothing to support that narrative. Curt remained silent.

"I said. You're American military, right?" Again, the gun butt smacked the back of his neck. This time, harder.

Curt responded. "What makes you think I am American military?"

The man reached down into his lap and flipped a coin onto the table. As it landed and bounced around, Curt recognized it. It wasn't money, but rather Chief Cologne's military 'challenge coin.' It was in his running shorts, along with some local pocket change. The coin had a U.S. Air Force insignia and information about the Djibouti military installation. Curt's eyes made no indication, but in his mind, he thought, *'Fuck.'*

Curt tried not to acknowledge it meant anything. "I found it long ago. Didn't know what it was, so I kept it."

The large man laughed across the table. He was convinced Curt was lying. He said something in Pashto. Curt's hood was placed back on, and he was thrown into a small room. The door slammed and locked. Curt removed his hood, but his hands were still tied together. As he sat in the dark room, Curt could hear the chatter outside. It was in Pashto or Dari. Curt was angry he'd made such little effort to retain the language. It was too late to worry about that, however.

Curt tried to think through what the others were doing. Mule must have survived, and he'd contact the others. Smitty, Buck, and Mule had to be working on a rescue plan. *'Yes,'* he thought. *'That had to be the plan. But how will they find me? There's no chance Mule followed the trucks-maybe they'd ask around, try to bribe low level Taliban to discover my location... I'm fucked.'*

As Curt stood in his dark room, he could hear the Taliban pound on the door, and he started to smell urine. They were pissing at the base of the door, as the urine seeped over the threshold into the room. He could hear voices laughing and yelling. The urine kept coming until he was standing in it, barefoot. The laughing died down and the urine flow stopped. Curt had experienced worse. Then it hit. Electrical charges were shot through the urine he was standing in. His leg muscles buckled uncontrollably. He fell sideways, with his torso and face landing in the urine. Now the muscles on the side of his body flexed uncontrollably, receiving massive jolts of electricity into the muscles. Involuntarily, he'd smack his head against the floor and walls. The volts and amps shot through his entire body. It continued for a full minute, but Curt would be unconscious before the end. An hour or so later, he'd awake. His body aching, electrical burns on his skin, and laying in a pool of Taliban piss.

****

The Frankfurt stock market opened the day relatively flat; however, Myer Pharmaceutical rose roughly 4% on strong trading. Over the past week, it had climbed nearly twenty percent. That increase was in line with many other big pharma stocks, which had all benefited from the scare of the poppy crisis. By the time Andrew awoke in Virginia, Myer had gained another 1.2%, now up 5.2% for the day.

He rolled out of bed, brushed his teeth, and then headed down to the kitchen for coffee. As it percolated, he checked his phone. John had sent a text.

'We're still climbin!'

Andrew ignored it and surfed through the news. Another American was killed in Afghanistan yesterday; shot dead, execution style. The female was caught visiting family. She was a dual Afghan and American citizen. U.S. political pundits on every major news outlet denounced the actions of the Taliban, to no effect. The Taliban had been denounced so often; they had grown immune to Western criticism. The mainstream media, however, ate up the pundit's comments. The talking heads also warned viewers about the disturbing video, but felt it was necessary to show it. The clip was the female American shot dead by the Taliban. They freeze the video once the first shot rang out but were clearly comfortable showing the parts of her screaming and begging for her life. It made for great ratings.

The video disgusted Andrew. To him, the Taliban's response was more severe than he'd expected from the herbicide attack. He thought, 'It is what it is,' however. Andrew checked his financial accounts. Specifically, he checked his portion of Myer shares. Andrew had made nearly 29% from the time that he purchased the shares. The stock was increasing so fast he couldn't keep track of how many millions that was in profit.

He took a shower, sat down, and ate breakfast with Becky. It was a lovely morning. Andrew and Becky shared a long discussion that morning, one about morals, ethics, right and wrong. It wasn't the normal topic Becky would raise and Andrew was unsure as to why it happened on that day at that time... but something in that discussion swayed his heart. Perhaps it was his concern about Smitty and Nover in Afghanistan. Maybe it was his disdain for Andrew Gerzema and the Taliban. Perhaps he'd been in the game just a little too long. Whatever it was, he would act upon it. A change was afoot.

After breakfast, he surfed on his computer and within a few minutes, found the contact information for Allison Nover. As the clock struck 0900Hrs, he called her.

"Hello?" Allison said, as she wiped sleep from her eyes.

"Ms. Nover?" Andrew asked.

"Yes. Who is this?" Allison did not recognize the number or the voice.

"I'm sorry. I believe I woke you. This is Andrew Denney. It's 9 AM, and I mistakenly presumed you'd be awake."

"Mr. Denney. Yes, I understand. I'm actually in Arizona now, visiting my parents. It's seven AM here."

"I understand. I'll call later."

"No, please. Really, I'm not sleeping well. I had a rough night."

"I'm sorry to hear that. I was hoping to speak with you about a story, and I believe you are the perfect journalist to write it."

"OK. I'm honored." Allision was excited about the chance. Andrew Denney was one of the wealthiest and most powerful men in the beltway. No matter the issue, it would be a desired story.

"I'm looking for someone to expose some monumental corruption. You have an excellent reputation as being a level-headed and fair journalist. I am willing to meet, present all the evidence, and answer any questions you may have."

Allison couldn't believe her ears. It was as if someone had just dropped manna from heaven into her lap. "Mr. Denney, when can we meet?"

"I'm at your disposal, but I assure you there is no rush. There's no one that will scoop you on this story, and the only timing issue is trying to get the story out by June, but that's not critical. Pease, enjoy the time with your parents, and when you get back to D.C., we can chat."

"Yes, Mr. Denney, and thank you for your trust in me." Allison hung up and rushed into the kitchen. She let out a soft scream of excitement, trying not to wake her parents. Then realized her excitement was a bit much as she ran to the toilet and began vomiting. Once cleaned up, she made some tea and began checking for flights back home. Eventually, her father heard the commotion and came out of his bedroom.

"What's going on?" Paul said.

"Dad! I got a line on a major story! I'm so excited! This could be HUGE!" She jumped up and kissed him on the cheek. "Oh, good morning, daddy!"

"Well. Good morning to you too," Paul responded. "Um. A few questions. Is there any danger associated with this story?"

"No, Dad."

"OK. Is there any over excitement or adrenaline associated with this story?"

"No, Dad."

"OK. Does this story risk the birth of my grandchild?"

Allison jumped up. "No, Daddy. Seriously! I'm OK."

"One last question. Can you brush your teeth? That puke breath is killing me."

"Shut up, Dad! Look, I'm gonna find tickets back to D.C. Can you drive me to the airport?"

"I'll drive you," Paul said, "But you'd better clear all this with your mom first. She's got plans for you out through the next two weeks."

"I will. Thanks again, Dad."

Allison strolled back to her room and began packing. There was a flight out around 1000Hrs, and she'd be on it. Mrs. Flaherty wouldn't be happy, but she'd understand, just like any other mom.

Chapter Thirty-eight
Exposure

Buck and Usman arrived at the ramp, prepared to work another day on the C-130. Raz met them at the aircraft, full of energy and happiness, still beaming from his solo engine starts the day prior.

"Good morning, Buck!"

"The Taliban captured one of our team down near Kandahar."

Raz's happiness dissipated rapidly. "No! What happened? Who captured him?"

"Raz, I couldn't name one Taliban in your country, and I don't know what happened. Smitty and Majeed left last night to go link up with the rest of the crew there."

"I'm so sorry. Is there anything we can do?"

"Not that I know of," Buck answered. "Let's try and focus on the aircraft. What's happened recently?"

"We are topped off with gas, as of last night. I went up and checked. All the tanks register full, and the cross-feed valves seem to be able to transfer fuel around," Raz said proudly.

"Good. Um. Hey, do you have anyone qualified to be a flight engineer or load master for our flight?" Buck's question was realistic. These crew positions would be important for the flight.

"I have a few which had some partial training, but they don't speak English."

"Well, I guess that's better than nothing. I want to troubleshoot engine two today. Can we find the potential engineer and load master then fire up the aircraft?"

Raz answered, "Sure." He barked out some commands, and the team scurried to prepare the aircraft. The two that would serve as flight crew reported in front of Raz, who gave them their commands.

"Raz, also have the crew chief confirm the boost hydraulic system is full of fluid. I want to try and get that online, too."

"Sure thing, boss." Again, Raz ensured the orders were translated and understood.

242

The aircrew all assumed their seats and started the three good engines. Once started, Buck asked Raz to contact the airport control and ask to taxi to the runway.

"Buck, they aren't going to let us take-off," Raz answered.

"Raz, we are not going to take-off. Please, just ask."

Raz did as requested, and the tower allowed the taxi request, but told Raz there was no flight plan in the system for the aircraft.

"Correct, Ground control. We just want to move the aircraft around a bit." Raz replied.

Buck turned on the taxi lights, signaling to the ground crew he'd be moving soon. In front of him, one Afghan ground crew helped guide him out, waving his arms over his head and turning him right onto the taxiway.

The C-130 slowly lumbered out of the parking ramp and down the taxiway, with three engines spinning and one propeller standing idle.

"OK, Raz. Here's what we're gonna try. We are going to request a high-speed taxi down the runway. We are NOT requesting take-off. Do you understand?"

"Yes. A high-speed taxi," Raz repeated.

"Good. During that event, we are going to attempt to windmill start the number two engine using the breeze."

"Can you do that?" Raz asked.

"Well, yes, it's doable and we have a checklist for that. But it requires that the engine is cooperative, and the problem is just the starter," said Buck.

Raz relayed to the tower what Buck told him. The tower was hesitant, but eventually granted approval. In most airports, taking a long time on a runway would be denied, but given the lack of flights in and out of Kabul since the return of the Taliban, there would be no problem deconflicting take-off or landing traffic.

Buck stopped the aircraft short of the pavement line separating the taxiway from the runway. Once there, Raz made another radio call requesting for the C-130 to take the active runway. The request was approved, and Buck taxied out into a position similar to taking off.

"OK, Raz. Are you ready?"

"Yes, sir."

Buck turned to his freshly minted flight engineer. "Are you ready?"

The perplexed flight engineer didn't understand but turned to Raz for help. After a quick translation, the flight engineer's head nodded up and down with a smile.

'Christ almighty, help me,' Buck thought as he adjusted the pitch of the number two propeller blades for the start, ensuring they'd grab the air and start spinning. He also set up number two to fire off once Raz introduced fuel into the engine at the prescribed RPMs.

Buck revved up the number one and four engines, leaving number three alone. The last thing he needed was to deal with asymmetrical thrust as he was trying to start an engine that had not worked for over a year. Once at max power, he released the brakes, and the plane lunged forward. As it gained speed, the flight engineer who was looking out the window began yelling into his boom mic, 'Spinning! Spinning!" He was referring to the number two engine propeller. It was the one word he'd learned specifically for this flight.

Raz watched the engine revolutions climb on the engine two gauge. Buck was driving the aircraft down the runway via the steering wheel, his feet on the rudder pedals, and he was also watching the RPM gauge and hydraulics. "Now, Raz!" he commanded over the intercom.

Raz turned on the fuel and within seconds, the engine lit off. "Hot Damn!" Buck yelled out as he pulled the number one and four engines back to idle and then used the engine's reverse thrust to slow the aircraft. As Buck retained control of the aircraft like a rodeo rider, Raz continued the starting engine checklist. The number two engine gauges climbed into parameters.

"Raz, don't forget," Buck said. "Ask for us to clear the runway and taxi back."

Raz was so excited about the engine start, he'd overlooked communicating with the tower. Raz requested clearance back to the parking ramp, which was granted.

Slowly, the C-130 lumbered down the taxiway and began her turn into parking. Buck could see the Afghan maintainers jumping and cheering. All four engines were running strong. The C-130 herk was alive.

"Raz, we have one last check. We aren't shutting down yet." Buck looked out the window and gave the signal for the ground crew chief to plug in on the headset. Quickly, he did so and said something in Pashto. "Raz, tell him we are going to do a full power engine run on number two."

Raz did as instructed, and the crew chief cleared the other maintainers away from the aircraft and also a suitable distance behind the number two engine. After a minute, the crew chief returned and gave a thumbs up.

Buck slowly changed the prop pitch until the blades were at max power. The plane bounced a bit, wanting to move. Both Buck and Raz kept their feet firmly on the rudder pedal brakes.

"Damn," Buck said. "Just as I expected."

Raz looked down and then looked at Buck. "What is it? Is there a problem?"

Buck pointed down at the number two engine bleed air temp. The temps kept climbing and were rising faster. Buck quickly eliminated the torque on the propeller.

"OK. Raz, shutting down number two. Now!" Buck pulled back number two, cutting fuel and letting it spin down. "Crew chief, can you plug in external power and watch number two? It may catch fire," Buck said in English, forgetting the ground crew chief barely understood.

When Raz heard fire, he spun his head left quickly. In multi-seat aircrew aviation, there was an unwritten. Never say the word 'fire' on the intercom unless there is a fire or potential fire on the aircraft. Raz began translating in a tone with far greater concern than which Buck relayed the original message.

External power was connected, and Buck directed the shutdown of the other three engines. Once the other three stopped spinning, Buck said, "Raz, tell the crew chief to put the scaffolding up on number two again."

Buck unstrapped from his seat, climbed down off the flight deck and walked off the aircraft. He checked the tires for dead

245

spots, given how long she'd sat. Luckily, there were none. He looked over the port wing control surfaces for pinching in the metal, as well as the number one and two engines for any signs of stress or leak. Everything looked in order, and he walked to the other side of the aircraft.

It was there that he found the next problem. Hydraulic fluid was pouring out of the seams of the starboard wing. It was excessive. "Well, I think we have found our boost pump problem," Buck said out loud. The boost pump operated off the number three and four engines. Clearly, a line within the wing was ruptured. Buck concluded that all of his efforts with the brakes, rudders, and other control surfaces as he did the high-speed taxi start forced the fluid from the system. It would need to be repaired.

Somewhat ironically, the slight leak out of the number three engine remained, but compared to what was seeping out of the wing seams, it was insignificant. He'd ask for the maintainers to investigate it, but the dripping was truly not an issue. Buck chuckled as he thought about one of his old instructors, Rob 'Rocco' Ricci, who used to say, "As long as it's leaking, we know there's still fluid in her. When it stops leaking, then we need to worry."

By the time he was done looking over the aircraft's outside, the scaffolding was under the number two engine. Buck climbed up and pulled the engine cowling. It was hot, and as it fell onto the scaffolding, steam and heat poured out of the compartment.

"Raz, come here. Bring your best engine crew chief," Buck belted out.

The two climbed up and Buck pointed into the compartment. "Look here." He was pointing at the bleed air duct. "Look at the scorching. It appears the small arms fire has not only destroyed the starter, but also created holes in the ducting. We need to find a way to seal this up. If we can't, the plane could catch fire at a relatively inconvenient time... like, when we are in the air," Buck chortled.

Raz relayed the information to his maintainers, who'd take care of it. At least Buck had solved the number two engine and boost pump issue. He wondered if Admiral Hershey could come through.

****

Smitty and Majeed arrived at the farm of Hakem's father. Mule provided a full back brief of the last day's events. Off to the side of the large center courtyard, Smitty saw a boy missing a leg. "Is that Noorullah?" he asked Mule.

"Yup. That's him."

"What condition is he in?" Mule relayed that story as well. Once Smitty had all the information, he and Mule inventoried their assets. Mule had kept the AK-47 from the Taliban he'd knocked out, but it had limited ammo. Smitty had his long and short guns. He also brought three night-vision devices: his, Majeed's and Usman's. The rest of the weapons and gear remained up north with Buck and Usman. Hakem displayed the weapons he'd retrieved from his house, most of which Smitty wouldn't touch. He did ask Hakem, however, for ammo. Unfortunately, the only ammo Hakem had was already in the weapons. It wouldn't be anywhere near enough. Smitty told Hakem and Majeed they'd need to go find ammo tomorrow, and lots of it. He handed Majeed three hundred dollars.

Smitty then walked over to the 4Runner and pulled out a cell phone and new SIM Card. Once the sim activated and connected to the network, he placed a call he didn't want to make.

"Hello?" the other party answered.

"Hey, Boss. Smitty here."

"Smitty! Are you guys out yet?" Admiral Hershey asked.

"Not yet, sir. We ran into a problem. The Taliban captured Curt."

"God Damn It! What happened?"

"They rolled up on him unexpected. There was no chance to engage. The rest of the team is OK."

"Do you know where they are keeping him?" inquired the Admiral.

"No, sir. We were hoping you'd be able to help with that." Smitty answered.

"That's a big ask. Let me see what I can do. When was he taken?"

"Sir, less than 24 hours ago. I drove down to his AOR (Area of Responsibility) as soon as I heard. Once here, I got an update from the rest of the team, then called you. He was rolled up in Qalat. That's your starting point. Admiral, they're killing Americans here for no reason."

The Admiral paused. "Yes. I'm aware. Is the number I called you on before still good?"

"Yes, sir, that's my terp. But this is a burner. I'll kill the SIM once we're done talking."

"Got it. Give me a day. Out." The Admiral hung up, then leaned back in his chair. His anger for John Gerzema and his ridiculous herbicide operation would have to be put on hold. He thought for a second, then belched out, "Alfi!"

Col Andrade entered, "Yes, Admiral?"

"I need a secure video conference with Gen Etcher down at SOCOM ASAP."

"Will make it happen, sir," Alfi responded and walked out.

Admiral Hershey called Kathy, his wife. "Hey Kat," he greeted her, "How are you doing?"

"I'm good. How are things at the office?"

"Crazy as usual. Hey, are you still in contact with that gal, Allison Nover?"

"I still have her contact but haven't checked in. Last I talked to her was my trip to Tucson that you ordered," she said sarcastically.

"Yeah. OK. Well, just want to make sure you sti…" The Admiral stopped speaking as Alfi walked into the office.

"Admiral, General Etcher is waiting on your secure video conference monitor."

"Already?" The Admiral said. Getting time on any four-star flag officer's calendar usually takes days, if not weeks, even for other four-star generals. Admiral Hershey expected to wait hours, but Alfi was a talented executive officer.

"Sir, he had a wedge of ten minutes in his calendar," Alfi said as she was starting up the Admiral's video conference system.

"Kat," the Admiral said to his wife, "I'll call you back later."

248

He didn't wait to hear her goodbye. He then turned to his video system. General Etcher was on the screen with his staff at the table.

"Glenn, thanks so much for taking this call."

"For you Chairman, anytime. What's the issue?"

Admiral Hershey looked at the group with General Etcher. It was too many. "Glenn, any chance we can go four eyes?" A military term for a meeting between just two people.

General Etcher had no qualms and his staff quickly got up and departed. "OK, sir. Just us. What's up?"

"A former SEAL has been captured by the Taliban near Kandahar."

"That's not good," the General responded.

"Concur. And it's the same guy who helped us deescalate the issue with NISSASSA as well as the situation in Kosovo," the Chairman said.

"Nover? That's horrible news. Good guy, as I recall."

"Glenn. I need to ask, and I understand if you can't tell me outright, but are you running any ops in Afghanistan?" The Admiral was 99% sure he knew the answer. Normally he'd know of such things, but perhaps, by luck, there was one he was unaware of.

"Chairman, I'm sorry, but I am fairly certain we aren't," General Etcher replied. "If we were, it would be one of our Central Command forward deployed SOF units. I can reach down to the teams there and ask, but I believe I'm going to get the same answer."

"I understand," the Chairman answered. "Yes, please reach down to them."

"Admiral, just to be clear, do you want me to start working up a plan to go get him?"

Admiral Hershey sighed. "Glenn, I'd love you to, but I can't justify it at this point. We don't know where he is, we don't know if he's even still alive. Starting a plan at this point is far too late in the game."

"Admiral, I agree. Maybe with any luck there's a team there. Let me get back to you."

"Thanks, Glenn." The Admiral hung up on the VTC. He got

up from his chair, walked out of his office and through the CJCS front office. "Alfi, I'm going to the gym. Need to work off some stress."

Alfi looked down at the Chairman's calendar. It was packed for the next two hours, with many meetings. "Yes, sir." It was the only correct response. Once the Admiral was out of earshot, Alfi and the deputy executive officer began calling the officials with appointments and rescheduling. Such was the life of an exec.

Down in Tampa at MacDill Air Force Base, General Etcher directed his staff to set up a VTC with the forward deployed special ops units and base commands in the Central Command Area. Because of the time difference, the call would be the next day at 0700Hrs Eastern Time. General Etcher said a small prayer and headed home.

****

The Chairman was finishing up his workout at the Pentagon Athletic Center, running on a treadmill. Simultaneously, Allison's was walking through Reagan National Airport to recover her luggage.

As she walked, a crowd had gathered around one of the TVs. Breaking news on the mainstream media showed a captured American by the Taliban. A former Navy SEAL. Then the individual's photo was pushed on the screen. It was Curt. Allison fell to the floor in the middle of the airport. Pale and as if she'd seen a ghost. Quickly, airport security came to assist.

Admiral Hershey was also watching the TV in the Pentagon gym as he ran on the treadmill. He gritted his teeth, pushed stop and stormed back to the locker room.

In Arizona, Paul Flaherty saw the news as well. He turned off the TV before his wife could see the broadcast. A tear fell from his eye as anger ranged inside. It was the first one he'd shed in years. He was concerned for his little girl. He was concerned for Curt. Immediately, he booked the next flight to D.C.. He knew Allison needed him. He'd not let her down.

Andrew also saw the news. He knew Smitty had asked for

funds to go, but hoped his denial kept the team out. Now that he knew Curt's life was in danger, he felt even worse about his plan with John Gerzema. He knew he had made the right decision to call Allison and offer the story. This news cemented his decision.

At Masirah Island, Dirty also saw the news, and figured out why he was staying on the base. He'd tell Sleazy about the news. Sleazy, after watching it for a while would reach out to John Gerzema, his father, and ask what he should do.

"Dad, they got a SEAL," Sleazy said.

"I heard. I'm working on it," John replied. He was unsure what to do, but he was a savvy enough politician to realize he should never let a crisis go to waste. "Stay put. I'll come up with something."

It was late at Camp Lemonnier in Djibouti, but Command Chief Cologne was awake and also saw the news. He was still in his office. There was little else to do while deployed than work. Command Chief Cologne got up and walked down the hall to the commander, his boss. "Sir, did you see the news?"

"Yeah, Command Chief. I have a feeling it's why SOCOM called a meeting for all of us tomorrow at 0700 hours Eastern Time."

"Copy. Can I sit in that meeting? I think I have some relevant info."

"You do? Mind sharing it?" The commander asked.

Jason Cologne explained his relationship with the team in Afghanistan. The commander would ensure Jason had a seat on the VTC.

The Command Chief returned to his office and began working frantically on his computer. It would be a long night.

Chapter Thirty-nine
Technological Advantages

Usman and Buck sat at their safe-house for most of the day. Raz had invited the Taliban leadership to come out and see the C-130 repairs. Eight of them showed up. Raz and his group of maintainers stood around in traditional dress. No one dared wear their Afghan National Army uniforms. Even without uniforms, however, there clearly was a military culture in their actions. The team stood in a line, and every time Raz barked out a command, they'd respond quickly.

"Raz," one of the Taliban officials said in Pashto, "You and your team have done very well here."

"Thank you, sir. It was all with Allah's help and guidance," Raz replied. Raz partially believed that, but more importantly, the Taliban leadership needed to hear it.

Inside the aircraft, a few of the officials would go up on the flight deck. Power was on the plane, and one could see the critical instruments for flight; a gyro, altimeter, speed indicators, and such. However, several radios were pulled out, to include the Ultra High Frequency radios that could receive encryption or coded U.S. keying systems. Where the radios once sat were open holes with a few cables. Same problem with the navigator panel's INS and GPS systems. The officials were pleased with what they saw and returned to the ramp outside where Raz stood.

Raz again spoke, "Would you like to see me start the engines?" Raz pointed to go up into the aircraft again. Part of him wanted to do it.

"No, Raz. That is not necessary. But tell me," said the same Taliban official who had previously visited previously, "Can the aircraft fly?"

"Sir, right now, no. We only have three of the four engines running, and even with a fourth engine, we have a major bleed air and hydraulic leak. Once those are repaired, we still have no navigation systems and only a VHF and HF radio. Why do you ask?" Raz was curious if the Taliban commander wanted to fly.

"We have started socializing the fact we have a C-130 for potential sale to some customers. There is interest and some have asked if they can see it. As we first discussed, we must bring revenue into the government given what the infidel Americans have done to our crop. Sadly, their indiscriminate poisoning has also killed all the wheat, corn, and other crops vital to feed our people." This, of course, was not true. Such crops had never grown in the deserts of Afghanistan, even after years of USAID irrigation and soil projects to facilitate their growth. The truth mattered little, though. It was an easy way for the Taliban to create blame for the coming year's famine. It wouldn't be the Taliban's fault, but rather Americas.

"Sir," answered Raz, to the potential sale of the C-130. "Praise be to Allah! This is great news! It's not flyable yet. Perhaps the potential buyers can come once it flies? I want to have it as clean as possible and in the best shape. As you can see from the outside, we still need a few parts for the second engine, but those we hope can come in a few weeks."

"Raz, they will be here in a few days from Moscow. And according to them, three engines is enough." Although the Taliban official wasn't an aviator, he was right. A C-130 could theoretically take-off with three engines. Raz knew this. He also knew it was unsafe. Technically, most multi-engine aircraft can take-off with one engine. One would require only a low level of intellect to arrive at such a decision, however.

"Yes, I have heard of such, but it is extremely dangerous. I don't recommend it."

"Raz, I understand, but this is not your concern, or mine. If they pay, I don't care if they fly it or set it on fire." The other Taliban officials laughed, but the maintainers who worked for days to get the plane ready gritted their teeth.

Raz tried to fake his response. "Yes, sir. Of course, that makes sense."

"Raz, one more question," the man said. "Where is your South African friend? I wish to thank him for all his help."

"Sir, he is feeling better, but not here right now."

"It seems odd that you'd schedule such a high-level meeting with our delegation and not have him here."

Raz didn't know how to answer. Just then, a Toyota 4Runner approached, honking its horn. They all turned. It was Usman and Buck. Raz's eyes grew as wide as saucers, as did the rest of his Afghan team.

The car parked, and Buck walked over. "Hey, sorry, I wasn't here earlier. Still trying to get over this... illness. A bugger of an infection." Buck rubbed his stomach. "Loose bowels, ya know. Been shittin' nonstop for 'bout a week. A huge arsefire if you know what I mean, mate!" Buck extended his hand to the Taliban official, which was reluctantly accepted.

"Ahhh, it is good to see you. I've told my colleagues here all about you. By the way, you wouldn't have some sort of identification." It wasn't a request, but rather a demand.

"Sure do, mate!" Buck reached into his pockets, searching around, then finding it. He pulled out a ragged and used South African Passport. The man looked a bit surprised, handing it to one of the others for a closer look.

"Ah, yes, South Africa. What part do you come from?"

"Grew up on Jeffrey's Bay, on the water. Surfing wasn't my bag-a bit frightful of the sharks, mate. Mountains and deserts are my game. It's why I'm here." Buck's story was tight, and his accent had improved. There'd be no way to question him unless any of the Taliban had personal knowledge of the South African southern coast. None of them did.

Buck's passport was returned, and he put it in his pocket. The Taliban official, now somewhat appeased that Buck wasn't American, shifted his questioning. "Raz says the aircraft isn't flyable right now. Do you agree?"

Buck looked at Raz, proud he'd answered correctly. "Raz is right. I wouldn't fly this thing right now. Currently, we only have three engines and one hydraulic system. The booster hydraulic system is dead. There's likely a massive leak somewhere in the wing line. Also have a bleed air issue. We are waiting on parts. Also, not sure if you heard, but we got the number two engine started on a high-speed taxi. Clearly the starter is shot, but even with that the bleed air ducting started overheating immediately. She's far better than she was, but we just aren't there yet."

"OK. That's helpful. Thank you. And on behalf of the Taliban, I want you to have something." He waved his hand at a lower-level colleague who ran back to the cars, pulled something out, and ran back. It was a small wooden plaque with a Taliban Afghan symbol in the middle.

Buck took it graciously as if it were a gift he would treasure forever. "Sir, I don't know what to say. Thank you for this."

"Allah has blessed us with you. It is the least we can do is share in His blessing. Gentlemen, we must leave. Inshallah, we will soon have our aircraft sold. Perhaps after this you can work on the other aircraft."

Buck spoke quickly. "Sir, that would be wonderful. I'd love to help and perhaps we can talk about some small amount of compensation. I want to do all I can to help the Taliban gain a flying ability."

"Buck, that's a very nice offer," Raz replied.

The Taliban official stopped in his tracks. A stern look grew on his face. "Buck? Who is Buck?"

Raz's eyes grew into saucers. He'd just screwed up Buck's alibi.

Buck spoke, "Sir, I am. Buck is my callsign. My real name is Daniel Hejda, just as Raz introduced me. Funny story. Once I made a pancake the size of a manhole cover, just like John Candy's character, 'Uncle Buck.' Since then, everyone has called me 'Buck.' Nothing much to it."

The official was not truly convinced, but had no information counter to Buck's claim. "Well, yes. Mr. Buck, yes. We can discuss further cooperation. You are too kind." With that, the Taliban group departed and would certainly run a full background check on 'Daniel Hejda' from South Africa.

Buck turned to Raz. "How did I do?"

"Buck, you were incredible, but where did you g......

Buck cut him off. "Usman is the MAN! One of his contacts finally found a counterfeit South African passport."

"OK," answered Raz. "But your British dialect, your friendliness and the offer to help? It was such a good act."

"Buddy, I may be a bit of a nut, but right now, I want to kill every Taliban I see. I just keep thinking we're pirating that

255

airplane out of here and taking millions out of the Taliban's checkbook."

"Well, I'm glad you did well. But what is a checkbook?"

Buck chuckled and put his arm around Raz. "OK. Let's try another high-speed taxi, fire up that number two engine, and check the duct work repair."

"Yes, sir. But the boost pump lines are not fixed."

"Not an issue. Utility hydraulics are good enough for now. Let's just leave the boost pump reservoir empty until the lines are repaired. No need to piss hydraulic fluid all over the airfield. Come on! Let's fire her up!"

****

General Etcher sat at the end of his conference table. Across from him were numerous flat screens on the wall, each with conference tables at other locations, all identified at the bottom of each screen: SOCCENT (Central Command Special Operations Command), Pentagon, the service's SOF entities-AFSOC, USASOC, USNSWC, MARSOC, then the in-theater small locations like Djibouti and others. At each table sat a few folks. The atmosphere in each room was somber. Everyone knew about Curt's abduction, and they were all aware as to what his future would hold without some form of intervention.

"Good morning to those on this side of noon, and good afternoon to those on the other," General Etcher started. "Please look around your rooms. This meeting is classified at the Top-Secret level and specific to only Afghan and CENTCOM clandestine operations." There was a pause to make sure only the folks with the right 'tickets' were in the rooms. "I wish to begin with an intel brief to ensure everyone is on the same sheet of music as we progress through this. Before that starts, however, I'm fully aware many of you know Curt Nover, and I know how you feel. But I implore you, this is not the time or place to let your emotions dictate decisions." General Etcher paused to ensure his message got through. "OK. Please begin with the intel brief."

Over the next ten minutes, a SOF intel officer gave as much detail as possible about the abduction. Many pieces were missing, which was part of the reason for the videoconference. After finishing, the intel officer offered to take questions. There'd be none. Most of what was in the briefing was also available in the local media.

General Etcher began again. "So. Now that we are all synced up, the Chairman has asked what options we as a community may have to assist in this situation. I owe him a response in a few hours. My first question is, does anyone have current ground ops in Afghanistan?"

Slowly, each location checked in. "No, sir." "No, General," No, sir." After a brief while, each had checked in. It was clear. There were no ongoing ops.

"OK. Does anyone have teams that are able to move on an objective in twelve hours?" He asked.

A visible sigh was let out from each location. The General had tipped off he wasn't sure Curt would live beyond the next twelve hours. From initiation to target, twelve hours was unrealistic even for U.S. SOF. Again, all the answers were 'no.'

"I understand," the General responded. He was frustrated, but there was no one to blame. It was what it was. "Look, we know Dr. Nover was part of a small team. He was the only one captured. We have limited comms with the remaining team members. They include a former SEAL, former Army Special Forces bubba and an Air Force AFSOC pilot. Is there any way we could provide them with overhead support via a UAV or other assets?"

"Sir, Pentagon here. We may have some imagery we can share, but we'd need to get it declassified, or we'd need to get it to the team members via a secure means, which unfortunately, I don't believe exists in that country any longer. And even if we had a drone overhead, I am not sure what medium we have to push the info to them. Do we know what radios they have?" The Pentagon official was correct. Even if imagery existed, there was no conduit to push it to them.

General Etcher was running out of options. "Pentagon, you're right. At this point, I'm grasping at straws. OK. I'll make

257

this as broad as I can make it. Does anyone have anything?"

"General Etcher, sir, Brigadier General Hill here in Djibouti. I think we may have something, and I'd like to turn the mic over to Command Chief Cologne."

"OK, Command Chief," General Etcher said. "What do you got?"

"General Etcher, sir. Good morning. On the way into Afghanistan, Dr. Nover and his crew came through here. We helped them secure resources and seek further travel. They were equipped with JTRS radios, which answers the Pentagon's question. But there's more. Before they left, I gave them each one of my challenge coins and pleaded with them for each to carry it as a gift to me. Well, those weren't run-of-the-mill challenge coins. While deployed here, I worked with a young airman who's a tech wiz, Senior Airman Gonzalez. In his free time, he learned how to crack Apple AirTags. He also figured out how to access the coding, allowing him to disable their reporting function to unpaired iPhones. For fun, I asked if he could imbed the AirTag chips into a few of my challenge coins. He did it, and those are the coins I gave Dr. Nover and the team. Upon hearing the news about the abduction, I searched for those four AirTags on my Apple account. I'm showing two in the vicinity of Qalat, one in Kabul, and one in Kandahar." The video conference operator in Djibouti flashed a screen grab from Chief Colon's phone. Jason continued. "Based on the intelligence briefing, I believe the AirTag that was with Dr. Nover is the one in Kandahar, and if it is still on him, he's within three meters of the device as of 15 minutes ago. Sir, Djibouti, over." Jason hit the mute button and sat back.

Lieutenant General North, the AFSOC Commander had heard enough. "General Etcher, sir, AFSOC here, Lieutenant General North. I apologize for this intrusion and want you to know, I in no way authorized the use of such experiments. Hell, for all we know, the Taliban could have tracked him down from these AirTags." Lieutenant General North could not have been further off base or failed worse at reading a room or a videoconference room.

"Gerry," General Etcher said, addressing Lieutenant General

North. "Stand down." Many of the eyes on the video conference screens tried very hard to hide their shock. In the civilian world, those words meant nothing, but in the military, that was a public dressing down of a Lieutenant General from a General, about as rare as a Wookie sighting. Lieutenant General North fumed. After the VTC, he'd remedy the situation with Command Chief Cologne, he thought. None of his subordinates would upstage him.

General Etcher continued, "Command Chief. How certain are you of this? I confess, I'm not well read on the AirTag device. Can you explain it further?"

"Sure, sir," Jason responded. "AirTags work in a fairly passive mode, relying on nearby iPhone or Wi-Fi devices. Every so often, they 'ping' a local device, then report their location passively through that device to their owner's Apple account. Given they work on the same frequency as Wi-Fi and at a minimal power and pulse duration, they are extremely hard to track, especially if they are in the vicinity of an iPhone or a dense Wi-Fi environment. In Afghanistan, the networks aren't that great, so I don't have continuous access to the AirTags. That said, there seems to be enough, and ironically the Taliban smart phones are likely the culprits exposing Dr. Nover's location. As of right now, the most recent ping update shows five minutes ago. Oh, and the password I used for these is 256bit encrypted, which is fairly standard. I'm not sure the Taliban, or anyone for that matter could crack it, especially in a few weeks."

General Etcher was elated. "OK, Command Chief and Djibouti, you stay on the videoconference. All other stations disconnect."

Lieutenant General North wasn't pleased. "General Etcher, I'd like to remain connected if able."

"Gerry, I understand that, but I'd rather have a smaller group given the sensitivities of this issue. I'm sure you understand."

Lieutenant General North didn't. He desperately wanted to remain on that conference call. "Of course, General," he said as his staff began the process to disconnect from the call.

General Etcher and Jason continued speaking, now the only two remaining. Over the course of the discussion, General

Etcher would bring some Electronic Warfare Officers and Cyber Officers into the video conference room. As the conversation progressed, he grew more and more convinced he could soon deliver at least something to the Chairman.

Chapter Forty
Caring for the Novers

Curt awoke, cold and shaking. A bucket of water was splashed over him as the door was opened. He was drug out from the room, hands still tied, and placed in the same chair he was interrogated at before.

"Dr. Curt Nover. Well, it is nice to see you again. And such an amazing resume. Navy SEAL, medical doctor, and a national hero for being global do-gooder." His interrogator slapped down an iPad onto the desk showing news articles with Curt's photo. There was no way to hide his identity. At this point, if he wanted to make things better, he'd need to begin to communicate. "Yes. That is who I am."

"Very good. I'm glad you've found your vocal cords. Now, can you tell me why you and your nation destroyed our crops?"

"Sir, I have no knowledge of the crop destruction. I am no longer in the government and took no part in that. I am not even certain it was the United States."

A large two by four swung around, slamming Curt in the back. Clearly, his answer was not believed.

"I will ask you again....

Curt cut him off. "My answer won't change. I won't lie to you. It serves neither of us any purpose. I am not protected by the Geneva Convention and even if I was, you don't recognize it. If you ask me the same question, you will get the same answer. You appear to be a smart man. Even if the U.S. did this, it would take thousands and thousands of pounds of chemicals, and hundreds of people to disburse it. You found me alone with a small boy. Hundreds of people versus me and a small boy? The stories don't match, and it would take a stretch to get them even close. I had nothing to do with your crops. If you don't believe me, fine, but please, save us time and beat me until I pass out again."

The Taliban interrogator smiled. He was impressed with the answer. "OK, Dr. Nover. Why are you here? How many are here with you and what do you know of the man Hakem who was protecting you?"

Curt took a pause. He now had to find a way to not lie but also protect his friends. "Sir. I came here with two others. I didn't know them well. We all came to meet and seek out someone. In my case, that was Noorullah, a Kochi child. I'd helped him years ago and wanted to see how he was doing. I had no nefarious plans." Curt tried hard to change the subject to Noorullah and away from his team.

The interrogator turned and grabbed a large backpack and dumped its contents onto the table. Curt's short gun, tactical radio, night-vision devices, body armor, and other pieces of military gear fell out. Secured alongside the bag was his rifle. It made a thud as the Taliban official dropped the bag onto the table. "OK. If you're telling the truth, explain this. Seems like a massive amount of firepower to find a small boy."

Curt looked nonchalantly at it. He was far less phased by the gear than the interrogator expected. "Sir, my story is the truth. I have these items because your country has recently not proven to be the most welcoming to Americans." Curt paused and looked around. "As one could surmise by my detainment."

Another whack of the board hit his back. Curt winced, but it was worth it. He smiled.

"You have not answered all my questions," the interrogator demanded. "Who did you come with and what of Hakem?"

"Sir, I've answered. My focus was on finding Noorullah. I was captured alone. I don't know where the others went and, to be fair, they don't know where I went. It's not the easiest to get into your country. The man with the mules at the border was where I met them."

"What man with mules?" The interrogator asked.

Curt, in great detail, shared all he could about crossing the border. He knew he was giving up a friend of Majeed's but that was a far better discussion than giving up Majeed himself, or Hakem. Curt described the house, the town, the safe-houses on either side, the color of the mules, what the mules ate, how they navigated the pass.

After five minutes, the interrogator had heard more than he desired about the mule man. "Enough. You're stalling. This man, Hakem. What do you know about him?"

"I know very little," Curt said calmly. "I held a gun to his head and made him take me in. Once I was inside, he fled." This was clearly a lie, and one that would be risky should Hakem ever be caught.

"I don't believe you!" the interrogator said, as he stood, pushing the chair back. Two of the goons ripped Curt up out of the chair, flipped him over, and shoved him down onto his face. Two more Taliban converged over Curt, and all four held him down. The open lesions on his skin stung as they rubbed hard against the dirty table. Two of the Taliban ripped off his pants and grabbed a toilet scrubbing brush. Forcefully, they shoved it in and out of his anus. Curt could do nothing. The Taliban laughed and cheered. After they were done, one of them grabbed him by the nostrils and pulled his head back, forcing his mouth open as another held his chin. They then began shoving the brush in and out of his mouth. He'd gag on it until he began puking. Curt did not resist. It was pointless. He closed his eyes and blocked his mind from what was happening. The Taliban were subhuman to him. This was all a horrible nightmare.

The Taliban finished their ritual of humiliation and threw him back into his urine covered cell. After throwing him in, the interrogator stood at the door. "Pray to your God tonight, because tomorrow, you will die for your sins and the sins of your nation under the watch of my God."

The door closed. Curt laid there. It stank, and he was in pain. But he was finally alone. He tried to look around for any escape opportunity. He'd find none. He took the interrogator's suggestion though and prayed. He prayed hard, like he'd never prayed before.

****

Back in D.C., Kathy Hershey's phone buzzed. It was a text message from an unknown number with a 702 area code.

'Kathy,

I'm not sure you remember me, but I am Allison Nover's father, Paul Flaherty. You visited a week ago. Allison is now in Georgetown Medical Center. I'm on my way to D.C. now but would welcome anything you can do to help her.

Thank You
Paul'

Kathy immediately called the Admiral and informed him. Once the news about Curt became public, she'd called Allison many times with no answer. Now she knew why. Within fifteen minutes, she was out the door and on her way to Georgetown.

Upon arriving at the hospital, Kathy found Allison asleep in a bed, with an IV and other medical devices hooked up to her. Kathy stopped a floor nurse and demanded answers. "Hello," she said. "I'm friends with Allison, can you please..."

The nurse cut her off. "Are you family?"

"No, but they are on the way," she answered.

"I'm sorry. But I can only discuss the patient with the family."

"OK, fine, can you please tell me if the baby is OK?"

"Ma'am, I can't tell..."

"Look, God Damn it. The fetus does not have freaking HIPPA protection yet. It's not born! Tell me now, or I'll have fifty lawyers here crawling on this floor." Kathy belted out. "I'll play this freaking game with you all day long! Tell me if the baby is OK!" The nurse looked behind Kathy and saw two secret service members standing motionless, wearing sunglasses in the hospital. The threat was a bluff, but with two close protection team members, it was a good one.

The nurse was taken aback. "Yes. Yes, ma'am. The baby is fine. Ms. Nover is sedated and will probably not wake for a few more hours."

"Thank you," Kathy replied. "I appreciate it."

Kathy called the Chairman and shared what she'd learned. They agreed Kathy would remain at the hospital with Allison until Paul got there. It was the right thing to do. Paul was already on the red eye through the night. He couldn't wait until morning.

Chapter Forty-one
Not the A-Team

The phone on Colonel Andrade's desk rang. She answered as usual. The party on the other line jumped on, "Good morning, Colonel, this is the office of the Secretary of State. Would the Chairman be available to take the Secretary's call?"

"Please standby," Alfi answered and placed the call on hold. Next, she walked into the Chairman's office, disturbing a meeting with the Vice Chief. "Sir, I'm sorry to bother you, but Secretary of State Baker is on the line and has asked to speak with you."

The Vice Chairman jumped up and rapidly excused himself. Admiral Hershey raised the handset to his ear.

"Secretary Baker, good day. What can I do for you?"

"Admiral, hello. Yes. I wanted to talk to you about the American being held hostage in Afghanistan, a Dr. Nover. I understand you know him and, if I recall, I think he was the one who helped deescalate the Kosovo issue."

"Yes, ma'am, and expose Nissassa. He's the one."

"According to allied embassies in the area, we've learned the Taliban plan to execute Dr. Nover tomorrow. We've sent demarches and have sternly worded diplomatic messages demanding the immediate release and are doing everything we can."

"I appreciate that Madam Secretary. I don't suppose you have any assets in theater than could potentially help us."

"I'm sorry, we don't Admiral." The Secretary paused. "But I'd offer, I think you may want to speak to Gary up in McLean."

The Admiral's eyes popped open. *'Yes! Why hadn't I thought of that?'* "Great idea, ma'am. And please, keep the diplomatic pressure on."

"We will. Good luck." The Secretary hung up.

"Alfi!" The Admiral yelled. "Get me Director Hamilton on the STE (Secure Terminal Equipment / Phone)."

Alfi yelled back in, "Yes, sir!" After a few minutes, the phone patch was put through, and Admiral Hershey was speaking with the Director of the CIA.

"Gary, hey, thanks for taking the call. It's a bit pressing."

"I was wondering when you were going to call," Director Hamilton replied. "I have a few toys set up for you if you want them. To be clear, I can't pull any of my manpower off of their missions, but I have a few overhead assets that could be of use."

"Perfect. Last known location was around Qalat and Kandahar. I don't …"

Alfi knocked at the door. "Sir, there's a call."

"Not now, Alfi! I'm on with…"

Alfi stopped him. "Sir, I truly believe you'll want to take this."

The Admiral was annoyed but took Alfi's advice. "Gary, can you hold one second?" Director Hamilton agreed.

The video conference screen in his office came to life. "Admiral. General Etcher here. I have some news for you."

"Great. Glenn, what do you have? Please be quick, Director Hamilton is on the other line."

"Sure." The General switched his screen to a map display. "Sir, the circle is where we believe Dr. Nover is being held. 75% confidence."

"Jesus, Glenn! I have no idea how you do your shit, but I'm glad you're on our side. I gotta let you go. Send that to my high side email." 'High side,' was a common phrase muttered among military referring to their classified email and internet systems.

"Sir, already on its way."

The Admiral switched over. "Gary! OK. I have potential coordinates for where they're holding Nover. I'm going to send it to you. Can you set up an overhead watch for a while?"

"Sure. I'll have eyes over Kandahar in about three hours. Will let you know what we can assess." The two hung up.

"Alfi!" The Admiral again yelled.

Col. Andrade entered as she always did with a sense of haste, holding a notepad and pen in her hands. "Yes, Admiral?"

"Just wanted to say you're doing a good job." The Admiral smiled. So did Alfi. "Now, get me that number to the Afghan guy running around with Smitty."

Alfi did as requested, and within a few minutes, Majeed had handed the phone over Smitty, "Sir, Smitty here." The Admiral could sense the despair in his voice.

"Smitty, knock that attitude out of your mouth. Look. Get some paper. Let me know when you have it." The Admiral waited until Smitty was ready to write. "Good. Now, write your work cell phone number across the top starting with the 'seven.' After that, write any number between zero and nine NOT already used in numerical order." The Admiral was establishing a code. "I'm certain you'd be interested in going to the latitude that starts with your third number, the number 4, your seventh number, your fifth number, your ninth number...." The Admiral rattled off the exact latitude and longitude for the location for Curt. Smitty didn't ask how his boss knew, he was just happy he did. "OK, Smitty. Now, what parts do you need to make Buck's jalopy run?"

Smitty pulled out what Buck had sent earlier. "Sir, we need a number two starter and booster hydraulic system lines – a bunch of them. Does that make sense to you?"

Smitty, I'm in the Navy. I have no clue, but I know someone who will. Got it. Good luck." The Admiral hung up quickly. The Taliban's ability to track, trace and monitor calls was limited, but it existed. Again, Majeed deleted the call from his phone records.

"Mule, pack up. Let's go. I think I have a line on Curt's location."

"What?! Dude! Even if you do have his location, we can't just go in without a plan!"

"No shit, Sherlock," Smitty replied. "I want to drive by it, though, and see what we are looking at. Come on!"

Majeed, Smitty, and Mule loaded up and drove to Kandahar. At about a mile prior to the location, Smitty set his iPhone, still in airplane mode, up on the dash with video recording. "Drive slowly, Majeed. We're only passing this place once."

Majeed did as instructed. Mule and Smitty softly called out what appeared to be potential guards, providing overwatch. "First perimeter, two hundred meters, two men standing on the corner. One on the roof opposite side, 100 meters out." Smitty kept talking.

"Jesus, seven out front; three with visible rifles," Mule said.

"Keep driving Majeed. Keep driving. Don't stop. Even if they ask."

The vehicle passed with only a few odd looks. Majeed continued for a mile, then stopped on a desolate side street.

"Smitty. That was some serious firepower," Mule said.

"Yeah. I agree." Smitty thought for a second. "Majeed, drive back in, but go down the road on the back side of the building."

"Mr. Smitty. I can, but there are other buildings that back up to it. You won't see anything."

"Majeed," replied Smitty. "I hope so. I'm counting on it."

Again, Majeed drove back, and Smitty recorded. There were only two individuals who even remotely looked like they were part of the protection force. Once the team had the videos, they returned to the compound in Qalat, roughly an hour's drive. Smitty and Mule sat in the back, watching the video over and over, discussing tactics and options for the avenue of approach, access points, as well as an escape route. It wouldn't be easy, but they were determined to try.

****

The next call the Admiral made was to Masirah Island. "Dirty, Admiral Hershey here. I need you to get a number two starter and lines for the booster hydraulic system onto a flight from there to Kabul International. Can you do that?"

Dirty looked down the quickly pulled together the C-130 parts list from his fellow aircrew. "Admiral. There are three starters here, that's not a problem. We have nothing for the booster system. Sorry." Dirty continued. "If you want the starter, I need to get it to Muscat. That's the only way to get it to Kabul." There were a few flights off the island. It would take weeks to find a flight to Kabul. In Muscat, he'd have far better luck.

"OK. Do it. Let me know if you need any support," the Chairman said.

"Got it, sir, but I think I have the perfect guy for the job." Dirty hung up and asked his engineer to go fetch a port side starter unit for a number two engine. As the engineer ran off,

Dirty picked up the phone. "Hey, Sleazy. How are ya!? I think I have a new mission for ya."

Admiral Hershey sat back in his chair. He heard a gentle knock on the door. "Sir. Do you have a minute?" Alfi said.

"Sure, please, come in. What is it?"

Alfi didn't say anything as she turned on the Admiral's TV and changed the channel to the news. Scrolling across the bottom was a banner which stated the Taliban would behead Curt live on one of their websites at midnight in Afghanistan, which would be roughly noon the next day in D.C., just over twenty-seven hours from the current time.

The Chairman's heart climbed into his throat. "Thanks, Alfi."

Chapter Forty-two
Calming A Storm

"Mr. Flaherty?" A voice called out in the hospital hallway. Kathy Hershey recognized Allison's father from her short stint in Arizona.

"Yes. Ma'am. Hello. Please call me Paul. Are you here for Allison, too?" Paul was somewhat surprised.

"Paul, yes, of course. The military may be massive, but we are family, and we always come together at times like this."

Her looking after his baby girl reassured Paul, but he was still concerned. "How is she?"

"She's sleeping. The baby is fine. She's in the next room down. The nurses are monitoring both her vitals and the baby's."

"Great. I'd like to go in, thanks," Paul said, then repeated himself. "Thanks again." Kathy nodded. Paul walked in and saw Allison. She looked so peaceful, but he knew she was anything but. He pulled up a chair next to her bed, held her hand, and gently ran his hand through her hair.

Slowly, Allison woke. She saw him and slowly said, "Daddy."

"Yes, my princess. I'm right here. Like I always promised you I would be."

Allison smiled. It felt good to be loved. As she grew more aware of her surroundings, her eyes opened wider, and she called out, "What about Curt?"

"He's alive," Paul answered firmly.

"Dad, how do you know?" She questioned.

"Because I believe it, and I have no information to the contrary. And I need you to believe this too. Allison, Princess, you are a strong girl. It's how I raised you. I'm here, and I will always be here, but you need to believe in Curt. I know he believes in you, and he's leveraging every ounce of love you've ever given him to fight to get home. He's not giving up. And neither are you."

Allison cried.

He stood up from the chair, leaned over the bed, and held

270

her. "I know it's hard, Alli."

"Dad. I just want to hold him! I want to know he's going to be there to see our baby."

"Alli, I want that too. Almost just as much as you do. And I'm holding onto every ounce of belief he will."

Kathy stood in the corner. She was crying. She'd been with more than a dozen Gold Star spouses who'd lost loved ones in military operations. It never gets easier. Husbands lost. Wives lost. Families torn apart. Kathy left the room. She walked down to the hospital chapel. She prayed hard to God that she would not have to witness the loss of yet another military loved one to combat operations. After grabbing something to eat, she would return to the room, allowing Paul to have some time with his daughter.

Back in the room, the nurse's station was alerted to Allison's increased heart rate and other vitals, suggesting she'd awakened. Within minutes, they were in the room, speaking to her, asking if she had any cramps or blood spotting. Allison was in the first trimester of her pregnancy, and it was the riskiest. Luckily, everything was going well from a pregnancy perspective, but it also created complications on what medications the doctor could prescribe to keep her calm. The entire medical staff was grateful for Paul's presence. He clearly was the foundation that would help Allison get through this event, no matter how it turned out.

****

Back at the compound of Hakem's father, Smitty, Mule, Hakem, Majeed and Usman were on their eighth evolution, running through the hastily crafted rescue. It would take all of them to pull this off. In the courtyard dirt, they'd scribbled a large layout of the streets and buildings. Each was walking in slow motion, mimicking their movements.

"No! Usman!," Smitty snapped. "I need you to drive your 4Runner THIS way! You need to make this turn. If you pass it, you'll need to go another entire block away, and that's time we can't afford."

271

"Sorry, Mr. Smitty." Usman was embarrassed and frustrated, and everyone could sense it.

Smitty took a deep breath. He was demanding Special Forces level effort from a civilian Afghan. If this was to work, Smitty needed to adjust his expectations. "No, Usman. I'm sorry. You are doing great. I shouldn't have yelled. I know you can do this. Everyone, let's take a break. Usman, can you get Raz on the phone? I'd like to talk to Buck."

Usman dialed the number, and quickly spoke to Raz in Pashto then handed the phone to Smitty. "Here, sir."

Smitty thanked Usman, then spoke into the phone. "Buck, Smitty here."

"Yeah. How are you guys doing?"

"We're going tonight. After that, we're gonna try to drive to your location in the two vehicles."

Buck thought about it, and the more he thought, the more he realized this was a horrible plan. "Smitty, you wanna break out the Taliban's public enemy number one, then go through a dozen checkpoints for over ten hours with him? Look, I'm a stupid pilot, but man, that sounds like a suicide mission."

"Yeah, well, I don't have many other plans."

"Why don't you get him out and just hole down somewhere?"

"Buck, you do flying shit. I do ground shit. Everywhere within a hundred miles, the Taliban will be searching like cockroaches. I need to get to you."

Buck turned to Raz and said something, then returned to the phone call. "Smitty, once you successfully get Curt, and you will be successful, don't come here. Go north out of Kandahar to the men who stormed the halls of Montezuma."

"Halls of Montezuma?" Smitty responded.

"Yes, if we're being monitored, I want to have at least a hint of protection. Think about it. You'll get it," he said again.

"OK. I'll try to figure it out."

"Good. I'll see ya an hour before daybreak. I gotta go. Lots of work to do here." Buck hung up and looked at Raz. "Raz, we're going tonight. Get your family and have them here by zero three hundred. Also, tell the airport to top off the plane with as much gas as possible. Tell them we will be doing engine runs again tomorrow."

Raz agreed. He headed home.

Buck stayed on the aircraft. He sat in the pilot seat, opened an old copy of the Instrument Flight Rules Supplement (IFR Sup). He flipped to the Global High Frequency (HF) radio stations. Because of the atmospheric expansion and contraction of the ionosphere, HF signals 'bounced' off the atmospheric layer and allowed for global communications. Unfortunately, there was little ability to predict the ionosphere thickness, making it difficult to know which frequencies would work and which ones would not. The rule of thumb suggested low frequencies in the morning and higher ones in the afternoon, but that really was not accurate because common sense dictated that if one side of the world was experiencing morning, the other side was evening.

Buck dialed in the first frequency and transmitted, "Any Command Post, any command post, Buck Zero One. Any command post, Buck Zero One."

Buck released the microphone and listened. There was significant static and what sounded like bubbles underwater. It was no wonder why aircrew hated to use HF. As for the callsign, Buck 01, should a command post try to find that callsign associated with an existing global flight plan, they would turn up nothing. Also, a '01' callsign numeric was usually the designator for a commander, at least a lieutenant colonel or higher. A wise enlisted airman at any command post would be foolish to ignore the call. Buck was counting on.

Nothing was heard after a few more attempts. Buck dialed in another frequency and tried. Again, there was nothing. While discouraged, he knew this was the game of HF communications. He looked in the IFR Sup and found another frequency. Once dialed in, he again tried the transmission.

A faint response came back, "Buck Zero One, this is Lajes Field Command Post, go."

Buck sprung up in his seat. "Lajes Field, Buck Zero One!" He yelled back into the radio. "Request a TCON (telephone communications) message transfer. Please advise when ready

273

to copy."

The young airman at Lajes Field grabbed a piece of paper. This was the first TCON request she'd received in over a year and was shocked Buck 01 was asking for one. That said, she was bored, there was little work to do, and this was at least something to do. "Buck Zero One, go with your request."

"Please call 520-555-3825 and relay the following to Allison. 'Buck passes, tanker request, 0800 Local, 60 miles feet wet from Pansi, Pakistan.' Read back request."

The airman read everything back correctly. As frail as this communication system was, the message she'd be passing was vital to the entire group's survival.

"Readback correct. Thanks, Lajes Command Post. Buck Zero One standing by this frequency for any further traffic." Buck prayed the message would go through quickly and he'd get some form of confirmation. He knew; however, his time was limited. As the ionosphere's shape shifted, the signal bounce would also shift, making Lajes Field unreachable.

The Airman began following the instructions, dialing the number. A female voice answered. "Allison Nover," she said.

"Yes, Allison, my name is Airman Henderson. I am assigned to Lajes Field, in the Azores of Portugal."

"Yes, Airman Henderson," Allison responded, a bit puzzled by the call. Both Paul and Kathy were sitting there and had heard her response. They, too, were confused. "Yes. Hold on.... Dad, I need a pen and paper."

Paul handed them both over. As Allison wrote, she spoke out loud as she wrote. "Buck Zero One, yes, zero eight hundred local with a tanker request. Yes, sixty miles, wet feet, Pansi, Pakistan."

Kath had heard enough of her husband's conversations that she knew this was something important. She called the Admiral. "Hey, I think you need to hear this."

Admiral Hershey listened to his wife try to relay the message, and his eyes lit up. After a quick phone call to the Pentagon command post, the Chairman of the Joint Chiefs was linked with Airman Henderson, who was shaking as she read the message back, word for word. "Airman Henderson, can you please check.

Did the aircraft say 'wet feet?" The Admiral couldn't understand that portion of the message.

Airman Henderson's heart froze. She'd passed the message incorrectly, and now the Chairman was on the line. "Sir?" she said, as soft and scared as a mouse.

"Yes, Airman? He responded quickly.

"I think I meant 'feet wet' not wet feet."

"Perfect!" The Admiral yelled. He needed to make sure. "Now, Airman Henderson! Please, call back the aircraft and tell them the message was received by me and we are working it!"

Airman Henderson lit back up. Never in her short Air Force career had one of her superiors been so excited about her error. She'd not be losing her job or getting an Article 15. "Yes, sir!" she replied. The line went dead before she finished.

"Buck Zero One, Lajes Field Command Post." Airman Henderson transmitted. There was no response. She tried again. And again. And again. Buck would never know if his message went through. As she called, Buck sat in his plane, listening to the static and odd sounds one hears on an HF radio. They lulled him to sleep. He'd not leave the plane.

As Airman Henderson tried in vain, Admiral Hershey googled Pakistan. There was no other easy way out of Afghanistan. If he overflew Iran, he'd be shot down. India was too far to the east. North would put him in 'no man's land' with Ashgabat, Turkmenistan, or Dushanbe, Tajikistan. Neither was too enticing. Buck had to be going south. 'Feet wet' was a military term for a flight that transitioned from over land to over water, but what did Buck mean by 'Pansi' the Admiral thought. As he looked along the coast, he found the Pakistani city of Pasni. 'That must be it!' he thought. Buck needs a tanker at 0800L at his time 60 miles off the coast of Pasni. Admiral Hershey got it right, and every other HAM (Home amateur) radio operator in the world that intercepted the transmission would still try to find Buck 01 in the flight system. There was nearly zero chance anyone else would figure it out, and there were none that would even consider calling Allison's number to put the pieces together.

Chapter Forty-three
High-Level Talks

While she slept in her hospital bed, Allison's phone rang. Paul reached out to answer it quickly, hoping it wouldn't wake his daughter.

"Allison Donley's, er uh, Allison Nover's phone," he said.

"Yes. My name is Andrew Denney. Excuse me, who am I speaking with?"

"My name is Paul Flaherty. I'm Allison's father. Allison is in the hospital and asleep right now."

"Oh, my God. Is she OK?"

"Yes. She's fine. We are going through a tough time as a family," Paul explained. He didn't know Andrew, nor did he know how much he could share.

"I can imagine. I've seen the news. I want you and her to know I am praying. Hard. Curt is a great man. This is all too much for many. Can you please tell me what hospital she's in? I'd like to send her some flowers."

"Yes, we are at MedStar Georgetown University Hospital, but I am not sure how much longer we are going to be here. It's only two PM so maybe they'll let her out today. Physically, Allison is fine, and so is the baby." As soon as Paul said it, he realized he shouldn't have. "Uh. Sorry. That's supposed to be close hold info."

"Your secret is safe with me," Andrew replied.

"Paul, please pass along to Allison that I called. I won't keep you any longer. Take care of yourself and your family."

Paul replied with a sincere thank you and then hung up. Andrew was growing more angered by the entire evolution. He picked up the phone and called John Gerzema. "John. We need to talk."

"Sure, Andrew." John was clearly happy. "Have you seen the Pharma sector today? It's climbing as if it were a Sherpa on Mt. Everest!"

"Yes. I've seen it. Have you seen the news about Curt Nover?" Andrew replied.

John 'read the room,' and toned down his elation. "Yes, Andrew. I have. It's upsetting. He seemed like a good kid. Really helped us out of a bind in the Balkans."

"Seemed?," Andrew said. "He's still on this earth. There's no need for past tense."

"Yes, of course," John replied. "That's what I meant."

"John, we need to figure something out. It's less than 24 hours now and that kid's gonna have his God Damn head cut off." Andrew was again growing more angered.

"Andrew. I understand your frustration. Many Americans are frustrated. The entire Afghanistan withdrawal thing is still an open wound. This just exacerbates the situation."

"Please don't placate me with your political narratives," Andrew snapped. "I want you to do something."

John chuckled under his breath. "What do you suggest I do?"

"I don't know," Andrew started out softly, then his tone slowly grew. "I'm not you, who is the former Secretary of Defense and now the President's Special National Security Advisor. When you ask me about the market and what we can do, I have an answer... always. When I ask you about military and security issues, I expect some fucking reciprocity."

After a brief pause, John responded. "OK, Andrew, let me make some calls. But seriously, you want me to rescue a man literally on the other side of the globe in under 24 hours? That's a tall order. Let me find out if anyone has an operation going on."

"I want a call back before the close of business today." Andrew hung up without waiting for a response.

John took a deep breath, got up from his desk, and walked down to the Oval Office. He sat in the waiting area, hoping Steve would eventually pop his head out. As luck would have it, Steve did just that, about five minutes after John's arrival. "Steve, do you have a minute?"

There was little love loss between Steve and John, but Steve also knew the President was loyal to him for some reason. He'd need to play nice. "Sure, sir. I got one. What do you need?"

"This Nover thing in Afghanistan. Is the U.S. doing anything?"

Steve's initial reaction was one of surprise. "John? Nover is an American Citizen. He's not in the military any longer. Why on earth he went INTO Afghanistan while we are still trying to get all our AMCITS (American Citizens) out is beyond me. I can tell you this-the President has not authorized any special mission dedicated to the recovery of Mr. Nover. If the DoD has anything cooking with an overarching mission in the area that could be applied to Mr. Nover, I don't know. We are aware of some missions in the area. I do not know, however, if Acting Secretary Crawford can even redirect them over."

"OK. I understand, Steve. Thanks for your time. Please tell the boss I'm standing by if he needs anything."

Steve looked at John and could not pass up the opportunity at a small dig. "Oh, sir. I think he knows." It was as far as Steve could go in his position.

✳✳

Earlier in the day, Ashton 'Sleazy' Beasley was on the ground in Muscat, trying to figure out how to get the number two starter onto a flight to Kabul. According to the schedule, there was a flight on the books, and he was already on the cargo side of the ramp. A good start. Eventually, he found an Omani whom he could bribe with $300 to get it onto the aircraft. Sleazy took down the man's name and number along with information on the manifest. The starter was wrapped in brown paper with an obvious note that stated it was a part for the C-130 on the Kabul ramp. The chances of this starter getting to Buck via that logistic trail were far less than 50/50.

Once complete, Sleazy took a cab back over to the passenger terminal and flew back to Masirah. It was a short flight and by dinner he was back and having a lovely Omani meal with Dirty at the local restaurant just outside the main gate. As Sleazy sat there, his phone rang. He recognized the number immediately and answered excitedly. "Hey dad! How are you!?" It was still daytime in D.C. given the time difference.

"I'm good, uh, son. Good." John Gerzema responded. Every time he heard the word 'dad' it stung with an uncomfortable feeling. "Ashton, where are you now?"

"I'm still on Masirah Island. Why?" Sleazy asked.

"Oh, nothing really. One more question. On the island, have you seen any guys that look like Special Forces in the past few days?"

"Nope. It's really quiet. Just a stuck C-130 crew and me hanging out. They've been ordered to stay on the island until the Chairman releases them though. Weird, given their plane was already fixed by a team from Ramstein Air Base, in Germany." Ash answered.

It was the most information John would get. "Thanks Ashton. I appreciate it."

"Anytime, dad. Hey! Dad! Guess what, I got a callsign from the...."

John cut him off. "Ashton. I don't have time for nonsense. I need to go. Goodbye."

Dejected, Sleazy stopped speaking and set the phone down.

"Your old man?" Dirty asked.

"Yeah. He's really important. I get he doesn't have time for me." It was the same rationale Sleazy had used for so long, he believed it.

"Yeah. You told us during your callsign night. Frankly, I think it's all bullshit," Dirty said. "Buddy, just my two cents, but you need to reevaluate this entire thing."

"What do you mean?" Sleazy responded.

"Look, nearly every kid of a famous person I know rides that gravy train so hard it destroys most of them. Drugs. Booze. Fame. They all turn into assholes. You? Not only do you not ride it, but you also let your old man pound your dick flat and hold you down." Dirty paused, then continued. "Seriously, how long do you plan to stay in his shadow? I mean, I don't want you to turn into a drugged out, infamous alcoholic, but there's got to be a healthy balance regarding the fame of you father and your life."

Sleazy tried to provide the standard answer to such a comment "But he told me it would be better for my mom and I if I kept it quiet."

Dirty just stared at Sleazy. "Better for who?"

"Whom. You mean whom?" responded Sleazy.

"Dude. Hide behind your Ivy league education. I have zero fucks to give about this. You and I both know what's going on. Sleazy, I just know this. It's almost impossible for a human to rise to their true potential when they're being held down, especially by their own parents." Dirty waived his hand and asked for the bill, which arrived quickly. From that phrase on, the two would not speak again until they said good night.

****

As John and Sleazy were speaking, Andrew was driving to the Georgetown hospital. His emotions were overwhelming. Should anything happen to Curt, part of him felt responsible. The next person he spoke to needed to be Allison. Andrew parked, walked into the hospital, hoping she'd not already been discharged.

Allison was, in fact, still in the hospital. Earlier in the day, Kathy and her full security detail hovering around had spoken 'to' the doctor, requesting if Allison could stay a few days longer. Kathy gently explained that the 'most famous American in Afghanistan,' Curt Nover, was in fact the husband of his patient. Should anything happen to that baby because of world events, Kathy and her security detail would hold that doctor fully responsible. It was more of a one-way communication. The doctor's decision was an easy one.

"Allison Nover's room, please?" Andrew asked at the receptionist.

"Yes, sir, hold on. It's right here, 314, but please, visiting hours end in an hour."

"I only need fifteen minutes," Andrew said as he walked away to catch the elevator.

Andrew found the room. The door was open. He gently knocked on the door and stuck his head in. Allison was awake. She'd clearly just ended one of her many crying sessions for the day. "Yes?" She answered.

"Allison, I am sorry to bother you. My name is Andrew Denney. I'm the reason you flew back to D.C."

"Yes, Mr. Denney. Sorry. I'm in no condition to do the

interview. I apologize. Can we do it a little later?"

"Absolutely. I didn't expect to do the interview now. May I ask you a favor, though?" Andrew requested.

Allison looked at her father, who was indifferent. "Sure," she responded.

Andrew shared his request. "If you're up to talk, I'd like to chat one-on-one. I have some information I think that will strengthen you through your difficult time."

Allison looked at her dad, who was supportive of any effort that would help his little girl.

"I'll go get a coffee," Paul said, excusing himself.

After her hospital room door closed, Andrew began to speak. As he did, Allison's eyes grew. Then Andrew played segments of audio recordings. Her eyes widened further. At first, she was furious with Andrew, until she learned his long-term plan.

Andrew was right. The brief information he shared strengthened Allison's resolve. "Allison, there is far more, and it's all yours. I want you to know, as I flew out of Montenegro with that Serbian bitch who destroyed my son, Curt said something to me that I'll never forget. We were discussing many issues. My business, my deceased son, my life. At the time, Curt's words stung. Now they resonate. He said, *'It's never too late to make right.'* I've thought about that far more than I can explain. He was correct, and that is why I'm doing this."

As weak as Allison was, she was rarely prouder to be Ms. Curt Nover. Her husband was a treasure, not to just her, but to many more... perhaps the nation. "Mr. Denney. Curt is a great guy. Thanks for your words. I'm holding onto the hope that Admiral Hershey has a miracle or two. He's been working on something. Let's just pray."

"Yes," said Andrew. "Let's pray." He shook her hand, then leaned over to hug her. It was awkward, but not lacking emotion. A tear welled up in Andrew's eye. As they parted, he said, "Sorry for that. I just felt like I needed to hug you."

"I understand, sir. I really do. Have a good day. I'll be in touch with you in a few days."

Chapter Forty-four
Failed Diplomacy?

"Admiral, I understand your concern. But there truly is very little we can do," Secretary Baker said to a dejected chairman. They were speaking on a secure line between the Truman Building and the Pentagon.

"Given the existing sanctions on the Taliban, there really are no 'sticks' left for us to use from a diplomatic perspective to leverage a stoppage to Curt's murder. Additionally, in the current political climate, the White House is unwilling to offer me some 'carrots' fearing any might enrage public sentiment." Secretary Baker tried everything to calm the Chairman, even addressing him personally as a friend. "Truly Squirts, I'm sorry, but unfortunately, there is no diplomatic solution to Curt's situation."

"I understand. From what I can gather, the group he went in with will try some half-cocked rescue attempt, but we aren't offering any support. I don't have much confidence."

"Well, that information is quite helpful to me," Secretary Baker offered.

"I guess I'm lost," the Admiral relayed.

"I have a presser in five minutes. I'll make a powerful statement that there will be no effort from the U.S. to rescue him. If nothing else, it will lull the Taliban into believing there's no rescue. Technically, it's true. There is no U.S. Government sanctioned rescue."

"Marleen... er, uh, Madam Secretary, that's brilliant."

"Thanks, Squirts. And for this call and the gravity of it, first names and callsigns are completely authorized."

"Thanks," he replied. Then, the Admiral yelled out of his office, "Alfi! Get me the Pentagon Press Secretary on the line. Tell him to hold for me until I'm done with the Secretary!"

"Yes, sir." Alfi would take care of it.

The Admiral turned his attention back to the Secretary. "I also spoke with Gary at CIA. He hasn't much to offer either."

"Not surprising. I didn't think he would. Afghanistan was a

hell hole when we actually had assets there. I can't imagine what it's like now. There's no U.S. Government entity willing to even consider being there." Secretary Baker paused. "Squirts, do you know why he went there?"

The Admiral didn't fully know, but much like Curt, Smitty, Buck and Mule, the Admiral too had unfinished business in Afghanistan. Many service members did, but he didn't really know how to convey it. "Marleen, I don't know. I guess he needed to track down some Afghan ghosts."

As they spoke, another call rang into the Chairman's front office.

"Colonel Andrade, Chairman's office. Can I help you?"

"Yes, Colonel. This is Andrew Denney. I have information for the Chairman."

"Yes, sir. He's on an important call right now. May I take a message?"

"Colonel, I assure you, this information is time sensitive. Can you please tell him it's Mr. Denney?"

"Sir, I'm sure you believe your information is critical," Alfi replied, "But he's speaking to one of the Secretaries."

"OK. Colonel, we can do this one of two ways. You can tell him I'm on the phone, or I can call the President and get patched through. Your call."

Alfi thought about it for a millisecond. "Please stand by." She went into the Chairman's office and stood there as the Chairman was wrapping up his discussion with Secretary of State Baker. The Chairman hung up with Secretary Baker and Alfi relayed the message from Andrew.

"What on earth could he have?" The Chairman blurted out. "OK, put him through."

"Admiral, Andrew here. Any chance we can meet again, same place as last time. Say an hour?"

"Andrew, I'm extremely busy. Can it wait?" Responded the Admiral.

"I don't think so if I'm going to help you stop Nover's execution."

The Admiral perked up. "Andrew, make it thirty minutes." He hung up.

"Alfi!" The Admiral yelled.

"Sir, already on it. Your motorcade will be ready in five minutes."

"Great job, Alfi! Damn! Can we clone you?"

"Admiral," Colonel Andrade responded, "My parents swear when God made me, he broke the mold... on purpose." The two chuckled. The Admiral grabbed a few things from his office since he would be heading home after their meeting. It would be just like last time the two of them met, under the Marine Corps Memorial overlooking the Potomac River.

****

CIA Director Gary Hamilton's phone rang while he was driving home. He answered, "Hamilton."

"Sir, you requested a call when our eyes were good. Confirming it now."

"Great, thanks. Are you pushing that feed into the Puzzle Palace?" The Director asked. Puzzle Palace was an often used nickname for the Pentagon.

"Yes, sir," the person responded.

"Perfect. Good job," the Director said, then hung up. His team had placed national assets in a position to have continual 'eyes' or overhead surveillance of the location believed to be holding Curt Nover. That video was being pushed to the intelligence nets in the Pentagon along with many other command level units. Gary looked down and dialed another number.

"Squirts," Director Hamilton said.

"Yeah, Gary. What do you have?" Admiral Hershey responded as his motorcade progressed to the Marine Corps Memorial.

"We are eyes on right now for your priority. Feed is being pushed across the interagency but only to those with need to know caveats. It's the best I can do, Squirts. I wish I could do more."

"Great news, Gary. I appreciate it. And if you keep calling me Squirts, we're gonna have to get you a callsign."

284

Director Hamilton chuckled. "Who says I don't already have one? You aren't the first military buddy I've befriended."

The two laughed and hung up.

****

Andrew Denney stood underneath the massive monument, a sculpture of Marines raising the flag at Iwo Jima on Mount Suribachi. It was a nice day in May. He wore only dress slacks and a golf shirt. Andrew saw the motorcade pull up.

The Chairman approached. "Andrew. Hello. If you have anything for me, please make it fast. Time is precious, as you know."

"Yes. It's good to see you as well, Admiral Hershey." Andrew replied, clearly irritated by the expeditious nature of the Chairman. Ordering around others may work in the Pentagon, but it would not work on Andrew.

"Of course, Andrew. Apologies. I'm a bit on edge. How are you?" The Admiral backtracked.

Andrew was far more appreciative of this approach. "I just left visiting Allison Nover at the hospital. She'll be doing a story in a few weeks, that I think you'll find interesting, but that's not why I'm here. She alluded to an effort you may have going on in Afghanistan. Given Nover is an AMCIT and not military, and also considering the expeditious nature of the Taliban's desire to kill him, I'm going to guess your efforts could perhaps use help. If that is the case, I'm prepared to assist."

The Admiral was agitated. "You mean you have nothing for me?"

"No, Admiral. I have many things, and what I don't have can often be bought. I'm offering to help, but the globe is a big place. I'll need some information should I be able to offer support." Andrew was matter of fact, almost cold.

"Andrew, I appreciate your offer, and I remain grateful for your last assistance, but your money often has strings tied to it that I don't realize until far too late."

"Admiral. There are no strings," said Andrew convincingly. "I spoke with John Gerzema earlier and offered to help. He's clueless and clearly being isolated within the Executive Branch. Curt avenged the death of my son. Yes, there were many other issues there, and I'd rather avoid that discussion now. I won't offer again. Please provide me the details so I can help."

The Admiral had no other options. He only knew the plan loosely. If he had greater clarity, perhaps he would ignore the offer. The Chairman shared Curt's location and the information that there would likely be a rescue attempt and a C-130 flight out. It was all he knew.

"Thank you, Admiral. I will do everything I can."

"Andrew," the Admiral said with authority, "Do NOT intervene in any way that hinders their effort. If you are the reason this fails, I'll never forgive myself."

"Admiral, I assure you I don't intend for my efforts to interfere. But I will also say this, if I don't help, I'll never forgive myself." The two shook hands and parted. The Admiral walked back to his convoy. On the way, some tourists took his photo. Another tourist boldly asked for a selfie, which the Chairman graciously obliged.

Andrew stood looking at the Potomac. It was now under twenty hours until the Taliban would execute Curt. *'Perhaps Gerzema was right. Perhaps there is too little time,'* he thought. *'Perhaps money can't buy everything.'* There had to be something.

Andrew reset back to basics. He was desperate, flush with cash, and nearly willing to pay anything. Then it hit him like a freight train. Andrew needed to find someone in the same situation, but on the other end of the spectrum. He'd need to find someone without money, and desperate to do anything to get it.

He scrolled through his phone, then found the number. He dialed it and the other line answered in Farsi. It was Ali Farahmand.

"Ali. Hey. English, please. It's Andrew. Andrew Denney."

"Andrew! My friend! My, it has been a long time! How are you?" Ali asked.

"I'm great, but I'm curious how you are? I can imagine global sanctions against Iran are truly agonizing."

"Yes, Andrew. I make do with what I can. There are few choices. Our leadership is our leadership. I think American's understand the effects of terrible leaders." It was Ali's gentle dig at both U.S. and Iranian leaders, neither of which suffered from the actual sanctions. That was the Iranian population. In his country, however, that was about as far as anyone would go on record attacking the regime.

"Ali, I may be able to help with that," said Andrew. "Do you still have your Cayman account?"

Ali's voice got quieter. "Andrew, yes. But please, who are you with?"

"Ali. I am alone. Look. I don't have much time. I'm prepared to wire your account one million dollars within the next twenty-four hours." Andrew's voice was unflinching, and Ali knew it was not a bluff.

"A million dollars? Sir, what do you want me to do? Kill someone?" Ali asked.

"Actually, just the opposite. Save someone." Andrew relayed what was going on. Ali was aware of the pending execution, as was most of the world.

"That's in less than a day, Andrew," Ali answered as he thought about it. "Look, I can't get there, but I think I have a play. Make it two million. One for me and one for another guy. Is that a deal?"

Andrew didn't hesitate. "Deal. If Nover makes it out of Taliban hands and you can give me proof of helping, the money will be in your account in five minutes."

"Great. I must go! I have much to coordinate!" The two hung up. Money and power were the only two plays Andrew ever had, and he'd grown exceptional at leveraging them. He just put his chips on the table. He'd now have to watch the roulette ball roll. He chuckled as he thought to himself, '*I wonder what U.S. officials would think if they learned help was coming from Iran?*'

Andrew opened his brokerage account and sold two million dollars' worth of his pharma stocks. He had nearly doubled his money by now. Two million was nothing. He'd be selling much more soon.

****

The media's sensationalism was at a fevered pitch. Secretary Baker, the White House Press Secretary, the Chairman and the Pentagon Press Secretary all pounded home the key talking points: there would be no U.S. rescue effort, and the need for diplomacy at this 'critical hour' was vital. The video shot across every American TVs except one. Allison's hospital room was broadcasting an old Netflix film. Paul and Kathy were both there with her, sheltering her from the media onslaught.

Later that night, the Taliban posted a video of Curt eating his last meal. It was lunchtime in Afghanistan. Most of the U.S. was asleep. Europe was just waking up. The execution would take place hours later when the western world was awake. The Taliban wanted maximum exposure.

After eating, Curt read a statement from the Taliban which was also broadcast publicly. It was a list of demands, to include billions of dollars to make up for the lost poppy revenue, recognition of the Taliban at the U.N., and lifting all global sanctions. These were ludicrous demands, mostly leveraged on what the Taliban considered to be the worth of Curt Nover. Curt knew he was valuable, but also knew no one was that valuable.

Chapter Forty-five
The Infidel's Punishment
(Take Two)

The live video stream began with merely a black screen. An audio clip played Islamic music, as one would expect to hear broadcasting from mosque loudspeakers during any of the five daily prayer sessions. This, however, would not be a prayer session. The video transitioned from black as a dark piece of paper was pulled away from the camera lens in an amateurish production manner. The initial image was grainy, but clarity was not important. In the middle lower section of the image was a human on his knees, hands tied behind his back, wearing an orange prison jumpsuit. The face was not visible, as a black burlap sack covered the entire head. The body remained motionless. If the torso wasn't erect, one could easily question if it was even alive.

From the right side of the screen, another individual entered the picture. It appeared to be a man, but determining this was difficult. He wore a large piece of cloth over his mouth and nose. On his head was a traditional Taliban headdress matching his black abaya. He spoke in Pashto, reading from a piece of paper he held in his hand.

"All Praise Allah. When the Lord inspired the angels (saying) I am with you. So, make those who believe stand firm. I will throw fear into the hearts of those who disbelieve. Then smite the necks and smite of them each finger. (Koran 8:12)"

He paused. Long enough to pull out a large dagger style knife, then continued. "Now when ye meet in battle those who disbelieve, then it is smiting of the necks until, when ye have routed them, making fast of bonds; and afterward either grace or ransom 'til the war lay down its burdens. (Koran 47:4)"

He continued, "The accused has been charged and found guilty of numerous acts, from being an infidel to treason against our ways. He must no longer walk among us in this life. We send him to the great Allah who shall judge his sins against Islam."

The man put the paper down and lifted the burlap sack off Curt's head. The bright lights lit up his face and Curt's eyes squinted. His left eye was bruised, and the right side of his face showed signs of electrical burns.

Once accustomed to the light, Curt opened his eyes and held his head high. Staring directly into the camera. If this was truly the end, he'd face it like a warrior. Millions had tuned in to watch. Allison sat on her bed, holding her father's hands. Her TV was still broadcasting Netflix, but she could hear the other broadcast from the nurses' station, where the entire medical staff had congregated.

Chapter Forty-six
Flash Bang
(Three Hours Earlier)

In the darkness of Qalat, the two 4Runners departed Hakem's father's compound. One vehicle was pulling a donkey on a trailer. It was one of his father's. A good donkey with a friendly disposition. They slowly made their way to Kandahar. For the border between Kandahar and Zabul province, they'd be wearing night-vision devices to circumnavigate around the checkpoint. On the outskirts of town, Hakem, his wife, son, and father would exit a vehicle with Noorullah. They'd anxiously wait in a restaurant while giving Noorullah another dose of methadone. Thankfully, Noorullah's addiction was showing signs of weakening. Hakem and his father kissed their loving donkey on the head and went into the café.

Roughly a half mile from Curt's imprisonment, the two vehicles stopped. Smitty and Mule exited the vehicles, wearing full Afghan attire covering up their military gear. Both were heavily armed, but given the loose outer clothing, no one would suspect it. Their turbans hid small communication systems, with small earpieces hanging down. The rest of their gear would be carried in by the donkey, drawing suspicion from no one.

Smitty and Mule offloaded the donkey from the trailer, then placed large, prepacked burlap sacks on the donkey's back. After a few minutes, the two would be walking the streets of Kandahar with their trusty four-legged creature.

Usman would head to a point a mile north of the objective, while Majeed would drive by the target one more time. He'd take good mental notes on everything he saw, circling up the street on the back side of the house, again observing. After that, Majeed drove towards Smitty and Mule.

"Sir, there was one more out front, but no more on the back street. I could not find any on the roofs, though, but I couldn't look too much without crashing."

"Great job, Majeed. Now, go get in position." He paused and

then transmitted. Majeed, Usman. Remember, timing is important. You must get this right. I believe in both of you."

"Yes, sir!" Majeed responded, proudly. Usman did the same. For more times than Majeed and Usman could count, they'd watched U.S. military operations as an interpreter, but never participated, something they'd desperately wished to do. Their inclusion back then was forbidden due to the Laws of Armed Conflict. Today, those no longer applied. Today, they were legitimate combatants against the Taliban. Majeed drove away. It was an hour until midnight. Smitty and Mule would need to start moving if they were to save Curt.

It was a painfully slow walk for both of them. They were disguised as Afghan farmers, bringing their bounty into the city's markets. To be believable, they needed to walk at a pace commensurate with their cover and not as if they were on a mission to save their best friend's life. Things in Afghanistan operated at a far slower pace... uncomfortably slow. To many who served in the region, there was an old saying: *'In Afghanistan, we have the watch, but Afghans have the time.'* To others, it rarely made sense. To veterans of the Afghan war, it made perfect sense. Pace of life in that country was unique.

They passed others in the streets. Given the late hour, there were only a few. Some cafes were open, with a few hookah pipes burning tobacco and other smokable items. Most were plentiful with customers, as each location would soon show the execution. Smitty looked at his watch indiscreetly. He had thirty more minutes. Fifty meters ahead, he could see the turn they'd take to get into the back alley. As they proceeded, they'd pass the main street with the guards out front. Smitty stopped before crossing the street, as if he were on some sort of busy New York thoroughfare. As he looked towards the guards on the ground, he counted them. He then turned his attention to the roof. Up there, he saw none.

The two men and the donkey crossed the street, then turned into the narrow alley. The buildings on either side backed up tightly. There was one way in and out, with high walls on either side. Ideal to sneak in, horrible for getting out after losing the element of surprise. Smitty feared it might turn into a city version of the Khyber Pass. Slowly, they proceeded.

It was now twenty minutes until midnight. As Smitty and the 'Mules' (one human and one a donkey) positioned themselves directly behind the structure Curt was in, they nudged the burlap sack off the donkey which fell to the ground. The two stopped, pulled their donkey to the side and acted as if they were trying to reattach the sack. If anyone was observing, the scenario looked normal. The two watched left and right until no one was paying attention.

Hastily, they tied the donkey to the side of a building. Smitty patted the mule's head and in his best *Shrek* impression said quietly, "That'll do, Donkey. That'll do." It was his quirky way of saying thanks and goodbye.

Smitty vaulted Mule up to where he was standing on the donkey's back. Mule was high enough to see over the roofline and quickly survey the area. Standing off in the distance was one Taliban with a long gun providing overwatch above Curt's holding cell. Mule lifted himself over the ledge, gently lowering him onto the recessed roof. Once clear, he pulled up the burlap bag which their trusty steed had carried, and then Smitty. The two low crawled in the roof's recessed area below the ledge, maintaining cover. Mule's exceptional fitness would be a tremendous advantage. Once at the lip between the two buildings, he and Smitty observed the Taliban providing overwatch. Once the guard's back was turned, Mule silently vaulted across the ledge between the two buildings. Street noise from below provided excellent noise masking.

Smitty kept watching. Eventually, Mule low crawled across that building until he was in place. He was lying along the roof ledge of the house that butted up to the one Curt was in, less than twenty feet from the guard. It was go time.

Smitty threw his legs over the roof lip holding himself at the roof line by his waist. Loudly, he let out some intentional moans and grunts, which captured the attention of the roof Taliban guard. As planned, the guard approached Smitty, being lured past Mule, who was lying in wait behind a lip of the adjacent roof recess.

The Taliban guard yelled something as he continued towards

Smitty. Smitty, resting now on the edge of the roof, raised his hands in surrender as the Taliban continued. He would pose no threat.

In swift movement, Mule stood up, approached the Taliban overwatch from behind, grabbed his face, then slit his throat. The man would make no sound. As he bled out, Mule took the weapon from his hand and gently laid him down, to ensure no one inside the house suspected activity on the roof. Mule stared at the Taliban soldier as blood pulsed from his jugular. Death would be at his door in under fifteen seconds. The pulsing jugular slowed. He was dead.

Smitty jumped across the roofline given the coast was clear. He whispered to Curt, "Hey! What took you so long!? That goon was getting close!" Smitty whispered.

"I wanted to see if he'd really shoot you." Mule answered, as he smiled.

The two shed their Afghan attire, exposing militant uniforms and gear. They opened the burlap sack and quickly loaded up all their tactical gear. Body armor, weapons, helmets, night-vision devices, bandoleers. They dressed as fast as possible. Time was fleeting. They could hear the Islamic music playing from inside the house. Midnight was near.

The text message from Usman to Majeed only said "Go!" in Pashto. The two began driving towards each other on the street that was in front of where Curt was held. Accelerating, they crash into each other directly in front of that house. It was a minor accident; both would back their vehicles away from the other, ensuring a clear getaway path.

After placing his vehicle in park, Usman exited and began yelling at Majeed, who stood for none of it. He, too, exited his car, yelling right back. Such an occurrence and the way the two engaged was a daily occurrence in Afghanistan. As the two argued, the Taliban soldiers who were trying to secure the area waved their rifles and handguns as if to intimidate the two and hope they'd leave. Neither would be phased. This was Afghanistan. Brandishing a weapon meant nothing. No one was scared until a weapon was aimed, and if that was the case, the aggressor had better pull the trigger, because the likelihood of another being leveled in return was probable. Oddly, one could argue in such a circumstance, Afghans valued concern about their vehicle over their own life. The Taliban soldiers were understanding of the anger between Usman and Majeed. They also knew that after ten to fifteen minutes, they'd calm down and leave. No reason to escalate the issue. Usman and Majeed were exceptional, well deserving of any Hollywood award. Soon, they were both blaming the Taliban for having too many people in the street causing the accident.

On the roof, Smitty and Mule heard the crash and the arguing. It was time. They jumped off the roof into the narrow alley and stood outside a window from where the music was emerging. It was the best guess as to where Curt was being kept. Mule gently pushed the open window's curtain aside. He saw a knife being leveled onto Curt's exposed neck. He nodded quickly to Smitty, who quietly active a flash bang, slowly pushed his hand beyond the curtain, then dropped it inside the window.

BOOM! As the flash bang detonated, Mule vaulted Smitty into the room, following closely behind. Smitty rolled on the ground as he somersaulted in. He looked left and right, noting where seven Taliban. "SEVEN!" he yelled out. Rolling out onto the floor, he pointed his handgun, popping off four rounds, killing two Taliban. After disposing of that pair, Smitty quickly re-surveyed the situation. Three remained in the fight. One was struggling to hold onto Curt, who was now fighting, while the other two were trying to regain their bearings from the flash bang. He let out a quick prayer that the last two has fled as he had lost visual on them. If he were wrong it could prove fatal.

Mule lunged across the room spraying cover fire for himself and Smitty. Once on the other side, he tossed two live grenades through the doorway that led towards the front of the structure. It was the room between them and the street where Usman and Majeed had been arguing. The grenades would detonate roughly 10 seconds apart, killing or wounding those who'd taken sought cover there. It also would cause superficial wounding to Taliban soldiers in the street.

After tossing the grenades though the door, he intentionally tipped over a large piece of furniture in front of the doorway. It would serve as an obstacle to hinder any Taliban who survived the blast and wished to enter the shootout. As he tipped the furniture, he felt two rounds hit him squarely in the back. They both felt like kicks from an angry steer. The sappy plate caught both, knocking the wind out of him, breaking a rib and tossing him to the floor.

Meanwhile, Curt kept struggling, ducking his chin down to hide his exposed neck. He attempted to roll away from his captor while his hands were still tied behind him. Fighting for his life, he was able to break free from the man retaining him, but had fallen to the ground in the process. Curt, now on his back, hands tied behind his back, coiled his legs to his chest, then kicked his capture with all his rage and might. The man shot across the room like a cannon round. He hit the wall and unfortunately fell directly onto Smitty's back.

Curt watched the entire thing. "Smitty Behind You!" he yelled. It was too late; the man had grabbed Smitty by the hair and was already lowering the knife. Mule was lying on the ground, unable to see what was transpiring as a table in the middle of the room blocked his view. He had no shot.

Smitty fought hard, but his assailant had the advantage. Smitty waved his arms and tried to smack the man with the butt of his rifle, even trying to turn it for a shot. There was none. Curt struggled to get to his feet. If he could, he'd charge the man. His life be damned.

Smitty and the Taliban soldier fought. Smitty's neck began to show signs of blood beading off the knife. It was piercing his skin. As Smitty fought, he looked in front of him and now six feet away, he saw one of the two Taliban soldiers that he'd incorrectly presumed fled. The man raised a rifle right at Smitty's face.

Behind Smitty, he heard the bellowing laugh of his soon to be executioner. The Taliban thug dropped his knife and held Smitty's head still to receive a fatal gunshot from his Taliban colleague. In Pashto he yelled, "Kill him!"

It was the end. Smitty began saying the Lord's Prayer. If there ever was a time for forgiveness, it was now. "Our Father, who art in heaven..."

POP! POP! POP! Three shots. Smitty and his assailant fell to the floor together.

"Thy kingdom come, thy will be done," Smitty continued... then he realized. He'd not been shot.

He was alive! His assailant, however, was not as lucky. He lay dead on the floor with three new air-conditioning vents in his forehead. Smitty put the Lord's Prayer on hold, staring up at the Taliban soldier who'd just killed his attacker. The man's hand was extended to lift Smitty up and said, "Take my fucking hand now if you wish to live!" Confused, Smitty took his hand and rose to his feet. Now wasn't the time for questions.

On the other side of the room, Mule, laying on the ground, quickly rolled onto his back, wincing from the pain in his ribs. He pulled his long gun up and pointed it at the man who shot him. The last mistake that man would make was assuming Mule was dead. POP! POP! Two rounds. The Taliban fighter fell to the ground.

Mule scrambled to his feet and with Smitty's help, grabbed Curt, throwing him out the window. Hastily, the two followed. Before leaving, Smitty looked back. Two of the Taliban fighters, one of which saved Smitty, were also scurrying out the window. "We're coming with you," one of them said. The two clearly intended to escape with them. Given one had saved Smitty and there was little time to argue (or a common language in which to do so), Smitty and Mule allowed them to follow, remaining leery of their actual intent.

In front of the house, Taliban who heard the first flash bang ran into the house, only to be wounded or killed by the grenades. Few survived, and those that did began to flee. They'd do nothing to facilitate either saving their comrades or provide additional firepower to the fight.

Earlier in the street as the first flash bangs detonated, Majeed and Usman jumped into their cars and drove away, much like any Afghan would do in the midst of a firefight. Majeed headed back to get Hakem and his father.

Usman sped away from the crash location, then slowed quickly. He'd need to find the first cross street and not overpass it... just as they had practiced. This time, he'd not miss it. Slowly, he pulled his vehicle over to the right as the crossing alleyway approached. As he looked down the alleyway, he could see Smitty, Mule, and Curt running towards them. He also saw two other shadows and yelled. "Sir! Behind you!"

"SHHH!!!!! Usman! They're with us!" Smitty screamed in a whisper. As the five got to the vehicle, they threw Curt in the back with Smitty. The two unknown fighters opened doors, but before they got in, Mule demanded their guns. He'd not be riding shotgun in a vehicle with two armed Taliban behind him, even if they'd just saved Smitty's life. There was little time to argue. The men handed over their weapons and jumped in. Usman sped off to the rally point, hoping Majeed was able to get the others from the café.

****

For the rest of the world, the video would show a knife lowering to Curt's neck, then the crash of a window. Seconds later, a loud bang that would knock the camera over. Gunfire would erupt, and an unrecognizable voice screamed the word, seven. Then the video cutout.

In the Georgetown University Hospital nurses' station, a subdued cheer went up. Paul ran out to learn about the raid. The video clearly did not reveal that Curt was still alive, but it also didn't show his death. It was something, and that something was some hope that many who wanted to see Curt live held onto.

Across the world, rampant speculation exploded across the news, social media and elsewhere. The seconds long video played over and over. Each time, armchair soldiers would weigh in with their expert analysis as to what transpired. No one would actually get it right.

On a Top Secret overhead video feed, everyone watched Smitty and Mule pull out Curt with two others, then drive away. "They fucking got him," Admiral Hershey said. "I hope he's alive." Those authorized to view the feed across the interagency

298

generated one collective fist pump. The video provided hope, but there were many unanswered questions. Now was the time to get to work.

****

Smitty untied Curt in the back of the 4Runner and held him. "Missed ya, buddy." Smitty said.

Curt was shaking in shock. "You too," was all he could muster.

"Buddy. Lay down. We got this, you're safe. Hold my hand. OK?" Smitty told Curt.

As he said that, one of the two friendly Taliban turned around to Smitty. "Sir," he said in English with what sounded like a British dialect to Smitty, Mule, and Curt. "We'd like to get proof of life back to our boss." One thing was becoming clear: they were not Taliban.

Usman said from the driver's seat. "Persian?" To an Afghan, the dialect didn't sounded as if they were from Iran.

"Yes. We're former Islamic Revolutionary Guard. We were recruited to perform close protection for senior Taliban about a year ago. We received a call from an old friend who promised $500k to each of us if we helped secure your escape. It's why we ducked when you first entered."

Mule was in the front seat. "Man, no one's gonna believe this. The freaking IRGC!"

Smitty thought about it quickly. He didn't know who financed the help, but he was sure any photo of Curt alive would quickly get into the right hands. "Yeah. Take your photo."

Curt was laying in Smitty's arms in the cargo area, with a slight smile and a thumbs up. Smitty returned the gesture.

The photo transmitted quickly from the IRGC's phone back to Ali. From there, it went to Andrew.

Within seconds, two million dollars wired into a Caribbean account. Ali would be financially set for a while; U.S. sanctions would not be a concern for him or his family.

Andrew called the Chairman's office again. "Colonel, it's Andrew Denney. I'd like to speak with the Chairman."

"Yes, Mr. Denney." Alfi had no desire for a similar discussion as last time.

"Admiral, Andrew here, did you see the video?"

"Yes. And we've got other indications they may have gotten away." Admiral Hershey was referring to the full motion video provided by overhead.

"Well, I'm looking at a photo of Curt and Smitty, both with their thumbs up."

"Jesus! Can you send me that?"

"Sure. For a few million. That's what it cost me."

The Admiral fumed. "You fucking asshole! It's not all about money! You said you wanted to..."

Andrew cut him off. "Admiral, it was a joke. Tell your executive officer to check her email. Have a great day." Andrew hung up. He was partially joking, but he also wanted the Chairman to know he did in fact provide help, and his own funds. Andrew considered sharing it with Allison. He wanted to, but given the sources, methods and agents, it was perhaps better if it came from the Admiral.

Once the Admiral had the photo, he sent it to Kathy, who shared it with Allison. She cried, holding it close to her heart.

"Allison," Kathy said. "Hope is a powerful thing. You mustn't quit now. They are far from safe."

It didn't matter. Allison had finally seen yet one more smile on her husband's face. She'd not let go of Kathy's iPhone all night.

****

The two 4Runners pulled into a small market parking lot on the outskirts of town after a successful rejoin. It was now almost 0100Hrs. Everyone exited the vehicles.

Smitty and Mule examined Curt. He had been abused badly, and they knew it. They gave him some water. He moved slowly and wanted to constantly hug both of them and Noorullah. He wasn't talkative. Mostly zoned out and in shock.

"OK," said Mule. "Now what? Do we go back to the compound?"

Smitty responded. "No. Buck said we go north, out of Kandahar, so we go north. Evidently, we are supposed to go to the where the men of Montezuma are from, or something like that."

Mule spoke. "What did Buck say exactly?"

"He said go north to where the men of the Halls of Montezuma are. I don't get it. Dude with Montezuma's shitter revenge? Is there a Mexican restaurant around here? What's that mean? I figure we go north and..."

Curt interrupted him, almost whispering, "Leathernecks."

Smitty and Mule looked at each other. "Fuck! Camp Leatherneck! Shit! That's it!"

Camp Leatherneck was one of the first bases in Afghanistan, built by Marines, then turned over to the Spanish. It was long abandoned before the U.S. left Afghanistan.

The group loaded up into the vehicles. Smitty and Mule had helped Curt disrobe and get him into something fresher and less stenchy. Curt stood there looking at the pile of clothes he'd disrobed from. Smitty held out fresh attire for him, but Curt stood there naked, motionless, staring at the clothes. They were full of spit, dried Taliban urine, his blood and his own feces, which they'd rubbed on him from the toilet brush. Curt glared at the pile. He calmly, almost robotically, grabbed his penis and began pissing on them, slowly swaying the stream side to side ensuring the entire pile was covered. A scowl was chiseled into his face, as if it were stone. No one said anything, and no one rushed him. They'd have waited twenty minutes if needed. They all understood.

Chapter Forty-seven
Flight of the Valkyrie

The news of Curt's escape spread quickly across Afghanistan. Some news outlets reported an intended delay in the execution, requested by the U.S. and graciously granted by the Taliban to allow for negotiations. Whatever the reason, it was good enough for Buck to know something was up. Now it was his turn. Refreshed from a small nap, he climbed down off the flight deck, opened the crew entrance door, and walked out. He could not believe what he saw.

There, behind the plane, were 32 Afghans. Raz and his family, along with many of the maintainers who'd worked on the aircraft with their families. Additionally, there was Raz's friend, the local Taliban leader.

"Raz, what is this?" Buck asked.

"Buck, they all want to leave." Raz answered.

"Yes, but I can't guarantee they'll get into the U.S. We don't know if we can get number two started, and we have no hydraulic booster. Technically, this aircraft is not legal to fly."

"Buck," Raz answered. "They have no fascinations about getting into the U.S. All they know is they want out of here. Anywhere is better than here."

"Yes, but…," Buck was running out of words.

"Buck. They know the airplane. And they know it can easily carry this many passengers, and then some. They also know if they stay and the plane departs, the Taliban will presume they knew and kill them anyway."

"Raz, I get that. But look. This flight is literally doomed. We need a tanker to get across the Indian Ocean. If it's not there, we have to either ditch in the ocean or divert back to Karachi. If we divert into Pakistan, we will all be returned to the Taliban and killed. Our odds aren't good. I'm ok with killing myself, but all these folks and their families? I can't."

Raz turned to the crowd and yelled something in Pashto. They all listened.

"Buck, I told them everything you said. I told them if this was

302

too much risk, they could leave. No one left."

Just then, one of the younger maintainers jumped up and yelled, "You our John Wayne! You our hero!" The group then began chanting, "John Wayne! John Wayne!"

Buck was moved nearly to tears. "Well. OK. Let's go." Buck said out loud. Then he lowered his voice and, in his best John Wayne impression said, "You persistent little pilgrim."

Raz belted out the pre-flight order. The maintenance team loaded their family onto the aircraft and then prepped the aircraft for engine start.

The first engine started fine, and the crew chief unplugged the power cart.

Buck and Raz would start engines three and four, continuing through the checklist methodically.

Buck looked out his window. "Shit. Look, Raz," he said.

Raz looked away from the engine instruments and saw three police car's lights off in the distance charging towards the airfield. Raz's heart sank.

"Raz, I'm not giving up. I'm telling you and our flight engineer to move your asses faster. Tell the last maintainer to pull the fucking chocks and get in!"

Raz yelled in Pashto on the intercom. The last man climbed up into the aircraft, shutting the crew entrance door, and as it was closing, Buck was already taxiing the aircraft.

As they taxied, the flight engineer was flipping fuel dials and setting switches as fast as he could read his checklist. Raz reached down to the one VHF radio and was ready to transmit to ground control, requesting taxi and take-off clearance.

Buck slapped Raz with his right hand while his left steered the big aircraft. "Don't call the tower. First, I don't think anyone's there, and second, I'm not sure we want folks to know we're taking off." Buck smiled. The police cars were getting closer. He taxied as fast as he could, knowing he couldn't go too fast. With a full load of gas, that weight on the aircraft would require heavy braking in order to slow for turns. He didn't want to overheat the brakes before pulling the gear up into the wells. Airborne fires are not fun for anyone. As the taxi continued, Buck pulled out his hand-held Garmin, set it in on the dash, and loaded Camp Leatherneck into the waypoint. It would be his only navigational aid.

Buck got to the end of the runway and turned the nose down the line.

"Sir, they're too close. We don't have time to do a high-speed taxi and get the number two engine online."

"Raz, you are a quick learner. You're right. Tell everyone to hold on." Buck ran up engines one, three and four to take-off power, 100%. He then set the pitch on number two's propeller to spin in the breeze versus standing still.

Buck looked at Raz. "You ready to go flying!?" Buck was alive, and he could see the excitement in Raz's eyes.

"Inshallah! My friend! Inshallah!" Raz was scared shitless.

Buck released the brakes and the big girl lurched down the runway, accelerating and pushing hard to the left. The asymmetrical thrust of two vs one engine forced the aircraft sideways. Once Buck had enough wind over the rudder, he could compensate and get the aircraft back to the centerline. "Good Rudder, off the nose wheel," Buck called out. He saw one good hydraulic system. It was enough, he thought. It had to be.

The flight engineer pointed at the engine gauges between the two pilots and said something.

Raz translated, "Number two RPM climbing." At the end of the runway ahead of them, they could see the police cars, doors were opening.

"Number Two started!" Raz yelled.

"Of course it did," Buck replied, chuckling, "Now get me some energy out of her or this is gonna be a real short flight!"

Although nonstandard, Raz skipped the after starting engine checklist. He and the flight engineer immediately tweaked out the engine and began drawing power from her. It wasn't maximum torque, but it was as much as they were going to get without the engine warmed up.

Buck hit rotation speed and pulled back on the yoke. The aircraft's nose gently lifted into the air, and the main landing gears followed suit.

The small arms fire from the police quickly dissipated as the C-130 cleared the vehicles and the police officer by mere feet.

"Climbing out!" Buck yelled. He looked down at his altimeter and the Vertical Speed indicator. "Two positive rates of climb! Bring up the gear."

Raz grabbed the gear handle and lifted it. "Gear cycling."

The two of them stared at the gear indicator, praying the gear would come up and stow appropriately. After fifteen seconds, the nose gear display finally showed the gear was up. "That was too long, Raz. Let's keep watch on that. She's good now. We can worry about that later."

Buck dropped his night-vision device over his eyes and dimmed the cockpit lights. All the external lights remained off. To folks on the ground, a black blob flew out of the airfield. Buck placed the aircraft into a lazy turn towards Camp Leatherneck. They'd be there in an hour and a half, more than enough time for Smitty and the gang to get there ahead of him, he thought.

At altitude, Buck set the autopilot and unstrapped, "Your aircraft," he said to Raz and went to the back. Buck took a flashlight with him. He'd check everything. A quick look in the little windows that exposed the wheel wells, the flight cables overhead. He also checked the utility hydraulic reservoir. He'd looked at it before take-off and knew it was full. Now, it was about 10% low. Buck went to the back cargo area and grabbed a case of hydraulic oil cans. He brought it back up with him and handed it to one of the maintainers. Before Buck could say anything, the Afghani maintainer took out a can, cracked it open and began pouring it into the reservoir. *'He knew.'* Buck thought.

"Perfect!" Buck yelled to the Afghani over the noise of the engines, giving him a thumbs up. The Afghan maintainer smiled back at Buck, large as life and also returned the thumbs up.

****

The two 4runners arrived at Camp Leatherneck, finding it abandoned with a poorly locked gate. Much of the base was covered in overgrown weeds and grass. The buildings had a good number of windows broken out. It was a far cry from what the field was in its heyday.

"Usman, turn the car around and back into the gate, knocking it down," Mule directed.

Usman did as directed. Unfortunately, he was a little too aggressive and drove up over the gate. A barb from the associated concertina wire punctured the driver's side rear tire. The sound of the hiss was obvious.

"Shit! Sorry, sir!" Usman yelled.

"Usman. It's OK. This girl has a spare, and we got time." Mule got out and cleared away the gate wreckage. The two vehicles drove onto the base.

Mule walked over to Majeed, who'd turned on the vehicle's parking lights. He then jumped back in with Usman. "Usman, parking lights on, and go slow." As Mule was barking out commands, Smitty remained with Curt. The two IRGC men were staring out the windows, with long guns at the ready. Given their story, Smitty had returned their weapons. Frankly, he knew he may need their firepower. Neither of the Iranians had night-vision devices but were grateful to have their weapons back.

Mule directed the two cars to the end of the runway. They sat with their taillights facing away from the runway and their headlights shining down it. Next, he directed both to shut off the engines and completely turn off the lights.

They all opened the doors and got out. Curt hastily approached Noorullah and held him. "I promised you!" he said. "I promised you!"

Usman offered a translation, but one wasn't needed. Noorullah understood.

"Shhh!" Mule ordered. They sat there quietly. Mule stared up into the sky with his night-vision devices. "Sir," one of the Iranians said. "You'll hear it before you see it. Can we use your devices for overwatch? That is the priority." The IRGC soldier was right. Smitty handed his night-vision device over, as did Mule.

The two scurried out into the brush and set up overwatch points. Usman and Majeed feverishly worked to change out the flat. They'd have it done in ten minutes, discarding the dead tire in the grass.

****

Buck was roughly fifty miles from Leatherneck. He wanted to do a normal approach to save fuel, but that was tactically unwise. He hadn't seen Leatherneck in a long time and wanted to see what he would be dealing with on the ground. As he got closer, he descended to 10k feet. It was as close as he'd wanted to get without knowing what threat was on the ground.

"Buck," Raz asked. "How are you going to land without any landing aids?"

"Well, Raz," Buck said. "It won't be pretty, but we're gonna try. If we don't do well the first time, we'll go around and try again. OK?"

Raz nodded with concern. Multiple approaches took time and surrendered the element of surprise. It wasn't a great plan, but it was the only one.

At five miles, Buck could see a dark patch where the airfield was. There was no movement as part of him was pleased the Taliban were not lying in wait. Another part was concerned his friends hadn't made it.

On the ground, Mule said, "Shh!" He heard it, and so did Smitty. They smiled. "Usman, Majeed! NOW!" The two started the SUVs and turned on their high beam lights.

As Buck looked down, he saw the brake lights and then the runway threshold lit up. On sheer instinct, he dropped the nose and pulled the throttles, lowering the aircraft into an overhead pattern. There was no mistaking this. He knew exactly who it was. Raz saw it too. "Sir! It's them!"

"It sure as hell is Raz! It sure the hell is! Before landing checks! Run 'em, Raz!"

Raz called out all the actions, and Buck ensured they were done. Buck was now abreast the airfield, flying faster than normal, but under the conditions, it was the right call. The flaps and slats moved, and the gear churned down. Buck watched the utility hydraulics needle fluctuate, but after a few dips and climbs, she settled back into normal range. The checks were done, and Buck began his turn off the perch.

"Alright!" Mule yelled. "Everyone in the cars, now!" The two IRGC jumped out of their firing positions and ran to the vehicles. They all piled in while Usman and Majeed strapped in.

Mule watched out the back of the car and saw the landing lights of the Herk swing into sight. Once the Herk passed overhead. Mule yelled, "GO!"

Usman floored it, and Majeed was soon to follow. The two vehicles raced behind the C-130 that was speeding away from them. The headlights from behind helped light up the runway as Buck settled her onto the ground. Eventually, the 4Runners were closing on the aircraft and would soon catch her. Once the C-130 stopped, both Usman and Majeed pulled their vehicles off the runway and let Buck turn the aircraft around. As it spun, the aircraft ramp and door opened. Everyone fled from the cars.

Smitty looked back at Hakem, who was running right behind him. "Are you sure about this? Your business? Your carpets?"

"Mr. Smitty, those are things, not life. Plus, I will be killed by the Taliban." Hakem paused. "Mr. Smitty, do you not want us? Are we not invited?"

"No! Of course you are," Smitty proclaimed. "I just can't imagine giving up everything."

"Mr. Smitty. I am not giving up anything. I am choosing everything. I assure you, Afghanistan gave up on us long ago."

Soon, everyone was on the aircraft. The ramp and door closed, and Buck was soon rolling back down the runway with an opposite direction take-off. There was little chance the Taliban would be able to engage. The Taliban had no knowledge of what airfield they were going to and the entire evolution took roughly fifteen minutes.

Once airborne, Smitty ran up to the flight deck, stood behind Buck, and hugged him in the chair. "Buck, you crazy son of a bitch! God, I love you!!"

Buck struggled to keep the flight controls in his hand. "Yeah, easy buddy, these aircraft don't barrel roll all that well," Buck replied. "Hey, how's Curt?"

"He's alive. They fucked him up good, though. You want to go back and see him?" Smitty said.

"Yeah. Hey Raz, follow the Garmin south. The next waypoint is Pasni. Your aircraft."

"My Aircraft," Raz replied.

Buck unstrapped from the aircraft commander's seat and got up. "Smitty, sit in here and wear the nogs (night-vision goggles). You'll be able to see the ground fire or a missile far easier."

Smitty put on the nogs. "OK, but if I see one, what do I do?"

Buck smiled, "Point it out to Raz and pray he can defeat the threat. I recommend the prayer goes to Allah though since we're in his territory."

"Jesus." Smitty replied, rolling his eyes.

"No, Allah." Raz corrected him.

Buck got down off the flight deck and went to see Curt in the back. As he passed the utility hydraulic reservoir, he checked it again. Before he looked, he saw three empty cans and the same Afghan holding a fourth can at the ready. Buck shot him another thumbs up.

Curt was sitting on the seat webbing along the side of the aircraft, holding Noorullah. Buck sat down and put his arms around him. The engine noise in the fuselage was substantial, too hard to have a discussion over, especially the one Curt and Buck needed.

Curt, shaking with tears in his eyes, turned to Buck and yelled, "I'd do it again! I'd do it again to get Noorullah."

Buck just held him.

After twenty minutes with Curt, Buck looked at his watch. It was nearly five in the morning. He went back to the flight deck and assumed the controls. It would be a little over three hours to crossing the coast 'feet wet' out over the Indian Ocean, but it would be only forty-five more minutes until they crossed into Pakistani Airspace, and left Afghanistan for good.

Chapter Forty-eight
Diplo Dilemma

"Hello, Secretary Baker's office," the voice answered.

"Yes, this is Colonel Andrade from the Chairman's office. Is the Secretary available?"

"Hold one minute, please."

"Admiral, sir, pick up!" Alfi yelled from outside his office door.

The Admiral waited on hold for the Secretary. "Hello, Squirts."

"Yes, Marleen, have you followed on the overhead?"

"Yes. I'm working on it right now. We are engaging Islamabad and Karachi as we speak. I think I've got overflight secured. Well, it's not a dip clearance, but at least they won't shoot it down. Publicly, they'll make a protest at the U.N. after the flight has long departed their airspace. We can live with that."

"Thanks Marleen, I owe ya."

"Nonsense. I'm happy for you. At what point are you looping the President in on this? Something this big spanning across departments and the interagency, he's going to find out soon."

"You're right. I'll call him next." It was a call the Admiral was dreading.

"OK. Again. Best of luck. Your guys seem like they really have a chance. By the way, do you know where they plan to land?"

"I don't know for sure, but if I was going to guess, it would be Bahrain, UAE, or Oman. Depends on what amount of fuel they have."

"OK. We will tackle those diplomatic challenges next."

"Marleen, you're the best. I appreciate it."

"No worries. Just loop in POTUS and let me know when he's in." The two hung up.

There was a gentle knock on the Admiral's door. "Alfi! Not now!" The Admiral was trying to figure out how to shape this to the White House.

"Squirts, it's not Alfi." A voice said.

The Admiral looked up. It was the Acting Secretary of Defense, Stacy Crawford.

"Yes, Ma'am. Sorry. I didn't see."

"It's alright, Squirts. Why don't you come down to my office, fill me in and we can make that call together? You look exhausted."

"Ma'am, I'm not sure if I know exactly what sleep is." Admiral Hershey walked out of his office and past the two executive officer's desks. Then said, "Madam Secretary, how did you know...."

Secretary Crawford cut him off and turned towards Alfi. "Colonel Andrade, thanks for the call. I appreciate you looking out for my employees, even when they won't look out for themselves." The two ladies smiled at each other, somewhat devilishly.

"Absolutely, Madam Secretary," Colonel Andrade said.

"Alfi," the Chairman said, as if he'd answered his own question.

✳✳

Buck sat in the aircraft commander's seat, just as he'd done for thousands of hours before. It was eerily quiet. Raz, the flight engineer, and he scanned the instruments over and over as if they expected something to break. Everything was fine. The second engine ducting repair was holding well. The bleed air temps were slightly higher than the other engines but well within tolerances.

A break in the silence. "Unknown Rider, Unknown Rider, approaching from the 100 miles southwest of Kandahar. This is Pakistan Airspace Control on guard. Identify yourself."

Buck and Raz looked at each other. They both knew Pakistan had more than enough capability to shoot them out of the sky if they so desired.

Again, "Unknown Rider, Unknown Rider, approaching from the 100 miles southwest of Kandahar, this is Pakistan Airspace

311

Control on guard. Identify yourself."

Buck reached down and set the radio to the guard frequency, 121.5. "Pakistan Airspace Control, this is Buck Zero One on guard. Please pass an ident code."

"Buck Zero One, squawk 4754. Say intentions."

Buck dialed in the squawk and hit the ident button. He then looked at Raz and said, "Should I tell them our true intentions?"

"Probably not." Raz replied.

Buck didn't respond. Two minutes had gone by, and Buck watched the dot on his Garmin cross into Pakistani Airspace. They were now clearly out of Afghan airspace. Finally, Buck replied. "Pakistan Airspace Control, it appears we've unexpectedly ventured into your airspace. Greatest of apologies, request direct to Pasni to exit."

"Buck Zero One, standby."

Raz and Buck looked at each other. If there ever was a God, this was the fifth time he was needed to help the flight.

"Buck Zero One, you are cleared direct Pasni. Please share your tail number and point of destination so that the government of Pakistan can file a formal complaint against your violation."

In such a scenario, most pilots would be enraged. They were going to be cited for a flight violation, which sometimes is a career killer. Inside the C-130, Buck and Raz were high-fiving. The flight engineer didn't understand a lick of English but also joined in the jubilation. Buck gleefully passed the tail number and then relayed they intended to land at Masirah Island. Finally, Buck could share his escape plan with the rest of the world. It would greatly help those trying to assist.

For the next hour and a half, the aircraft would fly towards Pasni. Every so often drinking more hydraulic fluid.

****

The secure call was set up between the Defense Secretary's office and the Oval Office. After the technology processed through the security clearance filters, both the Chairman and the SECDEF were looking at the President and Steve.

The SECDEF relayed everything that had transpired, or at least what she understood of it, from Alfi and Admiral Hershey. After she finished, she asked the President, "Sir, how do you want to play this?" The Secretary muted her mic.

Under his breath, Admiral Hershey said, "BOHICA."

"Yup, here it comes," Stacy said.

Admiral Hershey's eyes widened. He had no clue she knew that term.

"What, you don't think I know your vulgar little acronyms?" She smiled. "Heck, I even use a few on occasion."

The two then focused on the President's response.

"Well, I'm furious that I was not in the loop on this. We have U.S. Government assets, MY assets helping this rescue, and I was unaware. That's a foul."

"Mr. President," Secretary Crawford said calmly. "That's on me then. And for what it's worth, other than this phone call, you still maintain plausible deniability in the event anything goes wrong. Lastly, to be clear, there were few details and a very low expectation of success. Should it have failed, and you were read in, it could have spelled political disaster."

Steve looked at the President and nodded.

"OK," the President said, "But, I'm calling the shots now. I want the two of you over here soonest, and let's pull together the NSC."

Secretary Crawford gently replied, "Sir? Is there a National Security Threat?"

Growing frustrated, the President demanded. "Explain yourself, Ms. Crawford."

"Sure, Mr. President. Right now, you have a couple of Secretaries involved in this and it's low on many radars. If you pull together the NSC, you're signaling across the entire government that this is a far greater issue in your mind than perhaps it really is. You're also exposing a small scale operation to many interagency entities that not only don't need exposure but will feel compelled to 'do something' which in most likelihood will only impede progress, not help it. I understand Secretary Baker is still working to get AMCITs out of Afghanistan.

May I ask, how many times has the Secretary of Energy helped with that effort? Or the Secretary of the Treasury?"

Admiral Hershey sat there, pinching his leg hard to keep the smirk off his face.

"Acting Secretary Crawford, you're on thin ice." the President said.

"I apologize, sir. I don't mean to be." she replied. Stacy had a wonderful way about her in which she could give the appearance of an apology, without actually meaning it. "Sir, you relieved my previous boss and put me in charge. Then you re-hired him to a new position and gave him security responsibility for a chunk of the world, with no coordinating efforts into my department. Now, he's caused a mess, and if rumors are true, you're planning to let him go again soon. Mr. President, up until this appointment I have never been a political hire, I'm a career government employee. I have served and continue to serve both parties, and more importantly, the United States and her citizens, to the best of my ability. If you wish to fire me, please let me know. You'll have my resignation in under 24 hours. Make no mistake, I love my job, but also know I'll triple my salary in the private sector. When I step down as the acting Secretary, the second firing of this position in under a year, it won't play well, and your poll numbers will show it."

The President stewed, but he knew everything she said was right. While irate, there was something about her blunt honesty he found refreshing. Very few who served presidents afforded such honesty.

Steve held up a piece of paper with one word on it. 'Gerzema.'

The President nodded. His anger was misplaced. There were two culprits to blame. They were John Gerzema and the President himself for the affair in the White House bedroom that caused this mess. He took a deep breath. "No... No. I don't think that is necessary. You're doing a fine job, Stacy. I was a bit out of line. Sorry, just on edge." The President paused, and then continued. "Stacy, you asked me how I'd like to proceed. May I ask you what you recommend?"

"No apology necessary, Mr. President," Stacy said in such a

way that even if it were required, she'd not accept it. "I think the best solution right now is to give the Defense Department lead and then supported by State to coordinate with other nations. Our two departments can manage this. And bring you a win."

A 'win,' was something the President desperately needed. "OK, Acting Secretary Crawford, you have lead. I'll call over to Secretary Baker and let her know to provide support. Are there any other agencies you need to assist?"

"No, Mr. President, we can manage."

"Great. I'd like an end of day brief on this issue passed through Steve. Is that clear?"

"Yes, sir. Admiral Hershey will cover down and ensure the Joint Staff gets you something daily. One last comment: please make sure that Secretary Baker knows she has your full support. From the videos we have, the C-130 has way more folks on it than just the four-man team that went in. She'll need a long leash if this is going to work."

The Chairman sat there. In all his days, he wasn't sure he'd ever seen an acting secretary barking orders to the President, and him taking them.

"Will do. White House, out." The video conference ended.

Admiral Hershey just stared at Stacy. "Madam Acting Secretary, that was unbelievable."

"Eh. It's easy when you know Gerzema has him by the balls for something. Anyway, it's Stacy to you Squirts. Let's go get our team home."

The Chairman's head spun. So much for having solid intelligence assets.

315

Chapter Forty-nine
Passin' Gas

As Buck and Raz flew south, the light of dawn crested over the horizon in the east. They'd been flying for roughly three hours since departing Camp Leatherneck. Buck kept looking at the fuel gauge. He'd done enough calculations to determine how far he could get from Karachi and how much he could glide. He needed that tanker.

Fifty miles off the nose was the shoreline, out to the Indian Ocean. Buck got out of his chair and played with some of the instruments at the navigation station, trying anything that could give him indications a tanker was waiting. He turned on the TACAN (Tactical Air Navigation) system and scrolled aimlessly through the channels, hoping one would cause the system to lock onto the tanker. Like a backwards clock, the needle just kept spinning. It didn't work.

They were so close to success, he thought. The tanker HAD to be there. Buck sat back down. "OK, Raz. Here's the plan. Once we are feet wet, I'm declaring an In-Flight Emergency and transmitting on guard. Hopefully, if the tanker is there, they'll hear us and push us to their frequency and their location. We literally have less than five minutes of gas to find it and then we must go to Karachi. Do you understand?"

"Yes," said Raz. "What's the emergency?"

Buck looked at him, puzzled. "What do you mean?"

Raz was flipping through the barber poled section of his checklist, the section that covered all emergencies. "You said we are declaring an emergency. What is it?"

Buck laughed. "God, I miss training Afghans. Raz, there is no actual emergency. Put your checklist down. Tell as many of your guys as you can to put their noses in windows and look for that tanker. He has to be out there."

Buck looked down out the window. As soon as they were over the water, he transmitted. "MAYDAY! MAYDAY! MAYDAY! This is Buck Zero One on guard, declaring an emergency over Pasni, Pakistan, heading southwest at Flight Level 2.5.0."

"Buck Zero One. This is Pakistan Control. Go with your emergency."

Buck ignored the call. He didn't want to talk to Pakistan, he wanted to talk to the Tanker.

He'd transmit again. "MAYDAY! MAYDAY! MAYDAY! This is Buck Zero One declaring an emergency over Pasni, Pakistan, heading southwest at Flight Level 2.3.0. Nature of emergency is low fuel." In the aviation world, there is either 'min fuel' or 'emergency fuel' but not 'low fuel.' As he transmitted on the international guard frequency of 121.5 Mhz, he knew all other aircraft were required to monitor the channel. If there was a refueling asset airborne and close enough, Buck was certain the tanker would hear him.

Again, Pakistan Control answered. Buck was distraught. Then he heard.

"Buck Zero One, this is Texaco Two Three on guard, push 123.5."

Buck jumped back on the radio, "Buck Zero One, WILCO (Will comply)." Buck reached down and changed the frequency quickly. "Texaco Two Three, Buck Zero One, say status.

"Buck Zero One, Texaco Two Three is marshaling at 17,000 feet, sixty miles on a 180 out of Pasni." It was exactly where Buck asked them to be, but they were too far.

"Texaco Two Three, can you work north? We are min fuel and have about three minutes left to find you."

"Texaco 23 swinging north, expediting." The lumbering KC-135 turned north as the pilots mashed the throttles forward.

"OK crew," Buck said. "Eyes out now!" The two airplanes were closing on each other fast. Buck had pulled the C-130 throttles back to idle and dropped the nose. In under a minute, he was nearing 16,000 feet in a shallow descent, trying to conserve fuel.

Two minutes had gone by, still no tanker. Everyone on the plane could sense how important this was.

"Texaco Two Three, Buck Zero One. Say status?"

"Buck Zero One, Texaco Two Three, still working north at 17,000 feet."

Buck didn't see them, and his window for the tanker closed.

If he stayed any longer, he jeopardized everyone's lives on the plane. Dejected, Buck placed the aircraft in a lazy turn to the west, towards Karachi.

His next transmission was somber. "Texaco Two Three, Buck Zero One. No Joy (we don't see you). Turning west to primary alternate of Kilo Hotel India." (KHI is the airfield designator for Karachi). As everyone onboard felt the plane turn, a sinking feeling came over the Afghans, who realized if they landed in Karachi, the Pakistan would likely return them to the Taliban.

"Raz, set up for an approach into Karachi." Buck said, not happy about the situation, but knowing full well aviation was an unforgiving business. There was no other choice. As Raz got out the approach plates and set up the aircraft, Buck reset the VHF radio to 121.5Mhz guard frequency and transmitted. "MAYDAY. MAYDAY. MAYDAY. This is Buck Zero One, emergency fuel, diverting to Kilo Hotel India. Descending out of 16,000 on a glide profile. 45 souls onboard." In all actuality, Buck had no clue how many souls were onboard, nor was he in the mood to count.

"Buck Zero One, Karachi Approach, please ident and switch to 148.1."

"148.1, Buck Zero One, switching."

Buck looked down between the two cockpit pilot chairs at the radio control, and began dialing in 148.1. As he did, the C-130 shook a bit and the pitch of noise from the engines began to shift from a whine to almost a growl.

Buck immediately grabbed the yoke, "My Aircraft!" he yelled, rapidly scanning the instruments.

"Your aircraft." Raz answered. The three of them were all heads down, frantically searching for the problem. Engine temps, hydraulics, power settings... everything was fine. The flight engineer then looked up from the panels at the front of the plane to his overhead panel. As he did, he saw a massive KC-135 out the front windscreen overtaking them about 500 feet above, with the fuel transfer boom flying just fifty meters ahead of them.

The flight engineer began poking both Buck and Raz yelling "Gooz! Gooz! Gooz!" The Pashto word for 'gas.'

The VHF guard channel cracked to live, "Anyone around here seen a C-130 that needs need some gas?"

"Halle – freaking – lujah!" Buck screamed.

"Allah Akbar!" Raz said.

Buck looked at him. "OK, this ONE time you can say that. It's growin' on me!"

The flight engineer set up the fuel panel and opened the receiver port, just as Buck had instructed

Buck was slowly flying the airplane into position. "Karachi Control, Buck Zero One, please cancel our emergency declaration. We'd like to request MARSA (Military Assumes Responsibility) on Texaco Two Three."

"Texaco Two Three, will assume MARSA," the navigator onboard the tanker said.

Buck snuggled the C-130 up under the tanker. He loved flying formation, and flew like a pro, as if he was riding a bike. He felt the boom slam into the receiver overhead. "Contact!" Buck said.

"Contact," the boom operator of Texaco Two Three said.

Raz watched the fuel panel and the flight engineer gave a thumbs up, "Sir, we're taking gas!" It was the first time Raz had ever seen it. He was truly amazed.

The pilot of Texaco 23 jumped on the boom intercom, talking internally between the two aircraft. "Buck 01? Is that right?"

"Yes, sir." Buck replied.

"I'm gonna start a slow turn back to the south. Did you declare Masirah is your final destination?"

"Correct," Buck said. As the fuel transferred into the C-130, controlling the girl became more and more challenging.

"How many Americans and how many Afghans do you have on the flight? State Department is asking."

"Smitty, are you up on headset?" Buck asked.

"Affirm, buddy." Smitty replied.

"OK," Buck said. "We had 32 Afghans and then me. How many did you bring on?"

"We brought six Afghans, four Americans and two Iranians." Smitty said. There was a long pause.

"Two, what?" Said the pilot of Texaco 23.

"Two Iranians. Former IRGC." Again, the pause. No one would discuss it further. There wasn't time.

"Copy, total 44 pax," the Texaco Navigator replied.

"Hey Texaco. FYI, we have one VHF and one HF radio, both are commercial grade. We have no navigation system other than a handheld Garmin. My plan is to land at Masirah for gas only then continue onto any friendly NATO country that will take us in, within range of one bag of gas. I won't be able to get another tanker, likely, and I don't think we need one. Can you pass that back to whomever in D.C. cares and can get us some help?"

"We can do that," said the pilot of Texaco 23. I'm having my nav put us on a direct heading for you to Masirah to help your nav solution. Once we dial that in, we'll start passing back your other info." There was a small pause. "I'm showing a full 15K fuel passed. That should get you to Masirah easy. Do you want more or need anything else?

"No," Buck said. "You guys were heroes today, thanks."

"Nope. We watched the news. You guys are heroes. Best of luck. Hey, our nav has something for ya."

The nav piped up. "Buck Zero One is now a legitimate call sign in the global air traffic system. Your new squawk will be 1594. It will get you to the Masirah ADIZ (Air Defense Identification Zone). You're cleared up to Fight Level 2.8.0."

"Thanks, Nav! Greatly appreciated. Request disconnect." Buck said.

"Disconnect." The Boom operator replied as he flew the boom up out of the receiver. Once the boom was clear, Texaco 23 began speeding up and climbing away in a slow bank east towards Al Udeid. Buck 01, now a legal flight callsign, also accelerated and began a climb to flight level 280 en route to Masirah Island, which was two hours away.

Chapter Fifty
12 Gun Salute

At Masirah Island, Dirty was sitting in front of his hooch on a self-made hammock. The sunshine was comforting, and he was enjoying the solitude. His enjoyment, however, would soon end as his phone rang. He saw the 703 area-code and knew it was likely the Pentagon.

"Lieutenant Colonel Sanchez," he said as he answered.

"Dirty, Chairman here. Hey. Need you to get on your horse. I'm sure you've seen the news. The group who sprung the American from the Taliban are on an Afghan C-130 inbound your location."

As soon as Dirty heard it, he sat up. "You're shitting me?"

"No. I need you to get them three things. Get them gas, some food/water and clearance to take-off. The first two be easy, the third one is going to be a diplomatic goat rope. State Department is working from their end. I don't know how many diplo skills you have, but whatever they are, break em out."

"Admiral, with a callsign like Dirty, I assure you, I have zero diplomatic bones in my body, but I have a guy here that I think can help. I'll keep you advised."

The Admiral was pleased. "Great. Please do." The Admiral hung up.

Dirty walked over to Sleazy's hooch. He, too, was enjoying the sun, also in a homemade hammock that Dirty taught him how to make.

"Sleazy, I've found your chance to shine. Go get cleaned up in your D.C. clothes. Meet me at the Ops building."

Sleazy rolled out of his hammock, excited about doing something that was far more entertaining than doing nothing. "Will do, boss." He replied.

Dirty reviewed the flight info for Buck 01 from the computer system, ordered 44 meals and drinks and a few extra cases of water. He loaded them into a small van and told one of his aircrew to drive it out to the aircraft once it landed.

Sleazy finally made it to the Ops center on Masirah Island.

Once Dirty shared what was going on, Sleazy was salivating at the chance to help some American heroes get home to the U.S. He just wasn't sure how.

"Dirty. What do I do? I mean, I want to do something."

"Well, Sleazy, I'd say this is perhaps a good chance to leverage the clout and power your family has. But it's up to you. You are the closest thing we have to a diplomat in Oman." This clearly wasn't the case. There was a U.S. Embassy in Muscat, along with an ambassador and full staff. But Sleazy didn't need to know that as far as Dirty was concerned. By the time Dirty had finished pumping him up, Sleazy could have played starting fullback for Notre Dame's Fighting Irish, at least in a diplomatic sense.

Out on the ramp, the van full of food and water waited for Buck 01. The driver pulled out his phone and called Dirty. "Sir, we have a problem. You need to get out here fast."

****

As Buck began the approach into Masirah Island, he was grateful to have plenty of fuel, four powerful engines, and one can of hydraulic fluid remaining. At ten miles out, Buck dropped the flaps, then the gear, preparing for the landing. Raz had secured approval from the tower.

Buck was also grateful for a real landing aid, which helped him maintain glide slope. His landing back at Leatherneck was scary and something he'd not share; at least until he was safely in a bar and bragging about the exploit. The C-130 settled onto the runway and slowed as Buck reversed the propeller's pitch, enabling reverse thrust. Buck turned off the runway and onto the hammerhead of the taxiway ramp. There, he was immediately greeted by three police cars, each with the doors open and four armed officers pointing weapons at the plane.

"Not what I'd call a friendly welcoming committee," Buck said to Raz on the intercom. Buck transmitted out onto the VHF radio to the tower. "Tower, Buck Zero One. There appears to be a few vehicles in our way. Please advise on taxi procedures."

"Buck Zero One, shut down at your current location. Your aircraft is being impounded by the Omani government."

"Tower, Buck Zero One. I'm happy to do as you say, but if I shut down right here and lose my air conditioning, there will be 44 dead bodies on this aircraft in under an hour."

"Buck Zero One, shut down your engines immediately or the officers will be ordered to fire on your aircraft."

"Buck Zero One. WILCO." Buck and Raz began shutting down the engines, one at a time in hopes of prolonging the cooling. Once they were done, Buck looked at Raz. "Buddy, run to the back and pop the overhead escape hatch, also crack the paratroop doors just a little. I'll grab this one and also open the swing windows. We need to do everything to keep this thing cool."

The last engine on the C-130 had barely finished spinning when Dirty pulled up in a staff car. He looked at all the Omani Security and yelled.

"Lower your guns! Jesus! Are you going to shoot an airplane with a freaking handgun?"

None of them budged.

"Does anyone speak English?" He said.

Again, none of them moved.

Dirty pulled out his cell phone and redialed the last number from the Chairman.

"Good morning, Chairman's Office, Colonel Andrade speaking. Can I help you?"

"Yeah, this is Dirty in Oman. We have a slight problem. Is the Chairman in?"

"Dirty, he's on with the SEC STATE right now. Tell me what's going on," Alfi requested.

"Well, the plane was stopped on the ramp by security. There are 12 guns pointed at the plane. The temperature is rapidly rising in that plane, and they have no air-conditioning." The concern in Dirty's voice was clear.

"Got it. Stand by." Alfi went into the Chairman's office with a note describing Dirty's dilemma and showed it to the Admiral, who was on the conference call. He muted it and said to Alfi,

"Tell him to call back in 15 minutes. Secretary Baker is working it right now with the Omani Minister of Foreign Affairs."

Alfi departed the room and did as requested. Dirty was furious, but there was little he could do.

The Chairman again unmuted the call.

Foreign Minister Mohammed Albusaidi was speaking. "Yes, Secretary Baker. I understand your concern, but we have reached out to the Taliban, and they have made an attractive offer for the aircraft which we have accepted. It is ours now, and therefore, it will not leave Omani soil. We have prison buses on the way to get the passengers. The U.S. can send another aircraft to fly them out, but they are not welcome to stay here."

Secretary Baker had heard enough. "Minister Albusaidi, I appreciate your offer to house our Americans, who've committed no criminal act, in a prison. How gracious of you. I'd ask you and your government to strongly reconsider the purchase of this aircraft. I have both the Acting Secretary of Defense and the Chairman on the line and they both can explain the future challenges you may face should you continue down this path."

Acting Secretary Crawford began, "Minister Albusaidi, greetings from the Pentagon. I wanted to relay that our President has given both Secretary Baker and I significant authority regarding this issue. Now, I see two approaches, one positive and the other less so. Regarding the latter, I don't think anyone wins. You see, the F-16s you currently fly were purchased under a Foreign Military Sales contract with the United States. One clause of that contract clearly stipulates the U.S. can recall those aircraft at any time, for any reason. That clause also covers your other C-130s as well. Hence, you could keep this old C-130, but you would likely lose the remainder of your entire air force."

The minister jumped in. "Madam Secretary, I don't enjoy idle threats. I strongly doubt the U.S. would take such action, knowing they'd be forced to reimburse our nation for taking our aircraft." He was clearly agitated and from the rustling of papers in the background on his end of the line, looking for the contracts. Being of Arabian decent, he also was agitated by being forced to negotiate with a female.

"Yes, of course. You are correct. That clause does state the U.S. would be obligated to pay a portion of the original contract cost for your usage. To be fair, we would welcome that opportunity. I have the contract right in front of me. I can send it over if you wish. As for the U.S. payment, you do realize, it won't be the U.S. paying. There is currently a waiting list of nations, good allies and partners of the U.S., who desperately desire F-16s and C-130s. Your aircraft will simply alleviate a portion of that waiting list. Admiral Hershey, isn't that correct?"

The Admiral jumped in. "Madam Secretary, that is correct. Currently Headquarters U.S. Air Force and the Secretary of the Air Force reported to Congress there is over a one year wait to get F-16s, with three countries all on contract for well over 30 aircraft."

"Thanks Admiral, that's helpful information. So, Minister, as I mentioned, there is also a positive approach. As I see it, your military has submitted a request to procure Blackhawk helicopters, but that request is caught up in D.C. red tape. And you are one of the nations on a fairly long waiting list. Should you choose to refuel our aircraft, allow our local staff to tend for and care for our aircrew, and let it take-off, I'd be happy to look into the status of that purchase and see what can be done to help expedite it. Madam Secretary Baker, that's all we have from the Pentagon."

"Thanks, Madam Secretary Crawford," she replied. "Minister Albusaidi, we have worked together for a long time, and the U.S. has not forgotten how much Oman assisted with our efforts in the region. I understand Secretary Crawford's negative scenario is perhaps distasteful, but her interpretation of the contract is accurate. I'd rather we just ignore that portion of the conversation and look for ways to build a better relationship with Oman versus allowing opportunities to erode our friendship. Minister, please. I welcome your thoughts."

Minister Albusaidi was frustrated. Hours earlier, he'd promised his Prince they'd be gaining a used C-130 at a bargain. It was quickly becoming clear he'd not be able to fulfill that promise. That discussion would have to wait. "Secretary Baker, yes. I agree. Secretary Crawford's first approach is unwelcome and perhaps inappropriate for a dignified diplomatic discussion at our level. I do, however, gravitate towards her positive approach. I will speak with the Prince at once and share your gracious offer, then I will get back to you."

"Minister Albusaidi, please forgive my intrusion. I have word from our folks on the Island that the aircraft is at gunpoint and the passengers are being forced to remain on an aircraft in the sun without power or air conditioning. Surely this wasn't your request, and perhaps there were some overzealous security personnel. Could you please remedy this situation before you engage with the Prince?" The Chairman was doing his best diplomatic effort, which was actually quite good. One doesn't become the Chairman of the Joint Chiefs on military skills alone.

"Yes, Admiral. We will at once. I thank you all for your time." The parties disconnected from the call. The Admiral yelled, "Alfi! Get in here!"

Colonel Andrade strolled in. "Yes, Admiral?"

"When Dirty calls back, tell him things should change quickly. If they don't change in under ten minutes, let me know." The Admiral's orders were clear. Alfi walked back to her desk out in the front receiving room of the Chairman's office.

****

Back on the Island, a new development had arisen. Sleazy pulled up in another staff car, holding his cell phone out as if he were taking a selfie. He emerged from the car, and it was clear from his actions he was making a video.

"This scene is unacceptable and as the son of current Special National Security Advisor to the President, John Gerzema, I DEMAND the Omani's call off these security officials and allow the passengers to get off that hot plane!" Sleazy was live streaming the aircraft and the security members, none of which welcomed being filmed.

"Sleazy, what are you doing?" Dirty asked as he walked up.

"Why are you filming this?"

"Ah!" Sleazy said into the camera. "My good friend, Lieutenant Colonel Sanchez, is also here on the ramp and can attest to this situation. Sir, I'm live on YouTube. Can you verify what's going on?"

Dirty reached up, grabbed Sleazy's phone and ripped it out of his hands, then stopped the YouTube stream. "What on EARTH are you doing? Son, sometimes I think you are all thrust, no vector."

Sleazy was angered. "I'm following your request! You told me to leverage my power and I am."

Just then, the guns lowered, and the security personnel entered back into their cars. One of them nodded to Dirty, waving approval for him to go near the aircraft. The three cars pulled away.

Dirty thought to himself, *'There's no freaking way Sleazy did this. Is there?'* That didn't matter, because to Sleazy, he was certain the most recent developments were the result of his efforts. He bowed his back, popped out his chest, re-caged his streaming video camera and walked up the C-130 entrance door and knocked. "You can open up! It's safe to come out!"

The doors opened and the 44 personnel on board stumbled off the aircraft. It had gotten warm but not miserably hot yet.

Sleazy greeted each one, hand shaking with them as if he were a politician welcoming back a flight of military personnel from war. He relished it.

Soon, an aircraft tug arrived and would pull the C-130 to a more appropriate ramp to begin fueling it. As that happened, a bus arrived and took everyone other than Buck to a lounge in the Ops center. Buck rode separately with Dirty after their introductions and a brief chat about the previous flight.

"So, how's the bird?" Dirty asked.

"I've seen better and a few worse, but from the condition we found her in until now, she's a beaut." Buck replied.

Dirty nodded. "Is there anything you need for her before you take-off?"

"Actually, we could use an engine starter, and booster hydraulic pump lines and a box of hydraulic oil cans. Only way to get number two going is an air start or high-speed taxi and she's drinkin' hydraulic fluid like a 2nd Lieutenant downing beers at the Officers Club on a Friday night."

Dirty laughed. "So, you flew this thing with only one hydraulic system? And, I guess you didn't get the starter we sent to Kabul yesterday."

Buck also laughed. "It was either fly her or die in Afghanistan. So, yup. Flew her here. And no, we didn't get the starter. I confess, though, I had little desire to stick around and wait for it."

"Understood. Well, I can't get you the booster parts, but we have a few more starters. Also, more hydraulic oil than you could ever desire. Hold on." Dirty called one of his crew members, who rounded up another starter and scaffolding. He also would have a case of oil placed into the cargo area.

After the refueling, a few of the Afghan maintainers headed out to the aircraft and within an hour, had the starter install complete. Buck and Dirty were filing the flight plan, trying to find a location that would accept the aircraft. Unfortunately, every flight plan was denied. Again, Dirty pulled out his phone and dialed Alfi.

"Colonel Andrade, hello again from Oman. Hey, everything here is far better, but the aircrew for that bird can't find a country they can fly into. Do you guys have any suggestions?"

Alfi told him to hold and explained the situation to the Chairman. He said to her, "Tell them to get to Souda Bay. I have a plan."

Alfi did as requested. Unfortunately, again, the aircraft was denied flight approval into Greece. Buck and Dirty sat there. The day was getting long, and Buck wanted to get as far away from the nation that greeted him with a twelve-gun welcoming committee.

"Buck, I have an idea. Any objections to taking off VFR (Visual Flight Rules)?"

Buck thought about it. He was already in Omani airspace and could fly over their country without an issue. Saudi Arabia would be angered by an unauthorized overflight, but as long as they didn't land, it would be similar to Pakistan. Once over the

Mediterranean Sea, if need be, he could declare an emergency. It was far from orthodox and somewhat unethical, but Buck had few options left. "I'm good. Do you have an idea to get me outta here?"

"Too easy," Dirty replied. The two rounded up the passengers and helped them get onboard. Dirty sent out his aircrew to help with the engine start checklist, dragging the start cart from their aircraft over to the Afghanistan aircraft.

Buck and Raz were in the seats. "Raz, how about a bet? $10 that the number two engine won't start. How much faith do you have in your maintainers?"

Raz looked at Buck, "Make it $20."

"Alright! Clear number two for engine start!" Buck looked out the window, raised two fingers, then awaited a thumbs up from the ground crew. It was there in five seconds.

"You ready, Raz."

"Yes, sir!" he replied.

Buck pushed the starter button, "Turning!"

"Timing!" Raz responded with authority.

Buck stared out the window and then began shaking his head side to side as if the propeller didn't spin.

"Hide your bullshit, Buck, I see the RPM gauge climbing!" Then the igniters lit off. "Engine Start!" Raz shouted proudly.

"Raz, I wasn't shaking my head for a failed engine start. I just don't have $20," replied Buck. The two laughed.

The plane taxied out and took off, circled back, flying by the runway and rocking her wings. Dirty and Sleazy looked up and waved. Buck 01 was on its way.

Chapter Fifty-one
Dirty Deals, Done Dirt Cheap

The Chairman pulled out his cell phone, closed his office door and placed a call.

The other party answered. "Squirts! My God! It's been forever. How are you?"

"Prime Minister Pisanos, it's great to hear your voice. You are correct, it has been too long."

"Please, Squirts! Call me Zap!" the man said. It was the Prime Minister of Greece, Zephyrus Pisanos, formerly Lieutenant General Pisanos from the Greek Air Force. The two, as Lieutenant Colonels, attended the International College of Armed Forces together, years ago, and since then, the Admiral would always try to take any ship he was on into the Greek Isles to visit his long-time friend.

"Will do Zap, but given you're a polished politician, I never know where I stand with you."

"Ha! Always as my friend. I still remember you standing up in the hot tub on Santorini, trying to sing the Greek national anthem, wearing nothing but the wine bottle you held over your privates!" The story was true, and one which had not been exposed to others in the U.S. military.

"Yes. Thanks for reminding me. Hey, Zap. I have a time sensitive offer and I'm bringing it to you first."

"OK. Shoot. What is it?"

The Admiral explained the situation and that a C-130 was on its way to Souda Bay, likely landing in a few hours. Greece could impound the plane, as the Taliban would never be able to come get it, and then negotiate a great deal for the aircraft.

"Squirts. This all sounds too good to be true. If there's one thing I learned in America, it is there is always a catch."

"Zap, well, yes, but a small one. The plane has 44 personnel on board. Mostly Afghans, a few Americans and two former Iranians who were former Islamic Revolutionary Guard. I need your help getting them cared for until I can get another military flight down to them, then back to the U.S."

"Two IRGC? You're going to bring two IRGC back to the

U.S.?"

"Former IRGC, Zap. Former. Let me worry about that. Can you help me? It's really a win / win. I know Greece has been looking to buy a C-130J for a while. Frankly, that's not a great deal. You'd have a mixed fleet of C-130s. The maintenance, logistics and training issues as well as costs would be excessive. This gets you a common frame C-130, like your others, with low flying hours at a song of a price.

Prime Minister Pisanos thought about it for a while. "Squirts, get it to Souda. I'll open our airspace. I also promise I will take care of your crew. There's a pleasant hotel off the base called The Royal Sun, where we bedded down many of your aircrew for years. Years ago, I was the Souda Bay base commander and remember it like yesterday. They will be well cared for. As for the purchase, we will see. Getting money out of my Parliament is not easy, and our current President loves trees more than planes. That is for me to figure out, though."

"Zap, you are freaking awesome. I owe you."

"Eh, you always owe me. But I am blessed to have a friend like you." Zephyrus replied.

"The feeling is mutual, my friend. Take care, and thanks," replied the Admiral. They both hung up. Zap made a few phone calls and magically the airspace would open and permission to land would be granted.

Admiral Hershey relayed the good news to Secretary Baker and Crawford. Things were coming together.

****

The news of the wayward C-130, however, was no longer the lead mainstream news. The fast-churning media cycle had bitten onto the now viral YouTube video of Sleazy, and the questions were pouring into the White House Press Secretary's office from every outlet in the world. *'Is this person on the video your son?'*

John had seen the video. After calming down, he called Ashton. "Ashton! What have you done?"

"Dad, I'm an adult now, and I'm sick of living in the shadows.

331

If you're proud of me, great. If you're not, I can live with that too, but I won't harbor your secret any longer." Sleazy was adamant.

"You're a fool! Do you have any idea what this means for our family? For the power and strength we wield in D.C.?"

Sleazy chuckled. "You say 'our family' as if I grew up eating dinner every night at your kitchen table."

"Careful, young man. You and your mother were well cared for." John grew more angered.

"I guess. In your world, money can buy everything. In ours, it can't. Take care, Dad. When I get back, we can chat." Sleazy hung up.

Dirty was sitting across from Ash at the table. He gradually stood up and started slowly clapping until it turned into a standing ovation. "Well done, buddy. I'm proud of you."

Sleazy would be alright.

****

Allison had checked out of the hospital. Paul had taken her back to the row home in D.C. Once there, she'd gathered pens, paper, her laptop and other administrative accouterments. She'd be meeting Andrew Denney at the Starbucks on 8th Street SE, just one block over east.

Allison had seen Ashton's YouTube video as well, which she knew would only serve as another wooden stake to drive into the chest of the D.C. vampire John Gerzema. At the Starbucks, Andrew gave her everything. He transferred all their phone call audio files into her computer; he gave her copies of all the stock transactions and the overall plans to eliminate much of the heroin supply with the intent to corner the market on the sales of methadone.

Allison was floored. "Andrew, this is all too much, but I'm sorry, I must ask. Did you also invest in these companies? I find it hard to believe you knew of this plan and didn't also invest. Given the amount of money you already had, this would be a fortune for you."

Andrew grinned. "Allison. I will not discuss my finances, and

I would suggest you'd have a difficult time getting them on your own. I will say this though. You are looking at a different man. You needn't worry about my money."

Allison was unconvinced. "Sir, a story about exposing D.C. corruption from someone bathing in the swamp really doesn't sit well."

"I understand your plight. But I will share with you two things. First, I have no money invested at this time in MYER. That's significant, because as of the first of June, Myer Pharma is set to skyrocket when they are finally authorized to announce the sale of herbicides used in Afghanistan." Andrew paused as Allison wrote. It was true, Andrew that morning had finalized selling out of all his Pharma positions, unbeknownst to John Gerzema, who's money remained.

"And?" Allison said.

Quickly, Andrew responded. "And what?"

"Andrew, you said you had two things to share."

He pulled out his phone. "Yes, sorry. My memory isn't what it used to be." He pulled up a photo and as he passed the phone across the table, he said, "My personal funds facilitated this." It was the picture of Curt and Smitty in the back of the 4Runner. It was the same photo Kathy shared back in the hospital. It was private, and there were few ways Andrew could have a copy. The most logical one was he did, in fact, pay for Curt's rescue.

Allison looked up at Andrew as her hand slightly trembled. "If what you say is true, and I have little reason to doubt it isn't, thank you, sir."

Smiling, Andrew said, "You are welcome. After you publish your article, it is I that will thank you and Curt. You'll see."

The two finished up their meeting. Allison hugged Andrew, who wasn't expecting it. He hugged her back, this time far less awkwardly.

Chapter Fifty-two
Hydraulics? What Hydraulics?

After listening to the Saudi Air Traffic Controller berate the flight crew for airspace violations, Buck 01 had made it over the Red Sea and would now no longer need to listen about their Infidel flight.

Buck was on his third trip back to check the hydraulic reservoir, which was again being monitored by one dedicated Afghan maintainer. He was holding two cans now, even more ready. Buck chuckled.

Unfortunately, his jovialness would soon diminish. Buck looked down and saw half of the oil can pallet had been used. Buck ran back up to the flight deck and jumped into the seat. "My aircraft," he ordered.

"Your aircraft," Raz responded. "Hey Buck, while you were gone, we were given a flight clearance to overfly Egypt and to land in Souda Bay!" Raz was proud of himself.

"Yippee." Replied Buck, sarcastically. "That's great."

"Buck, what is wrong?" Raz asked.

"Oh. Nothing, Raz. Just a bit of the jitters. We are so close and all." Buck knew there was no reason to worry Raz.

Buck disengaged the autopilot and flew the aircraft manually, hoping he could induce fewer control movements than the autopilot. Each time he moved the yoke or rudder, he feared he was likely contributing to the leak.

The sun would set off in a few hours. Just about the time Buck 01 would land at Souda Bay Naval Air Station. It had been a long day for the crew. "Raz, can you do me a favor and try to get some sleep? We've been up for nearly 20 hours," requested Buck.

"Yes, sir." Raz leaned his chair back and flipped his sunglasses down.

****

Allison worked at a fevered pitch to complete her story. Now and then, the little one in her belly would demand food or sleep, but other than that, she was at the computer, typing away. The ringing of a cell phone startled her. It was Kathy Hershey.

"Kathy! How are you?" Allison asked.

"My dear. That's my question for you?" Kathy responded.

"Oh. I'm good. Working on a project and anxious for Curt's return. The baby is doing fine, and my dad is still here. He says he'll go home after Curt is back, but I doubt it." Allison smiled at her own joke.

"Well, all that sounds wonderful. Hey, I wanted to let you know. A little birdie told me that the C-130 will soon be on a U.S. military base called Souda Bay Naval Air Station. Once that happens, you can likely expect a call from Curt."

Allison's heart raced. "Really!?" she asked.

"Yes. Really," proclaimed Kathy. "I'm glad you're doing well. It's just a matter of waiting now until Curt is home. It's not fun, but far easier than the other challenges you've recently faced and conquered."

"Kathy. I really cannot thank you enough. I'm still relatively new to the whole military thing. I was hesitant at first and perhaps didn't give it the chance it deserved. If other military spouses are as dedicated as you, being a military spouse is truly an honor." Allison meant every word.

"Well, there's rotten apples in every bunch, but I'd suggest most of our apples are like me. I gotta run, Allison. Good luck with your next project. Keep me informed about the baby, because if you don't, I'm married to a guy who can get his hands on some nukes."

The two laughed. "I will. Take care, Kathy," Allison said as they hung up.

****

A note sat on John Gerzema's desk requesting he come to the Oval Office. He was sure he knew what it was for. As he walked into the waiting room, Steve was standing there. "John, he's waiting for you," Steve said, with what sounded like a hint of pleasure.

335

The two walked in. Steve didn't sit, and neither did John. The President was standing facing out the window, admiring the Rose Garden. In May, it was spectacular.

"Steve, please leave us," the President requested. Steve did as he was asked. He knew the request was coming as the President told him prior that the meeting would be 'Four Eyes.'

"John. Ya fucked up." The President said.

"Mr. President. I don't think this is a big deal, really it will blow over easy."

The President turned around, smiling. "Oh, I didn't mean with that illegitimate son. I meant with me." The President's smile turned to stern anger. "How fucking dare you blackmail me for the same deed you did?"

"Mr. President. No. Really. It's not like that."

"John, I'm giving you one chance. You will go out with the Press Secretary today. You will admit the boy is yours, illegitimate and the result of an affair. The issue with this other video ends, now. You will declare that you paid a high-tech computer firm to build a deep fake video, the one you have of my, shall we say, indiscretions?"

"I'm not doing that," said John bluntly. "You want me to put myself out like a sacrificial lamb with nothing in return?"

"Oh, I didn't say that. At that press conference, I am allowing you to announce the Afghan poppy operation. We're going public with it, and you get to own it. Frankly, I think this is a beautiful opportunity to assess your political skills. Will you be able to sway the public away from your indiscretions via your massive strike onto the Taliban economy? I don't know." The President paused, then continued. "Once you're done, the Press Secretary will say I cautiously supported your plan as did the rest of the U.S. Government, but it was your baby. Swimming or sinking, it is truly in your hands."

John sat there, trying to find another way out. There was none. "Mr. President, after the conference, what happens?"

"That's a good question, John. Frankly, that depends on your performance. I can't just go and fire the guy who society lauds as the man who got even with Afghanistan, can I? But I can dismiss the guy who considered extorting me with a deep fake.

Right?"

John stood there. His mind tried to look at the scenario from every different angle. He'd gotten lost in his mind until the President finally said. "The press conference starts in two hours. You may wish to take this time to prepare."

John nodded and left the Oval Office, passing Steve, who was waiting outside the door. Steve smiled as he walked by.

****

Buck 01 was descending into Souda Bay. They were roughly 80 miles out, descending at a shallow rate, gliding towards the island. Buck unbuckled from his seat one more time, intending to run back to check the hydraulic fluid level. He didn't need to go far. The Afghan who'd been monitoring it was at the base of the flight deck stair, holding two empty hydraulic oil cans. There was no more fluid.

Buck ran back up, sat down and switched the VHF radio to 121.5, the emergency frequency. Raz was clueless, just flying the approach. "MAYDAY! MAYDAY! MAYDAY. Buck Zero One, in a descent to Souda Bay, partial hydraulic failure, Two hours of fuel and 44 souls onboard." He switched to his intercom and said, "My aircraft."

"Your aircraft," Raz replied. "Sir, do we have a real emergency this time or is this one of the fake ones?"

"No Raz, this is real. Open your checklist. We've gone through all the hydraulic oil cans. There's no more. Clearly the old girl is drinking it faster than before."

Smitty ran up onto the flight deck. "Hydraulics? Dude, that sounds serious."

"Well, it's not as bad as a fire. Yet," Buck responded. "Smitty. Can you find about 10 feet of rope, fairly strong?"

"Easy. I have 550 chord and can quickly braid it," Smitty said, running to the back and grabbing it. In five minutes, he was back. The plane was now 30 miles out.

Buck wound the rope in front of the yoke and then put an end on either side of his chair. "Smitty, stand behind me and if I say pull, you pull. You got it? But dear God, do NOT pull unless I

337

tell you."

Smitty nodded.

Raz asked, "Do you want to run the before landing checks?"

Buck thought about it. Clearly, he'd have to run them at some point, but he wanted to wait. "Raz, let's hold off until five miles out. Also, let's get our clearance to land as well as crash and recovery vehicles at the end of the runway. OK?"

Raz nodded and coordinated that on the radio. Buck was still trying to nurse the big girl down with minimal control inputs. As he did, he saw the needle of the utility hydraulic gauge jump more and more. They were now within 10 miles and in two minutes would be at five.

"Raz, let's run everything for the Before Landing Checks except for flaps and gear." Buck, much like any pilot in that situation, was concerned how much those two actions would drain from the hydraulic system.

Raz ran the checklist, calling it complete minus the gear and flaps. "Hey," Buck said. "Can you ask the maintainer in Pashto how much fluid is still in the utility hydraulic reservoir?"

Raz did as requested, and his eyes bulged when he heard the answer. He looked at Buck. "Sir, there's none."

"Yeah. I figured. The controls are already getting mushy and tough. Not to mention the hydraulic indicator needle is jumping all over the place. Smitty, you still behind me?"

"Right with ya buddy," Smitty replied.

"Raz, fuck the flaps. And we're only dropping the gear via gravity. No stress on the hydraulics. Tell me my approach speeds."

Raz read the no flap approach speeds. They were far faster than a full or partial flap landing, which created other challenges. But Buck would rather wrestle with a runaway aircraft on the tarmac than be a passenger on a flying C-130 with a fully failed hydraulic system as it fell into the Mediterranean Sea.

They were now three miles out. "Raz, say a prayer. I'm dropping the gear with just gravity. Praying they go down."

"Gear Down," Raz repeated, then grabbed the gear handle and pulled, letting the gear free fall. As it fell, Buck kept repeating in his head, *'Come on. Good indicators. Good indicators.'* His eyes didn't move from the landing gear indicator panel. Both main landing gear registered 'down and locked;' however, the nose gear hung up for a while. Buck bunted the aircraft just a bit, and the nose wheel fell into place. Eventually, all three of the tricycle gear indicated down and locked. "Fucking Allah Akbar!" Buck shouted. As he did, Raz's head rapidly swiveled. Buck retorted, "I told you. It's growing on me."

Buck now struggled with the yoke. Fighting to keep the aircraft in a good attitude, as the nose kept falling. The loss of hydraulic pressure made the yoke nearly impossible to control. He needed thirty more seconds. The field was clearly in sight and the visual landing air slope indicators showed him on glidepath.

As the plane slowed, Raz called out, "Landing Speed."

The C-130's nose began to rise, "Push!" he yelled to Raz to help him on the yoke. The two shoved their respective yokes forward with a massive amount of effort, careful not to push too far. "Stop!" Buck demanded as the nose settled back to the correct attitude. "Now Pull it back to the middle!" He said. Raz and Buck strained to get it centered.

Holding the yoke steady as well as induce rudder inputs was becoming nearly impossible for one person to perform. The aircraft was now coming in low, but within tolerances; Buck didn't care. This was going to be his ugliest landing since flight school. Buck crossed the threshold, then slammed the throttles into idle. The nose began to drop, and he yelled, "SMITTY! PULL YOU SON OF A BITCH!"

Smitty braced his foot into the back of the pilot chair and pulled on both ends of the rope with all his might. Buck and Raz also yanked until the yoke was full aft. As desired, the elevators cut into the wind, slightly lifting the nose, and causing the main wings to stall. The C-130 slammed her main landing gear down onto the runway with authority.

"Raz! Reverse Thrust! Now!" Raz grabbed the propeller pitch controls, wound back the reverse thrust, and the aircraft slowed. After a few seconds and just as he'd been taught, Raz made an effort to take out the reverse thrusting.

Buck pushed Raz's hand away. "Dude! We have no brakes! Keep the reverse thrust in as long as possible!"

Raz looked down and saw Buck's feet pushing the rudder pedals to the floor. Out of instinct, Raz tried to pump the emergency brakes as much as possible, but it was little use. The hydraulics were gone and the indicator needle was now showing zero.

The plane was still slowing and Buck tried to gently swerve it with the nosewheel steering in hopes of bleeding off more speed. Ahead of him were fire trucks and a few Air Force staff cars, waiting to see the outcome of the emergency.

As Buck swerved, he transmitted to the tower, "Buck Zero One is no brakes." Within seconds, the fire trucks pulled off to the side of the runway, preparing to chase the C-130 off into the grass and perhaps worse, off the base.

Buck was now down to under fifteen miles an hour. The swerves were getting greater and greater. At five miles an hour left, Buck yelled, "Screw it," and turned the plane right towards one of the base staff cars. A crash at five miles an hour wouldn't kill anyone, but it would get the plane to stop. Slowly, the aircraft's nose gently kissed the car. Both would suffer cosmetic damage, but the plane stopped.

Exhausted, Buck said, "Shut 'em down, Raz." He would have been less tired if he'd run a marathon. The engines spun down and the end of the runway grew quiet.

From one of the staff cars emerged an Air Force Colonel, likely the one responsible for Air Force flight operations on the base. He was clearly displeased about the vehicle damage. Buck opened his swing window, stuck his head out partially and said in his best Rodney Dangerfield impression, "Hey! You scratched my anchor!" It was a famous line from the comedy classic Caddyshack.

The Colonel cracked a smile, as his anger dissipated. All in all, things could have been far worse.

The passengers climbed off the plane. Buck and Raz walked around and when they did, they found the primary leak. It was in the starboard wing line and appeared to be tied to aileron controls, as well as the trailing edge flaps. Had Buck tried to lower them, they all could very well be dead right now. Buck looked over. "Raz…. Allah Akbar."

Raz smiled. "No shit. Thank Fucking God."

Chapter Fifty-three
Hello

Allison was finishing up her article. She socialized it to the Washington Post editors, who salivated over it. She wanted another twenty-four hours to get it just right, but it was close, as written. Her phone rang. It was a number she didn't recognize. Given her discussion with Kathy earlier in the day, she rushed to grab it, then took a deep breath.

"Allison Nover," she said.

"I love you," is what she heard from a cracking voice. She could sense his fear.

"Curt! I love you too!" she screamed. "Come Home! Now!"

"I... I am," Curt paused. "I miss you." She could hear him weep.

"Curt, are you OK?" she asked.

"No. But I will be when I'm with you." Curt sniffled and wiped his nose.

"Baby, did you find Noorullah?"

"I did. He's with me. I'm bringing him back to the U.S. We will find a good family to care for him."

"No, Curt, he will stay with us."

Curt cried. "I can't do this anymore. I can't. I want to be home."

"I'm right here." Allison was nearly crying, too.

Smitty took the phone from Curt. "Hey, Allison, Smitty here."

"Smitty, is he ok? Please take care of him."

"The Taliban fucked him up pretty good. He'll come around, though. I've seen it before. He just needs time, and he needs you. According to what we are hearing, they're going to fly us up to Ramstein next and then catch a flight over to the U.S. Can you get to Frankfurt tomorrow? If so, you can drive over to Landstuhl Military Hospital and stay at the Fisher House. I know many buddies and their families who stayed there. It's world class. The staff is phenomenal and perhaps it would be a good place for you and Curt to meet up, away from the stress of D.C. The cost is free. Right now, I think it's almost certain they're going to take Curt in. I already told Squirts about him, and I think he's making the arrangements.

Allison wanted nothing more than to go, but there were complications. "Smitty, my dad is here, and I'm trying to get this story out."

"Bring your dad. Families are welcome at the Fisher House, and they have internet. I'll pay for your ticket. The only thing Curt needs right now is you."

"OK. I'll make it happen. Can you pass the phone to Curt?"

"Sure." Smitty said and handed the phone over.

"Curt. Baby. I'm coming to meet you in Germany."

He sat on the phone for a minute. "Thank you. I love you. Allison, do you want to say hi to someone?"

"Sure," she said.

"Haaalo!" the voice said.

"Hello. Is this Noorullah?

Allison listened. She heard in response. "Noorullah!"

"Allison. That's him. He's alive," Curt said.

"Yes, he is. Please, baby. Get some rest. I know it is late there. I'll see you soon. Curt, I love you."

"I love you, too." Curt said and hung up.

Allison bought plane tickets for both of them. Paul was excited about the travel opportunity. It was too late to catch the afternoon flights out of Dulles, but they'd be on the earliest ones tomorrow, arriving in Germany the following day given the overnight flights crossing the Atlantic to the east.

For the rest of the night, Allison worked on her article. She would look at it one more time the following day before departing for the airport. The article was already exceptional. It would shock America.

****

The White House Press Conference was packed. John Gerzema was introduced, and he fought for his political career. A seasoned politician, he did quite well, considering everything. In fact, at the end, it appeared the American public would be sympathetic to his misgivings, given the Afghanistan issue. The notion of sticking it to the Taliban and decimating their heroin crop resonated well with the American public. Of course, John promised to be more of a father, and publicly shared his pride in his son, often hidden from the public over the years. As for the deep fake video, he also apologized, attributing it to his desire to function and survive in a tragically corrupt D.C. political world. He was also extremely grateful that the deep fake video never saw the light of day.

Inside one of D.C.'s finer watering holes, The Dignitary, a grumpy Eastern Europe looking man sat at the bar. He'd been watching Gerzema's press briefing. As he heard about the video being false, he fumed. The man, Russian Ambassador Tarlov, was the one who's GRU units acquired the video. In Russian, he scowled angrily. No one understood him. After downing a neat glass of $250 vodka, he thought, *'I will find revenge. I will find revenge for Mother Russia.'*

****

The Greek embassy in Islamabad, Pakistan was the acting embassy for Afghanistan, because of the Taliban takeover. Few embassies actually remained in Afghanistan. The Ambassador had scheduled a call to the Taliban leadership for the morning. The embassy switchboard set up the call and connected the Taliban leadership, who sat in a conference room, as did the Ambassador with his team.

"Good Morning to you in Kabul. How are you today?"

"We are good, and we thank you for the opportunity to speak." The Taliban rarely were able to engage diplomatically because of sanctions and shunning from the west.

"Yes. Well, we wish we had better information to share, but we have a concern that we need to provide. It appears one of your aircraft has been abandoned at our airfield in Souda Bay. We will be billing you 1000 euros per day until you can get it off our base."

"Mr. Ambassador, we did not take the aircraft there and thus, we are not liable for that bill."

"I understand you did not bring it here, but the aircraft has your flag on it, and it is your responsibility. We are only charging you the rates we charge any other entity that beds down their aircraft here." This was untrue. The cost was exorbitant, but the Ambassador correctly presumed the Taliban were clueless regarding airport fees.

The Taliban spoke amongst themselves, then the lead member again spoke. "Mr. Ambassador, I understand you have C-130's in your Air Force. Would it be possible for your pilots to fly the aircraft back to Kabul? Unfortunately, we have no remaining aircrew in our country."

The Ambassador pulled out a sheet of paper from a stack. "We have taken the liberty of drawing up the charges associated with that. Unfortunately, the aircraft was damaged upon landing. The repair costs, as well as new hydraulic lines in the right wing will cost 1.5 million euros. A flight back from our country would be possible, but you would need to secure the diplomatic overflights of all nations in between, cover fuel costs and pay for the time our crew was flying. We estimate that to be roughly 200,000 euros."

Again, the Taliban discussed amongst themselves for a brief moment. Even if they could pay the bill, Afghanistan had zero diplomatic clout and would struggle to secure safe passage over all the nations. "Mr. Ambassador, we are curious. Would Greece have any interest in purchasing the aircraft?"

The Ambassador pulled out another sheet of paper and began speaking. "Gentlemen, our country has also investigated this option as well. We are prepared to offer $9.5 million for the aircraft in an 'as is' status and absolve you of any current parking fees or fines associated with the aircraft on the ground."

The Taliban were furious. The plane was easily worth $25 million. "What fine are you talking about?" One of them blurted out.

The Ambassador held up a photo of the right wing leaking hydraulic fluid onto the ground. "Well, this hydraulic leak, per European Union regulations, is a finable environmental offense. Currently, our ground personnel are trying to manage the leak and the spill, but it is clearly over 10,000 euros. You may not see this as an issue, but our current President has a very strong

345

environmental agenda. To her, this is a problem."

Again, the Taliban conversed. "Ambassador, may we send a team of mechanics to come, disassemble the aircraft and then ship the pieces back?"

"Why yes," the Ambassador replied. "However, whomever you send will need to have the ability to come into the European Union. Currently, many of the Taliban, unfortunately most of you as well, are banned from entry. We would also need assurances that whomever you send from Afghanistan will not flee their duties and attempt to declare refugee status."

The Taliban were screwed. They begrudgingly settled for the $9.5 million offer. All associated paperwork would be finalized in Islamabad the next week. Prime Minister Pisanos was notified immediately of the deal. He shot a text message out to the Admiral.

> *'Squirts,*
> *We got a steal on that Herk. $9.5M.*
>
> > *Many Thanks,*
> > *Zap'*

The Chairman saw the note the next morning. He replied,

> *'If you stop telling the Santorini story, we can call it even. Congrats to the Greek Air Force and to our Alliance. It's a win for the good guys.*
> > *Squirts'*

Chapter Fifty-four
The Table's Set

Allison was finishing packing. She'd grabbed things for Curt as well. Before departing the house, she fired off the article to her Washington Post editor. He confirmed receipt and informed her that it would run the next morning, Eastern Time. By then, Allison would be on the ground in Germany, hopefully holding Curt. She and her father took a cab to the airport and hopped a flight to Frankfurt. As they drove to the airport, Allison placed a call.

"Allison! Great to hear from you! Did Curt call you?" Kathy asked.

"Yes, Kathy, he did," responded Allison. "But Smitty says he's kinda messed up. My dad and I are on the way to Frankfurt and are planning to stay at the Fisher House. Before I get there, do you have any recommendations for me?"

"The Admiral told me he'd heard Curt was a bit shaken. I understand they are all going to get checked at Landstuhl, to include the Afghans. I can tell you the Fisher House there is a world class facility and the first point of care location for most of our wounded who came out of Iraq and Afghanistan. You will be in good hands. Did you get a reservation at the Fisher House yet?

"No, I didn't know if I could before Curt checked in and I don't know what to do with Noorullah."

"Who is Noorullah?" Kathy asked.

"He is the Afghan boy Curt went to find. Evidently, he's bringing him home. I think he's going to live with us," she answered.

"Oh. Ok. Anyway, yes, you can make reservations, but don't worry. One of my old friends runs it. I'll call her now and get you and Noorullah rooms. Leave it to me."

"Thanks, Kathy. I don't know what to say."

"Say nothing. And please keep us posted. Both of us are very fond of you and Curt. Lastly, if you need anything, don't hesitate to call. Again, I can get Nukes."

"I will, Kathy. I really appreciate it. Goodbye." The two hung up.

Allison shot off a text before her flight. She wanted to get it out while she was still in the U.S.

> 'Andrew,
> Article runs tomorrow AM. I'm throwing numerous haymakers. I hope I do justice to your story.
> Allison'

****

The news for the day was relatively favorable for John Gerzema. He'd done enough to weather the storm, and polling suggested Americans were grateful to see the nation take action against the Taliban. Throughout the day, he'd work in as many photo ops as he could with Sleazy, his son. While the images were all smiles, the tension between the two was clear.

John Gerzema was completely unaware of the fate he would suffer when the morning news broke.

****

That evening at Ramstein Air Base, Germany, a C-17 departed for Souda Bay Naval Air Station. It landed and the crew would spend the night. The next morning, they'd depart with the group of passengers, returning to Ramstein. There was still concern over the Iranians, the German government would not let them off the base and there were sensitivities letting them into the U.S. After a few debriefs with the U.S. officials at Souda Bay, it was clear these men were both $500k wealthier, their ties to the money in the Caymans was legit, and they were prepared to spend whatever they needed to live outside of Iran. Some puzzle pieces would still need to be worked, but it would eventually be doable. Andrew would assist where he could, and Andrew's assistance was always beneficial.

Chapter Fifty-five
The Rise & Fall of Kings

It was 0800Hrs when the Lufthansa flight landed at Frankfurt International. Paul and Allison were able to get a small amount of sleep on the plane. They were groggy, but the morning sunlight in Europe helped them awaken.

They collected their bags from the luggage carousel, then, planned on stopping at the Hertz rental car counter to grab a vehicle. Paul had done all the route planning the day before. It was roughly a little more than an hour to get to the Ramstein / Landstuhl area.

As they walked out of the baggage claim, they both saw a young airman holding a large sign that said, "Allison Nover." She approached and said, "I'm Allison Nover."

The young airman snapped to attention. "Ma'am, Good morning. I am your driver to get you to the Fisher House. Do you need help with your bags?"

"No. No. I'm fine. This is so kind. Please, lead the way."

The Airman led her and Paul to a blue van, double parked just outside the terminal with the hazard lights on. Once onboard, they were off, finally heading to see Curt, and whatever that might bring.

Allison pulled out her phone and connected to the German network. She checked the Washington Post website. Her story hadn't broke yet. She also checked her email account. It was clear the editors had done a good job keeping a lid on the story, as none of her journalist friends had reached out to chat about it. Allison took a quick last look at social media. Again, there was not a peep about the story. When D.C. woke up, she was going to shock the world.

****

The C-17 departed Souda Bay Naval Air Station at roughly 0900Hrs. Buck, Smitty, and Mule tried to care for not only Curt but also the entire group of Afghans who'd left everything behind. The C-17 was far bigger and more powerful that the C-130. It was also far more reliable than the ramshackle sleigh that had gotten them from Afghanistan to Greece.

Buck leaned down to Raz. "Hey, come with me."

Raz got up from his seat and Buck lead him to the C-17 flight deck. Raz walked up, and his chin hit the floor. He'd only seen such things in photos.

The C-17 cockpit didn't have a yoke, but a joystick like a small aircraft. Displays in front of the crew were all glass with digital displays. The windows were enormous, and the visibility was amazing. As a true aviator, Raz was in heaven. The copilot leaned back and gave Raz an extra headset.

"Raz, you up?" the copilot asked.

"Yes, sir. This is amazing," Raz answered back.

The aircraft commander in the left seat then spoke. "Raz, I understand from Buck here you are a trained Afghan pilot, qualified on the C-130. I also understand you're one of the guys who landed that C-130 in Crete with barely any hydraulics. That is one impressive display of flying, my friend."

Raz pushed out his chest with pride. "Yes, I helped, but it was Buck who was in command."

Buck wasn't on a headset, so he couldn't hear the discussion. He just stood there with a smile.

"Well, Raz," the aircraft commander said. "If you're that good, perhaps you could fly this old girl for a bit. Would you like that?"

Raz nearly relieved his bladder uncontrollably from the excitement. "Are you serious?" He asked, but it was clear that the copilot was already vacating his seat.

Raz sat down in the seat, adjusted it a bit, looked over the gauges, then placed his hand around the stick, careful not to touch it, but rather be ready when he was told.

"You ready, Raz?" the pilot asked.

"Yes, sir!"

The pilot smiled at Raz. "Your aircraft."

"My aircraft!" replied Raz. His hand gripped the stick. Raz was now flying the most advanced cargo aircraft in the U.S. Air Force inventory, perhaps the world. They'd need twenty men to get him out of that seat. Raz gently banked left and right a few times. He'd fidget with the trim button and do other gentle flight maneuvers, as to not upset the passengers. That said, if it were just him, he would have put her through her paces. Buck took at least three dozen photos.

Five minutes passed, and the copilot returned from his bathroom break. Raz reluctantly got up and begrudgingly returned the copilot's seat. Once out, he high fived Buck, who'd been the individual to arrange the event. Raz would be forever grateful.

After a few hours, the aircraft began its descent into Ramstein. The landing was uneventful and as they taxied to parking, buses along with some fans showed up on the ramp to cheer. There were welcome signs in English and Pashto as the story had truly gained significance over the past 48 hours. Also waiting on the ramp were Allison and Paul.

The C-17 came to a stop, and the engines wound down. Allison and Paul were escorted toward the airplane and waited just out front for Curt.

He was one of the last to get off, and he was also helping Noorullah down the steps and off the plane with his makeshift prostatic leg. As soon as Allison saw him, she ran up. "Curt!" she yelled.

Curt stood there. His eyes watered. As soon as Allison put her arms around him, a wave of calm swept over him. He knew he'd be OK. It would take time, but he was finally safe again. Curt was in the safest place in his world.

After a long hug, they separated, "Allison, I want you to meet Noorullah."

Allison reached out to shake his hand. Noorullah returned the favor and said loudly, "Noorullah!"

Allison chuckled and said, "Yes!"

Then Curt looked at Noorullah and said, "Allison." He emphasized it as if trying to signal something to him.

Noorullah's eyes lit up. He then said. "Allison. Sahnkt Euw."

Allison, too, began to cry. She hugged him and said, "You're welcome."

Buses would take the Afghans away and a few vans would

take the Americans. Evidently, there was a documentation error by the Germans and the two Iranians were 'misidentified' as Americans. Once off the flight line, they'd rented a car at the Ramstein Hertz counter and drove away, disappearing into the German countryside, just as planned.

Curt, Allison, Paul, and Noorullah would take a van directly to Landstuhl. The ride took roughly 15 minutes, and no one spoke. As they arrived, an Afghan interpreter and care giver met them to assist with Noorullah. Paul would settle the bags into the Fisher House while Curt and Allison checked into the hospital.

Curt sat in his room. He'd been given a sedative to calm him along with some other medications. He was not groggy, but relaxed.

"Dr. Nover, sir. Hello, I'm Dr. Tanner. I'm a psychologist and started out as a social worker for the military. I want you to know, many of us are truly grateful for the work you've done back in D.C. regarding Veteran care. But today, let's try to help you. How are you feeling?"

"Better. But I know what I need to do. So please, pull up a chair. The only way I get through this is to confront it. It's how it worked for me before, and I know it will work again. What kind of leader would I be at the VA if I didn't practice what I preached?"

Dr. Tanner responded. "That's quite brave of you. Are you sure you're ready?"

"Yes. Let's rip this thing open and start healing."

Allison got up as if to leave. "No!" Curt said. "I can't do this alone. I need you here. Will you please stay?"

Allison nodded, sat down next to the bed, and held Curt's hand.

Through a rollercoaster of emotions and the shock of the story, Curt explained what had happened to him, how it made him feel, and what he was mentally experiencing. Allison's hand was sweating in his. At times, she couldn't begin to understand how Curt handled it all, the urine, the toilet brush and the other traumas. Dr. Tanner sat there attentively, trying to hide any expressions of shock or judgement. After two hours, Curt stopped speaking. He was nowhere near healed, but he was clearly on a good path to find peace.

Curt was exhausted and begged to try to sleep. He also begged Allison not to go. He'd have nightmares, no doubt, and needed her. Allison promised, but asked to step out with the doctor for a brief chat. Curt agreed.

"Doctor Tanner. I'm really new to all this military and war stuff. I think I may need some help to deal with just hearing what Curt went through. Is my husband going to be OK?"

Dr. Tanner placed his hand on Allison's shoulder. "Ms. Nover. I've read your husband's chart, going back to before you were married. He's one of the toughest men I've ever encountered. I have great faith he will eventually be OK. He's a fighter, and he wants you in his corner. That's half the battle. Many of our service members who suffer something like Curt's experience isolate themselves, refuse treatment and destroy their families. Don't get me wrong, the road to recovery is long and isn't always easy. But you've got a great start. Now, can we get you some help?"

"Yes, Doctor, perhaps tomorrow. Can I get a day or two to process all this?"

"Sure. We are going to give a sedative to Curt right now. Would you like to spend some time with Noorullah and his care giver & interpreter?"

"That would be great."

Allison was led to a youthful looking elementary schoolish room in the hospital where Noorullah and his interpreter were staying. As soon as he saw Allison, he jumped up and began yelling in Pashto. She didn't know what he was saying, but she could clearly sense his anger and rage.

Noorullah's interpreter, another man, attempted to interject himself. He then turned to Allison, "Please, ma'am, can you leave. He's scared of his new surroundings and he's not really seen women in western dress. You are offending him."

Before Allison could leave, Noorullah began throwing things. His pupils dilated. He was enraged. The interpreter smashed his hand onto a call button. Immediately, a siren and lights fired off in the ward. While the hospital staff didn't know it, Noorullah was again experiencing heroin withdrawal and the only person

353

who did know was Curt, comfortably sleeping down the hall. Within seconds, two security personnel were on top of Noorullah, holding him down, or at least trying to. Eventually, another nurse ran into the room and injected a sedative into him. He too would be spending the night in the hospital.

Allison watched the entire scene unfold. She was nearly in shock. The individual Curt brought back to be part of their family wanted to kill her.

After roughly an hour, Noorullah was asleep on a hospital bed and wheeled into Curt's room. As the ward nurses brought him in, Allison was sitting next to Curt who was resting but awake.

"Sir and ma'am, you two are the only ones he knows here. The doctor thought it best if he remain in here with you.

"Of course!" Curt responded, unaware of the earlier altercation. He looked at Noorullah sleeping peacefully on the bed. Then he gazed at Allison. "Look at him. Isn't he great?"

Allison attempted to manage a reassuring smile. "He's really something." The emotions running through her were a mess. She was relieved the man she loved was safe, but realizes now he's damaged to a point she can't recognize. She's excited to be bringing a new child into the world, yet in utter horror thinking about a life with Noorullah in their family would offer. She squeezed Curt's hand as the two stared at Noorullah.

****

Allison laid in the bed next to Curt, awake as she stared at him. Her phone vibrated in her pocked and she dismissed it, sure she'd get it later. Then again, and again. Soon, it didn't stop vibrating.

'Shit!' she thought. 'The Article!'

Allison slithered out of the bed and sat in a recliner that was in the room. The article was on the Washington Post front page and being picked up by the AP. It would soon be global. Emails and tweets poured into her account. Her mom tried to call from Tucson but couldn't get through. Allison was the number one journalist in the world for that day.

Myer stock price plummeted, falling nearly 25%. It would continue falling while the Frankfurt exchange remained open and then fall even further in after-hours trading. The entire Pharma sector would suffer a tough day once the U.S. markets opened.

Numerous news outlets were scrambling to interview John Gerzema, whom just a day prior, was a hero. Today, he'd meet the President at 1000Hrs. The meeting was simple. John would present his resignation letter. John Gerzema's political career was now over.

****

At noon, the same day, Andrew Denney would appeal to his local Senator, stating he had further information. The Senator and he would appear on Fox News at mid-day. It was 1800Hrs in Germany, but Curt and Allison watched.

Andrew Denney outed himself as the source, giving full credit for the story to Allison. He additionally announced he'd accept any request by Congress to testify.

When asked if he'd made money on the stock trades, Andrew admitted he had, but everything from that trade would be transferred in a charitable donation to the Veterans Administration to help care for wounded warriors. His good deed quelled much of the outcry for him to spend time behind bars.

****

Back in D.C., Russian Ambassador Tarlov was finishing a long cable to Moscow. Earlier, he was furious that his primary leverage against the President, his 'Granddaughter's skating video,' was now politically impotent. Putting his emotions aside, he stewed over the situation. Then it hit him. A plan. A brilliant plan. The Ambassador devised a devilish plan on how to remedy the situation. Tarlov crafted a plot that would bring to bear the full value of that video again. It would also bring the United States to her knees. The timing was perfect. The more he contemplated it, the more he was certain this was the key.

Ambassador Tarlov leaned back at his desk, took one last draw on his cigar, then hit 'send' on his highly secure communication device. Layers of encryption systems pushed the electrons across a communication channel that operated only between his embassy and the Kremlin. Within seconds, his screen displayed a message stating the secure cable was successfully sent. Tarlov smiled.

The End.

Note from the Author:

The character of Noorullah is based on actual events that took place in Afghanistan in 2007. Here is a link to that article.

Afghan government helps save boy's life
By Air Force Capt. Bob Everdeen
Qalat Provincial Reconstruction Team
https://www.dvidshub.net/news/10109/afghan-government-helps-save-boys-life

To all who struggle with PTSD, please remember, help is never further than a phone call away.

The Veteran's Crisis Help Line: 1-800-273-8255

The National Suicide Prevention Lifeline: 1-800-273-8255

You are not alone

****

Thanks for reading. Please consider leaving a review on Amazon:

Appendix of Acronyms

ACOG	Advance Combat Optical Gunsight
AFSOC	Air Force Special Operations Command
MSH	Airfield Identifier for Masirah Island, Oman
USASOC	Army Special Operations Command
BOHICA	Bend over, here it comes again
CSAR	Combat Search and Rescue
DFAC	Dining Facility
EPA	Environmental Protection Agency
FOB	Forward Operating Base
HF	High Frequency
HVT	High Value Target
INS	Inertial Navigation System
JTRS	Joint Tactical Radio System
MARSOC	Marine Special Operations Command
KMSH	Masirah Island Airfield Identifier
MiS	Mazar I Sharif
USNSWC	Navy Special Operations Command
PJ	Pararescuemen / Para-Jumpers
PSD	Personal Security Detail
PTSD	Post Traumatic Stress Disorder
RMO	Round Metal Objects
GRU	Russian Intelligence, modern form of KGB
SECDEF	Secretary of Defense
SOCOM	Special Operations Command
SOF	Special Operations Force
SOLO	Special Operations Liaison Officer
TACAN	Tactical Air Navigation
UHF	Ultra-High Frequency
VHF	Very High Frequency
VFR	Visual Flight Rules
WTFO	What the Fuck, Over?
WILCO	Will Comply
YGBSM	You Gotta Be Shitting Me

www.ingramcontent.com/pod-product-compliance
Lightning Source LLC
Chambersburg PA
CBHW022145010726

47493CB00002B/350